My Mother's Spear

Ishtar Watson

Special Thanks to Evan Schultheis for his help with Latin translations and Robin Greene for her thoughtful insights.

I hereby dedicate this book to...

The spirit of humanity, peace, and freedom for all forms of human expression. May we learn a little humility and compassion.

The LGBTQIA+ and Neurodivergent people of the world. We have always existed, and we always will.

The archaeologists of the world. Without your dedication and skill, I would have been lost.

My dear friends, who have breathed life into my world and made each day worth living.

To my father who accepted his daughter with a hug and compassion.

And to my spouse... thank you for being you.

Ishtar

Ishtar Watson

Dear Archaeologists

I am a computer scientist and an archaeology student. I have a university background in archaeology, anthropology, and computer science, and I have engaged in experimental archaeology to understand and properly depict the ancient world as accurately as possible. I have taken courses in radiometric dating, attended archaeology field school, and have a decade of EDXRF experience. I've worked in the field excavating and surveying, and labs and museums cleaning, analyzing, and preserving collections. Still, our understanding of the past is evolving, and some details from my story may prove incorrect, given time and research. You may also disagree with my treatment of Roman-occupied Britain, from religion to clothing, but please know that any mistakes you find were made in good faith and not for lack of research. Additionally, some gaps in our understanding required a bit of conjecture to create a proper narrative. In a formal paper we should present only the facts, while in fictional work such missing parts must be imagined, but done so using evidence-based speculation and with great care.

For those who read Latin, I hope that my attempt to depict its use accurately was successful. I have only two years of Latin education, and I hired a more knowledgeable person to assist me with translation. I am more familiar with classical Latin, while the common person of the period probably spoke with a little more slang and regional dialect. Regardless, any errors made were not due to a lack of effort or research. Audere est facere…

Ishtar

WARFARE

Dear reader,

War is hell. The term is often regarded as cliché, yet it does little service to the true horror our species unleashes upon itself. Nor does it consider the most common victims of conflict: women, children, other genders, the elderly, the sick, disabled, and marginalized peoples, not to mention the countless men and boys who die at the bidding of those in power. War isn't fun, glamorous, or some sort of exciting adventure. War is an orchestrated violence and loss of life followed by a lifetime of loss, suffering, and regret. Worse, those who instigate wars and make the choice to kill en masse rarely suffer the direct effects of war – leaders often shielded from the results of their prideful choices.

This author has been so fortunate to have never lived through a war. In my effort to accurately depict such scenes, I have drawn on both research from real soldiers' testimonies and my own experiences. It may come as a surprise, but I have had a firearm purposefully fired at me and I have been attacked by individuals apparently intent on ending my life, more than once. I also live with both PTSD and CPTSD. While my life experiences do not equal those of the survivors of war, I believe they have given me the tiniest mote of understanding from which to write this story with accuracy and compassion.

The reader should walk away with three important points: Firstly, humans don't generally want to harm each other, and without a significant personal reason or a wider sociocultural organization actively normalizing and incentivizing this behavior, humans largely avoid it. Secondly, war should be avoided at all costs as the price of war is humanity, and this is a price paid both by those who engage in war and those engaged by war. Lastly, the scars of war are often unseen yet not unfelt in the minds of those forever altered by such violence and suffering.

Ishtar

Trigger and Content Warning

Dear reader,

To bring you an exciting and accurate depiction of ancient Roman-occupied Britain, I need to depict some of the more tragic aspects of life in those times. I have done my best to balance accuracy with gratuitousness. The stark reality is that much worse happened than is depicted in the books, but I find no value in depicting such horrors without reason. The terrible ways humans can harm each other must not be celebrated nor glorified.

Triggering Themes

- Crucifixion (attempted)
- Enslaved people (historical context)
- Gore and Body Horror (warfare related)
- Military Sexual Trauma (implied, never seen)
- Non-Consent
- PTSD / CPTSD and associated symptoms
- Rape (attempted)
- Sexism
- Sexual assault
- Sexual scenes (consensual)
- Suicidal references
- Trauma, physical and psychological
- Violence (especially related to warfare)
- War (graphic depiction)

Introduction

Nudity

In our modern culture, nudity has become hyper-associated with sexuality, but the extreme nature of this relationship is a modern–recent–association. Social attitudes and the sexual relationship with nudity have arisen through historical, cultural, and religious means. While this may shock the reader, nudity is by no means out of place for the period in which this story is set. Therefore, it is important to cast aside our modern notions of modesty and sexuality when considering the social norms of an ancient society.

Romans

The Romans were a complex and dynamic culture–cultures really–beginning as a small kingdom in 753 BCE and ending as a mighty empire by 476 CE, though some scholars still debate the actual date and method of Rome's end. In our story, we only see a small sample of a massive empire, and that sample is set around a military frontier fort filled with jingoistic individuals. It should be noted that while Romans practiced many acts that, by today's standards, would be considered horrific, such as crucifixion, enslavement, or gladiatorial combat, their society was far more than just these cruel spectacles. Mothers, fathers, children, schools, arts and artists, and so many more facets of society existed yet are necessarily underrepresented in this work as a result of its militaristic setting. As you read this story, please keep this in mind, and don't let your view of such a complex culture be jaded.

Parentheses (these)

Ancient people often used different names and terms for things in their everyday world than we do. When this happens, a modern word in parentheses that the reader may be familiar with will accompany the more ancient word. For example, Vallum Antonini (Antonine's Wall), where Vallum Antonini is the ancient name of the wall, and Antonine's Wall is the modern version. While some may find the ample supplementary information within this book troublesome, it has been included to enrich the reader's experience and understanding of the past.

Please see the author's notes in the back of the book for more information

KEY PRONUNCIATIONS

Sei'ln Meala	She-lan Me-la
Cynna of Dacia	S-eye-nah of Day-see-ah
Damona	Dah-mo-na
Acilius	Ah-kil-ee-oos
Ail	Eye-l
Brynen	Bu'ren-in (rolled R)
Ci	Key
Eilun	Ae-lin (A, like ape and e, like eat)
Erbin	Air-bin
Gaius Pedius	Guy-use Ped-use
Julia	Joo-lee-ah
Rigandona	Ri-kan-dona (g sounds like k)
Ris	Reez
Sabina	Sah-bee-na
Titus Fabius Vibulanus	Tye-toos Fab-use Ve-boo-lan-us
Ucer	Oo-ser
Urth	Earth
Uuen	E-in
Vita	Vee-tah
Brigante	Brig-an-tea
Bynwerr	B-eyen-wir
Clan Braide	Br-eye-da
Dynen	Die-nin
Iazyges	Eye-az-ah-geez
Veluniate	Vay-lune-ee-ah-te
Voltadini	Voh-tah-dee-nee
Wenechon	Win-neck-on
Weryn	Wir-en

PROLOGUE

The warrior knelt before a cooking fire as the fellow men of her equites daci (Dacian cavalry) laughed and drank after a long day's patrol of the western wall. In her left hand, she held a bronze censor from which white puffs of smoldering hemp bud and the last of her catnip from her homeland billowed. Her cheeks bore twin black spirals, each meticulously painted with a few strands of dried grass in the old ways, as one did when working magic.

In the distance, she heard the faint sound of a buccina (a Roman military horn) calling soldiers to arms, likely a night drill. Ignoring the sounds, she traced seven circles around the fire as she whispered the cleansing words of her spell. Nearby, the few Dacian men who had taken note of her otherworldly actions turned their attention to drink or bed, none too interested in women's magic – nor this particular woman's blade. The warrior's freedom had been traded for a chance to escape death following a raid when she was barely a woman, but after many years of servitude, she found those chains too heavy to bear.

"Mother of Fire and creator of all, I tire of these ways... this life. I asked you once for a chance to flee, and you filled my body with hope. I beg you once more, spare me this prison. Pierce my heart with death or warm my spirit with love, but don't leave me as I am. My path is overgrown, and I cannot see the way... Burn my path clear, and I shall sacrifice the life of a worthy warrior in your name. This I swear."

The year is 160 CE – It is the 23rd year of the reign of Imperator Caesar Divi Filii Titus Aelius Hadrianus Antoninus Augustus Pius, more commonly known as Antoninus Pius. The mighty Roman Empire dominates much of the known world. From Western Europe to North Africa and to Britannia (now called Britain), Rome had extended her reach, conquering or allying with everyone she met. That was until Rome encountered the northern peoples of Caledonia (land occupying roughly contemporary Scotland).

Far from a single group, the peoples of Caledonia were made up of many different cultures. While a few interacted positively and even joined with the Romans, a fair number fought for centuries to keep their lands and repel the southern invaders, some eventually forming a confederation. Two centuries before the famous Pictish kingdoms arose, the many insular Celtic tribes of what is present-day Scotland lived, loved, and fought for their lands against the might of Rome. Perhaps their most remarkable achievement was holding onto their land against a vast and technologically superior empire, eventually being defeated by Rome, nearly vanishing from historical record, and later reemerging as the Picts, though never fully losing their lands to Rome.

Unable to readily defeat the peoples of Caledonia and with the resources beyond the walls not worth the major expenditure such a conquest would truly take, Rome constructed two major walls to tax trade and isolate the North: Hadrian's Wall (Vallum Hadriani) from what is now the western Solway Coast to Newcastle upon Tyne, followed by Antonine's Wall (Vallum Antonini), from the banks of the River Clyde at Old Kilpatrick, spanning all the way to the coast of the Firth of Forth, just west of Edinburgh. The walls ran from east to west coast and served as points of taxation, limited military protection, and anchors for Roman influence beyond the walls, at least as far as they dared. But building a wall never really solves such problems, as the Romans eventually learned.

***Our story begins along the shores of the Firth of Forth**, near the eastern terminus of Antonine's Wall, at a Roman legionary fort beside a small village named Veluniate, where Caledonian warriors approach the fort's gate from two sides. On either side of the gate stood twin defense towers, punctuating an earthen wall supported by a wooden palisade, standing over twice the height of a person. To the North, a deep trench was dug to stifle attacks, while pit traps with spikes buried within awaited those who stepped too thoughtlessly.*

Creeping along the edge of the wall in the darkness of night, over 200 warriors approach the gate from the East, while a similar number approach in the same manner from the West. Behind those walls, a Roman noble prepares to lead a small band of cavalry with the intention of meeting with a northern village leader who had sent word of land that the noble might wish to obtain in exchange for some petty favors and a little Roman gold. The lands this far east were generally regarded as safe. Unfortunately for him, the offer was a trick to lure the greedy fool from the safety of the Fort, and his ill-fated trip is now awaited by many... **including one young woman who really should not be there...**

12

CHAPTER 1
HER TURN TO DIE

"But they are a very warlike and fierce people, and arm only with a narrow shield and spear, and a sword hanging by their naked bodies" ~ Herodian's Roman History, Book III

It is a widely held belief that the Caledonians and later Picts fought naked. In truth, we don't know if they did. Several contemporary accounts, such as Herodian, Polybius, Diodorus Siculus, and Julius Caesar, explicitly state this. Herodian is likely speaking of the Caledonian Confederation, an alliance of tribes in Caledonia, while the others speak of mainland European Celts. While these authors each come with biases, problems with interpretation (what did "naked" mean), and the propagandist need to represent one's foe as lesser or uncivilized, there may be some truth to these claims. The later Pictish people, who likely (we are still unsure) descended from the Caledonians, depicted themselves nude in martial scenes carved into stones.

Anthropologically speaking, ritual nudity is common enough and practiced worldwide today, so the idea that the Caledonians may have performed this as a demonstration of their spiritual devotion and bravery or to simply intimidate their foes is reasonable. Thus, ritual nude combat is treated as a sacred part of their culture and depicted within this work in a ritual sense.

NORTHWEST OF VELUNIATE (CARRIDEN) FORT, EASTERN EDGE OF ANTONINE WALL, NORTHERN BRITANNIA – 10 PM, MARCH 11, 160 CE

"Meala, keep your head down, girl!" firmly whispered a gruff man named Ucer, though his gruffness made it sound more like a dog's bark than a suggestion. He was a distant relative of hers, through her father, if she recalled. The dark-haired man waved his hand back at the woman, hoping she would take the hint and keep her head down. In his battle-tested opinion, she was unfit to participate in such a dangerous raid, having not joined a warband and probably not having the traditional training of a warrior caste member. The front lines were for the warrior caste and other Highermen, while the Freemen caste of landed farmers usually comprised the rear of the battle lines. Nevertheless, little could be done this close to the fight. She had trailed his warband and joined at their meeting point just that afternoon, using her mother's name and bloodline to argue her way into the fight. It was far too late to address why she was there in detail, so he had agreed. Still, if she got their warbands seen by the night watch, many lives would be lost.

The Moon was nearly full that night but barely peeked above the tree line, east by southeast, clouds obscuring much of the light, and over four hundred warriors as they crept just beneath the Romans' noses. Cool, damp air danced across her skin, the smell of the sea mixing with the pungent smells of torches, the earthen smell of the Wall, body odor, and the faintest hint of what might be wine. Off in the distance, the sound of an owl preparing for a kill served as an immediate reminder of the cycle of life. On any other night, she might have imagined herself as an owl and rushed off into the forest to look for mice or some other mischief, her imagination often getting the better of her, but not tonight. For the longest waking period of her life, she was entirely focused on the here and now. The only question for her now was, who would be the owl and who would be the unfortunate mouse?

Sei'ln Meala (pronounced she-lan me-la), or "Meala" for short, ducked her head lower. She was nearly crawling on the ground but heeded the grizzled warrior's words. The late dark season (early spring) air was cold and damp, and she was glad she had worn brown woolen trousers under her knee-length dark woolen tunic. Both were simple twill woven by her mother that past dark season, the clothing of a farmer. Her feet were kept dry by a pair of well-oiled leather shoes, though with how far she had walked over the past few days to reach the fort, she was pretty sure the shoes would need mending or replacement before long. Such was the problem with leather when it got wet.

With extra care to keep her head low, Meala took in the surreal scene that had become her reality. Nearly 200 warriors crept along the edge of the wall, between said wall and a similar sized ditch that ran parallel, just a short walk East of the Roman fort of Veluniate; an equal number coming from the other direction. Behind her expanded the mouth of a massive fjord, a waterway opening into the great ocean. Before her, Ucer, a dozen men, two women, and a single weryn (analogous to a transgender man) from her war band lay ready for battle. Behind them, at least ten more warbands formed their raiding force. They were far too close to the front for her liking, but this was what she had chosen for herself. It was this or marriage.

The warriors had painted their bodies mostly black with ash to hide them. Most wore similar clothing to Meala, though one man in her warband, Urth, had left his clothing beside a tree not far to the Northwest. He crept entirely nude with a captured Roman ax in one hand and a large oval wooden shield in the other. His body was painted red and black, while his face was painted black. Most impressive were his five magical tattoos depicting animals. When exposed as they were, the power of the gods, the spirits of the animals, and his ancestors would fill him with strength, protecting him from harm – at least, they might. As she watched, the man breathed heavily, seemingly unaware of the cold or perhaps more aware of the battle to come.

She wondered if she could be so bold one day as to perform a ritual of such audacity. Few felt such bravery, perhaps no more than one in ten from their total force, though the cold might have been a greater motivating factor. Of course, women rarely performed the act as it was considered unacceptable for a woman to bare her body in full, and there were other dangers to being seen so obviously as a woman on a battlefield, though a few that night had also performed the rite, in full or at least in part. Of course, some stories spoke of warrior queens backed by enough glory to ignore such problems. Far from glory, Meala was not even supposed to be there, but she had followed the region's warbands against her mother and father's wishes. She had to either marry or have social standing not to, and this was the only way for her to gain that status in such a short time. Her thoughts were interrupted as someone ahead spoke.

"There… Titus Domitius, I bet. Dirty little pig come to suck Erp's tits for a bit of land," a man not far ahead whispered, pointing at the entry to the Fort as the large wooden doors began to open.

"Any man fool enough to think that drunk a leader deserves a good spear up his ass," another man said with a chuckle.

"Quiet or we'll all be pig food," Urth muttered. With that, the warbands slowed their approach, taking extra care to remain silent as the moment of battle arrived. It seemed like the informant's estimation of Titus's departure had been accurate… she hoped. Meala's heart beat so loudly that she worried the Roman guards on the wall might hear. Just then, a small caravan of a dozen mounted soldiers emerged from the door, flanking a far more lavishly garbed man riding a white pony of fine quality. Titus Domitius was an important man among the Romans, at least as far as her people knew. His death would send a message, acting as a deterrent to other wealthy nobles. More importantly, it would allow an opening in the wall and a straight path to the Fort a few Roman miles east – a spectacular raid if it worked.

In truth, such raids were reasonably common, and their results were as much a benefit to the reputations of the warbands as hindering the Roman advance. Usually, raids were carried out upon the different clans and tribes who lived north of the wall, but the Romans had been angering the tribal chiefs, and a price had to be paid. Whatever their loftily described motives, simple hatred of the Romans was the underlying pretext. The invaders had killed thousands along the lands just north of their wall, waged conflict after conflict, and enslaved thousands more, resulting in nearly every family within a tenday's horse ride having lost someone to a Roman blade or slaver's whip. Beside her, another man made the sound of a pig as still others nervously laughed as quietly as they could. They were frightened, and humor helped a bit, but only a little.

"All right, keep your heads down and your mouths shut until the cart is in the doorway. If they shut the gate, we won't have a chance. May the Highest Mother stand with us," Ucer growled. Meala barely heard sounds of acknowledgment from around as she fixated on the coming battle. Her hands trembled and sweat beaded at her brow, even in the cool night air. It wasn't the death part that frightened her so much as the pain of dying or even living with a grievous wound. She had seen amputees, people scarred and mutilated, and the other common horrors of war. The glory was appealing when sung around a fire with drink, but when the time to fight came, she knew only fear and the fragile feeling of mortality.

Meala held her old wooden spear with its rusted iron tip. She had found the tip the previous warm season, seemingly discarded at the festival grounds. It was hardly a good weapon, but it's what she had. In her other hand, she carried her father's old rickety shield, a rough approximation of a bee painted on it using some of her soot body paint. When he learned that it was missing, he would be quite angry. Of course, if she died, it wouldn't matter. If she lived, her achievement might be enough to quell that anger. Around her waist, a worn leather belt held a simple bronze dagger, wineskin of wine-fortified water, and a leather bag, the latter carrying a small amount of dried food. It wasn't much, but she didn't have much. If she survived the battle, her share of the spoils alone would be enough to have proper equipment made.

She might even be able to get her first magical tattoo. Her calves and biceps were marked with rich, black tattooed rings, while her shoulders sported swirl tattoos she had gotten only that last warm season. The most painful had been a swirl tattooed on her right hand, each tattoo made from black ash. She had traded her labor at her cousin's farm a short walk north of her family's homestead for the tattoos and had the most of anyone in her family. But none of these were magical... none would help her now. Her thoughts were dashed as she heard a woman cry out ahead.

"Now, now, now!"

She wasn't sure whether the Romans had spotted them or the caravan cart was in the proper position. Either way, everyone began a sudden and aggressive dash toward the doors before they could be closed. From the Fort, a horn blasted its call above the sounds of war cries and trilling. The sound had a distinct pattern, but Meala had no idea what it meant. Instead, she focused on keeping up as she let out a war cry and ran toward the door. Above, she heard Roman soldiers reacting to the scene below.

"Mandata Captate! Portam defendite!" came the cry from the wall above as the Romans began to react to the raid. Soldiers rushed forward to close the gate doors, but a large wooden cart pulled by a single horse blocked the door. The soldiers at the rear tried to push the cart outward, while the screaming and confusion in front of the caravan caused the horse to try and back away. From both sides, screaming warriors rushed to the gate, hoping for such a situation.

Seemingly realizing they would be caught with the door wedged open, the light Roman guard rushed forward with their large, oval shields and weapons in hand and formed a shield wall. While the few guards who had been on duty wore armor, more soldiers began to appear wearing simple tunics as though caught off guard. More rapidly than Meala had expected, they formed a defensive line two columns deep while their leaders screamed orders. The mass of warriors from both sides slammed into the wall of shields, nearly driving the Romans back through the gate, but the second column of soldiers braced the first as smoothly as if they had practiced reacting to such an attack. The raid on Veluniate had begun.

As she watched, a soldier was cleaved in the head by an ax. As he fell, another Roman stepped into his position before his shield could fall, holding their line. The sudden and grotesque scene took a moment to see but so much longer to process as Meala came to a stop. Piece by piece, what she had just witnessed began to construct into an almost post-hoc understanding of what had happened, the original scene far too shocking and unreal to comprehend in real time. The full realization of what was happening began to set in as war shifted from an abstract notion in her mind into a real and terrifying reality. This was why young warriors normally took part in cattle raids and other less intense confrontations before joining something as spectacular as a full raid against the Romans.

As she watched, arrows began to rain down from a handful of guards at the gate towers, taking their toll as more guards arrived, many carrying larger tower shields. Beside her, a man not much older than she made a strange sound, then collapsed to the ground with a Roman arrow lodged in his neck, his blood spraying and bubbling around the wound. He looked like the sort of young man who might flash her a smile when her family traded at a festival, a man who may have just married or would soon… no, no, he wouldn't, she realized. Shock and fear filled her as adrenalin flooded her veins, the absurdity of the violence making it hard for her to accept that it was real. The Romans were organized, efficient, and well-trained. This was not like the stories…

"Pila!" she heard screamed by at least a dozen voices. All around, everyone raised their shields, but these would do little to help against the nightmare the Romans had presumably unleashed. Pila were small javelins with wooden handles and long, thin, rod-like projections ending in a deadly point. They were thrown high above the shield wall toward the warriors, their long and thin shape easily penetrating shields and then flesh. The spear would bend once it hit, making it useless to throw back at the Romans and rendering shields perforated by the suddenly cumbersome weapons useless to hold. It was a one-shot technique used to demoralize and blunt the thrust of an enemy.

She could barely see the pila in the dark, so Meala slid to a halt and raised her small buckler-style shield against the invisible death. Her body tensed, and she issued a shrill scream as she waited to be pierced. All around her, warriors raised their shields, but the deadly spears easily pierced their wood frames, finding their way into the bodies of a dozen. Meala gasped as she heard the screams of the fallen, but then the moment passed, and she was still alive, though it sounded like some of her people were not. She had only lived nineteen years and had never experienced anything like the nightmare she had just willingly entered. It had to be fake–a dream she might awaken from–yet it was all around her. She could see it, feel it, smell it.

Though a Roman pilum (pl. pila) was deadly, they did little to slow the assault as her people were simply too worked up and focused on their prize. There might be several hundred Roman soldiers in Veluniate, but most would be caught off-guard at the fort proper and unable to reach the gate in time, many simply drunk, or asleep. It was an awful risk but a worthy prize. If they could penetrate the gates and overwhelm the Romans before they could arm and organize, they might have a chance of sacking a fort and, with it, whatever riches the invaders had amassed.

Meala watched as a young man rushed the shield wall, an ax in one hand, while his free hand grabbed the top of the Roman's tower shield, trying to pry it aside for a clear swing. With a swipe of the Roman's gladius across the shield's top, the young man's fingers left his hand in one quick, gruesome motion. He stumbled back in shock, but before he could even react, an arrow from the towers above plunged into his chest. He collapsed to the ground, screaming in agony like so many wounded warriors. A moment later, the top of the finger-cutting Roman's shield was pried downward and a spear inserted, ending his resistance. Yet the hole formed was instantly closed as the Romans tightened their ranks, their shields reacting like the scales of a mighty dragon.

There were many attackers but only a few could fit past the large wooden doors to engage the wall of Roman shields as the others stood in the open throwing javelins, firing arrows, or preparing for their turn against the shield wall. Above, arrows rained down and the sound of screaming and battle was deafening. Meala's heart pounded as warrior after warrior fell, taking their turn to break the cursed wall, or die trying. She shook her head, trying to stay focused and keep her nerve.

"Voca equitatum!" a Roman with a large plume atop his helmet yelled as the bloodshed continued. Meala stood toward the center of her people, holding her shield high to help block arrows as those before her took their place at the shield wall. As each warrior died, the next would take his, her, or their place in the limited space available. Below their feet lay the bodies of the fallen, many dead but still more wounded and trampled as their fellow warriors fought to break the Roman lines. It was insanity and yet it was also her reality.

When her turn came, she would face the wall – she had to, didn't she? If she ran, she would forever be branded a coward before her people, her watching ancestors, and gods. Fleeing might save her from marriage to a man, but only because she would be so despised. Yet warriors with far greater skill and experience fell one after the other. The realization that facing the wall was now her only real choice, she probably would not survive, and that her final moments would be a mixture of terror and agony brought tears to her eyes, born of panic. Her heart pounded in her ears as fear and fatigue caused her shield hand to shake as she held it overhead. She advanced on the wall, one foot after the next, fighting to keep from thinking lest she lose her nerve in the terrifying madness of battle as the dying shrieks of women and groans of men filled the night.

Next up, a large man with spiked hair, a full body of tattoos, and a heavy war spear tried to kick a shield aside with his strength, only for the raised shield to tip sideways, bracing against the Roman's body, and a gladius sword to plunge forward, catching him in the neck. The Roman's head was visible for a moment but hard to make out in the dark. Even as he fell, a woman dashed forward with a spear in hand, her shield studded with several arrows, fine embroidered clothing and a heavy silver chain around her neck marking her as a minor noble. She thrust her spear at the Roman's exposed head with a trilling scream. The Roman suddenly pivoted his tower shield up and almost over his head, catching her spear and deflecting it. At the same time, he ducked and stepped forward, stabbing her right in the chest with his short gladius, the blade held horizontal to ensure it passed right through her rib cage. With a kick of his foot, he freed the blade and slammed his tower shield once more into the ground, creating an impenetrable wall of wood, steel, and martial skill.

The woman grasped the gaping hole in her chest, turning her bewildered look toward Meala as she stumbled away and fell among the pile of those who had taken their turn moments before, her noble blood flowing just like any other warrior. Had she seen this woman before at a major festival? A memory of someone like her–maybe her–flashed, laughing and holding a cup of beer. Meala wasn't sure in the moment, but probably. These weren't just faceless people… no, these were her people; cousins, neighbors, members of her extended clan and region. Two more warriors took their turn, one staggering away wounded and the other tumbling to the side, his fate unknown. Then a space opened, **and it was Meala's turn to face the wall…**

She felt as though her heart might beat from her chest as it thudded in her ears. All around the battle sounds softened as her focus tunneled upon the one exposed tower shield, dozens of warriors fighting on either side. The shield was battered and damaged, its surface slick with blood that shone the Moon's light back at her, a macabre canvas painted with humanity. This was the moment she had come for. This was the moment to prove herself… to free herself or be freed from this world. All around, screams of death filled the night as people she had eaten a meal with earlier that night lay on the ground dead and dying. Before her stood a line of metal banded, wooden tower shields. This was her chance to change her fate or permanently escape it, one way or another. Adrenaline danced through her veins as she held her spear and began to advance. Her dream of escape had become a liminal nightmare. This was her turn to die.

"I am Sei'ln Meala, daughter of Ail Braide!" she screamed as she rushed forward, her fear seeming to melt into a numb, alternate reality as time slowed and sounds muffled. She thrust her spear through a gap between two shields in one smooth motion, hoping to score a hit. An arrow barely missed her as it flew by with a buzzing sound. Suddenly, the shield to her right moved sideways, pinning her spear between it and the neighboring shield. Then, the deadly gladius came from around the opposite side of the shield. Meala released her spear and twisted her body sideways just in time to avoid a blade to the gut, though the blade sliced her abdomen as it passed. Ignoring the pain, she tugged at her spear, trying to free it. Beside her, a man brought his ax down hard on the shielded Roman ahead of her. His ax crashed through the tower shield, fracturing it down the middle as the soldier raised it to catch the blow.

Seeing an opening, Meala dropped to her knees at the Roman's feet as she fumbled with her old bronze dagger, having trouble unsheathing it in the moment. In one adrenaline-fueled motion, she stabbed her small blade into the Roman's exposed leg, just above his sandals. The man may have screamed, but the sounds of battle drowned everything out as the man buckled under the vicious wound. Dropping his shield, he tumbled forward onto the ground, reaching for his wounded leg, all around dozens of warriors and soldiers fought, their screams filling the night.

This was her chance to kill a Roman as the man rolled in agony atop his shield right before her. With her left hand she grabbed the Roman's neck, his hand grasping hers in response. His eyes remained closed in agony, the pain of his wound overwhelming. With her right hand she made ready to stab the man in the neck, yet she hesitated as the sudden realization that she was about to kill a man gave her a moment's pause. Beside her, the man with the ax was hit with several arrows, staggering away to die. Behind her, the next man stepped forward to take his turn, probably thinking that she had been wounded or killed. As she looked, the Roman screamed in agony, as the sounds of fighting filled her ears. Before she could force herself to act, a woman planted her spear deep into the Roman's back, then flashed Meala a nearly fanatic smile. Her chance to take a Roman's life had ended, just like that. It had all happened in less time than it would have taken to say her full name, yet time seemed slower, thicker… like blood.

The rising Moon burst through the clouds illuminating the battlefield as the small Roman reaction force finally began to crumble beneath the onslaught. The line of battle had pushed nearly a man's length past her and into the gate as the Romans worked frantically to pull the wagon from the entry and close their door while her people began climbing the not-so-tall earthen wall in droves. Unfortunately, they were being hampered by iron caltrops, small four-pointed metal spikes that caused untold damage to a foot, a wooden palisade that ran the top of the wall, and an increasing number of Roman archers peppering the climbers with arrows.

Her body flooded with cortisol and adrenaline, and danced upon a blade's edge of fight or flight as Meala knelt on the ground surrounded by death. All around lay the casualties of a fight that had moved a short distance away, leaving only blood and screams. Her breathing came in rapid, heavy gasps like she was in a thick fog, and her ears rang from the sound and fear. Beside her lay the dead soldier she had nearly killed, a young man probably only a few years her elder, his body framed by a gruesome pile of her fallen kin. Blood pooled like a muddy field after a rainstorm, dark and shiny at night, but the tangy smell was unmistakable, sickening, and everywhere. She was dazed and confused, her world spinning around her. Everything was surreal, and none of it made any sense, yet here she knelt on the ground in a sea of humanity and suffering… none of it was real… it couldn't be real.

A fresh wave of nausea passed over her, and she doubled over, vomiting. A moment later, she caught her breath and shook herself, trying to recover from the moment. What was she supposed to be doing? She could barely remember as she fought against the fog in her mind. Finding and grasping her spear with a numb hand as she wiped the vomit from her lips, she turned toward a new sound coming from her right. What greeted her sparked a new wave of fear, banishing the nausea in an instant as raw adrenaline fought against her reaction to combat stress.

From the West, at least twenty cavalry raced along the edge of a deep ditch that hugged the wall's perimeter, headed straight for the fight. If that wasn't bad enough, the soldiers galloping toward them were clearly not Romans. Instead, they were the greatly feared Dacian cavalry – strange and lethal warriors from a faraway land who served the invaders. Meala had never seen them before in person, but she had heard tales of the mighty horseback archers, and the group coming her way fit those tales perfectly.

A few wore pointed metal helmets, some solid and some made from leather with metal bands wrapped around them, each with various feathers and decorations. Their bodies were cloaked in long cloth and leather jackets with what looked like trousers and boots. They were protected by scale armor of hundreds of pieces of overlapping bone or metal, which glistened in the walls' firelight torches like a swarm of little dragons. Many carried swords and axes, but their most fearsome weapons were small, recurved bows, long, heavy war lances, and the skill to use them.

Her childhood stories did little to prepare her for the reality of the mounted warriors. As she watched, the lead mounted archer fired four arrows as fast as she could count them, a frightening example of their prowess. Using his body to control the horse, he rode a wide arc around the battle, firing arrow after arrow into the warbands, his compatriots following close behind. Beside him, another rushed headlong into a group of her people, his mighty war lance, called a contus, impaling a man as he scattered the warriors.

Between the heavy losses at the gates, sudden arrival of elite cavalry, and the sounds of many more Romans arriving to fortify the doorway, the pace of the battle had clearly been lost. Panic and disorder quickly filled the battlefield as a disorganized rout began. She should have run, but she couldn't seem to compel herself to move, her legs momentarily frozen. As Meala watched, her people sounded the cry of retreat and began to scatter in all directions, leaving perhaps one-quarter of their number behind for the Romans to kill and torture or the birds to pick clean.

Get up... Get up... ***GET UP!!!***

Her mind fought against her body's growing shock, trying its best to pin her to the ground. She had stayed and fought, and now the main battle was over. With a shaking hand, she clumsily sheathed her dagger and stumbled to her feet on shaky legs; gone was her usual finesse and dexterity. With her spear in hand, her shield lost somewhere in the carnage, she began stumbling around the battlefield. Where had she lost her shield? She looked about but saw nothing familiar in the mass of death lit by a pale moonlight, her mind growing confused from the trauma and shock.

While she stood there trying to focus, the cavalry raced up and down the perimeter of the battlefield, firing at her people, driving them into a mass rout as their primary goal was to halt the attack. Worse, with her people routed and pressure taken away from the gateway, the soldiers fanned out to secure the entry, and waves of Roman soldiers from the fort swept onto the battlefield, slaughtering all who had yet to flee. Meala breathed hard, forcing herself to stay in the moment so she could focus and flee. Looking around, she saw Romans before her and to the left, and Dacians behind and to her right. It had taken only moments to regain her composure and stand, yet those moments had been far too long.

At least half of the warbands had fled, but many more were being massacred all around, and soon she would join them. The sudden realization that she was going to die hit her like an arrow… So that was it, then? She had thought that it would be during the attack in some honorable way, not just a mindless slaughter. But this entire raid had just been a mindless slaughter, on both sides, she realized. She had fled one terrible fate only to find another, more deadly one. Another nameless warrior to be dragged away and tossed onto a pyre. Would her family ever find out what happened to her? Would she cross into the Otherworld or simply vanish into nothingness? Worse, if she were wounded or captured… No, she would take her own life or die fighting before that fate.

Her body felt numb, almost tingly, as fear danced through her. *I am Sei'ln Meala, daughter of Ail Braide,* she thought, realizing that she had only one choice left. Oddly, that singular realization and resignation began to solidify her focus. She lifted her spear, her arm trembling yet strong from a life of farming. *I am Sei'ln Meala. I am daughter of Ail Braide…*

Just ahead, a mounted archer passed by, firing their bow. She wasn't making it out of here. She was going to die in a few moments, but she could die fleeing or standing tall under the watchful eyes of her ancestors. The thought was so profound that she turned away from it lest it overpower her self-control. *I am Sei'ln Meala, daughter of Ail Braide!* Instead, she raised her spear and took aim at the archer, her body numb and tears rolling down her cheeks while she chanted her name like a mantra, *I am Sei'ln Meala, daughter of Ail Braide!* She would pass, but not without leaving her mark for the Highest Mother and the Highest Father, no doubt watching. They would look poorly on the raid but not upon her bravery.

As she lifted her weapon, the archer turned, matching her gaze. Meala held her weapon awaiting the archer's recognition of her challenge. The ritual of challenge was to be her final, and she would do it right. In a sea of death and surrounded by her enemies, Meala stood tall with her spear in hand and her bravery for armor, the unmistakable challenge of a warrior in her stance. She would stand there and issue that final challenge for single combat – the way of the brave. Just then, the archer turned her way and began their approach, the final challenge accepted.

With all her might, she stepped forward and launched her spear at the mounted archer, a trilling war cry on her lips. *I am Sei'ln Meala, and I will die on my feet!* She watched as the spear flew directly at the archer. Almost beyond hope, the spear slammed into the archer's chest, causing them to lose their bow as they nearly tumbled from their mount, caught off guard by the heroic, if not absurd attack.

Unfortunately, a spear wasn't a javelin, and Meala wasn't as strong as those who trained to throw such weapons. The old iron spear skipped off the archer's scaled armor and tumbled to the ground. With expert skill, the archer recovered themselves and turned their horse to gallop toward Meala, quickly pulling a second bow free from its bowcase. *They have two bows?!* Seeing her end coming straight for her, Meala pulled free her bronze blade and prepared to face the warrior and her end, her body feeling almost light as though it might float and her thoughts growing detached as though she were living in a dream.

"I am Sei'ln Meala, daughter of Ail Braide, warrior of the Wood Owl clan of the Eastern Wenechon! I do not fear you! Ancestors hear me! Highest Mother, take my fear! Highest Father, guide my hand!" she cried, finishing with a warrior's trill. But before she could do anything, the archer whipped an arrow from their side quiver, took aim, and fired. It was so fast that Meala had not even chosen an action. Oddly, as the arrow flew, she once more caught sight of the archer's face, but they were much closer this time. She was a woman, her swirl-painted face and rich, dark eyes catching the Moonlight as the blur of the approaching arrow registered in her mind. She was captivating. The arrow cut into the very edge of her upper left abdomen, deflecting off her rib and emerging from the back. In shock, she stepped backward as she registered the hit like a punch to the side.

Looking down, she saw an arrow protruding from her left side, its goose fletching blowing in the light wind. She had been shot by an arrow, but before she could even react, the still charging cavalry woman passed, lifting her booted foot and kicking Meala square in the face. Everything exploded into stars, and the world became a dark, dizzy place. The next thing she knew, she was lying on the ground looking up at a sea of stars with a few clouds, an arrow fletching just visible in the lower left of her vision. A moment later, darkness came like a merciful blanket.

CHAPTER II

THE AMAZON WARRIOR

Sarmatian is a term that may be applied to a number of Iranian language family speaking iron age cultures in eastern and central Europe, particularly the Eurasian steppe (grasslands) from roughly the 3rd century BCE to the 4th century CE. Among the many cultures that made up the Sarmatian peoples were the Iazyges (Eye-az-ah-geez). This nomadic people spread from central Asia through what is now Ukraine. Cynna is one such Iazyges woman of noble blood. She was born and lived in Dacia, a land occupying parts of modern Ukraine, Moldova, Bulgaria, Serbia, Slovakia, and Hungary.

The Sarmatians inherited much of the culture of the previous Scythian peoples, the culture the Greeks based their "Amazones" upon. Like the Scythians, women were known to fight among their ranks. Also like the Scythians, Sarmatian cavalry was considered some of the deadliest for their time. By the 2nd century CE, Sarmatians were known for their elite use of the bow, typically the Hunnish Bow, and a long lance called a Contus. In 175 CE, just 15 years after this novel is set, 5,500 Sarmatian cavalry would be forced to serve in the Roman army, with thousands sent to the walls in Britain. Some may have found their way to Britain beforehand, though we have little evidence for this.

Note: Cynna is Dacian by locus of birth, but culturally Iazyges. She wouldn't have used the term Sarmatian or called herself a Dacian, except when speaking to people who would not likely know of her true people. Throughout the book you will hear several terms used for her based on how people would perceive her ethnicity and culture.

The Romans had nearly lost the gates by the time Cynna's unit had made it to the primary gate. With that entry blocked, they had been forced to gallop a full Roman mile to the next gate and then return, a strain on both time and their horses. Cynna had barely finished securing her armor and stringing her bow as they rode, something she had yet to see a Roman auxilia do; a fact she considered with a mix of pride and loathing. She drew another arrow as she watched the painted raiders fleeing before her. Her people were nomads of the steppe and ready for a raid at any time, though she was sure they would get little thanks from the Romans for their efforts. In truth, she barely cared at this point.

Nudging her horse with her knees, she turned 90 degrees, took aim, and fired an arrow, catching a wounded man in the neck. She had caught him with her lasso as he had tried to flee, then quickly wrapped the rope around her shoulder to brace as her pull caused him to fall. Pulling her bow from its bowcase on the horse's side, she quickly dispatched him. He was yet another of the strangely nude raiders. Most had common sense to wear clothing in the cold, and a few even wore minor examples of body armor, though most wore simple cloth tunics, braccae (trousers), and the occasional helmet. She could not understand the fanatical naked warriors, though thankfully, they numbered only a few. Whatever drove them, they seemed to be significantly more dangerous than their more properly clothed friends.

The Sarmatian warrior dropped the rope and slid her older backup bow into its holder on the side of her quiver, glancing down to see how bad the damage was. A poorly thrown spear with a heavy iron tip had dug a gash in her iron scales and cut her flesh just below her left breast. She couldn't remove her armor to check, but it felt shallow. The spear had penetrated both her armor and the hemp fiber kaftan long shirt beneath, and bit into her flesh, its force nearly knocking her from her horse. The wound was painful but probably wasn't an immediate problem and would likely heal well. The bigger problem was her missing bow that the warrior woman had caused her to lose. With a sigh, she approached the place where she had probably lost it, drawing her hand ax, and began scanning the battlefield for the precious bow in the moonlight.

While there had been many brave fighters that night on both sides, she still had not expected to face down a painted woman wearing the ragged woolen clothing of a peasant and wielding a spear she obviously had little skill using. Sure, the Barbari (barbarians), as the Romans called them, often counted women and other genders among their ranks, but most had better gear and a few more years on them. Curiously, this particular painted woman had stood her ground and bravely met her charge even when she had no chance at living. It almost seemed as though the woman had called her out for a sort of duel, something her kind seemed inclined to do. Whether it was the woman's fierce eyes or bravery in the face of death, Cynna couldn't say, but the woman's determined look kept coming to mind even as she felt the pain of the spear's sting. She shook her head, trying to dismiss the image of the brave woman.

"Ohe Cynna!" she heard from behind. Without even a word, her horse turned, feeling the slight movements of her legs against its side. Cynna had grown up in the vast Eurasian steppe, riding since she could stand. At this point, a horse was simply an extension of her body, as was her bow. Unfortunately, she recognized the face of Gaius Pedius, the optio principalis, a title marking him as second to the head centurion of the second cohort of the II Augusta legion. Gaius was a rather gruff and unkempt fellow with a leering smile that always unnerved her. He reminded her of a jackal with his predatory gaze, though he had a sort of Gaulish look about him, in her opinion.

He approached, holding a bloodied gladius in one hand and carrying the heads of two Caledonii men and a woman by their hair, and a collection of silver chains and a torc in the other, his simple tunic soaked in blood and gore. The optio had clearly been off duty when the attack began, yet his overly enthusiastic expression suggested that he hadn't minded. Frowning, she nodded to acknowledge that she had heard the man. He flashed her a smile and a wink, which made for a strange contrast with the macabre scene unfolding around her as Roman soldiers hurried about slaughtering or capturing the wounded raiders who had failed to escape. Just then, she spotted her bow lying on the ground only a short distance away. Wishing to avoid the violent and vile man and glad to have found her primary bow, she quickly dismounted, scooped up the weapon, and remounted the horse in a fluid, well-practiced motion, and left before he could speak. If nothing more, she wanted to escape the sounds and growing feculent smell of the dying.

It wouldn't be long until the townsfolk began stripping and looting the bodies of any belongings, then dragging away their corpses and clearing the field. But luckily, that was not work for the valuable cavalry woman. She had only just arrived at the wall a few months earlier. Still, it had already become apparent that her small unit was considered far too crucial for menial tasks yet too foreign to be given proper credit. Like other specialized soldiers, they were labeled "immunes" by the Romans and excluded from common labor.

Cynna sighed, her head hurting and her chest feeling quite bruised from a wound that could have killed her. She would need to get herself cleaned and have a drink to settle her nerves. Sadly, she had run out of hemp buds with her previous spell, and their effects had been cast aside by adrenalin. She could really have used the calming smoke after such a battle. As she slowly trotted forward toward the gate and her escape from this mess, she noticed one of the bodies moving in the dim moonlight at the edge of the battlefield. Pulling free her still-strung bow, she approached the wounded warrior. This was the part she hated, enemy or no.

Meala awoke feeling cold and pain. Her head hurt, her side hurt, her hip, chest, and, for that matter, nearly everywhere else, too. It was too dark to tell how badly she had been wounded with the sky clouding and the Moon now almost occulted, though she didn't feel immobile. Her mind was a blur, and she couldn't seem to remember how she had ended up on the ground. She vaguely recalled the battle, fear, and throwing her spear at a mounted female archer, but her thoughts were so foggy and hard to pin down.

As she cautiously looked around, she could see Roman soldiers moving about, stabbing the wounded, and dragging others away. Fear shot through her as she began to realize what was going on and reality began to set in. She had heard of the various tortures Romans would inflict upon the wounded and captured, and that terror filled her. It was one thing to be killed but quite a different thing to be wounded and left behind. She had expected to die, yet somehow, she lived, again, presenting new opportunities for terror, especially for a woman. That last thought haunted her more than any other as she realized how much her body had become a liability few men could ever understand. But the thought also brought with it more adrenaline, clearing her foggy mind, at least a little. How long that lasted would be down to luck, the gods, and her next actions.

Her first problem was the arrow in her chest. The shaft had entered and exited her chest on her left side, deflecting over her ribs and probably anything vital, almost like a bone sewing needle making a shallow stitch. No one knew what the various parts within the body were, but if they were damaged, it usually meant death. Still, the pain radiating from her side was tremendous, a mixture of intense, dull throbbing and sharp spikes whenever she breathed. Feeling behind her, she realized the arrowhead had snapped off, perhaps when she had fallen. That was probably what had caused her to blackout, as the pain of removing an arrow was well known among her people to be one of the worst pains, aside from childbirth. Unfortunately, that still left the lengthy shaft protruding from her chest.

Her wounds frightened her, but not nearly as much as the men now walking the battlefield with spears and ropes. If the Romans caught her, they might do any number of unspeakable horrors, then take what was left and nail her to a tree or an erected wooden pole. She had heard the stories as a child – they all had. She wouldn't escape the battlefield with the arrow in her side, and there was only one way to fix that problem. Just then, a Roman soldier approached and Meala closed her eyes, lying backward. The man stepped by, obviously looking for more lively targets, yet they would soon enough check her or simply stab her with a spear for good measure. Meala nearly whimpered in fear but held herself still enough in the dark. As soon as the man had passed, she forced some of her tunic into her mouth to bite on, grasped the shaft, and pulled.

A few moments later, her vision returned as she lay back, still reeling from the pain. The arrow had perhaps come out halfway, but the pain was almost worse than any death she could imagine. The only reason she had not cried out was the shock of the pain had been beyond her expectations. Every part of her wanted to just give up, but the sounds of wounded being dragged away and the horrors of crucifixion overcame her, driving her to grasp the shaft with shaking hands and pull once more. With a tortured pull, the arrow came free, and her vision darkened a third time.

A moment later, Meala lay on the ground recovering from pain she had never known could be felt. Had she cried out? She wasn't sure, but the Romans might be coming if she had. The sounds of the dying were fading, and with them, her chance of escape. Weak and wounded, Meala rolled over and slowly crawled on her hands and knees, keeping low to the ground as she attempted to escape the nightmare that had become her life. Just ahead lay her dagger, catching the faint moonlight. She fumbled for the weapon and slid it into its sheath at her hip, having trouble with what should have been a simple motion, but her hands would not stop shaking.

Just then, she noticed a fallen soldier lying next to her was still breathing. The faint mist of his warm breath caught the dim torchlight, like a beacon. It was hard to make out much in the dark, but she could see his pained face as he winced. His head sported a nasty gash that had probably knocked him out, and it looked like someone had put a spear tip into his right arm. He was clearly one of the cavalrymen assigned to guard Titus Domitius Ahenobarbus, given his lorica hamata (iron mail), calcei (leather boots), and the spatha sword lying beside him, its form resembling a gladius, but longer and better suited for combat from the saddle. But what caught her eye was the gold phalera disk attached to his armor, its golden surface depicting a woman's face with what might have been snakes for hair.

This sort of trophy might win her respect and honor, assuming she could make it from this cold sea of death alive. The man was alive, his eyes open and looking toward the stars, yet he seemed disoriented, probably from his head wound. He would probably recover, but right now, he was defenseless. She could put a hand over his mouth and cut his neck like an old ewe, he would die, and she could take the phalera… Meala's hand slid toward the dagger sheath. This is what she came for. This was the honor she sought – a physical manifestation of her bravery. Behind her, she heard the painful screams of a man as a Roman slowly sank his blade between his ribs. Her hand stopped.

Honor came in many ways, from a mother surviving birth or a farmer raising successful crops to a warrior defeating her foe. But in each of these, a risk was taken, a feat was performed, and a reward was earned. There was no honor in stabbing a defenseless man, enemy or not. The gods and ancestors would see, and they would not smile at such a petty theft. Stealing from an enemy could bring honor, but only if that was what one had originally intended. It wasn't just the act, it was the intention behind it, and opportunity theft was not the same as intentional theft, like a cattle raid. It might have been different if she had been one of those to bring him down, but now the battle was over, and she needed to escape. She turned away, letting mercy govern her actions as she instead focused on escape.

The land before her was open for quite a distance around the wall, but the clouds blocking much of the moonlight made the land dark enough that Meala thought she might have a chance. At least she had her bronze dagger. The old weapon had belonged to her grandmother and had been passed down the family line. It wasn't enough to defend herself in such a situation, but it was enough to take her life if the Romans caught her, assuming that she could even bring herself to do such a thing. That thought nearly caused her to gag as her stomach turned. Forcing her fears aside, she crawled as quickly as she dared across the open ground. Her chest throbbed in pain with each movement, and she was sure it was bleeding, but that was secondary to getting away.

Behind her, she heard the unmistakable sound of an approaching horse. Her fear and anxiety piqued, and she once again heard her heart beating in her ears as she stopped crawling and willed herself to lay completely still. She didn't dare look back lest the fort's firelight reflect in her eyes, giving away her position. Her hair, clothing, and body were coated in ash and now mud, and were hopefully much harder to see in the dark of night. The sound of the horse faded, then stopped. After a brief moment, finally knowing how a rabbit felt, she began crawling again, this time even slower.

Her chest hurt from the cold and the friction from crawling on the ground, and her body was beyond miserable from pain, strain, shock, and wounds, but she was now quite a distance from the wall, and soon, she would feel safe enough to stand and try and make a run for it, assuming she could run. But just as thoughts of freedom arose, so did the sounds of hoofs behind her. Too shaky and startled to stand or think straight, her mind fatigued from constant stress, Meala rolled over onto her back, propping herself up on her elbows. It was the wrong thing to do if one wanted to play dead, but her basic instincts took over before her mind caught up. Her breath was stolen as terror once more gripped her. A Dacian mounted archer in all her competently deadly glory towered over her. Her bow was knocked with an arrow, and she was ready to fire.

For a moment, she held her breath, her words all but stollen in the instant as she lay there expecting death, a fourth time. Yet oddly, the Dacian said nothing, merely observing Meala with her large, dark eyes. The archer's countenance held no anger or disgust but perhaps something more akin to curiosity… maybe even respect? Her face was painted with black swirls and her long, black, waist-length hair coiled in a thick braid down her back. Beneath her scale armor, she wore a long hemp shirt that ran down to her knees and a pair of woolen leggings below. Her feet were protected by rather elaborate leather riding boots, ankle length. Together with her lightly tanned skin, painted face, several quivers of arrows, and oddly small yet heavily curved bow with one limb longer than the other, she had a somewhat otherworldly appearance.

As Meala gazed at her executioner, she began to recognize the woman's face. To her shock, she looked like the same archer she had faced during the battle in single combat – the woman who had shot her with an arrow. There couldn't be many women among the ranks of the cavalry. It was hard to remember the details as her memory was currently as useful as a lame horse, yet she was sure this was the same woman. As the moments passed and the archer's arrow remained ready, but not drawn, Meala began to breathe, her eyes wet as she held back her tears unwilling to cry before her enemy. More moments passed and the archer lowered her arrow just a little.

Glancing down the woman's mighty form, she took note of the damaged scales where her spear had hit the woman's chest, right where her heart should be. Each iron scale was the width of two fingers and as long as her middle finger, yet one was missing. She had personally tried to kill this woman, and now she lay defenseless at her feet. The archer followed Meala's gaze down her armor and to the wound, then returned her curious stare, a mixture of shared recognition, challenge, and something else Meala couldn't quite place. Her dark eyes and intense stare elicited an unexpected series of conflicting feelings in what should have been, no, what was, a terrifying experience.

Meala was struck at the moment, both expecting to die yet curious of the woman who towered before her. She was pretty, but more than that, she was majestic, and Meala did not want to look away. It made no sense, yet a new battle raged in her mind between her need to escape and her growing desire to look at the archer, if not speak to her. The woman was imposing and dangerously competent as she towered over Meala with her bow and armor… and oh, was she breathtaking… Meala blinked, trying to understand the completely strange thoughts running through her addled mind. Normally, she would be shy speaking to another woman within the context of such feelings, yet their shared experience in battle seemed to have, quite literally, cut through such paltry worries.

It wasn't romance, a feeling so far removed from her situation as to be laughable, but something closer to the feeling of needing a hug, a nearly equally laughable idea. The archer was more like a grounding sight of shared humanity, which also made no sense. She supposed that her mind had been tossed around so many different ways that night that she was no longer thinking rationally, but that wouldn't matter soon. At least her final moments were relatively calm as her breathing became more stable and the moment of finality passed, leaving her still alive.

"I..." she began to say, then stopped as she realized the woman before her likely spoke none of her language, and worse, probably had no interest in women. None of the few women who lived near her had shown any interest, which was one of the many reasons she had remained single several years past when most had at least found a lover, if not more. Besides, even if the mighty warrior had such interests, she still might not find a bloody, muddy Meala worthy of her time. Also, what would she say? They were faced off at the edge of a battlefield, surrounded by death and Meala might be moments from taking her place among the fallen. It all felt so surreal and absurd, like being detached from reality. Then the Dacian spoke, her contralto voice soft and her timbre deep.

"Loquaris Latine?" Her words were heavily accented, and her cadence quite foreign, but her meaning was clear. She had asked if Meala spoke the words of the Romans. Oddly, she noticed the woman's voice was beautiful, deep, rich, and almost soothing. She pushed the odd thought aside and concentrated on the moment at hand. She was to be killed, and her oddly hard to look away from executioner was interested in a chat first. In fact, she knew the Roman language because of her mother, Ail, who had grown up behind the wall and learned it as a child. Having a common tongue was interesting, but she doubted her words would be mightier than the sword.

"Sic…" (yes), she replied, exhausted, weak, and unsure what to say.

⌖

As Cynna approached, the woman rolled over with the look of someone quite sure they were about to die, and rightfully so. She held her bow, preparing to do just that when the woman's eyes suddenly caught the tiniest bit of light from the all-but-faded Moon, and her face came into view. She frowned for a moment as she realized who she was looking at. This was none other than the same woman who had stood her ground – the same woman who had nearly put a spear through her chest. Cynna gazed down at the woman lying on the ground. She was probably three or four years younger and wearing ragged peasant clothing, no doubt soaked with blood from the arrow wound Cynna had given her. The warrior's loose hair was long and perhaps brown, though it was difficult to see in the dim light.

As pitiful as she now looked, her tear-streaked warpaint and ash smeared across her face, and blood from her brow where she had been kicked, the painted woman had stood her ground as others fled and had challenged Cynna to single combat. In fact, she had nearly killed Cynna. If the spear had impacted no more than the width of a fingernail to the left between two iron scale seams, it might have penetrated her armor, and she would be the one lying on the ground slowly cooling. The woman had nearly pierced her heart and delivered her from her many years of remaining service to the Romans. Just then, the words of her spell returned as she felt a rush of euphoria sweep across her body at the realization.

Pierce my heart with death or warm my spirit with love, but don't leave me as I am.

Had this woman been an answer from the Mother of Fire? Had she been meant to die this very night by her own spell? Her mind swam with the possibilities, though she kept her face neutral, passive as always. She had also given her oath to sacrifice a worthy warrior, a warrior like the woman lying before her. Perhaps this was her opportunity to do just that. If she dismounted and used her dagger, she could probably slice the woman's throat without much trouble, but her thoughts had grown conflicted within just those few moments. As she awaited her fate, the brave woman looked back at her, defiance and perhaps growing curiosity, if not something else, loomed in her wide eyes.

"Do you speak Latin?" Cynna asked before she realized that she had. She nearly broke her placid expression as she internally scolded herself for asking. What was she even going to ask this woman, a warrior she should be killing. For a brief moment, she held onto hope that the brave and beautiful warrior wouldn't answer… Wait, why had she thought of the warrior as beautiful? This was a battlefield, not a social meet. There were plenty of beautiful women in the town around the fort, women that Cynna had never pursued, yet here she was considering the aesthetics of what might very well be her final victim of the night. How could she objectify a warrior with such bravery as she lay helplessly at her feet. The power dynamic was… It felt… wrong?

A moment later, the painted woman responded to the affirmative, her voice higher pitched than she had expected, though her breathy, guttural accent made her reply sound odd. She stared momentarily at the painted warrior, her body exhausted from a long day of riding and a battle to punctuate her night. Her Roman masters would have her kill or capture this woman, but her pride as an Iazyges woman tingled with the memory of the woman bravely facing her death with honor, not to mention her own confusion at how closely the events had matched with her spell. Worse, when she made eye contact, a part of her fluttered most unexpectedly – though she supposed that was simply the tingles of the large bruise forming over her chest.

With her second major sigh of the night, Cynna came to an unexpected choice. It wasn't a smart idea, but a quick glance revealed no one nearby, at least no one still drawing breath. The saner part of her mind cried out not to proceed, but the timing of the spell, the near-death wound, and the brave, worthy warrior at her feet were too much to ignore. The signs of the ancestors, spirits, and even the highest powers were always present, or at least her mother had told her this as a child. Most failed to see them, but the chance to change their destiny was one of many results for those who did.

"If I let you leave, will you swear your oath to never return or raise your spear against Rome?" she asked the painted warrior, more out of curiosity than serious consideration, though her voice was grave and filled with the gravity of a life-or-death question. The young warrior glared back in defiance, her brow furrowing at merely the suggestion – a look far too pleasing for Cynna's liking. Her eyes filled with fear, yet also pride and honor, the look of one who knew the value of life, perhaps having learned that value this very night, yet knew the greater value of honor. She was afraid, but also brave.

"I will not swear. This is our land, and I will die to keep it so," she spoke in open defiance, though her hoarse throat distorted a few words. Cynna found the woman's bravery rather likable, if not inspiring. Among her steppe people, courage and honor were deeply respected in ways the Romans didn't seem to understand. She reminded Cynna of the stories of her tribe before the Romans. They had been free once, but pinned between the Alans, Dacians, and Romans, her Iazygean tribe (a Sarmatian people, not actually Dacian) had been scattered to the winds. What she chose next could get her in serious trouble, even killed, but the painted warrior had crawled so far from the battle that no one would likely see… she hoped.

"Go in peace, warrior," she spoke with a nod, then turned and galloped away. Behind her, the wounded painted woman stared completely at a loss for a moment before staggering to her feet and ambling toward the trees. Cynna shook her head. She was far too young to be this jaded, but several years in the Roman military could do that. She wasn't sure if it was compassion, her fear of what the Romans would do with a captive woman, or perhaps the woman's bravery that had inspired her actions. Either way, it was time for a stiff drink and hope of sleep. *I just saved you from a crucifixion, at the very least… Mother of Fire, please tell me if I made the right decision or if I am a fool.*

A short time later, Cynna sat on the small wood-framed bed in her unit's barracks just next to the stables, only a short walk from the fort proper, preparing for bed. Her bed was in the corner of the barracks, shielded by a worn horse blanket. She had removed her armor, leaving it beside her bed, then stepped out back of the stable and stripped. Two buckets of water had cleaned much of the blood and dirt from her skin, and a short time later, she had returned to her bed wearing her clean linen braies (underwear) and a woolen blanket. Modesty wasn't a big deal among her people, though it seemed like a significant concern among

Romans. Still, no matter how much trust she had in the men of her unit, she slept with a dagger under her pillow just the same.

Lying against the wooden wall with her head propped against a rolled blanket, she examined herself with a small oil lamp as she cleaned her single wound. Beside her left breast was a small gash where the iron tip of the spear had penetrated her scale. Placing her fingers gently against the already bruising flesh, she felt the beat of her heart just below, a reminder that she had nearly lost her life only a short time before. The blood still trickled and would until the morning, most likely. Luckily, her small unit would probably be given a few days of rest for their service, if nothing more.

Cynna would need to find a replacement scale and repair her armor in the morning, but for now, she needed to sit, drink, and forget that she still served Rome. She sipped tart wine, the cheap stuff her unit usually drank. She could afford better on the reasonable pay she earned as a cavalry woman of Rome, but tonight, she didn't feel like drinking quality. As the lip-puckering tart wine drizzled down her chin after a lengthy swig, thoughts of the painted warrior returned once again.

Non iurabo. Hae terrae nostrae sunt et retinere mortuus fueram. (I will not swear. This is our land, and I will die to keep it), she had spoken in heavily accented Latin. The words and her soft, soprano voice replayed over and over in Cynna's mind. Why did this woman interest her so, she wondered? Was it the spell or her bravery? Cynna had seen many brave warriors fall, including her former commander, not one moon after Cynna had arrived while her group escorted a trade caravan northwest of the wall. A simple ambush and he had been cut down without so much as a final word.

It wasn't even that she was a woman, as Cynna had faced women warriors of the painted people before. There had been several lying dead on the battlefield that very night, the same as their men. She had never killed one, but not for lack of trying. Even her looks made little sense, as Cynna paid no attention to how a person looked when her bow was drawn, and her blood was pumping. In battle, Cynna cared little what sex or gender her foe was, nor how they looked, as everyone's blade was sharp.

No, it was something more. Deep down, she knew that part of it was that the woman was pretty, but that couldn't be all of it. Life and death were not a competition of aesthetics in her mind, nor would she have spared an enemy merely for looking good – an absurd notion to the warrior. Besides, the measure of a warrior was her bravery and skill, not something as fleeting as pretty eyes. Yet every time she thought of the woman standing there with her spear facing her down, her heart fluttered like some dumb fool girl with her first crush on a foreign trader stopping by the village. Her face, hair, defiant bravery… everything about her was just so… Cynna loosed a low grumble in frustration.

Pressing a clean linen rag into her wound, she lay back and let the tart wine simmer in her belly like a hearth as she considered the painted warrior and why she had spared her life. In all honesty, she wasn't really sure, yet she had. Perhaps it was simply confronting the woman in a situation where sudden, lethal force wasn't needed that had forced Cynna to confront the painted warrior's humanity. She was an enemy of Rome, a land Cynna cared little for. Her face felt flushed as her emotions and the wine ate away at the barrier she had placed between her duty and her heart. Though perhaps that spear had cracked that armor, too.

"Well, Mother of Fire, it seems that I am a fool," she said and took another swig of the drink, finally letting go of the mask she wore when around others. She felt the first salty tear running down her cheek, then her chin. A moment later came a second. Thoughts of the painted woman's tear-streaked war paint returned, and a moment later, Cynna found herself sobbing as the horrors of the battlefield filled her mind. A human could only take so much death before dying inside.

Meala collapsed beside a large stone jutting from the soil at the edge of a thick forest, not half a night's walk west of the wall. Her hands shaking as much from the cold as from shock, she fumbled her belt open and began pulling off her tunic. Unfortunately, the physical act of pulling the clothing over her head proved to be too painful, so she settled for cutting her tunic open down the front with her dagger. A good tunic wasn't easy to make, and she would need to use her belt to keep it together as she walked, but right now, she needed to treat her wounds before the full Moon sank below the trees taking its pale light with it. Of course, she could also use a fire to see and to ward against brown bears and boars, but one life threatening problem at a time, she supposed.

Pulling the tunic aside, she exposed the disaster that was her abdomen. Midway down her abdomen, below her ribcage, ran a laceration nearly the length of her hand, the result of a nearly fatal brush with a gladius. It was shallow and was already only bleeding the smallest bit, but it hurt more than she cared to consider. Yet this was barely a scratch compared to the pair of holes in her left side and the untold damage to her ribs and the flesh around them, her ribcage luckily unpierced. The blood still flowed, mostly as a gentle trickle. But her tunic was soaked in the precious fluid, a worrisome sight.

No one knew what blood did, exactly, but it was known that losing too much of it meant death. Meala recalled as a child listening to an elder druid once at a dark solstice festival telling a story of how menstrual blood was used to create the first people and how blood was the medium for the spirit. Of course, she had heard several other creation stories, and the old woman was a bit past her mental prime, but it was still a fun story. Whatever its purpose, she needed to stop it from leaking before she lost too much. None of the women she knew were frightened of losing blood, a common event once a moon cycle, but this much blood was dangerous.

With her tunic slit, Meala fully removed the garment and unwound the long strip of fabric that supported her breasts. The cloth was made from a single panel of woven linen cut into strips as wide as her hand and the length of her arm, sewn into a single piece a little longer than she stood tall. The strip would be wound around her chest and tied in place, providing comfort and support. At this point, comfort while walking was the least of her concerns. A short time later, she had torn pieces of her tunic and folded them into small, soft squares. She placed a cloth square on each of the two wounds caused by the arrow and wrapped the cloth tightly around them. It wouldn't stop the bleeding by itself, but it would slow it enough for her body to, hopefully, heal.

A short time later, Meala lay against the rock, sipping what little of her fortified water remained after she had poured half of it on her wounds, yet again, more pain. It seemed like the only thing in her life that she had plenty of was pain, that and several days of walking home wounded, weakened, and without her supplies. Worse, when or if she made it home, she would have to explain to her parents why she had run off to join a raid and how the raid had failed, leaving her in such a sorry state. The one thing she would not mention was the hauntingly beautiful warrior who had spared her life.

Cynna of the Iazyges, of Dacia

Why had the woman shown her mercy? This wasn't the same as the Roman man she had spared. She had not faced him directly in battle, instead finding him weak and defenseless. Meala had been nearly defenseless but still had her dagger and could move. She had even challenged and fought the woman in single combat. The lines of honor were a bit grey in such situations, but the archer would have been within her honorable right to take Meala's life, yet she hadn't. Meala had not lost honor, either, given that she had refused to give up or give in and had faced her death, but now she was entirely spent. Her emotional quiver had run dry of arrows, and all she wanted to do was cry, but she was too parched and honestly too tired.

She closed her eyes, needing a short nap, but her mind's eye was filled with violent, gruesome imagery from the battle. Her eyes flew open, and she paused, letting her heart calm. How was she supposed to sleep if closing her eyes opened her mind to such nightmares? She tried once more but was again confronted by the trauma from the raid. She needed to rest, if not sleep, but her mind refused to let go of the horrors she had witnessed. Just then, an image of the majestic warrior looking down at her from her mighty black steed returned, and she focused upon it. At first, the other images tried to press their way into her thoughts, but the worst of them began to fade as she focused on the woman's words.

Speaking in her rich, deep voice, the archer's words sounded as clear as when she heard them. *If I let you leave, will you swear to never return or raise your spear against Rome?* Would she swear an oath, indeed? No, she had not accepted one last chance to dishonor herself before her gods and ancestors, but thanks… Insulting though the request had been, she couldn't stop thinking about the woman who had made it or her low, husky voice. As she replayed the memory, her mind began to calm, and her exhaustion took hold. She began to fade into a dark and dreamless sleep, but at least one where her heart still beat.

Chapter III

MY MOTHER'S SPEAR

"They likewise dye their skins with the pictures of various kinds of animals; which is one principle reason for their wearing no clothes, because they are loth to hide the fine paintings on the bodies." ~
Herodian's Roman History, Book III

Of all myths surrounding the Caledonians and the later Picts (several centuries later), one of the most pervasive is that they fought painted blue with tattooed bodies. Much of this myth comes from Julius Caesar's line in his Bello Gallico, where he speaks of the Britanni dying themselves with grass, a line historically interpreted as the blue dye of woad. But the actual evidence is non-existent. In practice, woad makes horrible tattoo ink, leaving the unfortunate user scarred. As skin dye, it doesn't change the skin color much, and as paint, it peels off quickly. It might have been applied as body paint, but to marginal effect. That said, woad was probably used for cloth dying, as it is well suited for that task.

Tattoos (of different colors) are reasonably supported as tattooed warriors were depicted by the later Picts on stones. Their auto-lithographical accounts, the fact that humans have been tattooing themselves for thousands of years prior, and their use of symbology in their artwork that reasonably matches outsider accounts make tattooing quite likely. However, these tattoos would probably have been mostly black, made from carbon from ash and soot, and absolutely not blue.

BRAIDE HOMESTEAD, WESTERN SHORE, FLOODING LAKE (LOCH LEVEN), 64 KM NORTHEAST OF ANTONINE WALL, CALEDONIA – 1 PM, AUGUST 29, 160 CE

The male sheep, called a ram, mounted the female sheep, called a ewe, and the action began. An act that might very well bring new life into the world was mostly ignored by the other sheep nearby as just a mundane happening on yet another lazy light season day in the southern fields, a short walk from her home. South by southeast in the distance lay a hill, one day known as Benarty Hill, but to the locals, it was a sacred place for solstice rituals, although some thought it looked more like the resting place of an ancient giant. Close to the shore along the Southern fields, a pair of red deer (Cervus elaphus scoticus) drank their fill of water entirely unconcerned on a lazy, light (summer) season day.

Meala sat beneath a tree, vaguely noticing the happenings of midday, entirely lost in thought. The tree's thick canopy provided ample shade for her to sit and do what she did best – ponder. Upon her lips, she sang a song her mother sometimes sang as she worked the fields. The original song involved a warrior man passing through a village, but Meala had always imagined the warrior as a mighty woman.

> Long hair and scars of battle,
> wooden shield painted blue.
> Like the Great Fjord in morning,
> I noticed you.
>
> Upon your dark riding steed,
> our village you rode through.
> Iron spear and chain of silver,
> I dreamt of you.
>
> A maiden fresh and fair.
> A warrior matched by few.
> A challenge I accepted.
> I called to you.
>
> You said, *No man is my equal.*
> I said, *I see no man in view.*
> To my home you did follow,
> so I lay with you.
>
> Now a warrior and a maiden,
> we are a clan of two.
> Our love is for the ages.
> My warrior maiden, I love you,
>
> forever more...

While she did, she casually played with a weed, twisting it into various shapes between her fingers while she continued the mind-numbing task of keeping the flock in order while her words became a simple hum. Often, she would fold the weeds and grass into the shapes of little people and let her imagination run wild with fantasy to entertain herself. On one side lay the vastness of the lake with its many farming families barely visible along the shores. On the other, her family's small tract of land lay filled with barley awaiting harvest just before the dark season. It was menial work, but it kept her away from the rest of her family and alone, something she had grown to appreciate since she returned. Off in the distance, the chirpy cries of a king bird (golden eagle) filled the sky as it hunted rabbits.

There was always work to be done, from tending the small family fields, caring for livestock, mending the roof or fences, to spinning and weaving cloth, grinding grain and mending leather. Their family owned a small plot of land and a humble crannog (house built over the water) on the southern shores of a lake, owing to her mother's family standing as landed warriors, at least originally. Over time, the Braide clan had split into two factions: the Western Braides being more in keeping with their warrior station and keeping their oaths to the local clan leader as Highermen, while the Eastern Braides leaned more upon their farming roots, slowly becoming Freemen, while remaining mostly independent as they had when the lands were more peaceful… before Roman steel.

As for Meala, she was less interested in being a warrior than in what the position brought her – freedom. Blood and iron were a means to an end, but they had also nearly been the means of her end. Unfortunately, while nearly five moons of healing had repaired her body, time seemed to have only partly helped her mind. The night terrors and nightmares had lessened, as had the flashbacks when she was awake, yet they still came. She might be using her knife to cut some cord for a fence when suddenly the memory of the gladius cutting her abdomen would flash through her mind, causing her to tense. It wasn't usually so much a visual memory as a visceral memory of the sensations of being wounded – as though some part of her remained within a violent shadow of the Otherworld (the afterlife).

Worse than the flashbacks had been the anxiety and plethora of feelings that she had experienced. She had felt shame and guilt for the soldier she had wounded, an act that had led to his death. In the sea of death that had been the cursed raid, one dead Roman seemed barely incidental, yet he had been a real man with hopes and dreams. Was he married? Did he have children? Meala had worked to push these thoughts from her mind, but it was harder to "other" someone when you had faced them in battle. She had smelled their scent, tasted their sweat, and wiped their blood from her hands. These were not abstract concepts; they were real people. Yet, her mother kept the skull of a Roman whose head she had taken in their home, a permanent reminder of her skill in battle.

Her mother had only been a few years older than her when she had taken that head in battle. Of course, Meala was now twenty years of age as of a few days before, and still, she had yet to find a mate, yet another problem. There were no laws compelling her to do so, but the social pressure was enormous, as was the stigma facing a woman who never married. There were plenty of men to choose from living in the region, a point her parents reminded her of nearly daily. But no man had ever really appealed. Sure, she had seen a few men in such physical condition that even she had to take note, but it was more of a recognition of their prowess than a real interest. She fidgeted with the weed, folding it into the shape of a little person, "a grass doll," she supposed. Meala loved dolls and had made them from whatever she could find when she was a child, her imagination turning her everyday world into a fantasy.

Among her people, a woman could marry a woman, but one first had to find such a woman. Of the twenty-eight families that made up the few farms and the small settlement surrounding the lake, she could only think of perhaps ten or twelve women near enough to her age to be viable, and most of them were either wed or soon would be. Likely, some of them also appreciated women, but they also faced pressure to find a man. Of course, there was always Derelei, a weaver who already had two husbands and was said to be flirting with local women, a household of four not being unheard of. She was influential in their area and easy on the eyes, but she was also her mother's age. Meala was looking for love, not just someone to warm her bed. She sighed and watched as a pair of butterflies flew by, no doubt also looking for flowers.

Her people were quite liberal about relations and polyamory and polygamy were commonplace for all genders. Still, the social pressure to have children forced many women to find a man, even if only for an evening, something her younger sister Rigandona had suggested. The problem wasn't worrying about homosexuality. Any fool could see the male sheep pairing off and realize it was perfectly normal. The problem was that parents wanted grandchildren – and not just for egotistical reasons, but also for more practical reasons of inheritance and clan structure. Inheritance followed the female line, and Meala had only one sister, further underscoring this point.

Properly joining a warband was also not on the table, given that her family's clan had little interest in fighting the Romans or other clans, especially given the disaster of the early spring raid. Highermen families trained children of all genders for war starting around their ninth or tenth year. Their children were expected to learn many feats of strength, prowess, and cunning, as well as singing, dancing, and other arts. These well-rounded fighters made up the warrior caste, her mother's original caste. Below the Highermen were the Freemen, landed farmers who made up the middle of society. Her father was a Freeman, and so she had become when her mother rejected her birthright as a Higherman.

Among Freemen families, the boys and weryn (a masculine third gender) tended to be trained for war, while girls and other genders were usually taught only basic skills for self-defense, as the laws of the high chiefs and druids declared that all who owned land should be able to use a weapon. This training was often avuncular, involving an uncle training their sister's children. Unfortunately, her maternal uncle had trained her elder brother and would soon train her younger brother, but none of the girls, a task left to her mother, when she had time. This left her as a lone young woman without station or property, with only the prospect of slowly aging as "Aunt Honeybee." She frowned, tossing the "grass doll" aside. Being a warrior was her birthright, yet her parents' choice to live as farmers had robbed her of that right. Without her parents' support, she would need to prove herself worthy, birthright or no.

The ram finished his deed and strutted away triumphantly while the ewe stood there, seeming less than impressed. If things didn't improve, she could see herself in the same role as that ewe. Cattle and horse raids were how most young warriors gained status, but that was denied to her as a Freeman. The only idea she still had was to return to the Roman fort, sneak inside, steal something of value, and return. If she did that and the stolen item was valuable enough to earn her some legitimate reputation among her clan, she would find herself in a far better position to dictate her future. Perhaps she could travel with a trade group where she might have a chance of finding someone to love or at least have enough clout to stay single. Still, sneaking into a Roman fort and taking something of worth was no small feat.

"At least you don't have to choose," she complained to the uncaring sheep. Thoughts of the Dacian cavalry woman danced across her mind like a sweet floral mote on the breeze. She had been majestic on her horse, almost like the animal was an extension of her body. She had ridden without even holding the reins, somehow imparting her will upon the animal. Meala had explored such memories with her hand beneath this very tree, her emotions confusing in their implications and pesky complexity, yet her body had been entirely sure of itself. There was something about the mighty warrior that had left its mark upon her memories and burned itself into her very soul.

What must it be like to ride such a powerful warhorse and command so much presence? Meala had ridden her family's horse since she was young, but only when they traveled to the meeting stone for the market, but the archer's skill was of another level. Thoughts of those dark eyes returned, perhaps the only memories from that night that didn't cause her anxiety. They had shared a long and rather breathtaking look, and for a brief moment, she had nearly forgotten that she had been lying on the ground at the warrior's mercy. Sure, it had been terrifying, but there had been more to it… emotions she couldn't reconcile.

Glancing down she gazed upon the black tattoo across her upper chest, just beneath her collarbone and stretching from side to side. It was a stylized bee made with black ink. Her name, Sei'ln Meala, meant "honeybee" (Apis mellifera mellifera). Unfortunately, Meala, the honeybee, had been stung that night by a warrior's iron arrow and infected by her memory. It was her only explanation for why she couldn't get that woman out of her mind.

"More like the sting of a wasp," she mumbled angrily at the woman who wouldn't leave her thoughts. While her parents were hardly enthusiastic when she returned a hungry, weakened, cold, and bloody mess from the failed raid, she had at least earned the right to wear a sacred tattoo. Her bloody wounds and blood-stained clothing had been more than enough proof of her deeds, as had the tales of the raid from others, which quickly spread throughout the farming communities, as did the wails of mourning mothers, fathers, wives and husbands. Sacred tattoos were an ancient and ritual practice for those who completed a brave act or significant challenge in life, such as birthing a child or surviving a battle. In fact, given how easily a woman could die giving birth, many considered birthing to be a form of battle – both activities overseen by the Highest Mother, one of the major gods.

Beyond merely a simple style element or a memory of what had happened, sacred tattoos held a special significance among her people. Only druids, sacred women, and those elders touched by the gods could practice the art, and it had been two full moons before Meala had been able to arrange the ritual, not to mention healing enough to endure it. The most important aspect of the tattoo was its magical powers that were said to protect the wearer, especially when visible. Of course, on a warm day like today, Meala wore only a woolen wrap skirt tied by a woven belt, making her bee and her three large scars quite visible, as well as her other mundane tattoos. Her thoughts returned to the present as she noticed the flock moving slightly as they reacted to someone approaching. One learned to see these things over the boring years.

"Meala!" she heard her mother's voice from down the path that led to the homestead. "My daughter, several traders from Devana are just up by the Stone. Maybe you should go have a look and see what they have for trade. Eyfe said that she had not seen such polished stone in a long time," Ail, her mother, called as she strode down the path with a basket in hand, obviously returning from gathering in the nearby wood. The "Stone" was a large carved stone near what passed as the most public location for all the families in the local area. Around it gathered a dozen roundhouses at the Northwestern edge of the lake, the closest village. As for trading, her mother's smile and knowing look told Meala precisely what her mother had meant by "polished stone" and "trade." If she didn't find some way to distinguish herself more significantly than just one tattoo... Her thoughts trailed off as she heard the ram making more noise. How could he be at it again so soon, she wondered?

"I am not ready for that sort of trade and I care little for polished stone," she called back, twisting another weed in her fingers. Ail approached and stopped just before her rebellious daughter, leveling a frown, though a bit overdramatically. While Meala had her father's green eyes and sharp jawline, her long, wavy auburn hair and stubborn demeanor were entirely from her mother. Ail wore a woolen dress belted by a hand-twined, deer-leather belt, her feet equally bare on the warm season day. Her mother's lengthy hair had been rolled into a loose-fitting bun, making daily work easier. Neither spoke momentarily as Ail caught her breath from the short walk up the slight hill to where Meala tended the flock – an awkward silence filling the midday air.

There had been several fights when she had returned, wounded and soiled, her father's old shield lost and nearly her life along with it. Her parents had wished to punish her, but she was of age, and the rules became less clear when one became a woman, no longer a girl. Unwed, she was still under their purview, though she supposed they had considered her ordeal enough punishment. If she were a young man, she would have been fully within her rights, but she wasn't a man, so her rights were partly curtailed. It wasn't fair, but it was the way of things. Oddly, it seemed like the sheep were watching the interaction, perhaps enjoying the drama unfolding; their amorous deeds once more ended.

"If you care not for stone, then perhaps you can see what else a young man has to offer," she suggested, this time more bluntly. Meala frowned, her face clearly burning that idea to the ground. Ail matched her look.

"So, you will not meet with those men for trade?" she finally asked, her tone almost accusative. Meala said nothing as she rose to meet her mother. With that silence, Ail continued.

"You are my eldest daughter. It's your responsibility to carry on our family line. You almost got yourself killed not that long ago, or have you already forgotten?" she prodded, scowling, her eyes drifting down across the thin but still visible scar around Meala's left abdomen and the thumbnail-sized scar on the left of her chest, its sister scar a hand's length behind it. Several moons ago, this would have heralded a major argument, but over the past five moons, things had calmed. The fights had become minor arguments and then mostly just avoided. Meala couldn't quite figure out what her mother's feelings were on the topic besides her more clearly vocalized anger and fear of having nearly lost her daughter. Whatever additional feelings she held were kept neatly packed away behind her stern, tattooed face.

"My rib still hurts, and I'm scarred," Meala sardonically retorted, patting her freshly healed chest where an arrow had nearly taken her life, not to mention the burning sweats that had followed for nearly ten days. She had been lucky to recover with just her mother and sister's household magics and plenty of ember barries (Rubus chamaemorus), highest mother's wart (Isatis tinctoria), and beer bud (Achillea millefolium). Thankfully, asking the details of her part in the raid before she was ready to speak them went against her people's customs, and she had not been in the mood to elaborate. *Mother, father... the raid failed, I nearly died, and I was all but seduced by a warrior woman who tried to kill me.'* At Meala's talk of pain, Ail's mirrored frown deepened.

"And let that pain remind you not to carry a spear," Ail replied sarcastically. Meala wanted to snap a reply and would have if she were a few years younger, especially during her early few years of bleeding. But her often sharp tongue had seemingly dulled upon a little maturity and Roman steel. Instead, she turned away from her mother toward the sheep, hoping Ail would take the hint. Mothers were said to be perceptive, at least in the stories. Beside her, she heard her mother shifting uneasily before letting out a deep sigh – the sort of sigh only a mother of many children could manage.

"Plenty of women fight the Romans, so why do you have to be one of them?" she asked, her tone less confrontational and more curious. Meala nearly turned back at the abrupt change in tone and candor. Their fights had started just like this so many times. But this was the first time her mother had asked why she had run away. Sure, Meala had told her parents she wanted to become a warrior, but never why. It wasn't a question a man would be asked, but men didn't seem to have as many boundaries or expectations. Instead of directly answering her question, Meala posed another, one she had wondered for many years.

"Why did you? Why did you fight?" The silence returned as quickly as it had left. Ail had been born before the wall was constructed, and to the South of where it would be built, as a member of the most southern of the eastern Braide clan in Roman-occupied land. At the age of seventeen, she had left and found her way north into eastern Wenech lands proper, where she had eventually made a family and settled down. At just twenty, she joined a warband and helped fight the Romans as they pushed northward, along the way meeting and marrying Uuen. It was a story she had told while quite drunk, and one Ail had hoped her daughter hadn't remembered. After the silence became almost too much for either woman to take, Ail answered.

"And who says I did?" she asked, her voice much less confident under scrutiny. Meala slowly turned to face her, dropping the second weed she had been fidgeting with and standing tall before her mother. She noticed that she was actually the thickness of a single finger taller than Ail. It felt like not so long ago when she had run across this very hill as a child, playing as her mother watched while spinning wool. A wave of complex and confusing emotion passed over Meala like a gust of wind over the grassy fields as the edges of her eyes wettened. Such unplaced and powerful emotions had become commonplace since the raid, and she quickly blinked the wetness away before replying.

"You did. Once when I was young…" she began, but Ail cut her off.

"You still are."

"…and you were very drunk," Meala continued, trying to hold back a smile. Her mother and father were known to drink heavily on certain holidays, especially harvest days and Mehet Sem (midsummer). When they did, her mother's tongue was quite loose, and her eyes became blurry from the drink. It seemed her memories were also a bit blurry. Her mother sighed, likely wishing nobody had remembered some of the things she said after a few cups of wine. Her daughter was far too good at remembering anything unfortunate that she said while ignoring anything she was supposed to remember. Unlike her other children, her wayward daughter rarely drank more than a cup of wine during most rituals, leaving her dangerously sober. It was one of Meala's more perplexing childhood oddities.

"Why… why did I fight?" Ail stood for a moment, seeming almost reluctant to continue, but after a moment to compose herself, she answered, "Because this is our land. Because they follow strange gods. Because some of the things I've seen them do," she spoke softly. If her wine-induced stories were correct, she had joined a local war band and had fought in two significant raids. She had often seen her mother partly unclothed, a common sight in the warm season. The tattoos etched into her back and arms were of the same magical nature as the bee tattoo Meala had received. Her mother had never spoken much about what had happened other than that she had met Meala's father during those dangerous times.

"You have never seen a crucifixion, have you?" Ail asked rhetorically, already knowing the answer.

"No," Meala replied, looking down. Of course, she knew what they were as the stories of Roman cruelty were commonplace, if not propagandistic. Of course, her own people ritually sacrificed humans when it was needed, an often-brutal affair. Yet, that was for the gods, for good reason, and performed by a skilled druid, a very different situation, in her opinion. Before Meala could say more, Ail continued, though her expression became troubled as though remembering something she wished to forget. That look Meala knew, for she too shared such memories.

"It can take days for you to die, whipped bloody and nailed bare as you were born to cold wooden beams... captives from battle, criminals, slaves… Men, women, and children, too. Crosses running along their roads for as far as the eye can see for anyone who displeases them… and their wretched emperor. The guards get tired after a while, and they do things… things to entertain themselves and cause the most pain. I've never heard such screaming… smelled such… I worried that you…" she finished as her voice trailed off and her hands clenched as her eyes dropped to the ground, tears falling. Ail stood for a moment, lost in some horrible memory she couldn't truly forget. She had obviously seen such torture firsthand, though Meala dared not ask more. After a moment, Ail looked up at the sky and whispered a prayer before sighing. A moment later, Meala reached forward and drew her mother into a hug.

A short time passed as mother and daughter simply held one another, their argument temporarily at a pause. Meala could feel the tension in Ail subside as she rested her head upon her mother's shoulder. Beneath everything, Meala knew her mother was right about the dangers – she had seen just a taste of them, and it had left her changed, wounded in body and spirit. But she needed her mother to understand why she had to pursue her dreams, even at such terrible risk. It wasn't just some prideful heroism. Rather, the risk of death was her only real chance at life. After a short time, Meala released her mother, and Ail leveled a weary, resigned look her way as she wiped her eyes.

"You aren't going to listen to anything I say, are you?" she asked, the basket hanging low in her hands as though it held the weight of her worry instead of the season's last harvest berries (Vaccinium myrtillus).

"I don't want a husband. I don't want a man… because I want to love a woman," Meala said before she realized what she had just admitted in the heightened moment. She had never spoken her feelings quite so straightforward, but the gods and ancestors seemed to have filled her with the spirit of truth since her ordeal. Ail frowned, giving Meala an almost sarcastic look as though she had already figured that obvious fact out long before. By the look of it, Meala's homosexual nature was hardly news. But sarcastic look or not, Ail wasn't in the mood to fight, and her poignant memories had weakened her resolve, at least for the moment.

"Then what do you want?" Ail asked. Oddly, she spoke to Meala for the first time more as an equal than as a mother. It wasn't so much her words as a slight change in her demeanor, but Meala noticed. She supposed that standing before her mother, slightly taller, wearing the scars of battle and tattooed like a proper warrior, had finally convinced Ail that she was no longer the rebellious child who dominated her mother's memories and impression of her. Part of her felt emboldened by her mother seeming to respect her more like the adult she had become, yet part of her felt the loss as she was no longer just a child.

"I want to be Meala, daughter of Ail Braide, a woman who makes her own choices… not just Meala. I want to wear a chain of glory and be seen by our ancestors. I want to make my own choices of who I love and where I go, just like any man," she said, referring to the iron, gold, and silver chains and torcs worn as status symbols among their people. Her mother had earned the right to wear such a chain, yet never had. Only those of higher status wore them, and a simple farmer wasn't such a person.

While her parents owned land, they were technically freemen, landed peasants, as her mother had never stepped up and asserted her heritage or sang of her deeds before the gathered clan at the Stone or a sacred grove, thus never fully attaining her rightful place as a higherman. It was an odd position, somewhere between landed peasant and the warrior caste, yet that is where she chose to remain. Though they lived each day of their own will, there was a regional chief they owed some level of fealty, but they had some independence because of her earlier glory and warrior heritage, unclaimed or not. If Meala could earn some glory for herself, she could capture that mantle and stand alone. For a long moment, her mother regarded her as though she saw something new that she had not seen before, perhaps something she had missed, her eyes narrowing.

"You want to be called warrior and claim your birthright?" she asked. Meala nodded. She had said this many times, but it seemed that her mother had only just begun to realize how serious she was and, more importantly, why she wanted this path. Still, her mother had been witness to many terrible sights during her two raids and a childhood spent living near the Romans, memories that had plagued her long after she had put down her spear. Her expression began to change as she considered this. Then, as though confronted by yet another bad memory, Ail's emotions seemed to spike.

"How many men, women, and others lie rotting in Roman pits who died for such dreams?" Ail spat, her eyes tearing as though some distant thoughts returned with her question. The look haunted Meala, but she stood resolute before her mother – the matron of her household.

"How many die with a never-born in their womb?" Meala retorted, unwilling to back down. Her comment seemed to strike something deep and unresolved within her mother, a chink in her emotional armor that sent a bolt of anger through her as though yet another memory had been struck like a drum. Ail's tears now flowed once more.

"Meala... I..." she began as she closed her eyes a brief moment seeming to recall a sad memory, but Meala cut her off before she could recover, delivering yet another blow.

"You wouldn't be stopping me if I were a man!" she spat, her anger mixed with plenty of unplaced emotion from five moons past. Her retort wasn't the petulant cry of a youth, but the bitter anger of a young woman ready to spread her wings and backed by the fires of trauma-induced emotion with no place to go and far too much potency. Ail's eyes narrowed at that, yet a sonderous mote briefly flashed across her face. It was only a moment, but it further weakened Ail's resolve.

"You can marry a man and a woman or take a lover. This is any freewoman's right. But there is only one way to have a child. A child is your legacy, a future! She can grow and carry our family forward!" Ail all but screamed, her basket falling to the ground, spilling berries across the field, along with her hopes for her eldest daughter's future. But Meala cast her arms wide in defiance, her bee tattoo underscoring the gravity of her words.

"And here I am... I am your legacy! Let me be who I am. Let me make that name. What is the point of a legacy if I cannot be who I am? Why do we even care for our land, our people if we do not embrace life? A life not lived might as well not even exist," she snapped, her voice dropping as her angry reply turned into a simple plea. Her words had been pure emotion and harsher than she had wished, yet she had spoken candidly and truthfully, something she had rarely done as a child, yet culturally significant among her people. Words spoken from the heart were considered to be the most honorable, being pure and true. It was how she felt, and if her night of terror at the wall had done anything, it had reminded her how short life was. The challenge of the young to the wise was as old as the ancient gods, and the implications hung in the air like a morning fog.

For a long moment, Ail stood merely looking at her daughter, the girl who played in the lake as a child and used to bring her goose feathers for her father's arrows and flowers in the early light season (spring)... the girl she had carried for nine moons, fed from her very body, and watched grow from an infant into a young woman, the woman who had taken a stand against the Romans, just as she had. It was as though she saw Meala for the first time–a worrisome reflection in the stream of life–and her emotions were a mixture of respect, fear, and uncertainty.

When Ail stepped forward, Meala almost stepped back. Her mother had never struck her, but her words had been intense and laced with fear and anger beyond those of a mother scolding a wayward child. But quite unexpectedly, Ail pulled her daughter into a second, deeper hug and held her for a time. There was silence a short time later as they picked up the fallen berries, filling the basket and then Ail left for home, her thoughts unspoken and very clearly a whirlwind. Meala watched her leave, her mind filled with trepidation, and her resolve to finish this conflict one way or another piqued. Off in the distance, several elk watched as they drank their fill by the lake, blissfully unaware of the happenings of humanity.

"I miss the lake, but Eilun hates the nippers (midges)," Ris said, reaching for a piece of bread. His beaming smile, framed by a slight beard, had come a long way from the eager young man Meala had played hide-and-seek with as a child. Now, he sported long, dark brown hair running down his back, piercing green eyes, and a sharp chin, a spitting image of her father, Uuen, when he was younger. Rumor had it that he was the most desired man at the lake, at least by his looks. Honestly, Meala was shocked that Eilun had let him out of her sight, though she had little worry about his fealty. Her elder brother had always been a man of honor, someone she had and still looked up to, though she would never tell him, lest his ego grow too large.

Her oldest brother and his wife lived three days' walk to the North along the old deer trails where Ail and Uuen had granted them a small plot of land and had begun raising a family. Ris would often stop by his family's lands when traveling with sheep to the trading grounds to the South, always a welcome visit, leaving Eilun and her eldest aunt to tend the farm. Though she liked Eilun in small doses, the woman could be aggravating with her particular need to comment on everyone else's business, making her nipper-related absence not unwelcome. Meala sometimes wondered if the woman hated nippers because they reminded her too much of herself.

"I think she just needs some time alone," Rigandona, or "Rig," for short, mused as she reached for the water beer. Ris laughed, far too mature to take the bait but appreciating his youngest sister's playful jest, nonetheless. Meala's younger sister bore a surprising resemblance to her, though her auburn hair was a little lighter, and her eyes had little gold rings around their edges. "Eye torcs," Rig had once called them. Their mother had said that her eyes must have belonged to a mighty warrior queen who had lost them in battle, each sporting a torc of bravery. It was one of those unimportant memories that seemed to never leave. Rig had been a bit less well-behaved than Meala, often getting into fights with her younger brother, Brynen. Still, she mostly remained on their father's good side, which seemed to matter little in the long run.

The family sat eating dinner around the central hearth of the Crannog, a circular, roundhouse structure with wooden beam floors covered in hay, wattle and daub walls, and a thatched roof supported by stilt-like wooden piles above the water at the edge of the lake. It was of sturdy construction and offered some protection should some of the northern or southwestern clans try and raid cattle or sheep, though that had never happened in Meala's lifetime. While her younger sister and brother sat close to the hearth, the adults mostly leaned against the central circle of support poles that ringed the hearth. It was the evening, and the new day would start as soon as the Sun set. A time for the family to relax, feast, and prepare for sleep and a new day.

Cordage and supplies hung from the wooden poles above and set under the conical roof all around, while the interior's outer edge was almost entirely made up of raised platforms used for sleep or work. Below, the sounds of the water gently lapping against the poles added the background music of life, while a fresh mixture of herbs Rig had gathered that early light season (spring), dried, and now sat smoldering by the hearth flooded the room with a pleasant scent as the new day's darkness rolled in.

"There's something to be said for a happy, married couple, don't you think," Uuen said, acknowledging his eldest son with a nod and referencing his recent union to Eilun. Across the hearth, Meala frowned, suspecting that her father's comment had been meant as a personal dig. She had kept her head down most of the meal, uninterested in conversation and unsure of her place in the family. Beside her, Ail seemed to have perked up with food and drink. Yet, she still seemed lost, as though her thoughts were spinning around some unknown problem. No, not unknown – the problem was Meala. Both mother and daughter were acutely aware of the growing tension and her father's words did little to ease the strain.

Around the hearth lay a spread of food, slightly better than normal given Ris's arrival. There were dishes made from polished wood or stone (cannel coal) and thick, mostly undecorated ceramics. Though a few ceramics had been meticulously painted with designs by Meala when she was younger, her artistic skills and tendency to use them liberally resulting in quite a few lovely pieces. In them were the remaining portions of roasted deer liver with wild onions, roasted hazelnuts, salted honey oat porridge, mussels from the lake, quail, deer, and bread with salted butter. Everything but a few of the spices and the stoneware had come from her family's land and had been made by their collective hard work. This was the glory of the Freemen, an honor Meala couldn't argue with, even if she craved more.

Meala's small, carved wooden dish held an unfinished piece of bread, just a bite really, and the remains of a roasted quail, the bones picked clean. She had been lost in the ephemeral bliss of imagination as she arranged the bones in the shape of a little person. Later, her mother would save and boil the bones to make soup or bone meal to add substance to their bread. Nothing was wasted, especially as the dark season (winter) loomed upon them. Even now, the Crannog was filled with drying supplies as the family worked to store up food for the coming cold. Normally, these last days of warmth were to be celebrated with harvest and festivals, but all Meala could think of was her chance to gain honor slipping away.

Try as she might to ignore the awkward dinner, Meala couldn't help but notice Ail flashing a stern glance at Uuen. She couldn't quite read her mother's look, yet the woman's eyes were deadly serious. Across the hearth, Uuen caught Ail's stern glare and looked down. Had they spoken about her earlier fight with her mother? It didn't seem likely, as both of her parents had been quite against her goal of becoming a warrior. But hadn't her mother seemed a bit different, earlier? Almost sympathetic?

Her mother's words returned: *Because this is our land.* The words made the little hairs on her body stand in attention. For a moment, all was calm, even if a bit awkward, then Rig spoke up, cutting through the silence.

"I plan to find someone at First Harvest. There are plenty of boys there each year, and this time, I will be noticed," Rigandona boasted between sips of beer. Beside her, Brynen chuckled, causing Rig to frown, but she remained resolute. The start of dark season (early autumn) was nearly upon them, and with it came the First Harvest festival, the first major holiday of the year. It was certainly a good time to find a lover, though Rig wasn't quite old enough to wed, having only seen fifteen years. Of course, the term "boys" would likely garner her father's approval, given that their people were matrilinear, and inheritance and status passed down the female line, making Rig the only hope of continuing the family if Meala continued her wayward behavior.

"Too young… won't last," Meala's younger brother Brynen quipped in an almost too serious tone. Rigandona lifted an eyebrow at the boy, her emotions caught somewhere between amused at his "wise beyond his years" tone, especially given his mere twelve years of life, and indignant toward his—entirely accurate—assessment of her age, being only fifteen. Barely two years beforehand she might have dove on the boy, starting a fight, but she was trying her hardest to remain as an "adult." An adult woman didn't punch men… unless she had a few too many, as was common enough outside the gather hall by the Stone.

"I didn't say I would marry him," she replied as Brynen scoffed, Ris restrained a chuckle, and Rigandona frowned as her proclamation teetered on the edge of being felled like a tree under an iron ax. Changing the subject before his youngest daughter lost her newfound maturity, Uuen addressed his eldest daughter, his tone jarring her from her inner thoughts. His heavy words silenced the banter as he put down his cup, content to relax after a long day in the field and a filling meal.

"Meala," he began, and without waiting for a reply, probably doubting he would get one, he turned his attention toward his eldest daughter, "have you given any thought to Aniel?" Sitting across from him and tending the hearth, Ail shot Uuen another strong glare. It was the sort of glare not meant to say anything but rather to underline and remind him of something previously spoken. It was as close to confirmation that they had discussed, or even fought, about the topic of their unwed daughter before dinner as she could imagine. Meala glanced up, meeting her father's gaze, her anger quickly getting the best of her.

"He's a good man, aye… another good man," she said, her tone shifting downward as she overly annunciated her final word, underscoring the problem. Around the hearth, everyone gathered remained quiet but for the sounds of chewing. For a moment, the silence lingered until Uuen broke it with a resigned groan, obviously growing tired of this subject and likely aggravated by whatever he and Ail had spoken about, earlier. He had kept his feelings mostly locked away since Meala had returned, initially more concerned that she might die from her wounds than taking the time to discuss what had driven her to suddenly run away. He had given Meala moon after moon of distance and time, yet she remained aloof and apparently resolute in defying the one thing he asked her to do. But now, five moons of silence had come to a head, and Uuen was no longer willing to sit on his words.

"You wish to fight like a man and take a bride," he began in a harsh voice, his words severe and filled with the weight of an unspoken yet obvious truth finally laid bare. "You would live as a man, even as you bleed with the Moon," he finished, his words harsh, even for him. Rigandona gasped at their father's blunt, crude words, unlike the normally kind man she called father. Across from him, Ail sat silent, still, and unreadable, like a stone monolith, her eyes narrowing. The tension that had built for five moons returned, yet there was a finality to it this time, as if all parties were ready to end this fight, once and for all.

"No, I do not wish to live as a man. I wish to live as a warrior… a woman of honor," she replied coolly, her anger seething under her father's degrading words. Nearby, her usually benevolent and confrontation-averse brother Ris looked like he might try to defuse the situation, but a cutting look from their mother held his tongue. It was almost as if Ail was purposefully allowing this argument to happen, by doing nothing that she normally would have to stop it.

"And how will you pay the dowry for your bride? This isn't your imagination, this is the real world!" he spoke, his mouth firm and his emotions clearly close to boiling over. Meala leveled her green eyes upon him—eyes the same color as his–her emotional control at its limit. She had faced death and the horrors of battle, which had taken the edge off the mundane intimidation of the larger man. It was a sort of maturity but at the cost of innocence. She had grown since that painful night, and her wounds had healed, at least physically. She now wore the tattoo of her namesake, an honor she had earned in blood, and she would no longer cower like a scolded child.

"I am no ewe to be traded…"

"You are a shepherd, not a warrior, and this is a farm, not some battlefield. I don't care if you wish to fight. You have responsibilities to…" he began, but Meala suddenly stood, her plate flying from her lap, and her woolen shawl cast aside as she rose to her full height, her scars, and magical tattoo clearly visible in the firelight. They had all seen the scars, but none had asked about them in detail, other than that she had taken part in a failed raid that had become the talk of the area. Among their people, it was considered a warrior's place to speak of their fight and far too personal a topic to casually ask about.

"You speak of women and war like day and night, but only two at this hearth have fought, and neither is a man. I may imagine much, but I don't have to imagine my honor. I wear it carved into my body! I do not just wish to fight. I *have* fought. I stood before the men of Rome and took my turn at the wall (shield wall). When my time came, I didn't run. I stood there and threw my spear at my enemy… our enemy!" she spat, her heart pumping and her hands clinching at the memories. Beside her, Rig and Brynen stared wide-eyed as Ris shifted uncomfortably.

"I stabbed my spear into a wall of Romans so close I could smell their breath. A Roman's blade cut me, but I cut him down with my blade. Another took his life," she said, running her finger across her abdomen, her skin going cold, "A Dacian horse archer's arrow bit my chest. But I faced that archer…" she began. Tears rolled down her face, and her breathing was becoming rapid as her thoughts returned to that night. It was finally coming out after five moons.

"I was terrified, but I am no coward. I faced that archer and called her to fight… I called for honor… and I lost. A shepherd? I faced my death and stood my ground. But there is honor in standing and fighting… even in dying," she finished, tears now flowing as a wave of nausea overcame her. Beside her, Ail watched, seeing more than her daughter standing before her. She saw herself those many years before when she had raised her spear in battle. But she had been trained by her maternal uncle and had joined a warband with the encouragement of her parents, while Meala had achieved her feat alone. But her thoughts lasted only a moment, as Meala was not quite finished. These emotions had been brewing, and they needed to come out, as holding them in had become far too painful.

"I swear an oath now before our ancestors that I did this family honor. If you won't recognize that honor, then perhaps you haven't had enough experience with it!" she spat, her words thrust like a spear to Uuen's chest, her anger turning to sorrow at the confusing memories of that horrible night. It was the harshest thing she had ever said to her father, yet she had meant every word of it. Rigandona cringed while Brynen sat entirely still, his mouth wide open. Ris merely looked down, unsure of what he could add that wouldn't make things so much worse.

Uuen rose from beside the hearth, his face a mixture of pain, anger, and something else… perhaps a mote of respect, though Meala failed to see it as she turned and stormed from the Crannog, leaving a trail of kicked-up hay in her wake. Her father spoke something in reply, his words quickly followed by a sharp comment from her mother, but Meala paid no heed as she cast aside the wooden framed door and left into the late evening for a walk. She had deliberated for moons, yet her final choice had been made on the spur of the moment. She would return to the Roman fort, sneak inside, and properly capture from her enemy something of significance and, with it, secure the mantle of warrior, her birthright, and the freedom that came with it. She needed to stop daydreaming as a shepherd and take her life by the horns.

The crannog was quiet but for the gentle wind and water lapping against the wooden piles as the new day's darkness approached its midpoint (midnight). It was a calming sound, one that had lulled Meala to sleep since childhood. Now, those sounds would provide just enough background to mask her as she crept out the door. It had been a difficult choice, but she had spent many long nights considering her future and how to achieve it. While her father's words had finally pushed her to act, her multiple brushes with death had solidified that choice. She had only one mortal life, and she would live it or lose it by her own deeds.

With her convictions, her small cloth bag of fresh clothes, what food and gear she could sneak from the family stores, and her trusty old bronze dagger, Meala crept across the darkened home toward the faintly glowing line demarking the doorway. During the dark season, it was well insulated, but at the height of the light season, cracks to allow air to pass were a welcome respite to the heat. Now, they outlined her freedom as she passed the now burned-down central hearth. All around, five people slept, the sounds of their beer-induced snores helping to mask the sounds of the old, wooden house.

Each footfall brought a creak or a grown in the old wooden floor, but a childhood spent in the crannog also came with an intimate knowledge of every possible source of sound. Sneaking about had become a key skill for each sibling growing up. Meala offhandedly wondered if her parents had sneaked around as children. It seemed likely, but she would never get them to admit it. As quiet as a tree rat (red squirrel), she opened the old wooden door and slipped into the night; the comfortable smells of hay, peat, and burned wood were quickly replaced by the warm, humid air and rich smells of the lake. With a barely audible thud, the door closed, and with it, her old life.

She stood on the circular wooden deck that ran around the perimeter of the crannog. Before her ran a sort of wooden bridge running the short distance from the circular, stilted home to the shore, a small wooden gate blocking it at night, mostly to keep animals out. If someone actually raided their homestead, they would probably just take livestock and not bother crossing the short stretch of water to the crannog. In that way, the bridge was more of a deterrent than a defensive structure. She advanced slowly, ensuring her steps didn't creak the wood, lest a loud enough creak awaken her family. She had already been lucky in avoiding her father that night, especially given their home was a single room. As soon as she was ashore, she would sneak down the coast toward the Roman fort as she pieced together how she would…

"A warrior must look both ahead and behind," came a stern voice as a form in the darkness stepped from behind and placed a hand over her mouth, muffling her scream of surprise. Meala would have fought to free herself from the unexpected person, but the familiar smell and sound of her mother were instantly recognized, stifling her fear. She spun, finding Ail standing before her and wrapped in a woolen blanket, her feet warmed by a pair of fur-lined shoes. The shock of coming face-to-face with her mother while in the middle of sneaking left her stunned and unable to speak as her mind made sense of the sudden change. It confirmed her suspicions that her mother had sneaked about as a child and seemed rather good at it.

"Sei'ln Meala, my foolish, brave daughter. If you are a woman and not a child, then you will hear my words," Ail whispered, her expression stern but oddly carrying a mote of respect that Meala was not used to hearing. Her heart fluttered, and her adrenaline danced through her veins, but Ail had not called out to her father or the rest of the family. She had merely asked for her words to be heard, the request made between two adults, not mother and child. Meala nodded, unsure what else to say, and caught entirely off guard and without many options, lest her mother alert the family to her abandonment. Together, they stood in the warm night air of the waning light season.

"I know that it may not seem like it, but your father loves you. He just wants you to be happy and secure, and thinks he knows what is best for you. To him, you are still a girl with the foolish dreams of a girl. He thinks he knows best, and he's..." she began but paused, seeing Meala's immediate and negative reaction to her words. With a great sigh, she gathered herself; Ail's emotions suddenly looked less controlled than she had initially seemed, though she barely repressed a sardonic smirk at her daughter's distaste before continuing.

"I have seen the look in your eyes, and it tells me more than any scars could. He knows what is best for a boy or a man. He isn't a woman and knows little of our lives. You mustn't blame him as he acts just like his father before him. This is the way of things. It is my place to help you live, but you are no longer a child," she finished, pausing yet never taking her hazel eyes from Meala. Many emotions passed through Meala's mind, yet there was truth in her mother's words. Her father was rough and a bit too direct, but he had always been a loving parent. Other than their disagreement over her future, they had always had a reasonable relationship. But, though this was their single significant point of disagreement, it seemed unreconcilable for both father and daughter.

"What do you think is best for me," Meala whispered, her voice more pleading than she had hoped to sound. She would leave that night no matter her mother's words, yet now that Ail had begun to truly speak to her as the woman she was, she had to know what her mother really thought, and she felt that she owed her at least that much. Ail considered her momentarily, seemingly pleased by the question but with far too many powerful emotions dancing behind her eyes.

"You are more like me than I would wish on anyone, Honeybee. You want to live your own life, and you should. It isn't what I would have chosen for you, but this is your life to live…" she paused, waxing moonlight catching her suddenly wet eyes, "…or lose," she finished, swallowing a lump. Meala wasn't sure what to say, so she stood very still, the would-be warrior momentarily turned into a startled rabbit. Ail breathed deeply, her emotions threatening to steal her breath, yet she needed to finish.

"Mother, I…" but this time Ail was the one to take advantage of an emotional moment, cutting right past Meala's reply.

"Your father and you are both right, but this is your life. I chose as you did once, and it was nearly my end. Those memories haunt me even now. But it was my choice to make. This is yours. If you mean to be a warrior and claim your birthright as my daughter, then so shall you. But I won't see my brave daughter going into battle or wherever it is that you are going without a proper weapon." She paused, once more swallowing the growing lump in her throat and mastering her tears, as Meala stood wide-eyed, unable to fully process what she was hearing. Why was she feeling a sudden wave of regret now that her mother was backing her?

"My old shield and spearhead are buried beneath the gnarled tree just south of the Southshore path. There is a large stone covering them. Whatever you decide, you will always have my love, Honeybee," Ail said as her voice wavered and tears flowed. Meala approached her mother, unsure of what to say, as the sudden change hit her like lightning. Now she too felt a lump in her throat after hearing her mother's words, her own tears beginning to flow. Off in the distance, an owl could be heard as they stood for a moment in mutual silence.

Ail had seen within her daughter the same fire and passion she had once felt when she was only a year or two older. She had realized the futility of trying to talk Meala out of what the girl, no, the woman, had decided. There was a time when every mother had to begin respecting that their child was no longer an adolescent. If Meala wished to prove herself as a warrior, it was her right to do so, even if the act came with such a heavy burden of fear and such awful risk. Besides, Meala had been right: she wouldn't have denied her eldest son if he had made the same request.

As mother and daughter embraced once more, Ail's tears flowed freely even as she smiled in admiration of the woman her daughter had become – the sort of woman who would stand up for herself and what she believed in and do so with honor. There was a chance that her choice would lead to her daughter's death, or far worse, yet each person's life was theirs to live. This was something the druids taught and a well-understood principle among the warrior caste. Mother and daughter held each other for a time, simply feeling each other's presence and hoping it wasn't the last time. In the distance, a wood owl (barn owl) regarded them as it kept an eye out for dinner.

Chapter IV

My Courage Is My Strength...

Gender is a social construct that may be informed by many factors, such as sex (or assumed sex), age, social status, or religious belief. Having more than two genders is commonplace within humanity and has been documented for thousands of years. Unfortunately, insular Celtic people left few clues to their understanding of gender. The three genders Meala's people recognize beyond the gender binary are unattested, yet the notion that more than two genders would be recognized in insular Celtic society is hardly unreasonable.

Bynwerr (roughly analogous to a transgender woman), Weryn (roughly analogous to a transgender man), and Dynen (roughly analogous to a non-binary person) are based loosely on the Proto-Indo-European, Proto-Celtic, and Welsh languages but wholly invented as we do not have enough information about the languages spoken by second-century insular Celts. They have been included because transgender and non-binary people have always existed.

"Hey there! I bet my bed is warmer than Dacia!" a legionary called out from a distance, his thick accent marking him as a proper Roman citizen, a Cives Romani.

"Basia culum meum..." Cynna mumbled profanely under her breath. She frowned at the Roman soldiers' constant lewd comments as she strode from the fort toward a small pond just South. In fact, Cynna was of the Iazyges (Eye-az-ah-geez) people, Sarmatian nomads who only happened to be living in Dacia, not actual Dacians. Most wouldn't consider the distinction important, but she did. Her family had lived on the edge of Dacian lands since she was a child, having traveled west. It was a beautiful place, though she was not sure she would ever return. As for the exotic northern lands, the countryside was stunning, and the weather seemed to bother her less than the Romans. Unfortunately, each day was filled with leering soldiers and commentary she wished she didn't understand. She was the only female "Dacian" in her cavalry group. However, women warriors were much more common in the lands where she came from, comprising perhaps one-third of warbands.

Her father had been the youngest son of a tribal chief, but he had fled when his father had allied with the Alans, a much more powerful group slightly to the North. Their small piece of the clan became entirely nomadic, moving farther westward. Her mother had been a warrior from a neighboring clan, who had left with the man she loved, Cynna's father. As a result, Cynna had been raised in the ways of the nobles, even as her family traveled from place to place with their herds and wagons. Unfortunately, her father had passed from an unknown sickness when she was young, but her mother had been a brave and wonderful teacher.

She had seen just seventeen winter solstices when the Alans had caught up with her clan and massacred them. The attack had been at night and most of her memory was a blur. But she could still remember her mother ordering her to flee as she grabbed her bow and faced down the onslaught. Obedient to her mother and terrified, Cynna had taken her mother's armor and a new horse and fled. Her mother had stood her ground and felled half a dozen Alan horsemen before she had fallen. She had given her life to distract the raiders long enough for Cynna to escape.

Several months later, she had found herself before the entry to the nearest Roman frontier outpost, signing up as an auxilia. The snobbish Romans had only taken her as they needed one final rider to form a proper turma (a unit of cavalry soldiers), and because she could speak Dacian, some Thracian, Iazyges, and rudimentary Latin, making her an effective translator. It wasn't long until she found herself on the other side of the Roman Empire, killing in the name of a people she now despised, who rejected her. Now, six years later, she was growing so tired and longing to escape her lengthy pledged service.

Cynna knelt beside the small pond and splashed water over her face, her actions causing a "ribbit frog" (Rana temporaria) to leap into the water. That wasn't what the locals or Romans called them, but she had always liked the expression. Not far away, her war horse, Tamura, stood looking for greenery to nibble, her armor and weapons still bound to the saddle. That morning's patrol had been long, and she was quite dusty. Worse, she had used most of her arrows fending off a group of locals who tried to waylay her group. This had made for a grim day and far too much dust, an uncomfortable feeling she had to clean before she could even consider getting some rest or tending to Tamura.

Of course, she had to be careful how she cleaned herself in the open, as the men were already rowdy as it was. Using an old linen cloth dipped in water, she wiped beneath her hemp fiber kaftan shirt, which opened in the front. As she did, she noticed a soldier's armor and equipment lying neatly on the shore at the pond's edge. In the water, Cynna noted the form of a Roman man swimming, probably cleaning off after a long day. Being able to swim alone and without worry of assault was one of the many privileges of being a man, it seemed.

While she cleaned, another woman came to stand not far away with a basket full of clothes to wash. Though a bush partly blocked her view of the washing woman, Cynna caught a few glances. She was a bit older with long, honey brown hair, dark green eyes, and a splash of freckles. She wore a dark brown wool blouse and a long wool skirt secured by a waist cord with the excess cloth rolled over the cord. Her feet were bare in the summer, a typical look for a local brigante woman. The woman flashed the archer a friendly smile and knelt to begin her work, probably feeling more secure with the powerful warrior woman nearby. Cynna took a breath and stretched before returning to her own cleaning. She briefly considered how different her world was from the peasant woman, being a warrior.

Glancing back toward Tamura, her eye caught the glimmer of the polished bronze scale she had attached to her armor where the spear six Roman months before had nearly caused her end. The almost golden colored scale stood out from the rest of the iron scale armor, a reminder of the dangers of battle but also a reminder of the warrior woman. As she cleaned, thoughts of the painted woman returned. She had been brave, bordering on reckless. She had appeared to have little skill in battle, yet she had stood there willing to face down a trained Iazyges archer, calling her out for single combat.

Cynna smiled as she considered how reckless that was, but part of her also found it alluring. She hadn't gotten a good look at the woman in what little moonlight remained when she had found her after the battle, but she had seen her quite clearly, if only briefly, in the bright light of the braziers and sconced torches at the gate as she threw her spear. Even now, six months later, her wounds had healed, but the memory still remained, like a scar upon her soul – a bronze scale in her very memories.

Her skin had been painted with black ash, probably to make seeing her people in the dark much more difficult. She had seen it all over the bodies the next day as the soldiers worked to dispose of the fallen. It was how they had gotten so close to the wall before being spotted. She had worn a badly frayed knee-length woolen tunic secured with a leather belt and a pair of woolen pants. She wore leather shoes on her feet, and her hair had flown loose, almost to her waist. It was wavy and thick and colored some shade of reddish brown, though she couldn't make out that detail with the ash. But she had seen those deep, rich green eyes, like the color of the endless fields of the European steppe, as they caught the torchlight.

Like her own people, the painted warrior had a few markings, either painted or tattooed, on her arms, legs, and shoulders. Looking down at her arms, she noted her tattoos – a series of spiral vines with the flowers of her homeland. The tattoos extended far beyond her arms covering her much of her body. Each flower held a memory, but also a reminder of its magical and practical use. Magic was practiced by any of her people, but it was said to be strongest among women, or at least that is what her mother had said. She had added much of it in her long years of service to the Romans, yet her arms held the oldest marks, those made by her mother. Marking the body was an important practice among her people and the local tribes, a curious coincidence.

Cynna shook her head, needing to return to the task at hand. How could she continue to see the brave woman's face even now? How had she made such a mark in just their brief encounter? Sure, the woman had been rather pretty… well, if she were being honest, the woman was downright captivating, but something about how she had looked at Cynna as she faced her imminent death had lit a fire within the archer. Her defiance and honor reminded Cynna of her people and had shaken her to the core. Was it her bravery or some human bond shared between those in battle? It made little sense, though thoughts of the brave raider continued to nag at her mind. *Mother of Fire and creator of all, why this woman? She neither brought me love nor pierced my heart... why do you leave me waiting?* She thought, glumly.

She had never considered taking a husband, nor had she ever really found men of much interest outside of friendly competition. Having an interest in women was hardly a concern among her people. The Romans seemed to allow such liberties among their men, something she had witnessed when she had seen two legionaries behind a building in each other's arms, swearing their undying love. As much as she had come to loathe the Romans, she had found their intimate embrace romantic and had quickly left to give them privacy. Sadly, it seemed that their liberties extended only to men. Until her twenty-five years of service ended, love wasn't foreseeable, and Cynna had little interest in any ephemeral relationship. With six years of service, and given her age, she would be 42 years of age when this...

Her thoughts were interrupted by the sound of a large splash followed by what sounded like nearby washing woman struggling. Glancing up from behind the bush, she found none other than optio Gaius Pedius standing partly in the water, struggling with the woman. It only took a moment for Cynna to realize that the optio's intentions were hardly friendly. He was nude and soaked, and had probably emerged from the water like the stories of crocodiles to attack his victim. The lascivious man ripped the wet cloth she had been washing from the woman's hand and held her arm quite firmly as he worked to force her to the ground. As Gaius laughed and taunted, the woman struggled, yet the fear in her eyes told Cynna that she knew what was about to come and that her struggles would do nothing to save her.

A legion optimally contained more than 5,000 men divided into ten cohorts, the first cohort being double strength, and hundreds to even thousands of additional auxilia. Each cohort was led by a Centurian with an optio principalis as his second. Moreover, this particular disgusting example of an optio was second to the first centurion of the second cohort of the legion, on detachment to the fort. In effect, that made him one of the most important members of the legion. A man of his power was effectively above the normal rules and would likely face no or little punishment for his ravishment, if the woman even reported it. The woman's face revealed that she fully understood the helpless situation she now faced at the mercy of people who tortured for sport and ruled by the sword. This wasn't just sex… no, this was a lust for power by a man who traded in blood and fear. Cynna's skin crawled...

This was the same man who had been leering and bothering her since she had first arrived. She had heard rumors that the optio was known to be rough with women and frequented the slave pens as the brothel had forbidden his return. This was one of many reasons that she had always steered clear of him. Watching him attack the peasant made her blood run cold when she considered how many times he had nearly put himself in a position to do the same thing to her. Fear of the man's position and all she had learned since her arrival told her that she should just turn and leave, but how could she allow something like this to happen? Killing an enemy was one thing, but there were things worse than death.

Gaius grabbed the woman's skirt before she could do anything and ripped it along the seams, tearing it wide open. The cloth fell aside, and the woman screamed, realizing that there would be no escape. With that final scream, Cynna stood from behind the bushes and approached the optio, her hands clenched and her heart pounding. Sometimes, one simply had to act, no matter the cost. Her mother had believed that, and it had cost her life but saved Cynna. Still, her mother had carried her honor into the next world, and that honor was worth more than any mortal life.

The woman looked pleadingly towards the archer when Cynna came into view, her eyes wild in shock. Noting a change in his victim, Gaius turned to face whomever the woman pleaded to for help, though he kept one strong hand firmly on her arm lest she try and flee. As he turned, he came face-to-face with the Sarmatian archer. With her long black hair tied in a single braid, dark hazel eyes staring almost predatorily, her tattooed and scarred body visibly muscular, and standing slightly taller than the optio, Cynna of Dacia was the sort of woman who gave most men the impetus to reconsider their words and deeds.

"Well, if it isn't the barbarian woman. Come to watch a real man? A Roman man? Fine by me, but it won't be like the barbarian scum you spread your legs for, I wager," he taunted with a twisted smile. Cynna gazed back at the man, her eyes like fire. She had seen men like Gaius many times before, and her hate for them was significant. Even caught in the act, he had no shame and absolute confidence in his privileged place in the jingoistic society of Rome, sure that she wouldn't dare stop an optio and full citizen. Beside him, the woman waited to learn her fate.

"Or… maybe you and I can enjoy this here fine day? What say you, Dacian? Maybe she can leave, and we..." he began to say when suddenly Cynna stepped forward and kicked with her foot as hard as she could, catching the man square between the legs. Normally, he would have had some clothing to cushion the blow, but in his present state it was like stomping on a summer flower. Her legs were powerful, honed from a life of riding, and slightly bowed. Gaius stumbled back, grabbing himself and wailing, all immediate thoughts of his victim gone in a single, painful act.

The peasant woman took hold of her torn skirt, pulling it up for modesty. She grabbed her basket of clothing with the other hand and gave Cynna a nod of thanks before rushing back toward the small civilian dwellings built around the fort, known as a canaba. Cynna let the woman flee a reasonable distance as she calmed herself. Slicing his throat wasn't worth the repercussions, but perhaps a little cold water would help. She twisted her body and kicked out, catching the man in the chest as he tried to recover and knocking him into the water with a splash. She would likely face some sort of disciplinary action, but it was worth it ten times over to put the man in his place and save the local woman.

"I am Cynna of the Iazyges, of Dacia. If I see you doing anything like that again, I'll geld you like a fucking warhorse so you can keep your mind where it needs to be," she spat in her deep, accented, husky voice, not even considering that the man likely had no idea what she had just said. When emotions ran high, people often spoke in their native tongue. As she watched, the optio crawled again from the water toward his equipment beside the pond, likely embarrassed, in significant pain, and ready to leave. If she were lucky, he might keep his mouth shut as reporting her would tacitly admit his attempted ravishment and being bested by a woman, the former likely carrying no penalty as the woman was probably provincia (a person from land under Roman rule, but not a citizen), and the latter resulting in a significant loss of status. Of course, revenge would be an issue, but that was a problem for another day, and yet another reason to sleep with a dagger under her pillow.

Just as she turned to leave, she heard splashes from behind. Spinning around, she caught the movement of optio Gaius swinging his large hastile staff, a mark of his station, barely missing her. Ignoring his clothes, it seemed that he had grabbed a weapon and charged after her, clearly more enraged than she had expected. She spun around, but Gaius swung again, his sword arm honed from a violent life in the legion. With a painful thud, the hastile clipped her left shoulder, causing little damage as her powerful shoulder muscles absorbed much of the impact, protecting her bone. He had aimed for her head, but she had ducked before the slower-moving staff could find its target. Looking slightly confused that a woman had shrugged aside his staff blow, the enraged optio dropped the staff and threw himself upon her, knocking the pair to the ground.

"You didn't catch me quite where you thought, you horse-fucking whore," he began as he struggled to pin Cynna's hands to her side. Her head hit the muddy ground hard enough to daze her, and she fought against the darkness that threatened to invade the sides of her vision.

"You let her go, so you take her place..." he continued, finding the archer a much more challenging victim. Her arms were strong from a life of archery, and her powerful legs fought for purchase against the slippery, muddy soil. Losing the test of raw strength as the warrior regained her faculties, the optio leaned forward, using his sheer body weight to try and overpower the woman. Within moments, he forced her arms aside once more as he taunted.

"Where's your horse and bow to make you strong? You horse fucking scum are nothing without them," he spat as he struggled to pin Cynna's arms to the ground, her strength simply not enough under the heavier man's rage-fueled assault. She suddenly realized she had been so focused on her arms that she had forgotten her legs. Lifting her legs, she wrapped them both around the body of the Roman and began to crush. Stirrups had not been invented so riders had to hold themselves to the horse by sharp balance and sheer leg strength. Cynna had ridden since she could walk, and her legs could apply a frightening amount of force.

The optio's angry visage abruptly changed to fear as he felt the vice-like grip wrap around his waist, just beneath his ribs, and begin to crush. Panic filled the man as he had never experienced anything quite like being squeezed to death. Realizing she was simply too strong for what he had planned, he let go of her arms and wrapped his hands around her neck, hoping to simply kill her. Without a moment's hesitation, Cynna returned the favor, grasping the optio's neck, and began squeezing back as she flexed her neck muscles, trying to resist his crushing hands. It was only a moment before she began to blackout from her restricted blood flow. Even as he wailed from the crushing, his face turning red, he was winning with his bare hands. She would soon leave this world if she kept up this contest of hand strength. Releasing his neck, Cynna placed both thumbs into his hate filled eyes and began pressing.

"Bitch... ahhh!" he began to scream as he let go of her neck and grasped her arms, but inward she pressed. While Cynna usually kept her nails short, her thumbnails were just long enough to press between the eyelids and into the soft, vulnerable orbs. Gaius screamed in horror, tearing her hands free with the power of his adrenaline, his body still locked in the vice-grip of her legs. Releasing her legs, she rolled away, gasping. Gaius rolled around in the mud just a few feet away, holding his ruined face and screaming unintelligibly.

She wasn't sure how wounded his eyes were or if he might be able to recover. Worse, she was dizzy and worried that she might faint, leaving such a predator potentially awake and in control. With her last gasp of energy, Cynna reached into her boot before he could recover and pulled free of its sheath a small knife she kept hidden – one could never have too many knives, in her opinion. She slammed the knife into the optio's neck and then rolled onto her back where she could breathe. Her neck hurt, and she had nearly blacked out, but the knife made sure there was no chance the man would recover.

"Quid est?" she heard but couldn't understand the words for a moment as her body recovered. When the man spoke again, she began to understand him, her oxygen-starved brain recovering. Opening her eyes to the bright blue sky above, the soft, puffy clouds and rich sky produced the illusion of calm that belied the truth of what would likely come next.

For a brief moment, she ignored the words and their grounding to reality as she noticed a single king bird (golden eagle) soaring overhead.

"What is this? What have you done?" she heard a man say and opened her eyes a few moments later to find three Roman soldiers had just arrived at the pond, probably noticing the fight from the distant village or fort. She tried to speak, but her throat still hurt from the man's iron grip. She didn't think anything was broken, but there would definitely be bruises. Glancing at Gaius's twitching body and hearing the strange gurgling sound from his throat, she suspected she had gotten the better end of their interaction. Summoning what little spit she had, she spat upon the dying man, her opinion made clear by deed. Her mother had told her when she was young that while many men were good, some, like optio Gaius, simply did not need to exist.

"My horse and bow are not my strength... My courage is my strength..." she whispered breathlessly at the dying man with what little whisper she could choke up. A moment later, she looked up to find even more Roman soldiers gathering around her. Without the ability to explain the situation, she let them pick her up and roughly carry her back to the fort. She hoped she could explain herself as soon as her voice fully returned. Behind them, the ribbit frog watched the scene unfold with mild interest.

As the Sun set low on the horizon, Meala stood by the gnarled tree where she had often played as a child. Beneath her feet lay her heritage, birthright, and way of life, long buried by her mother. There had been a rather pretty stone pushed into the ground. She had noticed it many times as a child but never thought anything of it. She now realized that it served as a marker, an indicator of something buried. Her family owned several iron hoes, though the only one she could seem to find had a poorly maintained wooden handle and would need to be repaired or replaced before the next planting. Regardless, it was good enough to dig through the soil in front of the tree.

Buried only two hands deep was a heavily oiled leather sack containing three gold Roman coins, an oval shield made from planks of wood connected by iron metal strips, and an iron spearhead. The sack had mostly decayed, but the iron was free from rust and looked well made. They were hardly legendary weapons, but they were her mother's, and that made them shine like polished bronze.

The shield wood was not in perfect condition, but the leather had been oiled and had resisted a lot of the water that might have otherwise destroyed it. Ail had also oiled the iron around the shield and the spearhead itself. There was a little discoloration, but most of the shield and the spearhead had survived intact. The shield appeared to have once been painted blue, probably woad, though most of that had faded. That was one of the many problems with woad, and perhaps one of the primary reasons it was rarely used as a paint, instead being used more commonly as a dye or medicine. Taking the weapons and her few possessions, she left the safety of the farm and made her way south, then east toward the fort.

Meala spent the rest of the night as she walked down the well-worn and familiar hunting trail until Sun rose, all the while scraping the spear tip with a flat, smooth stone until it displayed a reasonably good edge. As the Sun's light bathed the land, banishing the fog, she held the spear above her head, letting the light dance off its now clean, sharp edge. She had made good time and was probably far enough from home that her family would not pursue her, though she suspected that her mother's final acceptance would probably settle the matter with the family. As strong-willed as her father was, when Ail finally put her foot down about an issue, it usually stayed down.

Meala had spent many long days and sleepless nights considering when or if she should return to the Wall. The Wall was a place of both danger and opportunity. The adjacent fort, one of many, likely held at least 400 deadly Roman soldiers, with a few hundred peasants in the adjoining village, a treasure of opportunities for honor. She had heard tales as a child of sacred golden Roman birds (eagles), called Aquila, stollen in the Southeast lands. But petty theft wasn't enough. No, she would need to take from the most powerful people and do so daringly for this to count. A warrior's honor came from such dangerous deeds, which was the main reason for cattle raids among her people. That was why stealing the gold medallion from the fallen soldier six moons ago had been unacceptable. It was a risky long shot, but at this point, she could not accept the idea that she would lie in some man's bed, and nearly any option seemed a better choice.

Besides, she was a member of the regional Wenech people, a tribe of warriors who lived right at the edge of Roman-occupied lands. Much like the Caledon to the North or the Taksalee (Taexali) to the East, her people lived mostly in small villages and farmsteads, creating small but distributed communities that owed fealty to a regional chief and the high tribal chief of her people. Of course, most of her society were not warriors. At the bottom were the enslaved and indentured, those who were taken in cattle raids and warfare or merely usurped by a more powerful clan. Next were the peasants, who lived on others' land and gave a share of their herd and harvest to those above them. Enslaved and indentured were forbidden to own or use weapons, and peasants could only use them when called upon by the warrior caste.

Next were the Freemen, landed peasants who were required to have basic martial skills and made up the middle-class of her society. Above them were the Highermen, the warrior caste, who normally lived as Freemen but trained to be warriors when called upon. Above them still were the tribal chiefs and high chiefs. To the side, not exactly considered within the normal hierarchy, were the druids – a group of educated people who performed, understood, and administrated law, medical knowledge, banking, and religious beliefs. While many peasant farmers fought in raids and battles when called upon, they were led by an actual warrior caste who were better trained, wealthier, and well-equipped. Her society was quite hierarchical, yet upward mobility was possible, and a successful quest might be enough to grant Meala her birthright – to become a true, transcendent warrior.

The morning Sun rose in the East as Meala strode down a seldom-used trade path headed toward the Wall, the clouds changing to purple. She had walked much of the night, and now she would walk a good portion of the day before stopping at a small gully about one-fourth of the way for a long sleep. She wore a freshly woad-blue-dyed, wool, knee-length tunic. Tunics could be quite wide and bulky, but when held tightly to her waist with a leather belt, a tunic became comfortable and functional. Her feet were snug in leather shoes, while to her belt she had affixed a bag of dried meat and her three gold coins, water bladder, pouch of black paint, trusty bronze dagger, and a knotted climbing rope. In her hair she had affixed a wood owl (barn owl) feather that she had found along the way. Overhead, an owl sang a warrior's tune as she flew past.

Most importantly, she carried her mother's shield across her back and held the precious iron spearhead. Now, she needed to find a suitable tree branch to make a shaft. She supposed she might ask the pretty daru'bene (tree spirit) in the nearby oak forest for some help…

With a start, Meala awoke and nearly tumbled from her tree branch resting spot, her dreams regrettably ending before she could speak to the pretty tree spirit. She had been imagining herself as a tree spirit before she had dozed off. It had been a fun and relaxing daydream of a reality where she had no rules governing her actions and the freedom to flirt with every maiden who passed the woods. Unfortunately, it was time to wake up and face reality, daydreams and the fantasy of dreams providing only a limited escape.

Nearby, a startled tree rat (red squirrel) scurried away. She rubbed her eyes and gazed across the open field at the Wall with its ominous entryway, the sight of the raid. The oak tree grew just Northwest of the fort, not that far from where Urth had buried his gear before the raid last dark season. It was close enough that the guards would have spotted her if not for the heavy, verdant canopy. She had only meant to rest until the Sun was at its midpoint, but she had been more tired than she had thought, and her memories had wandered back to a few days before when she had dug up her mother's spear.

A short time later, Meala found herself walking down the main path that led to the Wall. It was a path frequented by traders, and several were making their way to and fro as the Sun passed high over the edge of the Wall. Try as she might, no real idea of how to sneak behind the Wall had seemed viable, but as she watched locals walk through the entryway and into the village, it occurred to her that she might just simply do the same. Of course, this meant that she needed a reason to enter. Thus, that morning before she had napped, the idea had come to her: she would be a woman desperate to trade for sheep for her family. Her family had been raided by another clan and her father was killed in the fight. With no money, her three coins secured within her strophium chest wrap and away from Roman eyes, she had taken her dead father's spear and shield to sell.

The plan was ad hoc, to say the least, and left her with a pang of guilt as she had to pretend her father had died. No matter how angry she was with the man, she didn't wish that, and lying was hardly honorable. Still, as far as she could tell, this was her only option, and it explained her presence with the weapons. But even with a solid plan, her anxiety had grown as she approached the gate. Not only because she would have to speak to Roman soldiers but also because this was the exact place where she had nearly died not so long before. Her hands clenched, and her heart pounded, but she kept her breathing steady as she took one step after the next toward the gates. Upon the walls perched a murder of crows watching the happenings.

Up ahead, the guards stood clothed in simple tunics, their upper bodies protected by "lamminata" armor (lorica segmentata) made up of strips of metal, like horizontal bands, forming a metal cuirass, and metal helmets, though Meala didn't know what they were called. The sight of the armor brought a sudden memory of screams, metal clinking against metal, and the impact of arrow against wooden shield. Meala shook the sounds away, trying to keep her nerve and remain calm. She supposed that her "father's passing" would be enough to explain why she probably looked terrified. If not, the archers upon the wooden gate towers would make fleeing useless. She could still remember them firing at her the night when…

"Alright, next up. You, girl… are you alone?" spoke a guard who sounded almost bored, as the large horse-drawn wagon ahead of her passed through the gates. Meala snapped back to the moment, flashing a startled look at the guards. So stunned was she that she didn't even register the man calling her puella, meaning "girl." Meala was hardly a "girl" and probably nearly the age of the youngest of the men, though she had only seen the guards' faces from a distance and had no interest in chancing a peek. There were four of them, one appearing to be of local stock and possibly an interpreter, and at least two archers overhead in the towers. Before she became any more awkward than she already was, Meala stepped forward, keeping her head down as she approached her enemy.

"Name and purpose," the man said, seeming not to care. Meala wasn't sure why he didn't react to her obvious fear and anxiety, but she began to speak hoping he remained apathetic. She glanced to her left, and a sinking feeling flooded her as she realized that she was barely the length of a horse from where she had faced the shield wall and nearly died, at least the first near death of the night. Ahead, she could hear the other guards quietly bantering and possibly even speaking about her, but she paid them no heed as her memories and anxiety took center place.

"Drusticc… Drusticc, daughter of Geal, from East Hills (Sidlaws Hills)," she began, pausing momentarily as her heart felt aflutter. The guard shifted, but she continued speaking before he spoke, hoping her words sounded believable.

"My father dead. Two ewe dead… raid. Mother sick. I come, sell father shield, buy ewe," she finished. She spoke in Latin, making sure that she added as much local accent, missing words, and grammatical errors with her speech as she could, not only to sound believable but also to discourage conversation. For a moment, the guard said nothing as Meala waited. Finding herself waiting for possible death at the same gate did little to calm her nerves as she fought to keep back a flood of memories from that cursed night. It had been like this for the first two moons at home, then began to fade. Now, at the same place, smelling the same air, and standing before the same men, or at least reasonable copies of them, Meala was finding it exceptionally hard to keep the intrusive imagery at bay. Her hands clinched while she fought to keep her arms from wrapping protectively around her body.

"Alright, I should charge you to pass, but no sense in a toll if you are poor and here to give up the sword. I'd be happy to see more of you with some sense. But… word of advice if your barbarian ears can understand me. Even a barbarian woman should not travel alone. Next time, find a man you like for company, or you might just find one you don't. Move along," he concluded, much to Meala's shock. Later, she would reflect on the absurdity of an armed invader commenting on her people's use of weapons, not to mention his ominous, if not creepy, warning, but at the moment, she only knew relief. Quickly, Meala passed through the stone and wooden gates and behind the Wall. Before her, just a short walk east down a well-paved Roman road and nestled beside the shore of the Great Sea, lay the mighty fortress of Veluniate (Carriden) and the adjoining village that had quickly grown around it. The village was known as

Veluniate Village, not terribly original in Meala's opinion, but her mother had called such a town a canaba.

"Ancestors and gods grant me strength," she whispered.

The walk from the wall to the fort was a bit longer than Meala had expected, though it gave her time to relax after the anxiety of the gate. A well-made, paved stone road stretched from the entry gate nearly two Roman miles to the Fort proper. As she approached from the West, the sheer scale of Veluniate became apparent.

Ahead and to the East stood a fort of massive rectangular buildings of a construction style she had never seen. They were surrounded by a thick ditch and small rampart on their western side, the single ditch becoming three smaller, parallel ditches as it ran to the South and around the Fort to her right. Also to her right and just South of the Fort, lay the start of a civilian town, called a canaba, that had formed around the Fort. Though blocked from view, the larger, less dense civilian farming settlement, called a vicus, extended from the initial canaba and stretched far to the East past the Fort. Far ahead and just beyond the vicus lay the parade grounds and the many fields that fed the population. To the North, on her left, lay the sea and reason most of the Fort's defenses lay to the West and South.

The small canaba that had grown around the Fort at Veluniate turned out to be quite a bustling place. As she approached, a large building with smoke seeming to come from its very walls stood prominently, men entering and exiting the structure for some unknown purpose. Behind the building ran a smaller rampart sealing off the odd structure, its purpose unknown to the Caledonian. Just ahead, over the larger fortress rampart wall lay many more rectangular buildings, perhaps of Roman style? A large stone and wood building, cubic in shape, stood at the center and visible above everything else, sporting many windows. Though she had no real idea what most buildings were, something told her that the large one was the regional chief's dwelling, or whatever Romans called their leaders. Offhandedly, she wondered how massive the Roman's high chief's fort must be in the distant land of "Roma," no doubt a massive hill fort. She noted the structure, as it was likely to be her prime target.

As she passed the strange wall-chimney building, she realized it was some sort of bathhouse, something she had heard from her mother's stories but had never properly envisioned. It was clearly the case, given the group of nude men who rushed from it, laughing and roughhousing, their bodies wet and oiled. They appeared to be soldiers, though they seemed less dangerous without their armor, weapons, and clothing. It disturbed her how much they resembled men from her own people, not just their bodies under that armor but also how they joked and played. The uncanniness bothered Meala on some level, though she couldn't quite decide why. She quickly dismissed a few intrusive images from the raid that tried to associate themselves with their faces, taking a breath.

Far too sapphic and triggered by her memories to care, Meala passed the odd building and headed toward the South of the canaba where she found many roundhouse-style buildings of her culture surrounding a smaller number of Roman-style buildings, like some kind of unintentional metaphor. The Roman-style buildings were mostly small, mostly wooden structures, some with stone walls and foundations, each made in a fashion she had never seen. She supposed this was typical Roman style, strong and brutish, like their people. Still, though it pained her to admit it, she found some of their sharp angles, colorful walls, and the occasionally vibrantly painted statue or statuette decorating their perimeter oddly beautiful. All around people busied themselves with daily life; blacksmiths hammered away while people gossiped, and children played.

There were a few dogs who rushed around seeking food and fun while an elder druidess passed by, apparently unbothered by the Romans. The woman's lovely grey and white hair was long and set in many braids, some with tiny songbird feathers, while her back was covered with a massive bird feather cloak. Her face was tattooed with many small animal symbols, their ink faded with the wisdom of age. Under this, she wore an off-white tunic and grey apron. She held a bleached wooden staff with a silver cap at its top and a chain of silver around her neck, her vestments marking her as noble and a bardic druid. She was majestic. The druidess gave Meala a smile and nod, which Meala quickly returned, already feeling calmer. Druids were the educated caste, serving as magistrates of law, teachers, bankers, bards, and keepers of history, and, of course, some served as the religious leaders of their society.

"Excuse me, miss," spoke a man as he nearly bumped into Meala, distracted as she was by the druidess. The man, a Roman by his looks, gave her a hearty smile and a nod, then passed by carrying a large sack with some unknown cargo. Glancing to her right, she caught sight of an older local man with his iron chisel and hammer working to carve what looked like a stone altar. Meala couldn't read, but she recognized the symbols as Roman. The work appeared unfinished, and a surge of curiosity took control of her mouth before she thought better.

I   O   M

VIKANI CoNSIS

"What does that say?" she asked the older man with the chisel. He turned from his concentration, initially looking annoyed, though the sight of a younger woman with interest in his craft seemed to quickly wash away his ire. He smiled, his ragged grey work tunic covered in dust, nearly the color of his grey and black, shoulder-length hair, his face framed by a small but neatly groomed beard.

"The words? Oh, well, it will read: *To Jupiter best and greatest, the villagers living at the fort of Veluniate,*" he paused and seemed to consider what he had said for a moment, "eh, Jupiter is some god the Romans like. Anyhow… *paid their vow joyfully and willingly, deservedly. Aelius Mansuetus taking care of the matter.* Good fellow that Aelius, and not light on the silver, if you know what I mean," he finished with a knowing wink. Meala almost laughed at the amusing man and the Roman god. Obviously, the Romans would fall for some powerful spirit posing as a deity.

"Thank you," Meala said, giving the man a nod, which he mirrored, then quickly returned to work, obviously deeply enthralled. Meala was sure that once the Romans were finally driven away from this land, their silly altar and the rest of their trappings would be destroyed, but for now, it seemed that life continued. Just ahead she saw two little girls playing with a small collection of wooden dolls, one girl clearly Roman with dark hair and olive skin, while the much paler brunette next to her was a local, perhaps Brigante, given her facial features. She supposed children were too innocent to know the horrors of the world, and a pang of regret briefly washed over her that she would never again be so innocent.

She frowned, pushing away such thoughts, instead looking toward a wooden building with a utility she thought she might recognize. While it was made in the larger, rectangular shape of a Roman building, the materials and style were distinctly local, a fusion of cultures. It was a wooden structure resembling a Gather Hall, where people from the local community drank, ate, and gathered. Such a building existed at the Stone, a small village northeast of her home where most families in her area lived and traded. She had only seen two similar structures, usually oval-shaped, but her father had described others. It seemed friendly enough, with a sign she couldn't read with the Roman symbols, LVPI TABERNA. Below this hung a stylized wooden wolf head.

Beside the entry stood a tired wooden bench on which a middle-aged drunk woman sat with a wooden cup in hand, her child playing happily beside her with small, clay animal toys, the pair probably awaiting her husband or some other family member before leaving. The scene was one of home, more or less, and one that brought a feeling of order – a sort of island of her culture among an Italic Sea.

Just then, she heard the sounds of distant screams and yelling. Along with others, she turned to see a woman and man apparently fighting beside a small pond a good distance southeast of the village. She could only hear the loudest of their sounds and barely make out what they were doing. Puzzled, she watched as a slightly darker-skinned woman fought what looked like a naked Roman man—what was with naked Roman men in this place?—while a local woman staggered off and tripped. After a moment, the two combatants also collapsed and wrestled briefly, then...

Wait... did the darker-skinned woman stab the man in the neck? Meala wondered with a cringe, unsure of what she may have just witnessed. All around, those gathered gasped at the brutal act. As she watched, Roman soldiers hurried toward the group while those gathered began gossiping. Meala simply stood there watching, as did many others, the next moon's worth of curiosity and intrigue having just played out.

It wasn't long before the local woman climbed to her feet and hurried off toward the village holding her torn dress closed with one hand and a basket in the other, followed by the darker-skinned woman being roughly frog-marched toward the Fort proper by several Roman soldiers and a single soldier leading what might have been the darker-skinned woman's horse. Was it Meala's imagination, or did the woman in the fight remind her of the beautiful Dacian archer? There were at least 400 soldiers here and perhaps as many locals and traders, so she could be wrong. Still, she looked like she had the right build, even from a distance. Unfortunately, the woman was surrounded by too many soldiers and approaching gawkers for a good view.

Her mind instantly returned to that cold night as it had so many times since she had survived the raid. Thoughts of the woman towering over her came to mind, her pulse quickening. Their war had suddenly stopped as they regarded each other in the moonlight… She shook the thoughts away, needing to focus on what she was doing here. She was tired, hungry, and needed to figure out what she would capture that was of value to the Romans before nightfall, her entire trip nearly improvisational and likely a misadventure. With a deep breath to steady herself, Meala strode to the gather hall and pushed the old wooden door open.

CHAPTER V

THE WOLF'S DEN

The edges of the Roman Empire, known as the "limes" of the Roman Frontier, extended more than 5,000 km from Britain to North Africa and as far as the Black Sea. Along these limes, watch towers, walls, forts, and other bastions of Roman power were set up to enforce Roman control and taxation of the land. When a large enough fort, a castrum, was constructed, it would usually be garrisoned by a sizable military force. These soldiers had many needs, and locals were often attracted to the forts to fill these needs for the right coin. Within a canaba, one could find blacksmiths, carpenters, artists, sex workers, religious services, money changers, and nearly anything else one might need.

Often, another settlement would spring up at a distance of a few kilometers from the canaba, usually spread more widely and purely civilian. These satellite communities were called vici (sg. Vicus). Those who worked in the canaba might find themselves living in the vicus, forming what is called settlement duality. Veluniate is a real vicus that actually existed. We know it was a vicus because an altar to Jupiter was found, naming it so in dedication. Notably, the fort would not have been properly called Veluniate; instead, it was called Castra Legionis (Legionary Fort). As a curious note: if you have ever lived by a contemporary military base, you may have noticed that many services can usually be found near the entrances. They provide the same utility as a canaba thousands of years later.

She was immediately confronted by the normal smells of a gather hall, but more intense. Oddly, mixed among them was a thick cut of body odor, the pungent smell of wine, not as common among her people, and the unmistakable smell of sex. That last smell surprised her, as such odors were not a thing one would find in a normal gather hall, a place usually adorned with smoldering herbs and a comfortable fire. One missing element was the sound of music, a commonplace theme in most gather halls when they hosted as many people as this place.

The room was eight paces deep and half that wide (12m x 6m), with two large, parallel wooden tables running down the length and long benches at their sides. At the back stood two wooden doors, each long overdue for repair, probably leading to ancillary rooms. The room was poorly lit in the late daylight, with a few small windows, oil lamps, and two central hearths, unlit. It had some of the trappings of a normal gather hall, but it was more like a poor replica. The walls had no horns or adornments, the tables had no carvings to show the splendor and adoration of the locals who made the hall, and the general atmosphere was more related to drinking than gathering and socializing.

Sitting at the tables was the most eclectic bunch she had ever seen. Off-duty Roman soldiers, local women and men with their worn laboring tunics, elders, and yet another druid with his shaven head and grey tunic. At their feet, several children played while a dog patrolled the tables looking for scraps. It was like a tiny version of the entire land's population, all reflected in a single place, with none fighting. While peace appealed to Meala, she supposed that getting the entire population of the land permanently drunk wasn't a viable method to ending the bloodshed, nor would it remove the Romans.

Curiously, she also noticed that most of the Roman soldiers were gathered at one end of the two tables, their hair mostly short or shaved, their faces either clean-shaven or sporting small, neat beards, a style that Meala still couldn't understand as her people's men wore their beards long and their hair longer. Near to and even mixed among the soldiers were several women whose behavior and dress made little sense to her. Their clothing was loose enough to make their bodies generously visible, several without upper garments. Their faces were painted, but not like one did for war or ritual. Instead, they were decorated with bright reddish cheeks and colors over their eyes. They were also openly flirting with the Romans, with some of the soldiers touching the women without care… and the women seemed to have no bother with this.

She shuddered at the thought. Such behavior made no sense to Meala, as the women of her people would never have allowed such interactions in such a public setting. For a seemingly unknown man, a foreign warrior, at that, to grope a woman in her society would have resulted in said man being challenged by the woman, her spouse, or family to single combat, yet these women invited it. The women were locals, too, possibly Brigante or Votadini, judging by their clan tattoos.

While she watched, one of the women turned her way and gave her a briefly odd look that quickly turned into a playful, knowing smile, a soldier's hand resting upon her breast. She could probably see the confused look from a woman who had clearly never been in a Roman town and seemed to find Meala's bewilderment briefly amusing. A moment later, the handsy soldier slapped some coins on the table before the woman, catching her attention. She promptly slid them into her waist pouch and stood, casting Meala an amused wink before the pair left together toward the door on the right.

Meala stood for a moment, perplexed. What had she just seen and why? Her more primal instincts told her that the man had just paid the woman for sex, but why would she have done that? A few people began to take note of the younger woman hesitating by the door, so Meala blinked twice, resetting her senses. She promptly strode toward the table on her right, where several local women and their children sat closer to the entry side of the building, and took a seat. Despite the similarities with her culture, Veluniate seemed like a very alien place. Luckily, she need only remain until it grew dark. For now, she needed to drink and eat to be ready for the lengthy walk back, as she wouldn't be spending even a full night here, if possible… assuming that she could sneak into someplace important and capture something valuable to the Romans.

Just then, the door opened, and what looked like the local woman from the events at the pond stepped in. She wore a dark brown woolen blouse with a slightly lighter colored woolen skirt that had clearly been torn and was now held in place with her waist cord and a spare bronze pin. Meala had seen her returning with a basket, though that was now missing. The woman brushed her long, honey-blonde hair aside, revealing dark green eyes and a splash of freckles. She was quite beautiful, though really Meala's taste, and, as usual, almost assuredly not into women. *They never are*, she sighed with a groan.

She looked to be about ten years Meala's elder, a woman in her prime. Her bare upper arm was slightly red and looked like it was bruising. Had the woman or the man at the pond attacked her? Her body language was closed and downtrodden, which made sense for someone who had clearly been assaulted, though Meala was unsure who had actually been the aggressor. Before she could ponder more, the mystery woman approached and sat next to Meala, her worried gaze falling briefly over the Romans at the end of the table.

"What will it be, then?" a woman's raspy voice nearly caused the already jumpy warrior to start, but Meala turned a forced, friendly look toward the elderly "gather maid," who had just appeared from behind. Normally, such people brought drink and food, and kept the gather halls in order, a sacred and honorable job. Food and drink were without cost, a show of hospitality expected to be given to those who came to your town and returned when you visited theirs. Those who attended brought food and drink to add to the mutual stores, or a war chief would supply the hall to demonstrate their import. But here in Veluniate, she had no real understanding of how things worked, no matter how similar they might seem.

"Ummm… beer and some food?" she asked, unsure of the proper wording as she spoke in Latin, guessing that most here knew Latin, and not knowing the woman's native tongue. She was unsure what to do as this already felt much different from a normal gather hall. The gather maid, if that was even what she was, gave her a curious and appraising look, then spoke.

"Four asses and I'll get you something warm. Traveled far?" she asked, obviously trying to be friendly. Meala wasn't sure how to answer nor what an "asses" was. She had found three gold coins with her mother's spear and shield. Both had what was clearly a Roman man's face on one side and on the other, a woman wearing a strange helmet, holding what looked like a spear with one hand and a small tree with the other, a rabbit at her feet, though one of the coins was in much worse shape.

"I'm from North, by Flooding Lake," she said, fumbling in her pouch for a gold coin and hoping it was enough. Meala had never used money, something a simple farmer's daughter had little use for. Most exchange among the farming communities was done by barter, though her father would trade at the Stone and her parents maintained a collection of the little metal pieces. Her people had once used metal rings as currency, or so she had once heard from a druid, though she had never seen one and had no idea why anyone would value such little scraps of silver or bronze.

"Flooding Lake? Of course you are with those lot," the woman laughed, nodding at her ample tattoos. While many locals had a single marking of their clan, Meala sported tattoos on each arm, leg, shoulder, and chest, just visible under her blue-dyed tunic. Meala had no real answer for the woman, smiling back and placing the gold coin on the table, now more conscious of her looks.

"Is this enough?" she asked, unsure of the coin's value. A strange look passed briefly over the gather maid's face, but Meala failed to recognize it. Oddly, the glimmer of gold seemed to catch the attention of the local woman who had just sat beside her, though she merely watched.

"Oh yes, that should be just enough to cover it…" she began, placing her hand on the coin, about to slip it off the table, when another hand overtook hers, slapping onto the coin. Meala and the maid looked up to find the honey-blonde woman leveling a serious gaze at the gather maid. She looked shaken and disheveled, yet there was a sort of irritation in her stern gaze, the look of someone not in the mood to entertain those who preyed on others.

"I think you may have mistaken the coin. That was all it was, right?" she asked in a variation of the local Celtic tongue, her level tone conveying more threat than question. Her accent was Novant or maybe Votadini? Either way, Meala saw the challenge in her icy stare, the sort a woman made before a fist flew. Looking back at the gather maid, she watched petty anger flash across the woman's face as her nostrils slightly flared, but even Meala could see that the maid was not actually considering confrontation. A local herself, the maid knew what acknowledging her apparently bad deed would entail. The older woman's reply was saccharinely sweet, and her forced smile didn't reach her eyes as she reached into her pouch and produced a handful of coins, quickly selecting a few.

"Yeah… nothing more than a mistake," she said, slapping the coins on the table more roughly than was polite. The honey-blonde woman released the gold coin, which the maid promptly took and left. In its place she left twenty-four silver coins, three larger brass coins, and a single copper coin, an unknown value to Meala. Seeing her confusion, the honey-blonde woman explained, a nervous smile returning to her face, though the act of helping someone seemed to bring her some comfort.

"Your gold aureus was worth 400 asses," she said to which Meala stared back blankly as she began to playfully stack the coins into various configurations. The woman cocked an eyebrow as if just starting to realize just how naive Meala was, what the Romans would call paganum.

"You don't know how their money works, do you?" she asked, and Meala shook her head, then frowned when her tiny tower of stacked coins fell. With a sigh followed by a relaxing smile, the woman pointed to the small copper coin as she explained in Latin.

"One copper 'as' is enough for a beer and something to eat. Sixteen asses make a silver denarius," she said, pointing to one of the twenty-four silver coins the troublesome gather maid had left. Seeing Meala's look of understanding as she realized just how close she had come to being robbed. "Your gold aureus is worth twenty-five denarii." Almost as an afterthought, she added "These large brass coins are sestertius, worth four asses each, so four sestertii make a denarius. They have other coins, but these are the most common around here." Meala produced her another aureus and examined the lady on the back. As she did, the still-nervous woman smiled and spoke once more.

"She is Minerva, Roman goddess of many crafts of mind and skill. Weaving, wisdom, music, poetry, and strategy in war," she explained, though she didn't hide her look of curiosity at a young Caledonian woman possessing multiple gold aurei.

"War… is war all they ever think about?" Meala asked, drawing a somewhat confused look from the woman, quickly becoming a slight smirk. Her smirk melted into an understanding smile as the woman seemed to consider who was asking and why she might come to such a conclusion.

"We think of many things and not all of them war. I am half Roman, by my father, and half Novant (local tribe) by my ma, so I understand a little of both peoples. Do not let the look of this place fool you. Not all Romans are soldiers, just like not all your people are warriors. Even your warriors don't run around raiding every day. You are in a canaba, a town that grows beside a fort like flies on a cow's ass. Rome's soldiers need many things, and people follow them," she said, turning a brief glance toward the sex worker women across the room. "This place has become so large that it is now a vicus," she said, then noticed Meala's confused look and added, "A vicus is a larger settlement. You know, like a farming town?" Meala nodded, now understanding. The honey-blonde smiled in return, but her body language didn't match the gesture. She was nervous, even if she seemed to be slightly calming.

"Thank you for that," Meala said, noting that the woman's arms quickly returned to the core of her body, folding around her chest as though she were cold. The torn dress, closed body language, and her forced calm troubled Meala, but she could help with that and return the favor as the woman sitting across from her had given her an education, a different perspective to consider, and had just saved her from being robbed, yet another alien concept. Theft among her people outside of the context of a formal raid or act of bravery, like what she was doing, could result in permanent loss of station or one's life.

After a few moments, a different woman came to deliver her food and drink, the first likely too ashamed to show her face, or so Meala supposed. She placed a wooden plate with roasted meat, probably mutton, a small hunk of bread and butter, and a large clay cup of what looked like beer before her. Speaking before the woman could leave, hoping to help the distraught local and not liking unpaid favors, Meala decided to make another order.

"A cup of beer for my friend," she said, dropping a single "sestertius" coin on the table. The woman nodded and deposited three copper as coins before she scurried off to fetch the beer. Glancing up, she noticed that the honey-blonde woman had not even noticed the order and was now fretting over her torn skirt. Digging into other people's business was not proper among her people, but Meala was also nervous and far too curious about the strange happenings at the pond. Besides, nothing else was normal about this oddly Roman-influenced place, and perhaps such inquiries were normal here.

"Thank you for helping me. I am Sei'ln Meala of the Flooding Lake, daughter of Ail Braide of East Wenechon, of the Wood Owl clan," she spoke firmly but quietly, lest the rest of the room hear. Her formal tone, full name, and clan affiliation briefly drew the honey blonde's attention, though the words seemed to almost take her a moment to process. After a brief instant, the woman let go of her torn skirt in frustration and leveled her dark green eyes at Meala. Her smile returned, but it once more seemed forced, like someone trying to reestablish their humor when they didn't fully feel like being humorous.

"Wood Owl clan? Well, at least that explains the feather," the woman mused, her eyes briefly glancing to the feather Meala had affixed to her hair with some pine tar and flax strands from her rope. Feathers were not uncommon to find adorning the hair of those from the country, though usually smaller songbird types.

"Well met, Sei'ln Meala. I am Julia of Muire Glen, daughter of Ana, of clan Luan," she replied, giving Meala a nod. Meala returned the nod, but not before a slight frown gave away her pause at hearing the name "Julia." Julia's smile became a genuinely amused smirk.

"I told you I was half Roman. My mother was clan Luan, of the Novant, to the West. My father was a Roman merchant who named me. It's a name that does not run off the tongue easily, but Roman names never do. Though I guess I shouldn't complain. The Romans haven't been that bad to me, mostly," she finished as her expression soured. Before Meala could reply, they were interrupted as the gather maid brought Julia her cup of beer, compliments of Meala. For a moment, Julia looked at the beer like it might bite, then caught sight of Meala's enthusiastic look, realizing the gift for what it was.

"Now, what's this for?" she asked, eyeing Meala as she took a heavy draw from the cup and let out a breath of relaxation.

"I saw you at the pond, and I…" but Julia cut her off with a cackling laugh, the alcohol quickly fixing her nerves like nothing else.

"So, you wanted to get me a beer to loosen my tongue, right? At least you aren't as much trouble as the soldiers. They'll buy you a beer to loosen much more if you let 'em," she laughed. Meala frowned, mostly sure she understood the woman's meaning, yet wishing she had not. For Julia, it wasn't a general lack of enthusiasm for men, especially sexually. It was more a revulsion with Romans soldiers in general.

"Well, one of them tried to… you know. I was by the pond washing clothes, one sestertius a basket is the going rate, and the soldiers will pay. But the one I ran into wanted more than some clothes. Over-sexed ox came out of the water like some sort of wild thing, too. If it hadn't been for that Amazonem, I'd have been..." she paused, her face suddenly sober. She quickly gulped the rest of her cup and called the maid for another. Meala continued to munch on her food, gulping it down rather quickly.

"You'll cover me for another, right?" she asked Meala, looking a little sheepish at having ordered before considering who would pay. Meala nodded, entirely confused by the woman yet worried that she understood what Julia was alluding to and still perplexed by the need to pay for anything.

"Did he take your coins? Is that what he was trying to do?" she asked? Julia gave Meala an appraising glance, then stifled a sardonic laugh.

"He tried to have his way with me like some bull in a field," she said flatly, realizing that innuendo wouldn't work. Meala winced, her suspicions unfortunately confirmed, but Julia continued, "but all he did was get himself killed and my bag of pay lost. Twenty denarii someplace in that foul ret of a pond. It's probably gone now with all those soldiers. I wouldn't go back, anyway. My husband was right..." she finished. Meala had more questions than answers at this point but tried to sort through those that would be acceptable to ask and not too probative of Julia's person, as her culture dictated a degree of privacy.

"Amazonem?" she asked, starting with the biggest question and one about someone else, thus less problematic. The server returned with the drink, and Julia happily took a long sip before answering, her entire thought train seeming to pause until the activity was complete. Meala almost laughed at the woman's antics as she handed the gather maid a single bronze as.

"The warrior woman, aye. They say she's from Dacia. Only one I've seen among the auxilia, too. She's built like a man, which is probably why I've never seen her with one. That and the soldiers are afraid of her. Honestly, if she were a little more masculine, I'd consider asking my husbands if they wouldn't mind some company," she said, her beer mixed with an empty stomach loosening her tongue. Meala's thoughts wandered at the mention of an Amazon. Almost assuredly, that was the warrior who had captured her imagination, stolen her heart, and nearly taken her life.

"My husband is finishing up his trades about now, I suppose. This is where we were supposed to meet up at sunset. We live up north a bit and come down to trade for a few days before the dark season. I try and make some coin on the side, but I think I am going to stay right here until he is ready to leave," Julia continued, but Meala was having trouble focusing as her mind continued to wander toward the Dacian. What would happen to her? Was she in trouble? And why did Meala even care? Her attention returned at the mention of gold.

"If I had some of that gold the new governor has, I'd never have to come to this sorry place again. Not like he needs it. He's got lots of it, they say. The governor might use it to buy some friends. He'd need it to get anyone to eat with his vicious wife, Vita," Julia said.

"Gold?" Meala asked, now curious and hoping for something to distract her from the Dacian. She continued working on her food and drink, though her plate quickly became bare.

"Oh, you wouldn't know. Well, Rome sent a new governor to Brittania. The man is a fool, and his wife is like a badger. She had her last body slave whipped to death for some minor incident. Who does that? Anyway, the gold is supposed to belong to Rome, but rumor has it that he has taken it and wants to use it to buy influence. The man cannot even afford to have a southern villa made. He isn't even staying in the capital city. He hides in the castrum's principia (main military building of a fort), probably too scared to leave. It's that big building in the Fort. I'm sure the Legatus appreciates his personal rooms being taken. The big question is: how does he stay in the same building as his nasty wife?" she finished, speaking far too openly about a leader for Meala's liking, but no one else seemed to notice or care. She scratched at her scalp for the third time, the lack of a bath in the lake starting to bother her.

"You seem to have caught an itch," Julia said, sipping away at her beer. Meala glanced up, taking a moment to process Julia's Latin words.

"It has been a few days since I swam," she admitted. Normally, when warm, Meala would wash every day or every other day in the lake, and when cold, she would clean her body with water and cloth every few days. But she had spent several days of hard walking getting to the Wall, and it seemed the dirt and oil were finally catching up. Julia's expression suddenly changed to excitement, the drink obviously doing much to unwind her.

"We should visit the baths!" she exclaimed very excitedly, her beer-laced emotions quickly brightening at the prospect.

"Baths?" Meala asked, wondering if she meant the bathhouse her mother had spoken of.

"Baths… You know! The bathhouse is open to soldiers most of the day, but in the evening, it opens only to women. It's cheap enough to get in if you don't mind helping me out," she finished, looking a little morose at the end, likely realizing that she had saved Meala from one person taking her money only to become the next. Still, the idea of water and cleaning sounded lovely to the Caledonian, and a moment later, she stood.

"Julia of Muire Glen, daughter of Ana, of clan Luan… please take me to the baths," Meala said, her country formality catching the slightly intoxicated and far less formal woman off guard, but a moment later, Julia burst into laughter and nodded her ascent.

A short time later Meala and Julia found themselves walking down the main path of the canaba approaching the bathhouse. Meala needed to waste a little more time as the Sun sank lower in the sky but she also needed to relax. She had already considered the main building of the Fort to be her most likely target, and the mention of prized gold made her choice even more tempting, if not intimidating. But first, she would clean. The pair approached the building with the smoky walls, which Meala supposed were small chimneys in the walls, if that even made sense. At the entryway and sitting on an old wooden stool was an older lady who looked so bored that Meala worried she might slump over. Yet, as they arrived, she seemed to perk up, quickly evaluating the pair.

"One 'as' a head," she said, her words rhythmic and nearly slurred together, like someone who had said the same salutation for far too long. Meala furled her brow, somewhat perplexed by the use of the word "caput," meaning head, but supposed that it meant "per person."

"Two," Julia replied, then added, "and we need oil and a scrape," her words leaving Meala confused.

"That's one more each," the woman said, so Meala handed her a single sestertius, unsure what they had just paid for but suspecting that she would find out. Beside her, Julia made a little clapping sound with her hands, both a bit inebriated and apparently quite excited about a bath. With their entry paid, Julia quickly led Meala through the stone and wood entryway and into the bathhouse, a sudden gust of warm, wet air and damp-fragrant smells enveloping both women.

The building turned out to be subdivided into many smaller rooms, the walls made from wood and stone, something Meala had never seen before. The first room they entered had long wooden benches supported by stone blocks, with little wooden storage spaces. Julia called the room an apodyterium, though the word meant nothing to Meala, whose Latin vocabulary was only barely conversational. In the room were several women in the middle of dressing and undressing, the utility of the room immediately apparent. Julia stepped over to a bench and sat to begin removing her clothes.

Meala was surprised that she would wish for something like a public bath after what she had endured, but the beer seemed to calm her. Though it appeared from what she had seen that the Roman had not done more than menace her before the "Amazonem" had stopped him. Besides, if she did live up north, this might be her only chance with such a luxury for some time. She wondered what Julia's husband would think when he got to the Gather and she wasn't there. She supposed Julia had some sort of arrangement, or he would just have to wait. Either way, that was Julia's problem. Putting that out of her mind, Meala placed her supplies, bag with her spear point and shield, and shoes into the space under her seat and prepared to remove her tunic, but someone caught her eye.

"This place costs nearly four times what it should, but it's the only bathhouse. They don't even have a capsarius (enslaved bath attendant), but this bath is far too small. The main pool is only a tepidarium (warm water pool). They don't have a proper caldarium (hot water pool). After a hot soak, we can cool off in the frigidarium (cool water pool). When I was younger, mother took me to the baths in Eboracum, and they had…" Julia was saying, but Meala had difficulty paying attention to translating a second language and the many-ariums when the body language she was just noticing from another in the apodyterium was extremely blunt.

Across the room, Meala saw a woman glancing at her, but something felt… different. Sure, several women had glanced her way and a few had downright stared, but something about the mystery woman's curious eyes felt more personal. She turned to regard the onlooker openly, finding a woman who appeared to be about her age, though clearly from somewhere else. If she had to guess, she would say the woman was Roman, her hair dark brown and wavy, eyes a light brown, and her bare skin several shades darker than Meala's and the Roman soldiers. Her general look was like that of many of the soldiers, yet slightly sharper in features, and oh so feminine – so much less threatening. The woman gazed back again as she watched, matching Meala's gaze. Then, slowly, the woman blinked her dark eyes, then stood and strode from the room toward what Meala suspected were the pools, leaving her clothing behind, her naked form alluring and difficult to look away from.

"…anyway, if anyone steals your things, you can ask Minerva for help smiting them. She's that woman on the coin you had…" Meala watched the woman leave, feeling an odd mix of emotions. She had no idea who the person was, but she had only experienced such attention from women twice, the other being at the point of an arrow. Her most basic instincts were alight at the prospect of such a woman, yet that same spark of exhilaration and weakness had not overcome her as it had with the Dacian. She had been wounded, traumatized, and facing death, yet all she could do at that moment had been to stare into the eyes of her executioner, like the frighteningly calm eye of a mighty storm. This woman was pretty, but that same flame didn't seem to light.

"Oh, so you like women, is it?" The comment snapped Meala back from her introspection, thoughts too private to share with anyone and, depending on her mood, even with herself. She turned a slightly embarrassed look at Julia, only to find the woman smiling at her ruefully and seemingly unbothered. But upon seeing Meala's sheepish look, Julia's smile became the sad face of worry.

"Aww, did you think I would care? I cannot imagine why anyone would ever want to marry a woman when such men as I have seen roam these lands, but love is love," Julia explained, returning to a smile as she waved away any worries. Meala blushed, her much lighter skin quickly turning red at having been noticed, yet Julia's words of acceptance did much to relax her. Among her people, homosexuality was entirely normal and only problematic when issues of inheritance came up, but she had not known the Roman position on the topic. Putting aside the rest of their many problems, it seemed that Romans were not bothered with same-sex attraction, as far as she could tell, though she also considered that Julia's half-Roman opinion might not encapsulate the collective opinions of Rome.

A short time later, Meala stepped toward the doorway to the main pool, her skin smeared with scented oil, a mixture of olive and rose. The oil had been scraped mostly free using a strange tool slightly resembling an iron sickle or bent sword called a strigilis. The curved, dulled blade was scraped along the skin to remove dirt and excess oil, thus cleaning much of Meala's body. The entire process was quite strange, and made more so by Julia seemingly mistaking Meala's apprehension over using the strigilis as some odd worry over it being more perceived as a man's tool, which made no sense to the Caledonian. Yet another cultural confusion, she supposed.

As Meala entered the pool room a moment later, what Julia had called a tepidarium, she was shocked to find the floors warm as though they were heated from below, while the walls emitted heat as well. The air was warm, and the steam coming from the pool suggested it was, too. The thought of having such luxury in the colder seasons nearly sent a shiver down her spine. Julia quickly pranced over to the pool and slid into the warm waters, issuing a series of odd sounds as she adjusted to the heat of the water. A dozen women sat in the pool, relaxing, chatting, and washing. Around the outside, children ran and played while mothers occasionally scolded bad or risky behavior.

Meala caught sight of the pretty woman from earlier sitting on one of the raised platforms, allowing bathers to sit in the pool with their upper bodies above the water. She reminded Meala of an elegant water bird sunning itself by the lake. When the woman turned, she caught sight of Meala's bare form, her eyes widening as she switched from a playful glance to openly regarding. The warrior was pale, her body heavily tattooed with a large, stylized bee across her chest and a rustic barn owl feather in her hair. Meala was visibly muscular and bore several scars from life as a farmer and those of battle. The worst was clearly an arrow wound on her left abdomen, with a matching exit wound just behind it.

Almost as if on instinct, the woman adjusted her position, spreading her arms behind herself and over the lip of the pool, a much more open pose that was clearly meant to be a very direct invitation. Meala wasn't sure why the woman would be so captivated by a rustic farmer-warrior. The Roman was smooth, elegant, and quite feminine. Meala was rough and strong, her body scarred and inked, something she would not have expected the Roman to appreciate, though she knew little of such foreign tastes. She offhandedly wondered if it might be that she had few choices available. Of course, a bigger question was, how did the woman even realize that Meala was sapphic? She supposed that was a question for another day but something to consider.

Choosing to ignore the woman's amorous attention, Meala stepped toward where Julia now sat on a submerged platform and dipped her toe in the water. It was much hotter than the water she was used to swimming in. Yet, as she slowly lowered herself into the enveloping warmth, the feeling made her skin bristle with little bumps. With a gasp, she slid into the water and lowered herself to her neck, feeling the wonderous sensation of warmth. Most women she knew complained about the cold far more frequently than the men, aside from her sister, Rigandona, who seemed largely immune to the cold. The feeling of such absolute heat, the steam washing over her face, was the strangest form of platonic ecstasy she had felt.

"Your moaning..." Julia whispered, sounding quite amused, and Meala quickly stopped, not having realized that she was issuing a soft, content sound. Looking around, she noticed many women similarly relaxing, some chatting, and a few casting her curious gazes. Her eyes once more caught the amorous Roman woman, who now seemed even more enthralled, likely from the moaning, a sound that annoyed some women but had quite a different effect on men and those of a more sapphic nature. A part of her wanted to swim over to the Roman and stand before her just to see what she might do. Would the Roman woman make a move? The playful thoughts almost distracted her from her worries. A few sensual tingles accompanied the seductive thoughts, and Meala quickly dunked her head under the hot water and scrubbed her scalp clean.

At first, she imagined herself as a fish swimming in a strange sea, but her playful imagination and the very warm water quickly changed the "sea" into a pot of stew. A moment later, Meala, the fish, surfaced with a splash, grasping her long hair and pulling it into a single column. She squeezed the water from her hair, her face still aching from the heat, yet she felt so much cleaner than she had in days. As she opened her eyes, the Roman woman was letting out a deep breath, seemingly enjoying herself, Meala supposed. The woman's body was so much more delicate than her own, her bone structure more visible than Meala's. Among her own people, having a little more body weight was considered more attractive, though the slender woman's almost delicate physique seemed to work well with her foreign appeal.

Perhaps even stranger was her lack of significant body hair. Among Meala's people, body hair was a sign of adulthood. Women sometimes plucked the occasional hair that became annoying, but their legs, underarms, and other areas had the natural hair the gods had given them. Yet, these strange Roman women had little body hair. Meala wondered if they had some way to remove hair or if they were naturally this way. It certainly added to the local woman's mysterious look, though it seemed a bit odd. She decided the woman reminded her more of the stories she had heard as a child of sea spirits with fish tails and the upper bodies of beautiful maidens who lured men to their deaths.

"It looks like they just changed the water. It gets dirty, you know? A slick of oil," Julia was saying. The part of her who wanted to flirt with the Roman woman was held in check by a mixture of bad memories, anxiety over what was to come in a short time, and the woman's very identity as a Roman, assuming that she even was. Of course, Julia was also Roman, yet she was also half Novant, and that seemed to make a difference. So much for conquering the invader, she supposed. She was supposed to be wasting a little time until the new day (nightfall), then sneaking into the building she suspected held the greatest treasures of these foreign people, at least according to Julia. There, she would take something of true greatness from the Romans and escape.

The idea was essentially the same as the raids clans made against each other for livestock but on a grander scale. It was risky and there was a good chance she might not live through the night, a sobering thought.

Of course, on occasion, a younger man out to prove himself during a cattle raid might find an arrow in the back. If men took such a risk on their path to becoming a full warrior, so should she. She supposed that she should also be performing a ritual for assistance or at least mentally preparing. Instead, she sat soaking with Julia and flirting with a Roman woman.

"This takes the years right off. If I could get Erbin to try it… but they are always so wrapped up in their craft. Of course, Acilius has used the baths many times, but he just doesn't seem to appreciate the experience like I do," Julia said, naming people Meala didn't know and wasn't going to ask about. Instead, she lay back and let the heat melt away her physical tension as she considered her current situation. When she had first come to the Wall, she had considered all Romans to be the same: mindless, brutal men who dressed and acted strangely. She still found that description apt for some of their soldiers, but there seemed to be more to their society than she had first considered.

"… so I told her to go find a craftsman, like a blacksmith. They are also quite strong, and they can actually marry. A retired soldier is a different matter, but the ones at the garrisons are so… moody, you know. Always glum, like someone stole their strawberries. But Porcia just has no taste, so the very next day…" Julia continued, her voice oddly relaxing, if not pervasive. Meala absently splashed at the water, playfully. If no one else were here, she would probably imagine herself to be a slippery fish and swim in the giant stew pot of the whatever-it-was-arium. She had learned to control her powerful imagination, yet such a fanciful medium made it difficult. Still, several of the elder women cast her disparaging looks, though none of them dared to bother the muscular, clearly battle scarred, and tattooed woman.

Meala supposed that some Romans were good and some were bad, much like her own people. Her people's clans sometimes fought over land and other disputes, too. Perhaps it was better to look upon the Romans like a rival clan, just very large and different. As she turned to look, the pretty Roman woman slowly blinked back at her once more, yet another probably flirtatious gesture. A slightly euphoric feeling slowly built within her as she realized that she could simply swim over to the beautiful local and see what the woman wanted. Her own people engaged in openly sexual encounters during several rituals and feasts, and physical intimacy for the purpose of joy was hardly frowned upon. Moreover, Meala was quite single.

"… Of course, we have not seen any fruit from the South in a while. Lots of raids on caravans, you know. Too many dead on all sides, I guess. Of course, this new fool governor and his nasty wife will just make things worse, and you can take that to the altar…" Julia's words faded into untranslated Latin as Meala held her gaze upon the mystery woman across the pool, her base instincts at odds with her nerves. But her mood started to darken as she considered Julia's words, "Too many dead." Meala's thoughts paused upon those words. Her people had fought here many times and died. She clenched her fingers into fists as memories began to return, her anxiety now beginning to take over as her dominant feeling.

How could she be sitting in hot water… Roman water… inside a Roman vica, canaba, or whatever it was, beside a Roman fort and chatting with a half-Roman while another Roman, maybe, flirted with–at–her? The bodies of those she had fought beside had probably been buried or burned just west of where she now sat, and who knows what had happened to those captured. The same soldiers who had taken so many of her people's lives may very well have bathed in this same water, washing her people's blood away. Suddenly, the water felt… dirty.

Just then, the memory of a man being struck in the chest with a spear returned, filling Meala with a sick feeling. She opened her eyes, unable to process and translate Julia's words. Turning, she caught sight of an older woman across the pool. Her mind flashed to the older minor noblewoman staggering away, a vicious sword wound in her chest and her lungs filling with blood. She could still remember the woman's pleading eyes as her lifeblood and everything she was drained from her body. Meala realized she was having a flashback and not one of the minor ones. It would only grow worse until she was fully panicking unless she escaped whatever was triggering it. Turning and grasping Julia, she fought to remember the words in Latin to speak but did a poor job.

"Julia... have to go... thank you... bye," she said, abruptly bursting from the pool in a single, swift leap, rushing off into the apodyterium changing room, and collapsing to her knees, breathing hard as the cooler air covered her body.

"What about the Frigidarium?" Julia called, but she had already left. She placed her hand on her chest and felt the drum of her heartbeat as she fought to recover. Perhaps the heat had been too much, or maybe being within the very wolf's den, surrounded by her enemy. It had been a surreal experience that she had no interest in repeating. Behind her, she heard what had probably been several woman changing as she rushed into the room, likely spooked by the sudden, single barbarian invasion. But her vision had tunneled, and the images of battle had been all that she could see. *Breathe in, breathe out...* Meala placed her hands on the floor and worked to calm herself as she had learned to do.

After a few moments, the nausea and the images faded, though her anxiety lingered. She had faced such feelings several times after the raid, but they had mostly calmed to occasional intrusive thoughts, bad dreams now and then, and some unfortunate reminders. Maybe, if she could just take a moment...

"Hey, you alright?" The sweet and melodic sound of a highly accented woman's voice filled the otherwise empty room like a bird call in the forest. For a moment, Meala remained on her hands and knees, her heart calming and her breathing coming under control. Whoever the woman was, she wasn't the most important thing on Meala's mind. A moment later, two lightly tanned feet came into the edge of her view, a thin copper ring around one of them, some sort of decoration. A moment later, she felt a hand gently touching her shoulder.

"Do you need help?" the voice spoke once more. Meala took a deep breath as she lifted her head toward the voice. The woman's lightly tanned legs were far less muscular, and her body curvier than Meala's. As her eyes drifted upward, she realized that the concerned citizen was none other than the mysterious Roman. Her dark eyes held what looked like genuine concern, but that empathy barely masked her naked desire. A thin sliver of euphoria ran down her spine, cutting through the despair and trauma like a lightning bolt at night.

"Sea spirit?," she spoke in her language, then switched to Latin. "I... The water is... hot..." was all that Meala managed, though she was quickly starting to recover. The possibly sapphic nature of the strikingly beautiful woman in such proximity was a bit too much for her to ignore.

"Yeah, that is how baths work," the woman replied, her accented words filled with snark, yet her countenance held a warm smile. Before Meala could respond, the woman knelt before her with a small huff. She stretched like a wildcat, lithe yet mysterious. Meala hated to stare, but it was hard to ignore such a display – one almost certainly intended to be seen, given the woman's proximity.

"Mocked by a sea spirit," she mumbled in her native tongue.

"What? Oh, Terentia Sabina," she said, which sounded like a name.

"Sei'ln Meala of the Flooding Lake, daughter of Ail Braide, of the East Wenechon… Wood Owl clan," Meala replied, lifting herself into a sitting position with her back against the stone wall of the apodyterium, her world finally making sense. She closed her eyes for a moment, letting herself be at peace amidst what had been some sort of flashback from the battle. She took a deep breath and opened her eyes only to find the beautiful Roman staring at her. Abruptly, the kneeling woman leaned onto her hands and knees and crawled toward her, body language saying everything.

"Umm… Terenia…"

"Terentia, but please call me Sabina," the woman purred, entirely undaunted by the mispronunciation and far too enthusiastic to be anything but romantically playful. It definitely sounded like a sea spirit sort of name, in Meala's opinion.

"Sabina, what is it you want from me?" she asked, her strength beginning to return. Undaunted by Meala's confusion, Sabina shuffled to kneel just beside Meala. The Caledonian swallowed hard as she lay against the wall, her mind still cloudy and her nerves alight. Sabina smiled, seeming satisfied by her responses. If the Caledonian had been uninterested in women, her reaction to a nude woman crawling toward her would have been much different. She had experienced that before, but the Caledonian before her was clearly in need of some distraction and couldn't keep her lovely green eyes from drifting over her body, her cheeks and chest blushing adorably.

"This might seem a bit direct, but I wanted to kiss you," she said, her wide, dark eyes somewhere between predatory and alluring. Definite sea spirit vibes, Meala concluded, her imagination oddly ignited by the beautiful woman and the confusing emotions. Her breathing hitched as her mind began to re-hone, her primal instincts drifting from fight, flight, or freeze to the visceral longing that came with the sight of a very alluring woman kneeling quite nude before her. Her life had changed so much in so little time: not but a few days before, she was being treated as a girl and living under the rule of her parents, a ewe to be shepherded and far too many rams awaiting their turn. Now, she was a warrior, a woman of her own destiny, her life very literally in her hands. She could leave if she wished or simply lean forward and kiss the pretty, sea-spirit-looking Roman woman.

"Kiss me? Why would you want to kiss me?" she asked, wanting more of a reality check than a real answer. She was the enemy of Rome, and she didn't even know this woman. Yet, she had never heard of Roman women warriors, nor did their women seem to hold much power. So, was it really fair to include Roman women among her enemies? That was a question for another day, a day when her mind was clearer. Sabina made a pouty frown, but there was a smile mixed with it. Meala wasn't sure, but the Roman looked to be making the "how adorable" expression, and it bothered her warrior pride more than she had expected.

"Why would I not? I saw how your eyes took their time when you saw me. You do like women, right?" she asked.

"I do," Meala replied, feeling tingles of pleasure and want dance up and down her spine. She had wanted to keep that bit of information to herself, but her people's code of ethics demanded that she answer such a challenge directly, especially if she was to embrace her warrior caste heritage. Every part of her primal self begged her to give in to the beautiful woman, yet her logical mind was skeptical.

"Then why not a kiss? It's not like you'll risk a child from this. What does it matter?" she asked and leaned closer. Well, this definitely explained why warriors were lured into the sea-by-sea spirits. Her left hand extended slowly, cautiously toward Meala's face. Just before touching, Sabina paused, her gaze moving from warrior to hand, then back, a question unspoken but not unasked. This was the moment when she should say "no," her higher-order brain cried, but the sudden irrationality that came with the expectation of romance and intimacy did wonders to soothe her stress and anxiety and ground her. When confronted so directly by the promise of immediate and desired intimacy, especially when she had no other in her life to disappoint or harm by her actions, her will to say no faded like dew in the warm Sun.

Sabina's lips were warm and soft, and their feeling seemed to encompass Meala's entire body as they pressed delicately. Kiss after thoughtful kiss, Sabina explored Meala's lips as a warmth filled Meala's chest, sinking down her body and tingling twixed her legs. Sabina lifted her right leg a moment later and wrapped it over Meala's legs, straddling the warrior. Facing Meala and sitting in her lap, the feel of the smaller woman's weight on her waist was far more intimate than she had expected. As the woman leaned in closer, their bodies began to touch, first their waists, then their breasts, as the Roman pressed her tongue against Meala's lips until they parted. As soon as the smaller woman was inside, her hand softly grasped one of the Caledonian's breasts and began gently cupping and stroking it.

Meala realized that she was in the presence of someone with far more experience than she had, which was none. Part of her wanted to take control and let her instincts guide her touch, yet she was still recovering and there was something to be said for letting the more experienced woman do as she pleased. Just then, all thoughts left her mind as an exploring thumb found her right nipple and began to softly stroke circles around her most tender parts. For some reason, the feeling of her nipples touched left her boneless, her body suddenly weak and happily so.

Two women entered the room to grab their belongings but quickly left, paying the sapphic duo little attention, as sexual relations within a bathhouse were hardly uncommon nor considered out of line. Meala didn't pay them any mind, but she noticed when Sabina abruptly stopped kissing. Giving the woman a worried, pleading look, Sabina merely smiled and winked, then began kissing her way down Meala's neck, sternum, and tummy, her head going lower and lower as her fingers continued their magic.

"Wow, you are ready so soon," Sabina mused between kisses.

"What... I..." Meala began, confused, but Sabina merely giggled, probably realizing that Meala had never done something like this before. But the Caledonian's protests ended a moment later as the Roman kissed her delicately around the outside of her labia, blazing a tender trail around her most sensitive parts as Meala all but cried out for more. With a final, overly playful giggle, Sabina began to use her tongue as she had when kissing, yet in a very different sort of kiss. Meala cried out, then placed her hand over her mouth as she tried to fathom the sensations she was feeling. She had seen women doing such things to men at festivals but never realized that a woman could do the same to her.

Sabina's tongue was soft, wet, and with just enough pressure to feel amazing. As she kissed, if that was even the right word to describe what was happening, Meala felt wave after wave of pleasure dancing through her body. Her legs spread of their own accord, and she moaned, her hand no longer covering her mouth as her body responded to the impossibly wonderful sensation. It was all new, sudden, and unexpected, like the first warm day of the early light season (Spring). Should she even be doing this? But why not… her thoughts quickly vanished as the more vital parts of her mind surrendered to the moment's thrill.

Just as she wondered how long it would continue, Sabina's left hand snaked its way up her body, softly grasping her left breast just as her right, and both fingers began to twist and flick her sensitive nipples. Meala cried out from the sudden, geometric increase in pleasure, yet she couldn't bring herself to stop the woman. The small part of her mind that had tried to find some reason to stop had long since failed as she lay against the wall, simply feeling the moment.

As if sensing something changing, Sabina began to issue aggressive and throaty moans and grunts, her calls not from her own pleasure but a means to an end. The sounds, her nipples, and that oh-so-experienced tongue flicking and stroking, and Meala felt herself building toward a climax. She had felt these before under the tree while exploring her feelings, but they were never… her thoughts went blank as the climax suddenly came upon her, a small pulse of pleasure, followed by a much larger one, and then a greater one, a supreme release of joy. She grasped the sea spirit's head, her fingers tangled in Sabina's long, dark, curly hair as she cried out. Part of her wanted to break free, the sensations too much as they grew, yet part of her was unwilling to stop.

The feeling began to subside after much longer than any touch under the tree had ever lasted. Meala's body relaxed, every negative thought melting away like the last snow on a sunny day. When she opened her eyes once more, she found Sabina's dark eyes staring back at her, a smile on her lips. Before Meala could speak, the woman lifted her body, shuffling more gracefully than Meala expected until they were face to face. Meala wasn't sure what to do next, this being the first time she had ever been intimate with anyone, but Sabina seemed at ease with directing, oddly. She took Meala's hand and brought it down between her straddling legs.

"There, just use a finger, you know? Maybe two," she suggested with a playful wink as she returned her attention to kissing the Caledonian. Her eyes were large, dark, and filled with want, and her lips were still wet from Meala's joy. She leaned forward, her lips meeting Meala's, her playful tongue plunging deeper. This time, her kisses were not so much gentle passion but more like hungry desire. The Roman kissed as though she were submerged within a sea of need, and Meala was her only gasp of air. Daringly, Meala playfully nipped at her lower lip as her free hand cupped Sabina's right breast, her thumb softly stroking the sensitive nipple. Sabina gasped, her pleasure oh so genuine and primal.

Meala was quite winded from her exertions, yet enthusiasm filled her as her hand began to explore the warm wetness of another woman. As she pressed her finger within, Sabina softly moaned, her earlier guttural cries replaced with genuine sounds of joy. Meala had great difficulty keeping her attention on her fingers as Sabina passionately kissed her like the world was about to end, the Roman now extremely aroused. Meala pressed onward, pushing inward toward a slightly rough spot she had found on herself, quickly discovering it to hold the same magic in the Roman.

"Oh… Me…la…" she moaned, her lips coming free from Meala's for a moment. Her outstretched hands pressed against the wall as she leaned forward, straddling Meala, her smaller breasts almost in Meala's face. As she did, Meala lowered her head, kissing a path of pleasure down the Roman's neck toward her chest. A moment later, she placed her lips around one soft nipple and began to flick her tongue. Sabina's moans changed to open yelps of pleasure as Meala's finger gently stroked and her tongue flicked. Meala could feel Sabina's body tensing, so she synchronized her movements, her thumb and tongue tracing soft circles as she fingered the woman into a fit of moans.

She felt the pressure as Sabina's warmest place pulsed with her release, new wetness covering her hand and waist until the woman collapsed a moment later into her arms. Both women lay against the wall for a moment, their bodies and hair wet and their want in cessation. In truth, Meala felt she could do that again, but she wouldn't push the issue. She had never been intimate with anyone before and was shocked at how wonderful it had felt. Yet, for all of the joy, it had not been as emotionally powerful as the deeply romantic feelings she had held for the Dacian. How actual sex was less intense than unrequited romance with a woman who had tried to kill her, she couldn't say, but…

"That was quick. I guess we were both worked up from the bath, you know? Still, that was the most fun I've had in days, and free of charge," Sabina said, taking a moment to stretch, her body a little shaky but quickly recovering. She flopped over to rest against the wall beside Meala, both women clearly winded. Meala sat back, stuck somewhere between remembering the amazing sensations she had just felt and beginning to consider what she had just heard. As she too stretched, feelings of elation flooded her body, leaving her desiring more and extremely relaxed. Her mind had gone from a descent into panic and anxiety to a massive release in mere moments, a rather jarring consideration… but so too was the confusing thing Sabina had just said.

"Free?" she spoke after a moment, a bit confused. Sabina stood and walked a short distance across the room, a sight Meala was still too worked up to ignore, and then returned, seemingly unwinding herself.

"Yeah. Eighteen asses for the night and four for something quick, but not this time. It's a lot, but I like to think the best wine costs the most, you know? Normally, it's older women who want to taste a different sort of wine. But you, no… I just wanted to kiss you," she said, as though that made it any less confusing. Meala hoisted herself onto the bench, her expression now perplexed.

"I don't understand," she said. Sabina stopped pacing and tossed her a skeptical look, hands now firmly upon sardonic hips. Meala had difficulty not staring as the beautiful woman stood before her shamelessly nude, her personality so different from the women Meala had known growing up. Her body cried out for another go as visceral memories of Sabina's probing tongue, fresh as early light season (Spring) rain filled her mind. But she had something important to do and couldn't afford to spend all night in the Roman's arms.

"Wait… you know that I am a meretrix, right?" she asked, but her skepticism quickly faded to humor as she realized that Meala had no idea what she was talking about. Sabina burst into laughter, and came to sit on the wooden benches where people dressed, patting one beside her. Meala stood and sat beside her, hoping to understand.

"I'm a meretrix. Well, really, I am a prostibulum, you know, but who's checking, right?" Meala did not appear to know, so she sighed and explained, "I am paid for sex and sometimes just for the company, you know? A few older women and a couple of men that come here pay me regularly. I get two silver quinarii and they get a special time at the bathhouse. No one minds, and I give a sestertius or two to the owner to keep her mouth shut to the aedilis (person who regulates public buildings, including prostitution)." Meala sat for a moment, processing what she had just learned. It explained why Sabina was so easy to approach and why she was both skilled and seemed unbothered by Meala's lack of skill.

"What, you have a problem with what I do?" Sabina asked as she took note of Meala's contemplative look. She appeared ready to be annoyed or worse – her face clearly spoke of someone used to being judged.

"Oh, no, it's just… I have never been with anyone before. I'm not sure how I feel, but it isn't bad. It's…"

"Wait, I was your first? Oh, by Luna's bosom, that's adorable. Definitely free – the 'first-time' discount, right?" she exclaimed, her annoyance instantly converting to amusement and perhaps even a little adoration. Meala ignored the woman's jovial reaction, bordering on mildly condescending, clearly a trait of sea spirits.

"Why do you have sex for coin?" Meala asked, unsure if her question was too personal but wanting to know. She had seen women doing this at the gather hall but had not thought much of it since. Sabina gave her a warm smile, now starting to realize just how different their worlds really were. With a sigh, she began to explain.

"My mother died long ago. She was a… well, she came from just east of Alexandrea, Aegyptus (Alexandria, Egypt). A small town near the fortress of the Romans… It is far to the South where it is very hot," she added, seeing Meala's confusion over the place name. "My father was part of Legio II Traiana Fortis. They didn't marry; rules, you know? But when he left after he served his time, he took me with him. He wasn't all that bad, I suppose," she said, her expression barely masking a deeper pain, yet Meala wasn't sure if it was for her father, mother, or perhaps her situation?

"My father died just six months ago. Left me our small house and some land he got from soldiering. I already sold the land to the neighbors to pay what he owed for the lot, and I have no plans to find a man. Sure, they pay well, but I can't see myself that way, long term, right?" She said, her expression growing whimsical, as though she remembered some deeper plans she had made for her future. Meala supposed everyone had such thoughts, though few probably reached their dreams. She nodded her understanding, feeling awkward as she considered the timing of Sabina's father's death. But Sabina took the nod as a prompt to continue, clearly unfinished.

"No, I'll find a woman someday and start a weaving trade," she said, looking down for a moment before continuing. "Weaving is what I like, you know? But I cannot afford the materials to get started. So, this is what I do. It pays fine, and it's pretty safe as long as I keep from the soldiers… Sorry, I didn't mean to speak about myself. I just wanted to kiss you," she said, suddenly shy. It was the first real emotional vulnerability she had shown. Though nude she was, Sabina wore a thick armor of deception over her emotions, shielding them from outsiders, yet Meala had broken through simply by listening, it seemed.

"How did he die?" Meala asked, a wave of dread passing over her as though she probably knew the answer but could not be sure. As she spoke, Meala slid over to her possessions and began to dress. Sabina merely sat there, apparently at ease in her current undress, though Romans did have rather confusing social mores concerning nudity, as far as Meala could tell.

"Died at the wall. One of your kind put a spear through his neck," she said, then noticed Meala's suddenly horrified expression and hastily added, "And a good thing, too. Man was a dirty pig most of the time. He used to be nicer, but he drank too much later on. He had another woman here, too, but she left as soon as he died. Took anything worth anything, you know? Naa. I'm glad one of you put a spear through him," she said. Meala stood for a moment, shocked as she listened to the real-life repercussions of the raid she had taken part in.

She couldn't bring herself to feel deep remorse over the deaths of Roman soldiers – invaders in her land who did such unspeakable horrors, but those soldiers left behind lovers, children, and others. Society, even Rome, was built from such social bonds, and a battle severed and destroyed so many of them. Yet, Sabina seemed at peace with this, a perplexing mystery, though one Meala felt it too personal to ask about, as well as the mysterious land of Aegyptus (Egypt). Wherever that was, it might explain why Sabina looked different from even the Romans.

"Well, I need to go and wash up. I'm expected to help 'wash' a special lady just before close. She tastes like old wood and smells like a stable half of the time, but she pays me double, and her grey eyes are rather pretty," she said, shrugging with a smile. "I'm glad I got to meet you, Meala of the Flooding Lake," she added, tossing Meala a wink, standing, then turning to leave. Now dressed and ready to leave, Meala lifted her gear, then paused, a thought coming to mind.

"Sabina, wait," she called, halting the woman at the door of the apodyterium. The curious woman turned to regard her, an almost sad look briefly passing across her face as though she wished for the chance to find out how far their paths could travel, yet knowing those paths would probably soon part, forever. Meala put down her gear and began to dig around for a moment until her fingers found the small, heavy object she sought. It wasn't much, but Sabina's story and wish to become a weaver had meant a lot to the Caledonian. She could understand all too well the need to escape one's situation, and that was something she might be able to actually help if nothing more. Besides, if she died shortly, a distinct possibility, she would not need her possessions, and if she succeeded, she could replace the small item.

She stood, gazing across the room at the lithe form of Sabina, a woman so feminine that Meala nearly expected rose petals to fall from her as she walked. Sabina wasn't the sort of woman Meala expected to spend her life with, but she seemed like a good person. Meala hoped she might find herself a good woman to settle down with, yet another desire they shared. She couldn't help with that, but there was something she could do.

"The first time was free, but may I give you a coin for one more kiss?" she asked, feeling daring even after their intimacy. Her words were clunky and sounded odd, but Sabina couldn't help but smile. Their paths were about to part, something unspoken yet clear to them both, but it seemed Sabina shared Meala's penchant for fun. She glided across the floor a moment later until she stood before the rustic warrior. Meala awkwardly leaned forward as Sabina passionately planted a kiss on her lips, a joyful and meaningful kiss. At the same time, Meala's free hand found Sabina's, and pressed a coin into the woman's palm. As their lips parted, Meala smiled as she lifted her gear again.

"A fair trade for your kiss," the Caledonian said, then turned and left before she thought better of it. She had come here on a quest of honor, and that had to come first. As she did, Sabina licked the kiss from her lips, quite sure she would have kissed Meala for free as many times as she wanted. Her dark eyes grew wide as she opened her hand, the light from the brazier reflecting off the gold of a single aureus coin. It was over twenty times what she charged her most engaging and wealthy clients and nearly 100 times what she would have charged someone for a simple encounter. More importantly, it was enough to buy the fiber she would need to start a small weaving operation.

Fairwell, beautiful sea spirit

CHAPTER VI

CRUCIFIXUS

Crucifixion is a form of capital punishment and public humiliation historically used by many cultures, including the Romans. Some prominent Romans, such as the famous senator Cicero, thought it too inhumane, yet it remained the supreme form of capital punishment for criminals and enemies of the state and a form of discouragement for others who witnessed the act. All genders, and even children, were subject to the practice, though Roman citizens were usually legally exempt.

When performed by Romans, the act began with the condemned being stripped and then publicly whipped with a multi-thonged whip called a scourge. This sometimes resulted in death from shock and blood loss, though women were usually spared the scourge. The victim would often be forced to carry the horizontal beam, a patibulum, easily weighing 45 kg, through the town or city to a place where the stipes, the vertical beam, was erected. Next, the victim would be tied, nailed, or both, to the patibulum, and hoisted up the stipes. The actual configuration of nails and ropes has been long debated, though evidence for many different configurations exist. Sometimes, a victim's legs would be broken to hasten death, called crurifragium, as they could no longer support themselves, their bodies suffocating under their own weight. A wooden placard, called a titulus, with the victim's name and list of crimes would be attached to the cross. They would be left on public display to die, a horrifying and humiliating process that could take many days, unless those tasked to guard the condemned hastened death with additional wounds.

"Gaius Pedius… Optio Principalis to the Pilus Prior, second to the head centurion of the second cohort of the mighty II Augusta legion. That is the man you murdered. One of Rome's finest men betrayed and murdered by a Dacian dog," Titus Fabius Vibulanus, acting governor of Roman Britannia, spoke with disgust as he held Cynna by the jaw, staring into her face, his long yellow dyed woolen robes a stark contrast to the otherwise dull hallway of the fort. He had only been appointed governor the year before following Gnaeus Julius Verus, the previous governor, and had yet to consolidate himself enough to set up a proper residence, let alone travel south like a proper governor. Of course, with the legion's second cohort camped in and near the fort, he was hardly in danger from the locals. Unfortunately, his grasp of political power was another issue.

"You should be sent to the mines to work until you join the piles of dust," he continued. Fear rippled through Cynna as thoughts of the mines flashed through her mind's eyes. Workers mined gold, tin, copper, silver, and lead until they simply died from malnutrition or the consumption of working underground, a place for the dead, not the living. It was a horrible fate for any man, and so much worse for a woman. But she kept her face neutral, not wishing to grant these men even the slightest twitch of reaction.

The Roman noble released the restrained Sarmatian, holding his hand out for an enslaved local woman to pour clean water upon and wipe his hand with a cloth as though his very skin was made filthy by touching her. In truth, Titus despised the barbarians, but he did like their gold and silver, and they made good enslaved people, a resource he was keen to exploit. While they had some precious metals from their own lands, much of what the painted lot hoarded was from Rome, captured and repurposed. In fact, a large pile of it lay in his private chambers awaiting his "analysis."

He had only examined half of the bullion captured by the third cohort earlier that month when the interruption had come, with the rest of it sitting on his desk. Instead of inventorying it, he found himself constantly bothered by what should have been trivial matters, matters he grew tired of attending. Typically, the legatus' (General) staff would have handled these matters, but he was away with his staff, leaving Titus to keep the order like some sort of common soldier, acting governor or not. Moreover, his wife, Vita, was bound to help herself to some of the bullion while he was distracted. She was as aptly named as she was troublesome. It was enough to make a man scream. Now, he stood before some filthy eastern woman who had just taken it upon herself to murder one of the few elite soldiers he had in a position to help keep good order – a costly man to replace, at that.

Following the death of Marcus Gavius Maximus, trusted advisor to the emperor, Titus' patron had evaporated like the cursed fog of this wretched land. Worse, if what his few friends in Rome had said was true, ambitious men like Lucius Volusius Maecianus and Marcus Statius Priscus had come to power in the void left by men like Maximus. If Titus didn't consolidate his power in the South soon enough, the ailing Caesar Antoninus Pius, a man of waning power as age crept upon him like a stalking lion, he might find himself without a governorship as quickly as he had found one. Luckily, keeping a portion of the gold collected from the North would provide ample resources for buying additional support back in Rome, not to mention a little extra for himself.

He operated several fledgling enterprises in Britannia and Caledonia, from lumber mills near Veluniate to lead mines near Epiacum (Alston, Cumbria). He had plenty of wealth, but most were tied up in enslaved workers, land, and materials. Governor or not, he had not received the money his station promised, and his finances were quickly dwindling. The thought of sending such an annoying woman to his lead mine briefly entered his consideration. The average enslaved worker lasted only a few months before the poisons of the soil claimed them, but it would certainly provide the Dacian with a potent education to carry with her into the beyond.

He had a long-held distaste for non-Roman soldiers serving in the legion, an unfortunate side effect of having such an expansive empire. However, he accepted their necessity as nothing more than a barely tenable pragmatism. But a woman? The idea was repulsive, and here stood an example of why women had no place in the legion. They were far too emotional and certainly irrational, in his opinion. It was as foolish as arming a slave or seeking council from a dog. Luckily, most of the more foreign auxilia had the good sense to leave their women at home where they belonged. Now, he was down an optio, a man who played a critical role in keeping legionary order, just when he needed to secure his authority.

Decimus Junius Juvenalis would have wept... he thought, sardonically, remembering the poet's sixth saturam (poetic satire), a work that reminded the reader of a woman's non-martial place in life. The very notion of a woman warrior was an abomination and a stain upon the honor of Rome – an empire built by the blood, sweat, and strength of Roman men. A woman had her place in society, an important place, too. Without women, there would be no Roman men, and a woman's place was sacred. Yet everything and everyone had their place in the larger picture of a functioning society. Here, he was governor, and this wasn't Themiscyra (legendary home of the amazons).

While patrician lineage afforded a certain degree of freedom, even a man like Titus had some disciplinary rules he must obey. Of course, a barbarian woman wasn't a proper Roman under the eyes of the law, and making an example of her would remove the only female soldier under his command while reminding those who were not citizens what their lack of discipline might lead to. If nothing more, there was a certain satisfaction in dealing heavy-handedly with yet another source of stress, like swatting a fly on a hot day with a war ax.

The barbarian woman stood before Titus, held by four soldiers, her face unreadable as he considered her fate. In fact, he had already decided upon hearing what had happened, a knee-jerk reaction that he had simply found post hoc justification for. Still, it served his purpose for his soldiers to see him appear to agonize over the decision. He needed to both be feared by them and earn their respect with a reputation as a thoughtful man who made careful decisions.

Exchanging a glance with the pilus prior, Marcus "Pugius" Quirinalis, he cleared his throat theatrically, preparing to render his decision. In all honesty, the woman had probably defended herself against the lascivious optio. Titus had never liked the man and was hardly upset at his demise, personally speaking. However, the lack of another leadership position was problematic, and optiones took time to train. He had tried to convince Marcus to select someone else many times in the past, though unwilling to order such an act for the purpose of morale. Morale was what kept the military together and kept things well-oiled. To lose the men's respect would mean his only grasp upon them was money and fear, a dangerous combination. With a final sigh, he rendered his verdict.

"Crucifixus…" he spoke, drawing a confused look from the guards.

"Crucifige (crucify her). Do it this very night. Put her in the courtyard where everyone will see. These people speak several barbarian languages, but they will understand this," he said flatly, noting their stunned looks. The guards remained confused, his verdict of death or banishment to the mines expected, but the summary nature of a death sentence for a soldier, foreign or not, was atypical. In spite of it all, Cynna remained stoic, her face betraying no fear, even as waves of adrenaline flooded through her body at the pronouncement, her legs growing weak.

"The day grows late, and the Sun is near set. Perhaps we could convene a trial in the morning, at least as a formality?" Marcus suggested, a bit out of place yet somewhat off put by the lack of protocol. He had expected she would be put to death, as was natural for a murderer, but he had not expected the most humiliating and painful method to be the mechanism, nor outside of the proper procedure. Crucifixion wasn't as much a method of execution as it was a method of setting an example to those who witnessed it. Seeing a soldier so reduced wasn't necessarily the best way to reinforce the power of the Roman army or the exceptionalism of Rome's citizens, but the governor's word was law.

"She's infames (disgraced) and peregrina (free non-citizen subject of Rome), at best, not a citizen. I assume that our second cohort is fully capable of handling a single woman, even in the night," Titus replied, matter of factly, wishing to end any worry over the overly-harsh sentence. Several of the men murmured in agreement, while those who didn't agree kept silent in the presence of such a powerful man whose name itself carried almost as much weight as his station.

"I am your governor, and it is within my rights to order summary judgment outside of any other judicial order. You shall perform this execution quickly and quietly," he spoke, turning to leave the room. It was evening, and there was still a significant amount of paperwork to be done, not to mention cataloging the remainder of the bullion before bed. That last thought crossed his mind, sparking one final consideration as he paused at the door. Much wax would be melted this night.

"Oh, one more thing. Make sure you gag her so I don't have to hear the screaming all night."

Cynna stood with her hands tied behind her back and four soldiers holding her steady. She had listened to what the man had said and understood his thickly accented Latin. She had seen crucifixion before on her way to Britannia and again after the raid six months ago with the few captured locals. Even now, the thought of what she had seen filled her with horror. She wanted to scream, wanted to beg for mercy, but she knew there was nothing she could do. She had left her home to escape death and start a new life, but it seemed she had made the wrong choice. She only hoped that the Mother of Fire would numb her body to the pain as she faced her end as bravely as her mother.

The sky became a dim, grey blue as the last light faded. The Sun set a short time beforehand as Meala stopped by a merchant and purchased some supplies. She now had a bag of dried meat, her wineskin refilled, a small clay jar of honey, a bee's wax candle, and a long wooden pole. The lot had cost her a mere twelve asses and three smaller coins that started with a "Q" sound that Julia had not explained. Meala had given the trader four denarii and bade him keep the change, much to the man's surprise. She had no real use for Roman money and wanted to get rid of the remaining coins.

Twelve asses were just a bit less than Sabina had claimed her payment usually was. Meala had no idea if she had been boasting or if that was a normal amount for such activities. She had certainly been beautiful and skilled, yet Meala could not imagine herself paying for sex. For her, sex was more about the emotional connection. She had no such connection with Sabina when they had met, but the sheer excitement and intensity of the woman had been enough to weaken her resolve. She hoped the woman found her way and that one of her gold coins would be enough to help her, but Sabina was clearly a woman of her own destiny, someone Meala could respect, and someone at odds with the seemingly male-dominated Rome. Thoughts of her encounter with Sabina occupied her mind as she prepared for what must come next.

While she had donned her clothing and just before she had kissed Sabina she had slipped her remaining gold aureus and most of her remaining coins into Julia's bag beneath the wooden bench where she had left it to say thanks for the woman's help, especially since Julia had already lost a little less than a gold coin when she was attacked, and had given Meala a good idea of where to look for her trophy. She had spared just four denarii for her purchases, assuming that would be enough. With the day now beginning once more with night's return, Meala left the main canaba path and slid behind a large roundhouse-style building and into the stone ruins of what might have been a granary. It was a safe place to prepare, though graffiti on the remaining stone walls and various objects scattered about suggested others had used it for shelter.

Meala hummed a tune to calm her growing nerves as she quickly fitted the shaft to her mother's spearhead, aided by the dim, flickering light of a beeswax candle. The wood was a little larger than the spearhead, requiring her to shave the excess with her bronze dagger. Before fitting the spearhead, she used her dagger tip to create a small hole in the wood, then fitted the iron tip and used her dagger's hilt to hammer the spear's bronze pin into the wood, securing the iron tip. As she worked, her mind drifted as she considered how best to break into the governor's home, which it seemed was in the center of the fort.

With her spear and shield ready, Meala knelt within the old granary before what remained of the tiny candle flame, digging a small hole in the ground with her dagger. As she did, she softly sang a prayer to the spirits of bees, her patron animal, and the Great Mother, hoping to take upon herself the spirit of the former and the good graces of the latter. In the hole, she placed the small ceramic pot of honey along with her petition for assistance from the divine and spirits. As the final flickers of candlelight faded, Meala removed the ash from her bag and drew a dark band across her face, passing over her eyes, then down her chin and neck, ending just before her tattoo.

As she painted, her mind descended back to the many stories she had been told as a child of mighty warriors returning from valiant battles to carry away their loving brides – a popular theme. Even as a child, she had wanted to be that loving bride. At first, her dreams had surrounded dashing men, though the men of her imagination had always been rather feminine. When she was nine or ten, she had laid eyes on her first warrior woman, a middle-aged Orrean from a closely associated clan returning from a raid to the Southwest. Even now, Meala could recall her stoic visage, three scars disfiguring the left side of her face, her body tough and strong. She held the overly stylized gladius of a higher-ranking Roman in hand, his head one of many in a large linen bag slung over her back.

This was a woman who quite literally took life by the hilt and called no one her master. With age, Meala understood that she probably owed some fealty to a local chief. Still, the powerful woman had left her mark on the Romans, the world, and Meala's imagination. Once she grew old enough and had bled for a full four years, the discussion of who she might wed began. Of course, she wouldn't have been wed until her body was ready, at least sixteen to twenty years, if not a little later, and she had already passed both ages, quite single. During that time, her body had switched from an existential form to a liability – worse, a commodity. Thoughts of Sabina monetizing her body briefly came to mind; a woman using patriarchal rules against themselves for her own benefit, yet her mind quickly reverted to the archer.

When she had faced off against the archer in battle, she had felt something more than just her need to escape her family's desires. More than even the physical intimacy she had shared with Sabina. It had been some sort of renewed drive to take life to its limits, at least once, simply to prove that she could. Perhaps it had been that sense of mutual respect between women unwilling to live mundane lives... women who defied tradition. The Dacian had tried to kill her and had gazed upon her as an enemy. She supposed it was strange to find respect for one's enemy, but feelings could be tricky. And now, she knelt in an abandoned structure preparing to risk her life for freedom, and all she could think of was the archer. The Dacian woman may have let her flee that night, but in truth, she had remained a captive… or at least captivated, ever since.

With the sunset began the darkness of a new day and the hope of a new life. The Path of the Ancestors (Milky Way) erupted from the Southwestern horizon, curving overhead like an arcing path, though slightly tilted to the South. To the Southeast, a full Moon lit the sky like a war chariot flanked by a mighty hero, bright in her gold armor (Jupiter). Under the heroic light of her mighty ancestors and heroes, Meala slowly crept around the edge of the canaba toward the fort. Of course, a new moon would have been a much smarter time to try this, but poor planning seemed in ample supply. The air was warm and humid, causing the stars to twinkle as she approached the edge of the Fort proper, just west of the village. Off in the distance, she caught a glimpse of a wildcat (Felis silvestris silvestris) likely prowling for mice.

Across her back, her mother's old shield sat firmly in place, held by a leather strap, while in her right hand, she carried her mother's spear, a warrior's weapon. With the spear, shield, and her face painted, she would no longer be able to explain away her actions if she were found. Bravery and risk were part of what conveyed honor, and her actions, witnessed by her ancestors, gods, and any spirits who wished to watch, were the purpose of what she now did. If she faced no risk then her triumph would be hollow and might be easily discovered if someone communed with the ancestors, her witnesses. With this in mind, the weight of her mother's spear gave her courage as she approached the fort.

The fort was mostly rectangular, with stone walls surrounding many smaller, elongated rectangular buildings, and likely roaming soldiers. Of course, her first problem was entering the fort. All four of the entryways to the fort were guarded by a handful of bored yet reasonably professional-looking soldiers. Meala knelt in the brush between the fort and village, looking for a way in yet finding none. Her first idea had been to sneak through an entry when no one was looking. Her second had been to climb over the crenulated stone walls. Still, the irregular guard rotations and soldiers posted by each entry quickly dispelled those ideas. Luckily, the guards were probably watching the North and Western lands for groups of invaders and were not likely to notice a single woman sneaking about behind the fort. Oddly, she noticed red deer (Cervus elaphus scoticus) near the fort grazing.

Sneaking around the perimeter, she emerged from behind a building and found herself much closer to the deer. It turned out they were not eating but drinking. Running from a small waterway fed by a nearby brook that opened into the mighty fjord, and all the way to the fort, was a stone channel cut into the ground through which fresh water flowed. The opening for the water was small, but Meala was pretty sure she could squeeze into it, assuming the actual entry for the water at the fort's wall wasn't any narrower. Most of the channel was open to the air from the stream to the edge of the fort, and she would probably only need to crawl a short distance through a tight spot, though the thought was hardly appealing. Of course, there was also the problem that she needed to approach the fort's walls unseen, and her clothes would be soaked, but the night was warm.

Realizing that this was probably her only option, Meala ducked as low as she could and began approaching the fort. Thankfully, the full Moon was occulted by the forts walls as she sneaked along the ground beside the water channel. Open fields were maintained around forts to make just such sneaking more difficult, but the bordering village had neutralized that defense. Of course, this was nothing like a hill fort. Though she had never seen one, her father had told her stories of massive hill forts that dotted the landscape, offering their high chiefs protection and prestige. Be it prestige or pragmatism, the open spaces definitely made approaching the fort much more difficult. Twice, she had seen movement upon the wall and was forced to drop flat lest she be noticed.

When she reached the fort's outer curtain wall, she found, as expected, that the channel ran right into the fort through a hole she could probably squeeze through. What she had not expected were the twin bronze bars blocking entry. A jolt of panic and anxiety rushed through her as she realized that her entire plan could be thwarted by a single pair of bronze rods. They were the thickness of her thumbs and solidly built into the stonework. Worse, even if she had the tools to remove them, the sound would attract the soldiers long before she could break through.

"Stupid Romans with their stupid walls!" she cursed as loudly as she dared and kicked out with her foot slamming into the bronze, expecting nothing more than a wet shoe and a jolt of pain. Instead, and much to her shock, the bars moved forward, and her foot went right through the entry. Shocked and a bit confused, Meala stepped into the water and reached forward, pulling on the bars. Oddly, they weren't actually sealed in place. Even stranger, it looked as though someone had carefully chiseled the stone around the bars and removed it, then replaced the stone with very flimsy mortar, making them a solid appearance and easily removable. As a farmer, smuggling did not come naturally to Meala's mind as a logical answer to this oddity, yet she didn't have time to consider her windfall.

Instead, she whispered her thanks to the gods and spirits of the bees and prepared to swim.

Of course, the tunnel was only wide enough for her to shimmy through, and if she encountered similar bars on the other side, and if they weren't easily opened like those on the outside, she might find herself stuck underwater and possibly unable to escape. Unfortunately, it was too dark to tell what was on the other end or how far it was, though she suspected it was three or four times the length of her body. This was yet another frightening leap of hope, but the spirits and gods had been good to her so far, and she would not fail them by letting her fear prevent her from her path forward.

Removing her wet tunic and gear, she wrapped them together and tied them with her length of hemp rope. She would need to be as slippery as an eel to make it through, and she could pull her belongings along afterward if she made it. Besides, if her belt were pulled loose while crawling, her baggy tunic would make crawling extremely difficult. Holding the other end of the rope, she climbed into the water, restraining a gasp at its coldness. She submerged herself with one deep breath and swam the unknown and narrow distance under the fort wall through the water. *Well, I always wanted to try life as an eel,* she mused.

On and on, Meala, the eel, crawled as the cold water ate away at her resolve, and her body quickly exhausted. The stone was tight against her bare skin, forcing her to shuffle her arms to pull herself through the narrow stone channel beneath the heavy stone wall. Anxiety grew, as did her panic, but the dark water ahead began to lighten as she continued. When she reached the end, she found two more bars, presumably bronze, blocking her way forward. She was nearly out of air, and her body instantly went into fight or flight, primal instincts against drowning kicking in. Meala grasped the bars and began to frantically tug, but to her horror, she found that they would not come free. Worse, in her panic, it felt as though what little space existed in the passage was growing narrower. Air burst from her mouth as bubbles, while terror began to fill her.

Panic made her struggle, and the harder she struggled, the worse she panicked, a deadly feedback loop as her vision started to darken. Just then, Meala's frantic tugging pushed the bars forward, and they began to loosen. Realizing her folly and that the bars pushed outward, not inward, she used the last of her air and strength to force them open and pulled herself through the opening. A moment later, she lay in a large pond-like pool made from stone, gasping for breath. The next, she pulled her belongings through and sneaked off before anyone heard or saw the "sea spirit" of a woman who had just washed up.

A short time later, Meala found herself behind a stack of hay, ringing out her clothing and reapplying her face paint as she took in the inside of Fort Veluniate. The elongated buildings she had seen from the outside continued with even more than she had realized, soldiers wandering in and out of them. They mostly lined the outer perimeter of the fort, while the center held an odd mixture of differently shaped buildings, most of heavier stone construction. Toward the center was a very official-looking building with well-painted doors and a second floor, likely the very building Julia had mentioned. Beside it was a drystone walled area, possibly a courtyard, and near that were the massive stables.

At the very top of the central building was a window where a flickering light could be seen. Most of the soldiers seemed to be sleeping or keeping a low profile, but whoever was in that room was somehow different. Perhaps a leader or whatever the Romans had for druids? Meala knew nothing of Roman forts, but if she were in charge, the highest structure with its inviting lights was where she would be, so that's where she would go. A Roman "hill fort" made from stone. Meala had not known what to expect when she arrived, only that she had hoped to grab something important and then make her way out, a boon that would signify her accomplishment.

Her clothing was soaked, but she wasn't in the mood to climb the main building walls in a Roman fort wearing only her undergarments, so she dealt with the wetness and shivered at the cold. The air was still warm in the late light season, but water was the enemy of warmth, aside from the bathhouse, she supposed. Maybe if she were lucky, she might find something warm and dry behind the mysterious window. But first, she would need to sneak from the edge of the fort's wall to the main building and then climb it.

⤳

"We had one of these things built for another guy just a few days ago, but the slimy son of a newt got away. Lucky for you, that means we were ready to hoist you up tonight," joked a Roman soldier with a chuckle as two of the four men dragged the sizeable wooden cross beam from beside the courtyard wall toward the courtyard's center in preparation for its latest victim. Normally, the victim would carry the patibulum (horizontal beam) to a location where stipites (vertical beams) would be set up for reuse, typically the Western fields along the road to The Wall where the locals could see the price of crossing Rome. But with the governor desiring the cross set up in the fort's courtyard, a new stipes (vertical beam) had to be put in place and a hole dug.

The yard had once been lovely, a place of meditation and respite from the otherwise dower fort. Now, all that remained of its flowers and aesthetic elements were the signs of disturbed soil at the perimeter and one small statue of a goddess, possibly Mellona or Flora, watching over the macabre scene with stark indifference as a Roman soldier finished digging a narrow, yet deep hole for the stipes while his compatriots dragged the cross beam and a ragged Dacian archer into the desecrated space.

"Your armor is worth more than you, I'd bet. Shame if any of it went missing. I got this off your horse just now, but who knows if it's still there tomorrow, eh?" another Roman laughed as he inspected Cynna's scale armor. He continued laughing as he carried the woman's gear, tossing it aside where they could pile it beneath her feet upon the cross after they were finished. Normally, the condemned would wear a titulus – a wooden plaque around their neck detailing their crime. Given the differing languages, the quickly spreading story of a Dacian murdering a Roman, and Titus' apparent need to prove himself in some way, the woman's armor and weapons would serve well enough as her titulus, and as a warning. Unfortunately for Cynna, this meant the tradition of the crucifixion detail sharing the spoils of their victim was off the table, leaving them extra grumpy and more inclined to be brutal.

Cynna tried to cry out in anguish, but her voice was still hoarse, and her neck ached from the attack. She wanted to say something, even if it was to anger the men into just killing her outright. Cynna wasn't afraid of death, a possibility she had faced every time she had donned her armor.

Rather, it was the dying part and the associated pain that she feared. Worse, perhaps aside from being burned alive or placed in the mines, few deaths were as horrible as the one a mildly bored looking Roman noble had sentenced almost casually. At least the bastard who started all of this was dead before her, though that did little to calm her as she lay on the ground, bound and gagged.

As she watched, three of the men worked to fit the rectangular hole in the center of the horizontal bar onto the top of the vertical bar and then secured the two pieces of wood using rope. But the hurried nature of the crucifixion and the need to erect a stipes right here in the small courtyard had made simply lifting the entire assembly into the hole slightly less trouble. Normally, the horizontal bar would be lifted with the victim already attached and lowered onto the vertical bar, but Cynna didn't even notice the atypical procedure as her world had become a living nightmare.

Beside her stood a single soldier, making sure that she stayed put. She wasn't going anywhere with her arms and legs bound, but the Romans tended to be pragmatic folk. Luckily, he was merely watching his fellow monsters work rather than taking any interest in her. At least her horse had been taken back to the stables where she would probably be cared for, Cynna hoped. Tamura was a wonderful horse, surefooted and brave, and the thought of some Roman taking her was upsetting, but at least Tamura would live to see another sunrise. Behind her, she heard the men laughing as they finished with the hole.

Having prepared the cross, the four soldiers detailed to her fate lifted Cynna, freeing her hands and then dragging her, struggling to escape, to the horizontal beam. It took one man sitting on her legs, and one man on each arm to hold her down while the Sarmatian struggled against the inevitable horror of what was to come. The men groaned as they restrained her, annoyed that they would have to remain on guard with her at least until the morning, lest some fool or even a lover try and rescue her. Until then, they would have to deal with her pained groans through her linen gag.

"No wonder Titus wanted her gagged," a man wearing the captured silver chain of a raider said with a laugh. An older bald man with a quickly greying beard and a tired look approached holding a hammer in one hand and dropping a leather bag to the ground from the other. The bag issued a strange metallic sound, like iron projectile points falling. The sound was jarring, quickly snapping Cynna back into the moment. It was all so fast and just too much to process.

"Yeah, no scourge for this one. She'd wake up half of the town, and then we'd have to answer to you know who," a soldier with tattooed fingers replied with a chuckle.

"Well, women don't get the scourge, you know… too delicate for the whip. It's no fun if they all die before we can even string them up," the soldier with the silver chain noted.

"Yeah, well she's no woman. She may look like one, but her kind has an evil in them. She'd have made a good sword in the ring (gladiatrix), though," the tattoo-fingered soldier laughed, leering at the woman as though considering doing just that.

"You gonna be her ludia (female fan of gladiators)?" the soldier with the silver chain quipped. The men laughed and spoke casually as they worked, preparing to nail Cynna to the cross. The mundane nature of it all was surreal, though Cynna could barely register what they said as her mind was too far down the snake hole of fear to translate their bastard language into something sensible. She tugged and pulled, knowing that it wouldn't be enough, yet unable to lie still in the face of such a fate. Her body would die high in the air, her bones never being placed underground, properly. She would wear no armor and have no weapons at her side. If she had fallen in battle, her armor and weapons would have spoken of her worth, but now she would be a naked, bloody, broken body without any mark of her worth. Would her spirit even find the afterlife?

Cynna's mind fought against the suddenness of it all trying to rationalize the irrational, her fear dancing through her veins. How could this be happening? She had awoken to a perfectly normal day. She had ridden with her turma (a unit of cavalry) along the edge of the great fjord following rumors of bandits only to find an ambush set up that cost her nearly two quivers of arrows to fend off. Still, she had ridden into danger on behalf of Rome and driven away the bandits, or whomever they actually were, and returned in good order. Her only "crime" had been saving a local woman from a terrible fate, and now suddenly she was here, lying on the ground, three men pinning her in place while a fourth…

That was when she realized what the bag held: nails. She knew how crucifixion worked, yet in fear, she simply had not wrapped her mind around the horror of what was to come. She had seen a row of nearly one hundred crucified people along a road on her long march west toward Brittania, some young, some old, every gender and sort of person – the result of a minor uprising, it had been said. The sight had been horrible, and she had kept her head down to avoid looking at the condemned. Her heart began to beat as fast as a wild horse as her mind frantically raced for a solution to a problem far beyond her control. This couldn't be how it ended… she had cast her spell and done everything right. Great Mother of Fire wouldn't let this be… couldn't let it be.

"Well, get her stripped and pin her arms and legs so I can nail them. Grab some rope so we can tie them proper. Just keep the pressure on her like she was a man. Careful with her legs, she's built like a war horse. Grab a club so we can break 'em if she doesn't settle down," the balding Roman said methodically as though asking someone to help him nail someone to a cross was as mundane as repairing a fence.

Cynna struggled desperately as the men worked to prepare her for crucifixion, though her efforts were useless against four strong men. Piece by piece, her garb was unfastened or cut from her body. Her clothing joined her armor and weapons, piled neatly beside what had probably been flower beds near where the men worked. Pilus Prior Marcus had specifically ordered her possessions put on display beneath her feet so that everyone who passed knew that this was not just some local woman or an unruly enslaved person, but an elite auxilium cavalry woman. The message was simple enough: anyone might find themselves in a painful situation if they didn't behave, and status alone might not be enough to spare them.

The bald, older man sighed as he reached into the bag, removing a few six-unciae (roughly 6 inches) iron nails. He frowned as he noted the pile of armor by the edge of the courtyard. Standard regulations would have seen her armor and weapons impounded immediately for security, then divided among the crucifixion detail. Leaving gear near a prisoner was a risk if she escaped and a foolish choice by the governor and lead centurion. He supposed that they had simply not believed it likely that a woman would break free from four men. To be fair, he shared the centurion's opinion, but he still found the breach of protocol, annoying.

Of course, after removing her possessions, he would have had her scourged like a man. But for her breasts and lack of member, her body otherwise resembled a man, in his opinion, and he was curious if she could stand the whip. Afterword, she should have been marched naked through the fort and village to the Eastern fields, then back once more to the Western field, dragging her patibulum, during the day when she could be seen for maximum effect on the populous, then hoisted up to one of the permanent stipes, as was normally done with the condemned. There she would hang for everyone to see the absurdity of a female warrior until her bones peeled from the cross. A conservative man of tradition, he wasn't pleased with the forced pace and poorly planned nature of this summary crucifixion, but orders were orders.

Regardless of the procedure, once the nails entered her flesh, she would lose any ability to use her hands or feet as her tendons were severed. After that, a little rope would be tied around her arms and maybe even around her torso holding her to the beam to ensure she didn't slide off if her flesh couldn't hold her weight. That was a problem with women, but a little experience got the job done. Of course, her nearly man-shaped body might not have that same problem. Different cohorts had different methods of crucifixion, and the variations were quite wide. Some hung the individual upside down, while others used only ropes and no nails. There were pros and cons to each method, he supposed, though at least his current method would leave four large nails to recover and sell for their medicinal value of having been used in a crucifixion. A man had to buy wine, he thought with amusement.

As the balding man approached, the Dacian woman turned toward him, catching sight of the nails, her eyes growing wild at the sight. Her panic turned into absolute horror as the men laughed at what was to come. Despite her injured throat, she screamed one painful, horrible sound that the gag barely stifled. The sounds had a distinctly feminine tone causing a slight pang of guilt within the man for the briefest of moments, but he quickly forced it aside. Duty came before compassion, and he heard tales of those slaughtered by the Easterners of her distant lands. This wasn't a woman – this was a barbarian, and she would give her life for the order and stability of Rome just as any soldier… well, perhaps not quite as a soldier, he supposed.

"Don't worry, you'll probably pass out after the first one. We'll wake you up when it's done, so you don't miss out on anything," the older man said as he knelt beside her, selecting the first nail to be placed directly through her wrist and into the wood. Off to the side, the silent marble goddess statue watched with apathy.

Closing her eyes and ignoring the taunts, jeers, and grabby men as they finished binding her to the cross, Cynna began whispering a chant to her gods, begging for a quick death. She had never found love, never been free, and had spent her life on horseback with a bow in hand and the smell of blood in the air. All she had ever wanted was to be free to live in peace and love, but that was not to be. Briefly, a thought of the painted warrior woman flashed before her eyes. She had thought herself about to die, but Cynna had spared her that fate. Sadly, it seemed that no one would spare Cynna.

CHAPTER VII

A TALE OF BARBARIAN WOMEN

A torc is a solid, ring-like metallic piece of jewelry that hangs around a neck with an opening in the front, forming a 'C' shape. The ends of the torc are called termini and are usually exaggerated or capped to prevent the metal from scratching the wearer's neck, and add flair to the torc. Made from silver, bronze, electrum, or gold, torcs were usually symbols of status in Celtic society, with their size and material often signaling one's status.

Within northern insular Celtic society, roughly corresponding to modern Scotland, large silver chains were significantly more commonplace than torcs. Each link could measure more than a centimeter in thickness, making them quite heavy. The increase in silver and other precious metals seems to have followed Rome's entry into Britain, with Roman coins being melted to supplement naturally existing supplies of gold and silver.

One way of obtaining a chain, or less commonly a torc, might involve being given and granted the right to wear one from someone of higher status, such as a minor chief bestowing a silver chain upon a warrior for their heroics or service. Or one might claim such an item in battle, which implied honor had been satisfied. In fact, the Romans were known to capture many torcs and chains as loot from Celtic warriors after battle. It may be a grim reciprocity, given the Celts often took Roman heads as trophies. As a note, the author wears a large silver torc around her neck daily and has yet to be challenged by a Roman soldier.

Meala reached the edge of the primary building with its gabled roof and mysterious window, pressing her body against the cool stone lower section and issuing a sigh of relief. The window faced the fort's rear, but it was dark, and no guards seemed nearby, at least for now. Her dark blue tunic and ash-covered body made her almost invisible in the dark of night unless someone came particularly close. Luckily, while she could hear soldiers not that far away, none of them seemed to be patrolling her area. She knew that would not last forever, so time became a critical resource.

Of course, the larger problem was that there was only one way to reach the fire-lit room above: climb. Between Meala and the window lay roughly thirty Roman feet of stone and wood, with few handholds and a sheer, perilous ascent. Unfortunately, Romans were reasonably good stone masons, so few handholds were present. There were many things that larger men could do that she would have trouble with, but there were also benefits to being light and nimble, both advantageous when it came to climbing. Moreover, her slender fingers and toes could fit in the few tiny crevices along the well-made building. However, she suffered a significant lack of upper body strength. Either way, she began to scale the wall, one hand after the next.

"Quid tunc?" The alien sound of the Roman tongue just beneath her startled Meala so badly that she nearly fell, one hand slipping free. Normally, she spoke their language enough to understand them, but with her concentration focused on not falling, she had none to spare. She was near the top, and a fall from this height would leave her either dead or severely injured and unable to flee, a fate far worse when found by the guards. Quickly finding purchase, Meala held completely still as the sounds of footfalls approached from beneath. *Don't look up...*

"De feminis indigenis dixi. Feminae barbarae dum dormis te interfecerint..." a man joked in what sounded like the end of some lengthy discussion.

Unfortunately, her sharp mind understood enough of the words that after a few seconds, she began to understand what they were saying – something about barbarian women and why they should be avoided. It wasn't pleasant to hear what came next as the men chatted, and she wished she hadn't understood the invaders. Still, it didn't sound like she had been spotted, so she waited.

Chancing a peek below, Meala saw two guards passing underneath, casually chatting with one another, entirely unaware of the woman clinging to the wall just above them like some sort of demented bat. Holding onto the stone was difficult in her current and precarious situation, but if she tried to move and slipped, they would likely hear her if she didn't just fall and land on them. On the side of the building, as high up as she was, Meala was a sitting duck for any spear, arrow, or pilum, and there would be no way for her to climb down quickly for an escape. Her shield and spear were tied to her back with hemp cord and useless as she clung to the wall.

Worse, her fingers began to throb as she waited for the men to slowly make their way past. As soon as the men–finally–passed, she resumed her climb, finding a solid handhold on the edge of the windowsill. She knew she was high up but dared not look down again lest she panic and fall. That was something she had learned as a girl climbing trees. Life seemed to be filled with dangers and horrors from every direction. If you didn't learn to accept and put them out of your mind, you might find it hard to even crawl from bed each morning.

Peering through the open window, she found a reasonably large room filled with objects she barely recognized having grown up as a simple farmer in a crannog. The room was much larger than her entire home and mostly empty in contrast to a cramped crannog. What looked like a bed stood against the right outer wall and centered – a raised rectangular wooden platform with elegantly carved legs and ample ornamentation, the top covered with beautifully embroidered fine bedding. It was so far removed from the wooden frame, and simple furs Meala slept on that she barely recognized it for what it was and would have taken it for a goddess' bed had she been told such.

All around hung tapestries adoring the walls, while beside the bed stood several wooden furniture pieces of mostly unknown utility, aside from a small table-like piece. Each was delicately carved in a cultural style that seemed neither Roman nor local, though Meala had no idea where it might be from and had never seen imported Egyptian furniture. A clay oil lamp with a wax tablet, stylus, and a few vellum pages lay on the table. Meala knew what writing was, though she couldn't write in the ways of Romans, merely knowing the runes used in magic, clan affiliations, and property markings.

Across the room, on the left outer wall, stood a large table with a much more utilitarian design, being sturdy and lacking the ornaments of the other furniture. Piled neatly on the table were many knickknacks and objects, some of them appearing to be silver and gold. Beside those sat a small wooden chest, the apparent source of the costly items – the very sort of things Meala had hoped to find and take. Unfortunately, standing in the middle of the room was a woman wearing a Roman noble's fine purple, silken robes. For a brief moment, Meala almost forgot that she was hanging outside a window over a Roman fort, being far too captivated by the gorgeous purple. The noble took a seat in a sort of chair a moment later, her back to the window.

Beside the noble stood what looked like an enslaved girl of perhaps fourteen or fifteen years of age. The girl wore a simple linen tunic with a small wooden plaque hanging from her neck proclaiming her as property. Meala couldn't read the writing on the plaque, and even if she could, doing so while hanging from a window would hardly be easy, but she knew of Roman slavery and basic customs, having lived her entire life only a few days' walk from their wall. Of course, her own people kept slaves, but the Romans had made an entire industry out of it, capturing and marching away thousands of her people to their cursed southern lands, never again to be seen. The idea of owning another human had always bothered her, regardless of what she had been taught.

The enslaved girl had pale skin and dark brown hair, a far contrast to the noble's light olive complexion and massive updo hairstyle with a bright reddish color more like blood than natural redheads Meala had seen. And though she only caught a side glance at the girl, her facial features were slightly different, both familiar and different simultaneously. She held a fine bone comb in her hand and stood beside the noble, obviously attending to the woman. It was a surreal scene, like a slice of life from another world, or perhaps even the lands of the gods. Even stories of the wealthiest chiefs she had been told had little resemblance to the room before her.

As she watched, half of her body protruding from the window, the tired-looking noblewoman removed a carved bone adornment from her hair and paused for a moment as though she were considering what to do. After a short moment, she leaned forward to put the bone hairpiece on a wooden table beside her bed. The enslaved girl reached forward with the comb and unfastened what turned out to be a wig, removing it from the noble to reveal shorter, curly brown hair neatly bound and pinned. After removing the pins, the girl attempted to comb the woman's hair, though her timing was poor, as the noble's head moved just as the girl began, catching a knot in the woman's hair. The noblewoman gasped as the comb caught her hair, probably painfully. She placed one hand on her hurt scalp and used the other to slap the girl, though her swing wasn't very strong, possibly owing to a long day or perhaps a few too many glasses of wine.

"Ouch! You stupid creature. Wait for my word before you start and hold my hair tightly so the knots won't hurt. I'm starting to think Titus had other motives for buying you. You have the skills of a goat," she spat, then took a moment to compose herself as the enslaved girl stepped back, her eyes down as she awaited her domina's next outburst. But the woman seemed tired, and the sharp pain faded with her anger as she continued, "Though I suppose it's our own fault, expecting a barbarian to be more than the trained animals you are. If he wishes you for company, so be it, but he could at least buy me a proper ornatrix (hairdresser). Either way, if you don't get your act together soon, you'll get another beating… but in the morning and by someone with a stronger arm, I should think."

Though the girl appeared less than pleased at being slapped, her lack of a real response implied that this wasn't the first time. The awful woman seemed so different from Julia or the flirty woman at the bathhouse. Her mother had even told tales of friendly encounters and relationships with Romans before leaving her home south of the Wall. It certainly was a mixture of messages. She wondered if this awful woman might be the "Vita" Julia had mentioned. She certainly seemed to fit the description.

She doubted all Romans were as cruel as the noble woman, though it seemed as though Rome had sent the cruelest ones to the Wall. Perhaps it was because they were the warriors of Rome and not whatever passed for Freemen? Either way, Meala felt sorry for the enslaved girl. So many villages had been raided, and the Romans had enslaved so many. This was yet another reason the Romans had to be driven from their lands. Unfortunately, a draft of wind reminded her that she was still hanging from a windowsill, peeping into another woman's home, one foot barely finding purchase on the edge of a wooden plank and the rest of her weight supported by her arms on the sill.

A moment later, the woman commanded the girl to sing and comb her hair as she lifted one of the vellum pages to read. The woman sat upon a chair of sorts with the enslaved girl behind her, both of their backs to the window Meala precariously hung from. The girl's voice was soft and low, yet her melody filled the room. It wasn't a song Meala recognized, though its cadence and tune reminded her of the songs druids sang during various ceremonies. The room was far from empty, but Meala's hands were now too fatigued to climb back down. Her load-bearing foot ached, and she couldn't hold on much longer. She could almost hear her father's voice fussing at her for yet another mistake. *Yes, father, I know I'm being foolish,* she self-chastised as she began to climb from the wolf's den into the lioness' den.

Slowly, Meala slid her torso halfway through the window and then precariously brought her foot through, all while trying not to make any sound. The singing, not words, just sounds, did their part to muffle the sound, but one could only be so quiet. Unfortunately, her plan went sour a moment later as her lengthy spear strapped to her back touched the edge of the window. The sound had been so slight, yet adrenaline flooded her body as she prepared for the worst. She turned to see the spear tip against the windowsill and carefully guided it into the room. Behind her, she could hear the tired Roman woman mumbling to herself about something, apparently not having noticed the armed intruder sliding into her window as the song continued. Meala took a deep breath and finished her less-than-nimble entry. Unfortunately, climbing was typically much more complicated than it initially looked. Her bare feet touched the smooth, polished wood of the floor as the scents of the room filled her nose, a mixture of exotic fragrances, oil, and soot. Her senses were alive and needed to stay that way if she wanted to remain so.

Meala looked back toward the room, hoping to spot something valuable and close that she could grab. The gold she had seen was enticing, yet too far to reach without alerting everyone. Unfortunately, as she turned, she realized that the enslaved girl was looking right at her, her song never missing a note. Meala's heart nearly stopped as their gazes met. Oddly enough, the girl, almost a young woman, continued to brush the noble's hair, as she watched. The girl regarded the intruder curiously while she skillfully worked to remove a kink in her Domina's (matron) hair. Meala slowly held her hands out, palms up, trying her best to indicate to the girl that she had no intention of harming her. Yet, she was painted with black ash with a spear and shield tied to her back, which did little to back up the friendly claims that her hands were making. Still, the girl continued combing as the noble read her velum and mumbled to herself about something that irritated her, unaware of the drama behind her.

To say the situation was precarious hardly did it justice, and the moment of truth was at hand. There was no time to flee if this went sour, and the girl was oddly still gazing at Meala curiously, if not almost hopefully. Meala closed her eyes for a moment, choosing how to best explain herself, silently. The enslaved girl turned a disgusted look at the noble and then hopeful at Meala. Meala lifted a fist and made what she hoped was the motion of knocking someone out, but the girl ever-so-slightly shook her head no. With one free hand, the girl put a finger to her neck and made a slitting motion. Was this woman the infamous Vita, a woman who beat her enslaved workers to death for minor mistakes? The despair creeping into the girl's face seemed to match that belief. Though Meala had spent plenty of time preparing herself for the act, killing another human would not be easy. Still, she couldn't think of any other way to proceed, and she would have killed a soldier if needed. Her snatch-and-run idea was already failing, and the woman would probably hear her with how this interaction was going or at least turn.

Meala slowly pointed at the noblewoman, whose back was to her, then used her finger to indicate the noble's throat being slit. Next, she pointed at the girl and then herself, waving her hand to, hopefully, indicate that they had no need to fight. Finally, she pointed toward the gold on the table, the real prize. She motioned that they might split the gold and flee through the window. Her motions were simple and her point clear enough that she suspected anyone would understand, regardless of culture or language. As she made the motions, the girl continued to softly sing and brush, her eyes never leaving Meala. When she had finished, her adrenalin rose as the girl's nearly placid face quirked ever so slightly, the only indication Meala had that she was considering her offer.

This was when the enslaved girl would either keep her mouth shut or alert her mistress. Meala stood there silently, her gaze pleading as she waited for the girl's response. For a brief moment, a girl who had no power in life suddenly held the lives of two people entirely in her hands. Time passed painfully slowly as the girl gently combed, each stroke of her brush a consideration of her fate. Thirteen strokes later, the girl slowly nodded her head in what appeared to be agreement. Holding back a sigh of relief, Meala slid free her bronze dagger and approached the noblewoman from behind and slightly to the woman's left.

As Meala approached, she could smell the woman's perfume, lavender, and hear her as she mumbled something to herself. Meala glanced at the girl, reading her face. Up close, she noted the girl's rich, brown eyes and slight freckles, but also the worn look in her eyes. She could see the girl was terrified, yet somehow holding her emotions tightly under a placid mask, likely a learned behavior while enslaved to Romans. She was so like many of the girls Meala used to play with when she was younger, yet this one wouldn't grow up to find love, marry, or have a life of her own. Meala's own quest for freedom filled her with sorrow as she gazed upon the frightened girl, and that horrible inequality began to provide the fuel for what she must do next… what she had come to do.

Taking a life was much harder than she imagined, but she had nearly done it during the battle. Unfortunately, her nerves were starting to fray as she kept readjusting the knife in her hand, her palms sweating. This wasn't like killing a warrior who was also trying to return the favor. This was an unarmed woman who didn't even know what was about to happen. She could smell the woman's scent, her perfume, and see the little pale hairs on her skin. Was this woman a mother? Did she have a family? Try as she might, Meala was starting to find the final act very difficult to perform, her humanity stepping in the way of what must be… must it?

The enslaved girl watched as the strange painted warrior prepared to act then hesitated. It was clear to see in her green eyes that the painted woman was almost as frightened as her and beginning to freeze up. Unfortunately, the warrior was now far too close for Domina to believe that she had not aided, or at least ignored, the warrior's approach. If the warrior fled, she might be beaten or even killed. She had held her tongue with the hope of a final, quick end. Domina would die, and the warrior would slit her throat next, a swift finale to her nightmare at the hands of a thief or whatever the mystery warrior woman was. She hadn't the courage to end it herself, but a little help would set her free. But none of this would happen if Domina Vita didn't die.

Summoning every drop of strength and courage in her body, the enslaved girl boldly reached forward, dropping the comb. She slapped her right hand over Domina Vita's mouth and wrapped her left arm around the woman's head, pulling it back as she lifted her knee and pressed her body weight against Vita, keeping her briefly seated. She felt as though she were about to have a panic attack, and she hated touching or being touched, yet she kept going, ignoring all her sensory distress as she committed herself to death. Vita pulled her head forward as she grasped at the girl's arms, but she jerked the noble's neck backward, making a primal, frightened gasp as she did. The noblewoman started screeching, but the sound was muffled as the strong hands of a girl used to hard work, day in and day out overpowered the softer, weaker hands of a noble who had to order an enslaved man to beat her because she couldn't do it.

"Do it..." she whispered as loudly as she could with a heavy accent, her words a plea. The noble switched from trying to remove the arms to trying to stand, likely realizing that others had to be in the room. Meala realized it was now or never and grasped the noble's hair. Her body tried to freeze, but the girl's pleading look kept her going. She placed the bronze dagger against the woman's throat and dug in as deeply as she could, just as she slaughtered sheep on the farm. It took two slices until the blood shot across the room, spraying part of the wall in one massive jet before dropping into smaller, pulsing spurts. As she stood back, the girl wept while she held the woman's head letting every drop of blood leave her wretched form. After a moment, the girl let the woman's body slide to the floor... Domina Vita was now Domina Mortis.

And then it was done.

"Domine..." the girl whispered. Meala could not believe how much blood had covered the wall. She should have been ready for it as she had watched her father kill so many animals on their farm and had even slaughtered a few animals herself, but it was still quite a scene, a scene that she had made. She felt a little queasy, though helping her father butcher animals as a child made things a little easier. Still, a strange sense of guilt filled her over the enormity of her actions. She turned to see the girl, realizing that she was hardly the most frightened of the pair. The girl openly wept as she collapsed to the floor and began rocking back and forth, her sorrow bursting from her masked emotions as violently as lightning. The girl said nothing for a moment, her emotions far too volatile as she quietly cried and rocked.

Unsure what to do and starting to feel the growing shock of her emotions rising, Meala dropped the dagger and sank to her knees, wrapping her arms around the girl. She wasn't sure why she did it, but simple human compassion overtook her. For a short time, she held the girl as they both cried for different reasons rooted in the same spray of blood. Beside them, a Roman noblewoman lay steadily cooling as her lifeblood trickled like spilled wine. After a short time, the girl spoke, her voice a whisper and oddly steady despite her clearly emotionally compromised situation.

"You… you must take my life. End this," she whispered, a plea in her voice.

"What?" Meala responded, unsure that she had heard the girl or perhaps she could not accept what she had said. A moment later, the girl repeated her request, her quiet voice carrying the powerful emotion of the moment, her words a mixture of Roman accent and something else Meala couldn't place. That the noblewoman had abused the girl enough for her to risk her own life in the act of murder was unsettling. But now she asked for death? It made no sense to Meala and wasn't something she was willing to do. Killing a powerful and abusive Roman woman was one thing, but killing a victimized and enslaved girl was not something that she could live with.

"No," she said flatly. The girl looked at her, stunned, her expression a mixture of fear and betrayal.

"You must… you owe me this. I held my tongue. You owe me… I…"

"Why? Why do you want to die? Why not escape just as I came in?" Meala asked, her mind swimming in confusion in the moment, and reality taking on a surreal feel as a pool of noble Roman blood slowly expanded before her. The girl looked weak, her strength finally giving out from mental exhaustion while the enormity of her situation sank in.

"When they find her dead, they will blame me. The price for killing a master is crucifixion for all slaves of a house. All… Dominus cannot afford that… but he will torture and kill me. I cannot escape as I don't know how to do such things. I am not from this place. I cannot take… I cannot end it. I've tried. Please! Please make it stop!" she begged as her words became a tearful whisper, "please, end it." Meala began to realize why the girl made such a request when she considered what "escape" entailed. She probably thought that she would need to scale a building, then sneak past dozens of soldiers, and flee into an unknown in the night. In her current state, Meala wasn't sure the girl could climb down the rope.

"No… No, you will not die here. I have a rope, and we can climb down and escape together. You can escape with me, not alone! I can get us out of here and help you get far from the Fort. You don't have to die," she whispered as the girl began to sob anew. For a short time longer, the girl rocked back and forth as she seemed to be working to stifle her tears. Meala's heart pounded as time passed and the risk of someone coming rose, yet she couldn't bring herself to rush the poor girl. After a short time, the girl stopped rocking and began to wipe her tears on her tunic, quickly restoring herself to as neutral an expression as she could afford, a trauma behavior that continued to trouble Meala. She made no eye contact, but began to speak, her voice soft and quiet.

"I will try if you promise you won't let them catch me. If we fail, you must promise me that you will take my life," the girl spoke, her last few words coming out with more tears. Meala frowned, wishing the girl wouldn't make such statements, yet she understood her fears, at least in concept. Reluctantly, and not entirely sure of her own truth, she nodded her agreement. Technically, she had given no formal and honor-bound oath, yet she knew her ancestors would see her nod as such. If that time came, Meala had no idea what she would do, but anything was better than leaving the girl to her fate – a fate Meala had forced upon her.

"Well, let's grab what we can and leave," Meala said, unsure what else to say in the awkward moment. Seeming more in control, at least in appearance, the girl nodded her agreement, and they began searching. The pair stood and began examining the room, gathering what could be easily carried of value. The girl moved slowly, her hands shaking and her wits not fully with her. She stumbled to the bed table and took a gold ring, vellum documents, tablet, and stylus. She put these items on the bed, tightened her waist cord, and then stuffed each item into her tunic. Behind her, Meala rushed toward the large table upon which lay a wooden box with dozens of gold and silver items, mostly looking like items from her people, probably looted treasure.

Somebody had been separating the loot into two piles and writing notes about them on a wax tablet. Meala had no idea what the notes said as she couldn't read, but she knew gold when she saw it. She quickly gathered all the precious metal items, piling them in the small box. Next, she ripped off a piece of the noble woman's palla (an outer cloth garment worn over a tunic and stola) and pressed it into the box tightly so that it would stop the gold and coins from rattling when they sneaked out. She secured the heavy box to her back over her shoulder using her last short piece of hemp rope. Every moment they stayed, their chance of capture rose. Meala was about to head to the window when her eyes caught sight of something fantastic.

Sitting on another table on the other side of the room near the window and partly obscured by a vase was a beautiful gold torc, the kind one would find around the neck of a chief. Unlike the more common silver chains her people wore, the thick torc had been meticulously forged to wear around the neck of a mighty warrior. More than even the small chest of loot, this was what she had come to find, a true symbol of power she could show to her people. This sort of boon could elevate her to warrior status and grant her enough say over her destiny to avoid her common fate. This was a physical manifestation of her freedom.

Hurrying over, she lifted the precious torc, marveling at its weight. Even in the dim lamp light, the torc twinkled in the way that only gold could. Meala placed the heavy torc around her neck, feeling its weight against her collarbone. Looking down, she could see the ends, called terminals, hanging just above her collarbone, with the edge of her magical bee tattoo just below, peeking out from beneath her tunic. A great feeling of pride overwhelmed her as she became lost in the moment until she heard the alarmed sounds of the girl calling for her. When she looked up from the torc, her eyes fell upon the blood-splattered wall, and a wave of nausea passed over her. She nearly vomited but held it back, looking away and breathing deeply.

Death was no stranger to her people. She had watched relatives die and even taken part in a battle, but it was still a difficult sight to behold. Looking away, she caught sight of the enslaved girl waving her hands. Following the girl's outstretched hand, she realized the problem: The woman's blood had pooled on the floor beside her body and was probably seeping through the wooden floorboards into whatever room was below. As soon as someone saw that…

"Yeah, let's get out of here," she said, panic setting in. A few frantic moments later, Meala had uncoiled her longer rope and secured it to the bed, hoping the heavy wooden object would hold their weight as they climbed down. She would have plenty of time to think about her success and reflect on her actions if she escaped, and every moment that she stayed in the room increased the likelihood that she wouldn't. Double checking that the small, but almost too heavy, wooden box was securely hung over her back, she approached the windows and looked to see if it was clear. Neither hearing nor seeing guards, she tossed the rope out the window, then awkwardly, with a spear, shield, and box strung to her back, began to climb out.

Surprisingly, the girl climbed out of the window just after her, even though she appeared terrified of the height. Meala had expected to need to help her, given her earlier fears. She wondered if the girl feared more the act of escaping and the enormity of it all than the actual physical actions. Perhaps she had suffered so much that her will to take such chances had been broken? Whatever the reason, the girl slowly climbed down the long rope, one hand at a time, as the pair left the building. After a few precarious moments and unexpected rotations, neither knew how to properly repel down a wall, the pair safely made it. Unfortunately, the rope would have to remain hanging from the window, meaning the next patrol to pass would likely notice it – if they didn't find the blood or the murdered woman first. This made a quick escape even more paramount.

A few moments later the pair were sneaking along the outskirts of the formal stone buildings built around the fort. She wasn't quite sure how they would escape the curtain wall or the actual wall to the West, especially with the rope now gone. They would need to replace the rope if they wished to pull their belongings through the water or find another way out, but, with an entire fort of sleeping people, there had to be some rope they could grab as they escaped. At least she and the girl…

"Hey, what is your name?" Meala asked the girl, realizing that she had no idea who the enslaved girl was, a formality she had forgotten during the intense actions of the evening. The girl looked spooked but replied to the question, sounding far calmer than she probably should, yet still not making eye contact. Again, Meala wondered what had made her so innately obedient and feared that she knew. Of course, autism, CPTSD, and PTSD would not be understood for nearly two millennia, but that wouldn't stop Meala from showing the clearly traumatized girl a little humanity and respect.

"They called me Alesia. I don't know what it means, but they always laughed when they told people my name," she said, her voice nearly a whisper. Meala frowned. She wanted the girl's real name, not the label the Romans had forced upon her.

"What was the name you were first given? Your real name," she asked, giving the girl a confident nod of respect. For a moment, the girl frowned, barely visible in the darkness behind the elongated buildings.

"Damona," she whispered, the name spoken with a strong, foreign accent. Meala forced a smile in kind, finding the name pleasing yet still quite flustered from the night's events. If she spent too long considering what had already happened, she worried that her flashbacks or simply a flood of tears might overcome her, so she concentrated on the name as a distraction.

"Damona? What a pretty name. Why did they change it?"

"They said it sounded too much like Domina," Damona replied, shyly.

"Hail and welcome Damona. I am Sei'ln Meala of the Flooding Lake, daughter of Ail Braide, of East Wenechon, of the Wood Owl clan," she said with a firm nod, her pleasant tone not quite matching the precarity of their night. Still, Meala had been raised better than not to introduce herself. For a moment, Meala waited, hoping Damona would say something, but the girl remained mostly frightened. She certainly couldn't blame her for that. A moment later, the pair continued tracing the outer perimeter of the fort wall, hoping to sneak past the stables and by what looked like a large courtyard, straight down the path Meala had taken, and right back to the stone fountain, where they could escape, at least from the fort proper. With luck, they would find rope along the way.

Meala caught sight of a dozen guards standing beside the edge of the wall up ahead. They appeared younger, less organized, and less experienced than the other guards. At the lead was a much older soldier barking orders, his face baring permanent frown lines. She wondered if they were new recruits, like the youths she had seen in training for a warband. She couldn't get a good look at them in the darkness and sparse torchlights. Either way, their avenue of escape had just become cut off.

"Ad due... Exi. Movete!" the older man barked, though she could barely hear him. A moment later, the group of spear-carrying soldiers began marching toward the main gate, leaving the intruders briefly alone.

"We are not going that way. Let's sneak around the backside of the fort and try the other side. I saw fewer places to hide, but maybe it won't have as many guards," Meala suggested, hoping to take a longer but safer way around before the Moon grew high enough to properly illuminate the interior of the fort. Damona nodded but said nothing more. She wasn't sure if the girl simply wasn't talkative or too afraid to speak. Either way, this was hardly the time or the place for conversation.

Sneaking around the stables, they found an open courtyard on the other side surrounded by smaller buildings. They would need to travel past or through the courtyard, down the path, and right through a group of the elongated buildings to reach the other side of the fort, definitely a good place to find rope, but also random encounters. As it was, Meala was amazed they had not yet been spotted or noticed the dead Roman woman. When they got to the other side, they could make a run for the wall, slip over in the dark, head south, then west, and backtrack later.

Oddly, Meala's playful imagination kept trying to imagine herself as a scurry mouse rushing to and fro through the Roman settlement, trying to avoid dogs, foxes, or wild cats. Given the horror of the night, she was surprised that her more playful side had surfaced, but perhaps it was her mind trying to detach. With a steadying breath, she rehoned her focus to the task at hand: living.

Keeping low against the courtyard wall, they made their way toward freedom. Suddenly, they heard a strange and slightly hoarse screech coming from the courtyard. Meala and Damona paused for a moment, exchanging confused glances. Meala's first instinct was simple – someone needs help, but a more frightened part of her mind reminded her that it was not her concern and that she should simply ignore the scream and continue with her escape. Unfortunately, curiosity, the drive to help those in need, and acting without fully thinking things through were somewhat hallmarks of the young woman's chaotic life. After an eye roll at her actions, she chose to at least take a look.

"Hey, can you wait here while I check to see what that sound was?" she asked. Damona's confused and suddenly anxious face revealed her displeasure at her rescuer's curiosity, but she was hardly in a place to do anything about it. She would need to get quite far from Roman-occupied land before she would be safe, and the strangely bold auburn-haired woman who now sported a mighty warrior's gold torc seemed to be her only chance. Ignoring her frightened companion, Meala placed one foot on a stone protruding from the low wall and lifted herself enough to see what was happening in the courtyard.

The sight that befell her was almost surreal and quite shocking, though she wasn't sure what she had expected. Before her lay a wooden cross like the Romans were said to use for execution. Partially strapped to the cross with rope was a struggling nude woman. Three Roman soldiers were trying to pin her down while a fourth held what looked like a hammer. It seemed the woman had gotten a hand free and had wrapped it around the neck of one of the men and was attempting to strangle him with a headlock. Another man punched her several times in the head until she let the man free. In response, she spat blood in their faces.

In the torchlight, Meala could see the woman's body clearly, though her face was blocked from view by the fourth man with the hammer. Strangely, the woman's chest had a recently healed and a rather deep-looking wound just below her left breast, as well as several other scars. The man with the hammer placed a nail just below her left wrist and lifted it to strike. Right as he began, the woman bucked her body with far more strength than Meala would have expected. For a brief moment, she caught sight of the woman's face… she had seen that face before.

The Amazon… it was her. Her heart sank as she remembered what she had seen by the pond. She had wondered when she had seen the distant woman but had not been sure until now. The archer had saved a local woman and killed a rather nasty Roman. She had saved her friend, Julia, and fought her attacker in honorable combat, and the idea that she would be blamed was foreign to Meala, yet that was what had happened. She had seen the men take the archer away, but she had not realized that this was what was to become of her – the woman who had haunted her dreams and spared her life was moments from being crucified.

Crucifixion wasn't just a death sentence; it was one of the most excruciating and long-lasting death sentences, meant to humiliate the victim in every way and cause horrendous pain and suffering. It was one of the many practices that instilled fear in her people, something the Romans used to discourage raids – something she had worried might happen when she had been wounded and struggling to escape the raid. What if a Roman had found her instead of the mysterious archer? Her heart welled up in her chest at the sight, her compassion lighting her aflame.

This very woman had chosen to spare her such a fate that night. As she watched, she realized that whatever struggles the woman was putting up were almost ending. There were four men, and they were moments from nailing her wrists to the wood. Not only had this woman spared her life when she had no valid reason, but Meala had been unable to forget that face… that strong, confident face. How could she let the Dacian die in such a horrifying way? And in such a disgraceful manner? It burned at her very core and filled her with rage. She had spared Meala – the sort of debt a warrior paid. She felt the weight of the gold torc around her collarbone and knew what needed to be done. Gold was not her true prize: honor had to be satisfied.

There were four men, and she was one woman. Even taken by surprise, this was an impossible set of odds. She had seen how fast Roman soldiers reacted, being quite well-trained. In fact, more than anything, it was their discipline and order that gave them strength. Meala needed something to counter that discipline, and one unorthodox idea came to mind. Dropping to a crouch, she began unfastening her belt as Damona looked on, her confusion growing when she realized what Meala was up to.

"There's someone in there I owe my life, and the dogs are going to nail her up. I can't let that happen… Here, you can put this on, and no one will recognize you," Meala said as she began removing her bulky tunic. She had seen enough, and she could do only one thing now. Damona stared back, shocked. She had heard enough tales of naked, fanatical Caledonii to guess what the warrior was up to, something her own Gaulish people did, as best as she could remember. The problem was that this "Meala" was her only way out of this mess, and if she ran away, was captured, or died, Damona would be alone and quickly found.

"You… you can't fight four of them... I can't wait for you!" she whispered fearfully. Meala had been her only way out, and now the fool woman was about to go get herself killed and leave Damona to fend for herself. Panic filled the girl, and her tears returned once more. She wasn't able to take her own life–she had tried–and when she was found, her Domina murdered… the wife of the governor of Brittania, dead... Ignoring Damona's growing nightmare, Meala handed her the overly large woad-dyed tunic she had borrowed from her mother and the small, yet quite heavy, box full of gold and silver. Her own tunic had yet to be repaired, a low priority in the warmer seasons when she rarely wore more than a wrap skirt.

"I would ask you to stay and wait for me, but if you become frightened or I fall, flee and take the gold with you. This is something I must do and the only way I will put my mind at rest. If you cannot escape with a rope, take what gold you can wear. There's a stone pond over that way," Meala said, gesturing just beyond the courtyard, "Head over there, climb into the water, and swim through the hole. There are bars, but they are loose. Just head south and disappear. I am sorry for this, but I cannot live without facing this trial," Meala explained, her voice trembling as fear gripped her just as it had nearly six moons before at this same fort.

With the mindless focus on her orders and nearly pathological repression of her sheer terror, Damona took the still-damp tunic and began to slide it over her very conspicuous linen slave tunic. Her wooden name tag had already been forgotten in a ditch near where they had first set foot on the ground. With the gold treasure, the local-style tunic, and simply keeping her head down, she had a reasonable chance of making it south and perhaps finding a boat that might take her North across the water, bypassing the walls, or anywhere else she wished.

Originally from Gaul (roughly modern France and surrounding region), Damona had been enslaved since childhood when her family was sold by a local chief into Roman hands. It had been a decade of suffering and fear, and the northern warrior was the first to truly show her kindness. She wanted nothing more than to flee the danger, but if she left before at least giving the painted warrior a chance, she would regret it. Besides, her legs were shaking from fear, and she felt like she might vomit. She could barely mask this level of terror and felt her tears rolling unbidden down her face. Wiping back tears as she had learned to do lest Domina had become angry, she decided to stay at least to see if the painted woman could win. It seemed impossible, but only an hour before, she had been slapped by her wretched domina, and now she was kneeling on the precipice of freedom. She just wanted it all to end, good or bad.

A moment later, Meala stood wearing her new gold torc and her linen strips of cloth that wound around her breasts and waist, providing support and modesty, but without her bulky, oversized tunic. Ritual combat did not require women to fully strip, though some did, though she had no intention of removing her undergarments. Of course, the men tended to go entirely nude, but that was also partly down to bravado, and she only had but so much bravery. All that was required was her tattoo being visible to her enemies and the ancestors. Her magical bee tattoo lay open to the night air, and her face, arms, and legs were painted black with ash and tattooed for all gods, spirits, and ancestors to see. The stories of chieftainess' and legendary warriors came to mind, like the Shadowed Maiden, a warrior from the northwest renowned for her martial skills, Boadicea, the Vengeful, or the intoxicating wolf-chieftainess Medu'ma.

Even as she felt fear gripping her spirit, new feelings began to rise — pride, empowerment, and the fervor of someone who knew the very gods and ancestors were watching. A single woman about to fight four armed Romans in their own fort… the gods themselves might very well spare a glance. She could almost feel her bee tattoo tingling at the prospect. She held her mother's small shield in her left hand and spear in her right. She stuffed her bronze dagger into its sheath and into her undergarment as she prepared for battle. Her skin beneath the tunic was pale, but she hadn't the time to fix that as the Dacian warrior's time ran short just beyond the stone wall of the courtyard. At least her bee tattoo would be fully exposed; a covered tattoo would not have the magical protection of an uncovered tattoo. Her battle would be as much a dedication to her ancestors and family as it was the most foolish act she had ever taken, a high bar.

With arms nearly trembling from fear and adrenalin, Meala stood ready to fight. She had imagined herself as a warrior fighting the Romans for glory or to rescue a lover, but never like this. She was terrified, but her mother had not raised a coward. Moreover, the man with the nails and hammer had just pressed his knee against the woman's hand and was preparing to drive the nail deep within. Meala glanced once more at Damona and gave her a forced wink. She hoped the girl would not just flee, taking the loot with her. Of course, if she were killed or captured, she hoped Damona would do just that. She paused at the last part, considering her fate if captured… no, she needed to stay focused lest her nerve break. Romans ruled by fear, and she could only be free of their oppression through courage and bravery.

"Ancestors, see me. Mother, see me. Father, see me…"

Chapter VIII

Puella Picta – A Painted Girl

The martial pursuits of women in antiquity were not merely confined to warfare, as was the case with female gladiators, sometimes called gladiatrices (sg. gladiatrix). Curiously, only one example of this word being used in ancient Rome is known. In fact, no formal or consistent term for female gladiators has been found. However, "ludia" is sometimes incorrectly used, but likely referred to a female enthusiast of gladiators. Regardless of what we call them, we know that Romans had female gladiators and considered them quite a spectacle.

Laws were passed to prevent women of higher birth from participating, and we have two pieces of art depicting female gladiators. The first is a relief showing two female gladiators named Amazon and Achilia, who may have ended their famous fight in a draw. We also have a bronze statuette of a woman holding a weapon and wearing a subligaculum, similar to how Meala now prepares to face the Romans. Unfortunately, the lives of women in much of the past have been far less documented than men, leaving scientists to piece together what few clues exists to gain an understanding of the past. Yet, women have played more than meek or domestic roles, from leaders and warriors, to gladiators and mercenaries. This text focuses more on the martial lives of ancient women, but the reader is encouraged to learn about all aspects of ancient women's lives.

Sadly, little is known of the struggles, bravery, sacrifice, and horror these women endured; women's history being largely forgotten. If the reader would like to learn more about the tragic and fascinating history of such women, they might consider reading the works of Dr. Anna McCullough and Adrienne Mayor.

"She squeezes pretty hard for a woman," the soldier with a scar beneath his eye laughed as he rubbed his throat. He had tried to hold the woman down, but she had torn her arm free and wrapped him in a vice-like headlock. Now, her right arm was tied tighter than a tourniquet, and her legs had just been bound, one on each side of the vertical beam, each awaiting a nail. Two of his compatriots laughed as they finished tying the overly strong woman down while the centurion, their de facto carpenter, prepared to nail her once and for all. Once the nails were driven between the bones just beneath the wrists, the woman's hands would become reasonably inoperable, and she would finally stop fighting. This had taken far too long already, and the centurion had taken it upon himself to finish the task personally. In the centurion's opinion, this entire affair was being poorly handled, but orders were orders.

Cynna breathed hard as tears blurred her vision, and terror flowed through her as though mixed with her very life force. She had fought the men with everything she had and interrupted three attempts to nail her, but she knew there was nothing she could do. She grunted as the bald man's knee pressed her left arm against the wood, and the point of the nail pressed against her wrist. From her tear-blurred eyes, she could see his hand lifting the hammer. She whispered a prayer to her gods that she might withstand the pain and not cry out. She didn't deserve the punishment she had been given. But she was also an Iazyges woman, a daughter of the sky and the steppe, and she would do everything in her power to rob these Romans of any satisfaction.

She clenched her eyes as the hammer rose and flinched as she heard the impact of metal against wood… but the pain never came. Instead, a strange wood against metal clanging sound began – a peculiar segway to what she had expected to be pain. All around, the Roman men appeared somewhat startled. Cynna turned her head, blinking her tears away, yet the sight that befell her was so unexpected that she wondered if it was some sort of delusion. The many torches illuminated a woman with long, dark auburn hair, green eyes like the steppe in spring, and wearing a heavy gold torc around her neck like some sort of high chief or hero. She stood not far from the men holding a shield and spear, her body tattooed, painted black, and otherwise dusted heavily with ash. But for her subligar (waist cloth) and strophium (breast bindings), she was otherwise bare, like a proper barbarian.

Almost immediately, Cynna recognized the woman. It couldn't be, and yet it also was… She had seen this woman once before, lying on the ground and clutching a wound Cynna had given her. In fact, the scars from that wound were plainly visible on her bare skin. This was the woman who had occupied her wayward thoughts for six moons, the warrior who had nearly taken her life. The brave warrior she had chosen to spare. And now she stood there like a hoplomachus gladiator facing down four well-trained Roman soldiers without even the sense to wear proper armor, much like the rest of her foolish, backward… honorable and brave people. As she watched, the woman slapped the spear against her shield repeatedly as she slowly approached the men.

Cynna blinked her eyes and shook her head, sure that she must be delirious or delusional. Had the nail already driven, and the pain forced her into delusion? She decided that if this was a delusion, it was better than a real crucifixion, and if it was real, she had to do everything she could to get free while the men were distracted. Just then, the man with the hammer lost his balance as he stood, turning to face the intruder, her bruised and painful hand suddenly coming free. She reached with her numb hand for one of the nails beside the bag, but she couldn't quite reach it. She began bending her legs, twisting against the ropes to free them. Years of holding her legs tightly against a horse had given her strong leg muscles, and she used them now to her advantage as she attempted to twist her feet free. Everything in her world vanished as darkness surrounded her vision but for the single Roman nail.

Meala slammed her spear against her shield repeatedly and rhythmically, capturing the men's attention. It would have been better to have stabbed one of them before the others realized, but the man with the hammer had been about to drive the nail when she had gotten there, and she had no time to capitalize on surprise. No part of this plan was sane nor practical, yet here she was doing it. She hoped to at least impress her ancestors, but without much hope of surviving. At this point, her ancestors were probably convinced that she was out of her mind, she thought wryly, something she could likely ask them about, shortly.

"Puella picta…" *(painted girl)* one man breathed.

"Puellam parvam gladiatricem pictus est non enim te missionem est," *(painted little girl fighter [gladiator], there is no reprieve for you)* another added with a chuckle, mocking Meala with the Roman term missio, a reprieve given to gladiators who were defeated but spared death.

"Ludiam tuam servare veniebas? Unam enim te facere possumus," *(You have come to save your ludia [person who likes gladiators]? We can make one for you)* another man sneered, nodding at the cross on the ground as he reached for a weapon. Meala snarled in response, but as the four Roman men stood, pulling their short swords free, Meala began to feel small by comparison. It wasn't just that each Roman man stood slightly taller with much larger muscles and weight; it was that they looked seasoned and tough, their bodies scarred from a life of combat. In truth, they were frightening, but so was she... she hoped.

Skipping the customary scream of her people and not wishing to awaken the entire fort, she dashed forward, leaping into the air and bringing her spear down in a bold thrusting move the first Roman had obviously not expected. He slashed wildly with his sword, but it bounced harmlessly off her shield, a gladius not particularly good at slashing. The spear struck the man in his neck muscle, and he stumbled backward, holding the superficial, yet likely painful wound.

Behind her, another man raced forward, thrusting his sword as hard as he could with his gladius' blade horizontal in the proper manner to puncture her organs through her ribs. Meala drew her shield against her side and rotated her body, causing the blade to skip harmlessly off the shield as she wasn't sure she could have stopped the blade directly. As she rotated, she retracted her spear from the stabbed man and swung it widely to ward off attacks toward her unguarded side. Before she could capitalize on the man's deflected sword, another stepped into the opening, their skills and training fighting as a team already starting to synchronize into a deadly dance.

Luckily, as the man lunged to take advantage of the opening, he tripped on one of the crucifixion ropes, stumbling to the ground, but not before his blade cut a slice in Meala's right arm. Behind her, she could hear the man she had stabbed in the neck coming. Ignoring her wound and not having time to use her spear on either the tripped or deflected men, Meala swung the spear butt backward at the man who was charging and slammed her shield as hard as she could into the neck of the man who had just tripped and fallen to the ground. She didn't have the upper body strength to break his neck with her shield strike, but any solid impact on a fragile neck was significant, causing him to curl into the fetal position, grasping his neck in pain. The spear missed the man coming up behind her, but it caused him to step back just in time to allow her to finish using her shield.

Meala skipped back a few paces, slamming her spear pole against the shield and smiling in a crazed, hungry way, hoping the absolute terror flowing through her body wasn't visible on her face. She dared not consider her wounded arm lest she panic more than she already was. It felt like a shallow laceration, but she could already feel the blood running down her arm. Before her lay one Roman man, not dead but obviously in grievous pain, another holding a bloody shoulder but ready to fight, while the obviously more experienced man with the scar beneath his eye and the bald man had stepped aside to grab shields that two of them had brought and compose themselves, professional fighters through and through.

So far, she had been exceptionally lucky, but she had failed to seize the initiative, and the men were no longer off-guard. As if to underscore that thought, the three men began encircling her with their swords ready and the two shielded men in a defensive pose. Oddly, not a single one of them had sounded an alarm. The sounds of struggle the woman had made when Meala first found her probably meant that those within the range of her voice would likely ignore the sounds of the fight, assuming them to be the crucified woman, but a Roman soldier screaming for help would be her immediate downfall. She wondered why they had not called for help, but she had a dreadful suspicion it was because they didn't think they needed it. Their smiles spoke of men who wanted the glory of the fight for themselves and were sure they would get it.

Cynna freed her leg from the partially tied ropes with a painful tug. She bent her leg backward, contorting herself until her left leg was nearly to her outstretched left arm, her body pushing to the right as she extended herself. She was flexible for sure, but there were already several tendons she was pretty sure would hurt tomorrow if she lived. With her toes, she touched the bag of nails and started trying to grasp one of the metal spikes. The pain was intense, but nothing else mattered at that point. All around, she heard men taunting and laughing at the painted woman, her one and only distraction and hope of escape. With one final exertion, she had managed to slip one of the nails lying on the ground between her toes. She grunted as she tried her best to bend her foot to her hand, but the human body could only bend so much. Suddenly, the tip of her finger touched the iron edge of the nail, and she grasped it, releasing her foot. Her back, neck, and legs ached from the contortion, but she now had a sharp piece of metal in her hand.

Ignoring the pain, she bent her left wrist and began scraping at the hemp rope binding her to the wooden beam. As she did, she watched as the valiant painted woman lunged with her spear several more times at the now-laughing Romans. They were taunting her, she could see. They probably hoped to tire her out and kill her, or worse, do the same to her as Cynna. Glancing up, she saw the woman's face in the torchlight. Her ash-streaked face bore a wolfish grin to frighten her enemies, but her eyes held the look of fear – of a wolf who knew she was cornered and ready to go out with blood. She was outnumbered and outmatched, yet she stood there with her spear, unwilling to back down. That same look had captivated the Sarmatian so many months before. It was that very look that she couldn't seem to forget. Cynna sawed at the ropes with renewed vigor.

With the ropes now fraying, she forced the nail between the plied rope strands and began twisting until one of the plies broke. Years of drawing a bow had left Cynna with significant finger strength, an oddity of her physiology that she now used to her advantage. She slid the nail between the final two plies and twisted a little more until suddenly her hand was free, the feel of the blood rushing back to her cold hand a welcome respite.

Her heart pounded with terror as she worked to free her second hand. The painted warrior cried out and the men grunted, but she fought to ignore these sounds as she broke one ply after another, and then both hands were free. Not even sparing a glance for the painted warrior, she quickly began working on freeing her right leg, then her left, which was much easier with both hands. At that moment, the bald man glanced her way and realized Cynna was freeing herself. His gaze snapped back to the painted woman as he turned to his side and then stepped backward to handle the Sarmatian, unwilling to show her his unguarded back but also unwilling to turn from the painted warrior. She was but a woman and would likely not recover quickly from her wounds, but he would still be cautious.

"Libera es…" he began to cry when his entire world exploded in a bright flash of light and sparkles that quickly faded into darkness. The hammer slammed into the side of the lead centurion's head, cracking his skull just beside his left eye. He fell to the ground, holding his head and gurgling as veins burst open and his brain began to swell. Cynna dropped to her knees, the hammer she had just used falling beside her. She needed more time to recover, and forcing her body into a sudden, adrenaline-fueled lunge had not helped. But she had no choice as the centurion had spotted her. He would have killed her momentarily, being the most capable and skilled of the men, but the centurion had misjudged her endurance or how free she had become, a fatal mistake. Rolling onto her side, she grasped the fallen gladius.

With great effort, she began to stand, though she almost stumbled several times due to the pain from injuries she had experienced being strapped to the wood. As she did, the painted woman took note. The ash-painted warrior lifted her shield and spear into the air and began shaking them around in some strange display that gave the men pause. It also kept their attention as the stiff, slow-moving Sarmatian slowly rose behind the next man. She could tell the Romans had about run out of patience. Still, try as they might, none of them had been able to score a second hit against the nimble barbarian.

One of them had a superficial wound to his trapezius shoulder muscle that would heal quickly, and another would have a sore neck for a few days and lay nearby recovering, but if they tired out the painted woman and captured or killed her, they would be rewarded, a greater prize. What they didn't know was that another of their group was silently dying on the ground behind them, and the sacrificial woman had just risen. One man attacked the painted warrior and missed, but the man with the captured silver chain saw the opening and drew back his blade to thrust forward. Cynna leapt for him and wrapped her left arm around his head as she plunged the gladius straight into his neck and downward, into his chest, the so-called "vital spot," with one strong, rage-induced motion, breaking the silver chain from his neck as its flexible clasp snapped.

"Placarentne tibi gladiatores? Inde ferram cape, porce!" (You like gladiators? Then take the iron, pig [a term used when vanquishing a gladiator]) she spat as the tattoo fingered man dropped to his knees, his body failing as his heart stopped. Filled with as much righteous schadenfreude as pain, Cynna kicked him forward with her numb foot just as the other man turned to see what had befallen his friend, the stabbed man making much more noise than the centurion had.

Meala watched the Dacian woman dispatch the bald man with a single blow to the head, then collapse. While she stumbled to rise again, Meala began waving her arms, lifting her spear and shield overhead to draw attention from the vulnerable woman. The Dacian had just reduced the fight to three-on-one, and hopefully, two-on-three, if she wasn't badly hurt. The men watched her, hunger in their eyes for blood or possibly a woman, and maybe even both. The fallen man she had hit in the neck would likely recover, and the two menacing Meala didn't know that their leader had already left the world of the living, their focus on the painted warrior.

One of the men lunged forward with his shield, suddenly driving the base into the ground and stopping it, momentum launching his body forward with his blade out to wound or kill Meala. With her arms high overhead, she wasn't in a good place to block the strike, but she twisted to her left, the blade just barely nicking her bare flesh as it passed. A moment later, her shield and spear plunged downward as she ducked, her token strike entirely missing the man as he recoiled behind his shield, almost on instinct. The second man sprung forward to take advantage of the opening, the Romans fighting as a single unit. His sword drew back, ready to thrust forward into Meala's entirely undefended right side…

Just then, the Dacian lurched forward wrapping her arm around the attacking man's head, a gladius in her hand and raised in the air, it's point angled downward. She was like a spirit of vengeance as she grabbed the surprised soldier entirely arresting his lunge and pressed her blade deep into his neck, a death far too quick for the soldier. The man with the shield turned back at hearing his companion's horrible gurgling sound, but this was a mistake. Just as he turned, he heard the sound of Meala's footfalls. He fought to pull his tower shield into her line of expected attack, but it was already too late. The spear flew through the air, gashing the side of the man's face as it partly deflected from the tower shield. Yet that was only the distraction.

Grabbing her bronze dagger, Meala dove under the defensively raised tower shield and stabbed her blade into the Roman's heel, causing the man to buckle and fall. She clumsily rolled aside and quickly rose into a crouch, coming to find herself kneeling over the wounded Roman. Her next act came almost before she could think, an instinct born of her body's primal urge to continue and the realization that her mercy now would be paid for with her blood if the man cried an alarm. She could see the shock and hate in his eyes as she brought her dagger down once more, closing one of his eyes forever and ending his fight.

Looking up, she found that the Dacian woman had just finished plunging her gladius into the wounded man Meala had hit in the neck, ending his painful night with a single thrust. She had slumped upon the ground afterward, surely weakened from the ordeal and needing a moment to recover. Meala reached forward and pulled the dagger from the twitching Roman soldier's eye with a grotesque sucking sound. A moment later, she was on her knees, trying to vomit her very soul upon the ground. The night had been bloody, and feelings Meala had never experienced danced along her spine, among them feelings of shame, confusion, and panic at what had happened. Her flashbacks had been driven back by adrenalin, but they wouldn't stay hidden for long.

Meala remained on her knees for a time, feeling the urge to wretch once more, but nothing came out as she dry heaved. Her vision had darkened, and she felt strange, tingly sensations all over her body, her emotions slowly coming under control. She had heard warriors speak of how this could happen after one's first battle, but this wasn't technically her first. Either way, she couldn't believe they had survived. Suddenly, she felt a hand on her shoulder. For a moment, she started, but when she looked up, fumbling with her dagger, she quickly realized that it was the gentle hand of Damona. In her other hand, she held a small clay jar, the kind that often held wine. For a moment, Meala was almost panicked, looking frantically in each direction, but her foes lay dead or badly wounded all around. Her fight-or-flight responses were all over the place, and her mind was having trouble controlling them.

"Drink this," she said, handing the container to Meala with a look somewhere between terrified and astounded, a look Meala understood from immediate personal experience. Meala still felt like she might vomit, but she took the clay container and put it to her lips, tasting the rich, almost painfully tart taste of low-quality wine. The men had obviously brought the jar expecting to spend the night guarding the crucified woman, and it took the edge off the moment. With a few swishes, she washed away the bad, foul taste of vomit and took another. The wine might help hold back the flashbacks and urge to curl into a ball or simply black out, but she could already feel her body shaking and her intrusive thoughts trying to get in.

Turning her attention to her right arm, she winced as she poured some wine on the wound. As the blood washed away, the cut turned out to be mostly superficial, yet she knew there would be another scar and plenty more blood before it healed. As she sat there, breathing hard and taking another sip, Damona rushed around looking for anything else of value while the mystery Dacian lay on her back, recuperating her strength. Meala watched as the girl pulled the coin pouch from one of the Roman men and tied it to a cord around her neck, stuffing it in her tunic. She didn't care if the girl kept the money as she probably needed it, but she decided to pretend that she hadn't seen it. She took another swig, swished it for a moment, and spit. It was time to meet the Dacian and settle her debt.

Cynna realized she was lying on her back, though she swore she had fallen facedown. Opening her eyes, she also realized someone was standing over her and looking down. Her vision was blurry, and her head felt like it was spinning, but as it focused, she began to realize who it was. Puella picta... no, she wasn't a painted girl, she was a painted woman, femina picta. She shook her head, wishing to banish the vile Roman words, yet quickly realizing that they might be her only shared language with her savior, assuming the woman could even speak the cursed tongue… yet had she not said that she could the night Cynna had spared her?

This time, the painted warrior woman whose life she had spared stood over her with a dagger, their roles entirely reversed. The woman was dusty, with a few speckles of blood, her face painted with black lines of ash, and her smaller, yet well-defined body smeared with dirt and sweat. She was glorious, a woman who had saved her and confronted four well-trained Roman men from the second cohort of the II Augusta legion, besting two of them in single combat. Of course, Cynna had killed the other two and finished the third, but her kills were taken entirely by surprise. But why had she returned and spared Cynna from her fate, and why did she stand over her with a bloody dagger in hand, her expression a mixture of painful emotions?

She supposed the woman had come back to kill her, perhaps some sort of warrior code. She knew the people of the North cared much for honor and bravery, much like her own kin. She might be able to lift herself to fight in a short time once she got her head to stop spinning, but for the moment, she was helpless. The prospect of having a dagger slowly pressed into her chest as she lay helpless was less than pleasant, yet it certainly beat dying on a cross, her body on display for the amusement of Roman men. Yet, the woman didn't move, simply watching her. Partly, the Caledonian seemed disoriented, overwhelmed, her emotions displayed on her painted face, clearly a whirling storm.

In truth, Cynna would rather be stabbed through the heart by the brave and beautiful painted woman than nailed to a cross to serve as the perverse ornament for an empire she could no longer serve. At least it would be quick and a lot less painful. Moreover, her death would mean something to the brave warrior, which was more than the mere evening of humor it provided the Romans. Was she Caledon? Wenech? Cynna couldn't place the tribe, though she supposed it didn't matter. She was so dizzy, her strength temporarily lost in the aftermath of her adrenaline and terror-mixed nightmare – a nightmare banished by a spirit of vengeance… no, by a flesh and blood woman. Beautiful and captivating as she might be, Cynna wasn't in the mood to delay her fate any longer.

"Procede… nam non Romana es," (Go ahead... at least you are not Roman) she spoke, spreading her arms wide and puffing out her chest, waiting for the blade. On her way to the Northwest from her homeland, she had watched gladiators fight in one of the smaller arenas at Aquileia. She had also watched fellow soldiers fall in battle and even her mother facing down a raiding horde, paying for precious moments for young Cynna to escape with her very life. She knew what an honorable death looked like and wouldn't beg, instead closing her eyes and awaiting the cold metal. The sound Cynna heard next was so unexpected that she took a moment to process what she was hearing.

Laughter abruptly filled the night. It was the sound of a woman laughing, a melodious sound to her ears, yet why? Opening her eyes, she found not an executioner with a blade but an outstretched hand from a still-laughing painted warrior, tears in the woman's emotionally compromised face. The shock of the juxtaposed emotion was so jarring that Cynna briefly forgot that she was supposed to be dying. Instead, she noticed how beautiful the woman's face was when she laughed, little dimples forming around her mouth as her tears flowed from humor, or perhaps the emotional release of having simply lived. After a moment, the warrior calmed enough to speak, her voice as high pitch as Cynna remembered from their first meeting.

"You spared my life when it was yours to take, by all rights. Now, I have spared yours. That makes us even," the painted warrior replied in Latin with a heavy accent, many of her words improperly spoken but understandable. For a moment, Cynna stared at the hand, unsure what to say. The painted woman frowned, her emotions finally beginning to steady. Her laugh had been a mixture of stress release, the buzz from so much adrenaline, and perhaps the very serious look on Cynna's face, though the Caledonian looked like she was still a bit nauseated.

"We don't have long, and we need to get out of here, so you might want to stand." Cynna took her offered hand–soft and warm–and slowly brought her aching body up to a sitting position, her head still spinning but improving quickly. A much younger woman, perhaps still a girl, wearing a blue-dyed tunic, approached carrying what looked like Cynna's armor and equipment. The younger woman deposited the garments and gear beside her and then stepped back, assuming the pose of a servant or an enslaved person ready to help Cynna dress. The painted woman glanced at the girl, then back at Cynna with a shrug.

"She helped me, and I promised I would rescue her, too," she said, noting the look of confusion on the Dacian's face at the girl's presence.

"Sei'ln Meala, daughter of Ail Braide, of East Wenechon, of clan Wood Owl, but most people call me Meala. The girl is Damona… just Damona," the painted warrior explained, poking her finger at herself and forcing a smile, though only barely.

"Meala?" the Dacian asked, her head still fuzzy.

"It means honeybee," Meala explained, glancing down at her bee tattoo. Cynna grimaced as she stretched her legs, her head finally seeming steady enough to stand.

"My name is Cynna of Dacia, of the Iazyges," the archer began, pausing to grimace as she lifted her shaking body to a kneeling position. "If we are to escape, we need to do it soon before a patrol arrives to find me not strung up and before they lose their bowels," Cynna spoke, nodding at the dead Romans, though her throat was hoarse. Meala could see bruise marks around her neck and cringed at the thought of how they had gotten there. She simply nodded, wanting nothing more than to talk with the beautiful archer but now was not the time. Both women were wounded, tired, emotionally damaged, and time was something they had little of. Besides, if Meala spent too much time talking, thinking, or even relaxing, she worried the flashbacks would start and she would be on her knees gagging.

No one spoke again for a short time while Cynna and Meala put their gear back on, though Damona looked quite reticent to remove the blue tunic, having obviously preferred it to her enslavement garb. Given their precarious location within the fort proper, there was a sense of urgency. All it would take would be for one patrol passing, and they would be done for. Even hiding out of sight would not be enough, as the Romans would likely expect either to see the crucified Dacian or people working towards that end, and someone would eventually notice the dead woman and her blood dripping through the ceiling.

Though it was cut down the front, Cynna donned her light grey woolen tunic. With a frown, she slipped on her long kaftan shirt and tied it tightly with a leather belt she took from a dead Roman, her shirt and former belt having been cut when she was stripped, and began wiggling into her scale armor. Damona instinctually helped hold the armor as she slid in, habits learned as an enslaved servant hard to break. Afterward, Cynna sat on the ground quickly re-tying her leggings with simple slip knots, as the cords that held them to her belt had also been cut, courtesy of Rome. It only took her a moment to restore her clothing, but she was clearly less than pleased. Around her neck she now wore the captured silver chain claimed from the body of the Roman she had killed, and likely from a Caledonian person before that.

Beside her, Meala knelt as she finished securing her shield. When she looked up, she noticed the spot where a bronze piece had been bound to the armor to replace an iron scale that had been destroyed when her spear had pierced it. It wasn't until that moment that Meala realized how close the spear had come to passing between two scales at their weakest point. In truth, had her aim been even slightly to the left as she had hurled the spear, the woman kneeling before her and wiggling into the heavy armor would have died that day. She had to have realized, yet she spared Meala that night.

Of course, Meala had spared a Roman's life, finding no glory in killing a wounded and defenseless man. Had that been all it was? Was the archer–Cynna, she corrected herself–just sparing a woman not worthy of killing? She had been quite a mess that night, wounded and lying on the ground. Yet each time their eyes had met, Meala had never seen pity or simple mercy. No, she had seen something so much more profound, but she still had no idea what emotions burned behind those rich, hazel eyes… like jasper. They were beautiful but held a sadness that danced on the edge of sight, teasing and frightening.

Her eyes wandered down the woman's clothing and then back up her arms, noting the intricate details of her finely woven fiber hemp kaftan shirt, beautiful blue and white striped cloth leggings, red woolen socks, and a pair of leather riding boots. Before the woman had reclothed, she had even caught sight of beautiful flower and vine tattoos covering her body. However, it had been too dark to see them in detail, and Meala had thought it inappropriate to stare at a woman after the Romans had specifically unclothed her for the purpose of ridicule and torture. Now dressed, she watched the curious sight of the Dacian woman gearing up more enthusiastically than expected.

She had formed crushes on people before, like Ana of Aelsegh, a woman only perhaps a year older who lived several farms to the West, and a much older Caledon woman who had seen many battles with the Romans. She had been majestic, with every visible part of her body tattooed with magical symbols and scars here and there telling her brave story. Around her neck, she had worn a heavy gold torc of the finest quality from the South. Of course, the warrior had been older than Meala's mother, but that hadn't stopped her wandering mind. Meala's gold torc would nearly command the same respect, especially given how it was obtained. Oddly, her new torc reminded her of the one the Caledon woman had worn, looking almost the same. Just then, the armor slid over the Sarmatian's head, and the woman looked up, meeting Meala's gaze. Her eyes were richly pigmented and full of life, yet sorrowful, and framed by light brown skin and long dark hair held in a single, thick braid.

At first, Meala's mouth opened as she was about to say something – to perhaps explain herself. But then she realized Cynna was looking at her in the same curious way. Instead of blinking or looking away, Meala gazed back with as much courage as she dared. Endorphins flowed through her bloodstream as her skin blushed. She continued to face the archer just as she had in battle, but the challenge in her eyes was very different. Why did this feel, somehow, more daring? She had faced soldiers, battle, and death, yet she was completely captivated by the same woman who had haunted her memories for six moons.

Breathing seemed a little harder, and she forgot about her body's many aches and pains. It was as though the world had slowed for a moment to stretch, banishing even the encroaching and intrusive thoughts, anxiety, and flashbacks. This was the third time they had faced off, but this time not as enemies. Part of her worried the Dacian would realize her amorous thoughts, perhaps thinking them unwanted or grossly inappropriate, especially given the circumstances. But another part of her feared the archer might not realize her interest, a bizarre mix of emotions.

Time ticked by at some unknown rate as Meala's grasp of reality became uncanny. Two warriors knelt upon the blood-soaked grass of a once beautiful garden, both enemies of mighty Rome and all but standing within the wolf's very den, yet their eyes continued to meet. After a long pause, the truth of their mutual interest became an unspoken acknowledgment, something they realized without a word, as there was no other way to explain such captivation amid death.

Slowly, Cynna began to lean forward, the sounds of her leather boots creaking and iron scales rubbing against each other as she approached until her lips were but an inch from Meala's. Cynna had hardly recovered from what had happened, especially emotionally. Her hands still trembled and her mind was a wash of thoughts that would probably haunt her until she finally passed. It had been a violation, a living nightmare, yet the green eyes of her rescuer were like rain washing away the dirt and blood. Gazing into those beautiful emerald orbs of the painted warrior filled her with calm; a respite from what had been hours of terror. She felt wetness dripping down her face like the river Danu Nazdya (Dniester River), each warm drop carrying away a mote of her pain.

It would be a while before she could feel safe enough to open herself to more than a simple kiss. This was hardly the context for anything else, yet there was something vital about the woman before her that calmed her pumping heart. What she needed now was grounding, so she banished her rational thoughts, what was left of them, anyway. She could feel the warm, moist air from the painted warrior's lips as her hand slowly extended, still trembling as though it were cold. Still, the painted warrior didn't move, her face a mixture of longing and wonder, so cute that Cynna wanted nothing more than to kiss her. It was like an escape from the darkest night… a vital beacon of fire in a blizzard or a single iris flower growing in a field of despair, each petal soft and kissed with dew.

When her fingers touched the warmth of Meala's arm, she found that her hand finally became still. It wasn't the rough, muscular pell of a Roman man's grasp but the soft, smooth feel of a woman. A moment later she caught the woman's scent, so very different from the smell of a man, fainter, less musky, safer. She had never wanted to embrace somebody more than this strange, brave, beautiful warrior. They had faced each other in battle and saved each other's lives. Now, their lips were so close that she could feel the heat. Her tears continued flowing as their breath danced across each other's lips, their hearts beating and…

"A patrol!" Damona whispered as loudly as she could, breaking the mood as fast as if cold water had been poured upon them. Shaking her head, Meala glanced up at the girl, almost momentarily confused as though she had forgotten what was happening. As she looked around to reestablish her surroundings, she saw the bodies of four Romans, and her memory of the fight returned like a hot arrow to the chest. Nearly falling backward, Meala stood, grabbing her spear and shield but hoping they could escape before anyone noticed. As the Dacian stood on shaky legs and turned to leave, Damona pointed toward the fort's entryway at a flickering light reflecting off the side of the building. It was growing in intensity with every moment as soldiers approached.

Fear once more became the dominant emotion as Meala saw the firelight approaching. When she turned back, she noticed the Dacian had disappeared. Looking in every direction, she began to panic as the patrol approached. The bodies of the Romans were everywhere, and there was simply no way to hide. Even if they had sneaked away, the patrol would find the bodies and no crucifixion, and alert the fort within moments. They could make a run for the wall, but she knew it was unlikely they could make it before a horn blew, and Meala doubted she could fight a patrol by herself or even with the Dacian. Just then, she thought she heard a woman shriek from the fort proper... Domina had likely just been found.

"Where did Cynna go?" she asked Damona, her mind nearly dizzy from the effects of battle, a moment of intimacy, and then back to alarm. Using her shield hand, she directed the girl to get behind her, preparing to meet the Romans head-on. The sudden renewal of danger had soured the brief sip of romance she had felt. In truth, the threat had never really left, but she had at least ignored it for a brief moment, lost in the most mind-twisting of escapes, like a snowflake upon the tongue during the warmest day.

"Over there, the stables... look," Damona said, pointing to her left into a darkened area beside a large building with a wooden overhang blocking enough torchlight that Meala couldn't make out any details when she glanced in that direction. As she looked, she swore she saw movement and heard a sound like a horse. Was this a Roman or something else, and where was Cynna? But before she could discern what was happening, she heard the sound of the Romans.

"Attende te! Femina Picta! Desisteque hastam demitte!" came a stark order as the four torch-bearing Roman legionaries rushed into the courtyard, a guard detail, it seemed. Meala stood before them, boldly slapping her mother's spear against her shield, indicating she had no intention of backing down. It was how her people prepared for battle and often used to initiate single combat. She had been lucky beyond reason with the crucifixion detail and had been helped. But now, she faced four trained men ready for action entirely by herself and wearing her thick tunic.

Unfortunately, unlike the overly confident crucifixion party, one of the soldiers had the good sense to call out an alarm, grasping a whistle from around his neck and blowing it four times as the four men quickly encircled the warrior. At the same time, the man beside him advanced to destroy the painted Northerner, likely thinking his odds against a younger woman were overly matched. As he cautiously advanced, Meala lunged with her spear. Unfortunately, the soldier had been expecting this and promptly swiveled his oval shield into place, using its momentum to deflect the spear while he thrust his gladius at her exposed neck. Luck was on Meala's side as the blade clipped her heavy torc, leaving a nick in the gold but harmlessly deflecting. The sword was typically used for impaling the body, not the neck.

Stepping backward, she faced off against the deadly and well-trained Romans. The four encircled her but stayed out of her spear's range, perhaps thinking better than attacking heedlessly, given the first man's failed probing attack and their four dead compatriots lying at Meala's feet. To her side, the other Romans approached with their swords and shields in the same stance, professional soldiers using proper tactics. How well-trained and regimental Romans could be was frightening when they were not caught off guard. Within moments, they had flanked her and were taking their time, probably hoping to wound and capture her. With two approaching her from each side, she knew she was done for, but she wouldn't go out without a fight. Looking back at the absolutely terrified Damona, she screamed a final command, hoping the girl would follow it.

"Run! Take the box and go! I'll hold them here!" But, surprisingly, the girl shook her head no. It wasn't so much that she bravely wished to make some final stand but more that she had no idea what else to do. She doubted she could run far enough and fast enough. Worse, now that Meala had taken back her blue tunic, she was again left wearing the garment of an enslaved girl. She knew that if she were caught, a fate as bad as crucifixion might very well be hers, and she was too frightened to take her own life. But perhaps the soldiers would simply end her suffering. From her perspective, death at the soldiers' hands seemed like the only real option.

Meala quickly turned her attention back to the soldiers, slamming her shield and spear together one more time and smiling at them as though she welcomed the fight, even though, deep down, she was absolutely terrified. With their eyes briefly turning towards their fallen comrades, the first two soldiers advanced using their shields as a wall. Meala held her shield before her, spear at the ready. They were trying to drive her back into the other two men at her rear. Worse, Damona was at her side, adding another variable to the mix. As soon as she attacked one of the Romans, the one beside him would move his shield aside and stab with his sword – a tactic she had seen several times, followed by those in the rear lunging forwards to kill her and Damona.

Meala twirled her spear in her hand, reversing it so the head faced behind her, and leapt forward slamming her shield into the shield of the Roman on her right. Sure enough, the Roman to her left rolled his shield aside and positioned his gladius for a strike. But Meala paid no heed as she used the momentum from the first Roman's rebuttal to propel herself 180 degrees in a circle, forcing her spear point directly into the suddenly exposed chest of the Roman on the left. She felt the sickening impact as her spear passed through the soldier's tunic and into his flesh. Kicking back with her foot, she freed the spear with a tug and skipped away, narrowly missing a gladius from the first Roman.

Meala barely dodged the weapon as she stumbled backward and tripped, falling onto her butt. Beside her, Damona screamed as one of the second pair of Romans rushed upon the downed barbarian, with his sword ready for the final thrust. Suddenly, with a wispy sound, an arrow seemed to all but appear in the man's neck. He dropped his sword and his shield and began grasping at the arrow while his blood sprayed into the warm light season air. Turning a glance, Meala heard the sound of a horse approaching. Exiting from the darkened area where Damona had seen the Dacian go, Cynna burst forth, riding a mighty black warhorse followed by a heavier, grey horse she had obviously been leading but released to use her bow. The mounted warrior quickly holstered her war bow into a special leather sheath that held it during battle and grabbed the pre-tied lasso from the other side of the horse in a nearly effortless act of dexterity Meala could only watch in awe.

Finally returned to her element and eager for revenge, the Dacian rode straight at them, whipping the lasso into the air in a mighty spin. The soldier she had shot in the neck had already fallen as his lifeblood painted the ground, while the soldier Meala wounded had dropped to a knee. The two uninjured men turned to meet the new threat, but before they could do anything, the lasso flew, catching one of them around the neck. Cynna wrapped the rope around her strong arms in one smooth motion. She trilled a war cry as the lasso pulled taut and her horse reared high, snapping the man's neck with a disturbing sound like a branch breaking from a tree. She held her body to the horse using the sheer force of her powerful legs, leaving her hands free for combat.

The final soldier stabbed his gladius into the dirt, reached for a set of small darts strapped to his inner shield, called plumbatae, and pulled one free. He hurled the dart at Cynna with a practiced aim, but the deadly dart deflected off her armor. Turning toward the new threat, Cynna snatched an arrow from her quiver with one hand while grabbing her bow from its case with the other, the deadly tools meeting in a skillful union overhead as she lowered them, in one motion drawing the bow and taking aim. The Roman lifted his shield, his plumbata in the other hand, and began backing from the courtyard. Just then, Cynna let fly her arrow. Without seeing if it hit, she pulled another, knocked it, took aim, and fired in the blink of an eye.

As the first arrow deflected off his shield, the Roman pulled aside his shield to toss his deadly dart, only to find another arrow following the first far sooner than he had thought possible. He dropped his dart, falling to his knees as his heart failed to beat. A few quick arrows later, eight Romans were scattered around a cross. For a moment, Meala and Damona both stood there recovering from the intense battle. Meala still felt waves of nausea, but they were lessened this time, perhaps because she was more numb to the violence or possibly just too tired to process everything. Either way, a moment later, the horse came to stand before the painted warrior, and once more, the mighty Dacian looked down at Meala, but this time, she was smiling.

"She's a strong horse, and she came when I called. The Romans obviously didn't remove her saddle or tie her down when they took her... fools. The pair of you cannot weigh more than 400 libra (~131 kg or 290 lbs.), too much for Tamura to carry. This packhorse will carry you well if you can ride?" Cynna spoke in not the best Latin. Meala gazed at Cynna's majestic horse, Tamura, then at Damona and finally Cynna, and nodded, taking a moment to compose herself enough to even reply.

"I can ride, but not well," she admitted, feeling slightly embarrassed at having no idea how much a Roman libra weighed and admitting her lack of skill in the face of the warrior who had just killed a man using a horse and not even holding the reins. Cynna gave her a curious look, ending in a lifted eyebrow and a smirk. There was little real humor behind it, both women far beyond their emotional limits, but such gestures kept one sane in the face of death, it seemed.

"Tamura is young and strong. While I was nursing, my mother carried me into battle riding Tamura's grandmother; the battle of The Three Nights. She can handle my weight, and I can take the lead. Mount up, fast. We must ride like the wind as a storm is coming," she finished boastfully, though Meala could hear the waver in her voice from the physical and emotional strain of her ordeal. A moment later, a series of horn blows issued from the fort proper, likely signaling the start of the official military response to the death of a Roman noble or the response to the whistles and the need for them to get going.

The pack horse was much larger than Cynna's war horse, with a powerful body, very large mane and tail, and large frame, though it was somewhat shorter. Its back was bare, Cynna not having time to saddle it, but it was probably their only way out. With the alarm horns blowing, sneaking was out of the question, and leaving on foot was far too slow for them to escape. So, after a few precarious moments, as both Meala and Damona discovered how difficult it was to actually mount a pack horse, the trio was ready to leave. Meala sat in the front, holding the reins while Damona held on from behind. Meala placed the small wooden chest before her, holding it with her right hand and the reins in her left, her spear slung over her shoulder with a leather cord. Behind her, Damona wore Meala's shield over her shoulder to protect her back, just in case they needed to make a run for it, and held Meala tightly.

Meala, the warrior, prepares for single combat

With likely the entire fort and this section of the wall having just been alerted, their chance of escape was dwindling by the moment. Even now, Meala could imagine Roman soldiers grabbing their armor and weapons, and the quick reaction forces they maintained day and night were likely forming up as they did the night she had raided the wall six moons beforehand. Between them and freedom stood the gates of the rest of the fort and the wall gates, and an unknown number of Roman soldiers ready to stop them. But before she could despair, Cynna adjusted her knees, and the mighty horse began to move – an unspoken command to begin their flight to freedom.

CHAPTER IX

ESCAPE!

Determining the breeds of horses used in the book is complex, given that Romans did not understand horse breeds as we now do. Romans categorized and bred horses based on physical characteristics, such as color, size, and endurance. As for insular Celts, we have virtually no evidence of how they interpreted horse breeds. To complicate matters, many breeds available to Romans and Celts no longer exist or have been significantly changed due to breeding. Still, a few guesses can be made concerning their apparent breeds.

Cynna's mighty warhorse Tamura was probably a Turkoman breed, similar to a modern Akhal-Teke. Fast, nimble, intelligent, and having a high endurance have made Akhal-Teke and their predecessors highly sought after and especially useful for steppe cultures. Black is an uncommon color for the Akhal-Teke, but it does exist. The coat of such horses famously exhibits an almost metallic sheen, making a horse like Tamura extremely beautiful and a perfect companion to a mounted archer. The packhorse stolen from the legionary fort was probably related to a Galloway Pony or a Fell Pony, though likely a predecessor breed. Shorter, rugged, and extremely hearty in the cold with their thick coat, mane, and tails, such horses would have been useful in the bitter Caledonian winters.

"A little girl with a doll could break their line." Valerius Pontius leaned against the stone of the Veluniate gate's entryway, watching his group of tirones (trainees) practicing their shield and defensive techniques. The spring raid had yet again demonstrated how important it was that the men guarding the gate were ready to form a strong shield wall if suddenly rushed at an untimely moment. Had several veterans not been on duty that night, they might have lost the gate, a disturbing prospect. Sadly, the fresh local men were still having trouble learning how to properly work together, and they would need much more work before they joined the ranks of the legion.

Valerius sighed, wishing he was back in his warm bed with a cup of wine. Unfortunately, nighttime was also the best time for training, as there were fewer higher-ranking individuals, such as centurions, who might find the personal need to come to add their opinions to the training. As it was, he already had to deal with the jeers from the four regular archers atop the gate, who looked on with amused interest. Luckily, he had heard of a crucifixion and planned to march his tirones passed when they were done practicing.

Such a grizzly and vivid image might help burn the training deeper into their minds and wake them to their new reality. Valerius found crucifixion distasteful and tried his best to avoid it, yet it served its purpose in frightening the locals into submission. Though he sometimes wondered if he would ever get some sights to leave his dreams when, or perhaps if, he finished his service and started a farm. Would he continue to see those many dead faces in his wife's eyes? Would he even be fit to find a wife by then, he wondered? Valerius breathed and cleared such thoughts from his mind as another man spoke.

"They will be mixed with regulars over the next few weeks, so maybe not so bad, right?" asked an archer standing beside him, absentmindedly working on a loose fletching on one of his arrows with a string. Valerius shrugged more board at this point than angry. He had served twenty-three of twenty-five years, and was much more concerned with making it another two cold seasons than the quality of his trainees.

"The weakest link breaks the chain," he retorted with a chuckle, recounting something his papa had said long ago. Suddenly, the sound of a warning horn, maybe a cornum or something local, rang through the night like thunder in the distance. Looking out across the open field, he saw nothing but the still of the night. Behind him, the sound rang again, begging for attention.

"It's coming from the fort!" the archer beside him spoke as they turned in the direction they had not expected to find an enemy. For a moment, they could see nothing but the fort, the sleeping village in the distance, and a few torches bustling about. There was the sound of men screaming and then the sound of horses approaching. They both looked onward from their wood and stone gate tower as the sounds of the tirones went quiet. Up ahead were growing sounds of voices, screams, and more torches. Someone or something was coming.

Beside him, the archers grabbed arrows, preparing to face whatever unknown threat approached. Valerius called down to the tirones to form a line facing inward toward the coming threat as the horn blew once more. There was no time to close the gate, but the few guards and archers were now supplemented by the force of tirones, who were normally not present. If he were really lucky, his small trainee force might have paid attention to their training. Suddenly, an arrow launched from the darkness, catching an archer in the face. The man grabbed the arrow, stumbling backward while screeching. Out of the dark, a horse galloped as fast as an arrow, its rider bent low, pointing a bow in his direction and firing. Valerius ducked to avoid the deadly missile, an arrow flying right past his head so close that the fletching brushed his cheek.

"Hastas praeparate! Tuos exercitationes memorare!" he screamed, even as he scrambled to his feet. When he did, a second archer fell, shrieking as an arrow protruded from his collarbone just above his tunic. Below, the mounted archer traced a circle around the backside of the gate, firing arrow after arrow at the men while maneuvering with only their legs, their arms busy with the bow. But why was the archer not trying to escape from the gate and riding in circles and why did they seem somehow different in body shape and armor?

That's when it struck him – this was a woman, her long braid flowing in the wind and her face far too feminine as he got a closer look. In fact, she was a woman he had seen with the auxilia only days before… the very woman to be crucified, if rumor were to be believed. But how had she gotten free from a crucifixion detail, become armed and armored, and where had she gotten her horse?

A moment later, a larger, slower horse came lumbering from the darkness carrying two riders, women by their look, and headed directly for the gate. They should have been easily killed with how straight and steady the large horse cantered toward the gate, its rider obviously unskilled. Yet no one could take that easy shot as the Dacian mounted archer ran one more circuit within the mustering area, suppressively firing her bow at anyone who dared try. With her final circuit complete, the Dacian sped toward the gate to join the slower horse. She held tightly to the nimble horse with the sheer force of her legs as they flew toward the entryway, her bow steady and unphased by the horse's movements as it tracked an archer for a kill shot as though she were standing still. She loosed her arrow and drew another in the blink of an eye.

Just ahead, the line of tirones began to form up as they were trained, each holding a wicker shield and a hasta (spear). Yet as they did, the Dacian warrior flew past the slower pack horse to meet the new threat head on, issuing a loud trilling sound and brandishing her bow. Behind her, the Wenech woman screamed a battle cry high enough pitched to rupture a man's eardrums. Together, they charged the tirones, unwilling to stop, a normally suicidal maneuver against a wall of proper soldiers. Had Valerius's men been trained, they might have locked shields and held their ground, spears wedged against the ground and pointed up and outward, as a horse wouldn't mindlessly ram a wall of shields and spears, but Valerius had tirones…

Valerius groaned as bile built up in his throat upon watching the young troops dive out of the way, one of them managing to knock over a large brazier set up for light and starting a small fire before the entry. Another stood his ground and thrust his spear, to his credit, but the poorly aimed weapon glanced off the Dacian's scale armor. As a further insult, the well-trained archer didn't even spend an arrow on a single tiro, content to leave them to their cowering. As luck had it, the fire illuminated a series of four-pronged caltrops in the road, small iron spikes that littered the field before the gate to impede attacks, especially at night. Cynna had not expected them and quickly called a warning to Meala before leaping over the fire and leaving the fort in her wake.

Their path illuminated by flame, Meala pulled on the reins, maneuvering her horse, passed the sprinkling of caltrops and past the fire, and into the night. As they passed, the archer twisted her body backward and fired three more arrows in rapid succession toward the remaining archer at the gate. The arrows missed their targets but suppressed the remaining archer long enough for the women to escape his range. And then they were gone into the night. Valerius turned his wary gaze to the remaining archer and shook his head.

"Titus was a fool to order her death for ridding us of that greater fool, Gaius. We need more of her kind... and I need a fucking drink." The archer nodded in agreement.

☽○☾

As the night rolled along, the trio followed the Southwestern bends of a great fjord known to the Romans as Bodotria and the locals as the Slow River (Firth of Forth), headed west, then northwest, roughly following the shoreline. After a short distance, Cynna led them due west, along the path of the Wall – a direction few fleeing Rome would choose, or so she had reasoned. At first, their horses cantered, neither Meala nor Damona confident in a gallop, but after a while, they slowed to a trot and then a walk as their distance grew. The night had just passed its midpoint when Cynna stopped before a small group of trees and held out her hand to indicate something, perhaps to stop? Meala figured it was some sort of military gesture, but she was too tired to worry about it.

The intrusive thoughts and images had come and filled her mind's eye with blood, death, and odd little motes of pain. Luckily, now away from the Fort and the Wall and with the cool, open night air around her, Meala had somewhat recovered. Her mind finding other parts of the night to dwell upon. She had nearly vomited several times, but little remained to be released. After many deep breaths and the silence accompanied by little more than horse hoofs, the hoots of owls, the almost hiss-like sound of hedgehogs, and the child-like sounds of foxes, Meala was finally regaining some control over her emotions.

The problem was those emotions were almost as chaotic as battle. She had finally met the woman who had occupied her mind for half a year and nearly kissed her, but they had hardly spoken since. They had shared four moments of vital intimacy: in single combat, at the point of an arrow, then the blade of a dagger, and finally, on their knees in the Fort. But even after such moments, Meala had no idea what to make of their encounter. Was this the spark of something greater or simply emotions so powerful they had caused the Dacian to feel and act irrationally?

She couldn't imagine a typical woman being so interested in kissing another woman, even if she had been extremely rattled, but could she be sure? They had only spoken for a moment since they had formally met.

Her feelings felt like leaves in a windstorm, blown about in the trauma and amorous-fueled insanity that had been her "raid" on the Fort. She should be happy that she escaped with her life or excited that she had found something of significance to ward off the will of her parents, but all she could think about was the beautiful archer just a little ahead with her hand held out, seemingly to halt the party. *Fuck...*

"What do you see?" she asked as her horse strode up to the archer, yet before Cynna could answer, Meala's horse stepped close enough, and she saw: The full Moon hung low in the sky, south by southeast, over Meala's left shoulder flooding the land with an eerie light. From that light, a small roundhouse sat nestled within a lowland, mostly obscured by the trees. Beside it stood pens for animals, what looked like a farm, and a smaller wooden structure on the bank that looked almost like a small house or hut. Such farmsteads adorned the lands, just like Meala's family farm, and the prospect of a real bed to sleep in held great appeal.

"We could ask them if we might stay the night," Meala offered, unsure how the Dacian might take it. She glanced at Cynna's armored visage, finding the warrior's scale and mighty appearance a bit hard to ignore. Her outfit didn't resemble a Roman soldier, and she certainly didn't look like one, but they were also not so far from the fort for either of their comforts. Of course, while Romans did business and even had farms north of the wall, they were less likely to send a large armed force after them at night, as the locals would likely take poorly to the intrusion and slowly pick the Romans off, one at a time.

"These are your people, correct?" Cynna asked, feeling a little dizzy and obviously exhausted. Cynna's deep, husky voice was a welcome reprieve from the mundane ambiance of the open lands at night. Still, Meala hesitated momentarily, unsure of a few key words in their shared language of Latin and how much information to speak. The problem was that clan relationships were… complicated… and explaining them could be time-consuming and frankly beyond her limited vocabulary of mostly regular speech. After a moment of hesitation, Cynna turned her a curious, if not appraising glance.

"These are the lands of the Damnone (Damnonii). They are different people. I am of the eastern Wenechon, Wood Owl clan. We are different peoples and different clans, but we are both of this land. My people are northeast," she began, unsure of how to explain kings, druids, local clans, regional clans, and alliances. "Romans call us all Caledonii, after the Caledon, but we are not the same. These people will not know me, but they will probably help us. It is our way to help travelers in need. We only kill the soldiers because they come in force and pay no respect to our land or our leaders. We don't harm merchants and those who ask permission, and harming those who are not our enemies and who are in need would be without honor," she finished, unsatisfied with her roundabout answer.

Cynna understood, her own Iazyges people often being lumped into one of several possible catch-all groups by the Romans, such as Dacian, Sarmatian, or just Barbarians. Cynna began to frown, that quickly became a slight smile as she watched Meala's face flash a worried look. Cynna's thoughts wanted nothing more than to sink into the depths of despair and confusion that her world had become, but Meala's eyes seemed to ground her and bring respite. She had the strangest urge to smile every time she gazed into those wide, green eyes, the only thing that seemed to bring her peace. Still, grounded or not, the fort felt far too close to be safe and her mind was a wash of horror and confusion from what had been the second worst night of her life.

"We should travel farther to be safe," Cynna began, but Meala cut her off, noting the exhaustion in the Dacian's eyes – eyes she had difficulty ignoring.

"Ideally, but we are tired and hungry. We must rest and eat. Besides, you are wounded," Meala added, nodding at Cynna. Her injuries were many, though mostly bruises and pulled muscles, nearly all hidden under her clothing. The Sarmatian returned Meala's nod with a smirk.

"So are you," she said, noting the visible and slightly bleeding cut on Meala's arm. They had both shed blood, and neither could claim to have a sound mind. While Damona seemed unharmed physically, her all too often blank stare and quiet demeanor spoke of a mind far more injured than either warrior. Neither woman knew how to help her, but getting off the horse and into a warm bed certainly wouldn't be a bad start.

"You are right, I am, so we must rest," Meala finished, nodding at the house and flashing a smile at the Sarmatian. Behind them, Damona remained quiet, a life of servitude enforcing a strict code of being seen but not heard. It would be a long time before someone like Damona undid the harm the Romans had done to her if she ever could, but Meala would give her as long as she needed, only asking her to speak when it was necessary and letting the girl have her privacy to process what had happened to her. Privacy was important to Meala's people.

Riding beside them, Cynna considered their distance from the fort and what the Romans might do in response to their actions, especially the death of Vita. Meala had filled her in on her exploits as they had fled, and to say that she had been shocked to hear of the governor's wife being killed was an understatement, though the vile woman had deserved it almost as much as the optio. Fleeing as far as possible was their best choice, but Meala was tired, Damona was mentally fatigued from her ordeal, and Cynna was worse than both of them combined. She hid her mental, emotional, and physical exhaustion well, but she wanted nothing more than to fall from her mount and lie on the ground for a full year, if possible.

Her arms and neck were bruised where men had held her down to… she couldn't even think about it without reflexively pulling her arms close. She tried to close her eyes, but intrusive images poured in, and she opened them quickly. Thoughts of the men sent shivers and sharp jerking reflexes down her body, Tamura reacting to the motions as she felt her rider twitching. It had been a violation, and it could have been so much worse. Luckily, the men who had done so were dead, which seemed to help. She had dealt with mental and physical trauma before as a warrior for the Romans, but she could only be strong for so long.

"Very well, we shall see if we can bargain to stay here," Cynna stated flatly. Meala held back a smile, finding Cynna's assumed command of their small group amusing but not wishing to contest it. None of them were in charge, though she supposed that Cynna probably had much more experience in command, which wasn't very difficult as the largest force Meala had ever commanded was a flock of sheep.

"I'm the only one of us who speaks the language of this land, right? So, I'll ask. You two stay back," Meala offered, nearly falling as she tried to dismount the horse with as much grace as a drunk old man trying to take a piss in a rainstorm. Cynna grimaced as she watched her stumble but nodded at the simple wisdom, wondering how anyone could possibly stumble while mounting or unmounting a horse.

"Hide that torc," Cynna added, considering anonymity a critical aspect of their immediate security, as she worked to remove her own silver chain. Meala stood, dusting herself off, and turned a curious look at the Sarmatian.

"Why would I hide this?" she asked, one hand touching the heavy gold torc, her brow furrowed as she was genuinely confused. Cynna cocked an eyebrow, unsure why the obvious wasn't obvious, and having little patients as she tried to mask her mental distress and frustration.

"They will ask a stranger with dirt and blood on her clothes how she got such gold. Your face is still painted for war. We will already attract far too much attention, and there will be too many questions. They may even try to take it from you. You should tell them that we were attacked by thieves and barely escaped and have nothing to trade," she finished. Now Meala frowned, perplexed by the Sarmatian's logic.

"You want me to lie to them?" she asked incredulously. Cynna slowly nodded her head, indicating that was exactly what she wanted.

"Lying is dishonorable," she retorted.

"More honor can be found if you live long enough to earn it," Cynna replied, ever the pragmatist.

"No, I will do no such thing. I will tell them where I got the torc and of my deeds. No one would take someone's torc. Such dishonor is… I cannot imagine someone from my lands doing that. They would be seen by the gods and ancestors. Such a boon is only given in honor or taken from another if won in battle or by a leader," she finished. For a moment, Cynna and Meala glared at each other, a point of cultural difference raising their mutual anger and fueled by exhaustion.

"Then do as you wish, but I will knock my bow," Cynna said, removing her main bow and quickly stringing it in case Meala needed help. The Caledonian woman was certainly brave, but that didn't mean she was invincible or had the best judgment, even when it came to her own people. Meala glared back at her for a moment with a mixture of quick anger and confusion, her own nerves wearing thin and her emotional capacity for handling conflict quite exhausted. She briefly closed her eyes and inhaled, letting the air out slowly as she regained her calm, then turned and strode toward the small farmstead.

The door to the roundhouse opened and Meala found herself staring at none other than a Roman-looking man. His complexion, facial shape, hair, and every other detail but for his local-style clothing could have been any other Roman. A brief jolt of fear ran through her, but she quickly controlled it, her exhaustion curiously aiding in the endeavor. For a moment, the man eyed the painted warrior, his eyes drifting from the dried blood and wounded arm to the smear of ash in the way of a warrior across her face and upper body and the massive gold torc around her neck. A Wenech warrior woman painted for battle gave the Roman a similar moment of pause. After an awkward moment he opened his mouth to speak, but another voice cut his words off.

"Meala!" came an unexpected voice that she recognized, followed a moment later by Julia, the woman she had aided at the canaba. The woman swept past the man and grabbed Meala, pulling her into a deep embrace. A short distance away, Cynna watched, turning a confused look at Damona, who shrugged in response. It seemed to Cynna that the locals were far more accommodating to each other than to her kind. Such an interaction with another tribe on the steppe would have been handled and responded to in a very different manner.

"Well, met Julia of Muire Glen, daughter of Ana, of clan Luan," Meala said as soon as the excited woman released her from a hearty embrace that her pained body could barely handle. She thoughtfully recited the woman's name, locus of life, and matronymic line, a custom of most of the people of her lands and an important skill to learn. Julia quickly stepped back to look at Meala in the dim hearth light but paused as her eyes fell upon the torc, blood, and paint.

"To you as well, Sei'ln Meala of Flooding Lake, the generous daughter of Ail Braide of the Wenechon," she replied, not quite getting Meala's location correct and omitting her clan, but continuing without realizing her err, "But what brings you to our little homestead, and… by the Great Mother, why are you painted like some sort of warrior? You couldn't have raided someone or done some other warrior thing this night.

I thought you just needed to… relieve yourself, but then you didn't come back. I went to the apodyterium, and you were gone. I only just got back home a short moment ago. And with the torc of a… and the Aureus! It made up for what I had lost and my trip to town…" Julia paused for a moment, sharing a look with the still unintroduced man. Her brow furrowed as her eyes narrowed.

"Are you a noblewoman from the West or South? Did something happen? Were you disguised when we met?" she began, ignoring her own cultural moors concerning privacy, it seemed. Meala supposed that Roman culture had rubbed off on poor Julia as she spat out question after question. Beside her, the patiently waiting man smiled and finally cut her off, clearly wanting to end the awkward part of the encounter, if for no other reason than common decency.

"Greetings Meala of the Flooding Lake, I am Acilius, once of Florentia (a Roman city), and now of clan Luan. My wife has spoken of your good deed, and we would welcome you in our home to speak, and some hospitality, if you wish," he finished, giving Julia a knowing look as speaking in the doorway was hardly the best way to greet a guest. Meala forced a smile, her mind and body close to giving out from exhaustion, but she hesitated. Among her people, secrets among friends and family were typically to be avoided.

"I have two others with me," she said, turning to briefly look toward the horses and riders a short distance away, then returned her gaze. "They are my friends Cynna of Dacia and Damona of Veluniate. We are tired, wounded, and in need of rest. But you must know that we flee the Fort. The Romans call us enemy and fought us in our escape. We took the life of a noble and caused them great woe. We have seen no pursuit, but I cannot swear an oath that none follow," she finished, being entirely truthful. Taking them in for the night was probably not very risky, but there was some risk. She would not hide this from Julia or her family, as to do so would be dishonorable. For a moment, Julia and Acilius exchanged glances, then nodded.

"They will not send a force out at night, not with the unrest to the West and the Bear clan patrolling the trails south. If they come for you, it would be in the day and only after careful planning," said Acilius, a little too familiar with Roman military policy for Meala's comfort. She supposed he was ex-military, explaining his presence this far north.

"Besides, it's not like you killed the legatus or the governor, right?" he added jokingly.

"Just his wife and a dozen soldiers," Meala said flatly. Acilius burst into laughter only to find that Meala had quite a sober expression.

"Hold up. You took the life of the Governor's wife and a contubernium (group of ten soldiers) of soldiers?" he asked incredulously. Meala nodded, though she had no idea what a contubernium was and merely guessed, given the word's context. Acilius and Julia shared another look, but Julia nodded again, and Acilius stepped aside with a half-smirk, then called out to Meala's friends on the rise.

"You there, come. We have beer and food. Welcome," he called.

"Please, let us put you up for the night and we can speak of this around our fire and a cup of beer," Julia offered, obviously working hard to curtail her interest, though her cultural moors against digging details out of people's personal lives were finally starting to win over. Not only did the honey-blonde woman need to repay a good deed and her need to learn the juiciest news for probably the next ten years, but her cultural customs demanded hospitality if asked, especially by those of honor – and the massive gold torc spoke of honor as brightly as the Sun spoke of day.

"I'll put some food over the fire and heat some water, then fetch Erbin to see if they can water and feed your horses. They probably fell asleep in the pottery again," Acilius said, referring to the small building beside the house, then giving a wary quick look at the unknown travelers in the darkness, then Julia, and finally a warm nod to Meala, before turning and leaving.

⤬

A short time later, six people sat around the central hearth of the roundhouse, sipping beer and talking. The night was late, and they would likely sleep far too late, but a full day of leisure was important occasionally. Downtime to talk, drink, and merrymake sharpened the mind – a dull knife was useless. And so the night went as Cynna watched Meala chatting with Julia, a woman she had apparently met once in the village adjoining the fort, and her husbands.

Of course, the initial meeting had been a double shock when Julia recognized Cynna as the woman who had saved her from ravishment by the late Gaius Pedius, the ill-fated optio principalis. Julia had tried to thank Cynna, but the archer had merely held up a single, wiry hand to halt the feisty woman before she could make even larger of a scene. Thankfully for Cynna, Julia and her husbands took the hint and dropped the topic, though Cynna kept noticing Julia peering at her with an almost reverent look as the night continued. Unfortunately, the attention and the constant reminder of what had happened did little to help Cynna's deteriorating mood.

It turned out that Julia had two husbands, multiple partners and marriages beyond the binary being not so uncommon among insular Celtic people. Her first had been Acilius, a talkative and reasonably jovial man with dark, shoulder-length hair and shadowy deep eyes. The man was built to be intimidating, yet he held a softness that Meala couldn't quite place. A former Roman legionary who had finished his twenty-five years of service and had taken his earnings to secure some land from the local clan to build a farm, Acilius had forsaken his family name and settled down at the farthest northern corner of the empire, seeking a calm life, free from conflict, a life goal Cynna could entirely understand. Though she considered herself a proven warrior, Cynna wanted nothing more than to leave that way of life behind. Every drop of blood she spilled seemed to take with it a piece of her.

Next had been Erbin, a freemen Caledon from farther north who seemed to be a consummate potter, given the many quality ceramic pieces adorning the small round house. They were what Meala's people called a "dynen," a third gender and one of three genders beyond the common man and woman. Of course, "maritus" and "marita," the Latin words for husband and wife, were ill-applied to a dynen spouse. Still, it seemed that Erbin had chosen maritus when speaking Latin as no term existed to describe them properly, a limitation of the language.

A quiet sort, their thinner features were accented by a thick mane of red hair running halfway down their back and a pair of rich, hazel eyes. Their arms were tattooed with black rings from shoulder to wrist, a painful expression of their spirit, yet quite lovely, in Cynna's opinion. As Acilius told it, Erbin had fallen for him while he traded in the village of

Tamia, North of their home and Meala's lake. Luckily, Julia had found herself equally smitten with the quiet but talented potter, and Erbin had joined their marriage. But it seemed their family wasn't finished, as Julia was also expecting a child, though she had only seen early indications of this. Humorously, neither husband was sure of the father, at least yet.

"I suspect we are both the fathers," Erbin laughed as Julia finished speaking of her family. But as the humor faded and Erbin took another deep swig of their beer, eyes began to fall upon Meala and Cynna. No one would pressure them to speak, but it was clear that those gathered would love a good story and to learn why two women and a girl had shown up painted and bloodied like the victors of a mighty battle and what had happened at the fort. This was the part Cynna had wanted to avoid, yet the gabby Meala seemed unable to understand why she thought this was such a bad idea. A pang of anger arose, something that normally didn't affect the usually even minded woman, but the stress of her day had been anything but normal, leaving her a wash of emotions.

Cynna quickly sipped her beer, wanting nothing to do with speaking of the day's horrors. In her opinion, telling outsiders of their exploits did nothing more than reduce their safety. Perhaps it was learned behavior from the barracks or a simple mistrust in humanity, but trusting others beyond the simple, martial trust as a soldier had always been a bad choice in her experience. Yet, the painted warrior seemed unable to keep her private affairs private as she quickly recounted their entire encounter at Veluniate in detail. Though to her benefit, Meala skimmed over the part about Cynna's crucifixion, merely indicating that she had been captured and not going into more detail. That one consideration meant a lot to the archer, yet her dower mood continued to simmer.

"You really took the life of the provisional governor's wife," Julia asked in shock as Meala paused for a sip. Part of her boisterous recounting was cultural and important to her people, yet she was also clearly tired and still quite disturbed by many aspects of her own tale. Still, she continued as a proper Wenech warrior should, speaking of her exploits in the proper boisterous and exaggerated way that such tales were supposed to be spoken. Her enthusiasm sounded a bit forced, perhaps some part of her culture driving her need to explain things, but the entire night felt to

Cynna like a dirty finger pressing into an open wound. She merely glared while Damona kept silent, having finished her second cup of beer.

"Damona held her vile head like an old ewe for the mutton, and it was done with a blade," Meala said, pausing to blink back her own horrible memories, her hands clenching at the thought of the blood and a quick wave of nausea returning, though the beer did a good job of calming her nerves. Her boisterous enthusiasm was hard to maintain, though it was the way of her people to speak of brave deeds in this way. Cynna grimaced as Damona winced at the memory.

"Then it seems that you have earned your gold (the torc)," said Erbin, lifting their cup high in acknowledgment, then taking a sip, followed by Julia and Acilius. Just then, Julia let loose a cheer for Meala, the sort of call one made at a gather hall after a successful boast. Meala smiled while the husbands and Julia laughed, even Damona finding herself smiling amid her displeasure at the memories, her stress and fear numbing as her mind stopped processing the day and night, the beer taking control. Beside them, Cynna nursed her beer, watching Meala and Julia, her mind far from calm. Speaking of these things felt wrong to her, and celebrating such horror made no sense. This was not how her people recounted such tales and to speak of them in such a grandiose way was nearly an affront to her sensibilities. Worse, Meala had ignored her warnings.

"Titus is a fool, and I rejoice that his reign will be shorter than the emperor's cock, especially once more news of his failings passes the Rubicon (a river in Rome), laughed Acilius. Suffering the effects of two mugs of beer on a stomach unused to such alcohol, Damona abruptly spoke, her words slurred and so unlike her typically demure nature.

"Is all the Empire evil? Is everyone so horrible?" At that, Acilius cast her a curious expression, while Cynna suddenly took notice, and everyone else just stared, unsure of what to say.

"You were a slave to the governor's wife, a noblewoman; a high and mighty patrician, even, or so she claimed… miserable cunt. I grew up the son of a leatherworker in Florentia. That's a city north of Roma, far, far south of us," he added, realizing that no one else present would know where that was. "My father was a good man. He never raised his hand to me, my mother, or my sisters. I joined at seventeen to see the world, and here I am. Served in the legion for twenty-five years, too." He turned a thoughtful expression toward Damona while Cynna continued to watch, her expression neutral but her mood quite poor.

The empire you know is the worst of it. The asshole of the bull, and the governor, it's cock. You know the life of a slave and of a woman. Worse, you have spent time around only the legion, some of the roughest of us. If you are a rabbit hunted by wolves, you may not believe me when I tell you that a mother wolf plays with her cubs and loves them as a human mother. She sleeps beside them, licks them clean, and even suckles them. The empire is like a wolf. She spends her day hunting and killing, but she isn't always vicious," he finished, sipping his beer. Damona remained neutral, but Meala could see her tipsy eyes moving slightly as though she were considering Acilius' words.

"I don't like wolves," she said after a moment, then sipped her beer again as a tear ran down her face. At that, Meala reached over and hugged the girl, soothing her as the first bit of her emotional dam began to break. A careful observer, Cynna could see that the girl wasn't a fan of being held, but she was also drunk and far too drained to do more than accept the hug. Damona would take a long time to undo years of learned placidity and timidity, but her first step was simply escaping. Cynna had also escaped – both she and the girl held by different ends of the same Roman chains. Unfortunately, the realization pushed her mood even further into the depths of depression, a feeling she could no longer avoid if she sat here being constantly reminded of the worst parts of life.

"I need to piss," Cynna abruptly spoke, interrupting the conversation a bit more harshly than she had wanted. She couldn't handle any more of this. She took her beer and an oil lamp and stepped to the door, quickly leaving the roundhouse without another word. Between her emotional ordeal, hearing about Rome, a land she despised, and watching Meala bonding with Damona and the locals, Cynna had about as much of the night as she could take. Her emotions were a confused whirlwind of misplaced anger, and she needed to vent before she screamed. Luckily, the warm night breeze felt calming on her skin as she stepped into the small, wooden-fenced yard before the roundhouse.

Meala watched the Sarmatian leave with a sense of loss. They had come so close to a kiss that the very thought of the archer's warm breath against her lips sent tingles through her body. Even now, after everything she had endured and her mind so overwhelmed with the enormity of the night's events that her very spirit begged for rest, the thought of those lips could stir something within her she had only felt once before… six moons before. What had that moment been? Was it the spark of something more or just the result of a woman being pushed to near insanity? Meala shook her head, trying to reorient herself.

"Fuck…" she muttered, her expression drowned out by the sounds of Erbin telling a joke as Julia poured herself another beer. Cynna had been nearly crucified. She had been tied to a cross and humiliated by those men. It didn't look like they had done anything else to her, but how close had Cynna come to being violated? Rape of prisoners was said to be commonplace, as was torture, and lying vulnerable near four men in foul moods at night was a sobering thought. Would having been a former soldier have protected her in any way? Meala doubted it. Had Cynna endured more than Meala had realized? It hadn't looked that way, and the men were still clothed, but such things could be hard to tell, and Meala certainly wasn't going to ask.

The thought of what might have happened, mixed with the memories of the kiss, poisoned the memory. How could she think of Cynna like that when the woman had just been so vulnerable? She had avoided looking at Cynna until the woman was dressed for that reason, and now she would avoid thinking about her in such a way if she could. A wave of shame washed over her, and she quickly drank the rest of her beer, quickly looking to Julia for another. She would be dehydrated tomorrow, but she needed to keep her mind away from such thoughts. *Fuck… fuck… fuck…*

A short time later, Cynna found herself kneeling beneath a sea of stars beside the resting horses, the small oil lamp flickering before her. Her hand hurt where she had fallen to her knees and punched the ground twice, but her emotions seemed to be calming with the wind. The farm dogs had come by shortly afterward and found places to nap beside her, seeming friendly, though she had not tried to pet them. Overhead, she watched as the stars slowly moved across the sky as she whispered a prayer to the matron goddess of the world, Tapeti.

Her father had prayed to the Mother of Fire on behalf of their people when she was a child, as was his right as the son of a high chief. She had often sneaked up to his tent and listened many long nights as he invoked the goddess to learn of safe routes through the steppe. So many long years later, Cynna had invoked the goddess once more as she asked for deliverance from her shackles in the service of Rome. Her emotions raged, fueled by the many horrible things that she had faced.

Did she really like Meala? Did Meala like her? The way the woman looked at her seemed to imply such shared feelings. But, if she did, why did she ignore her warning and tell Julia, her husband, and her pet Roman everything? Why did she comfort Damona but not her? She shook her head, banishing the last of her petulant complaints, knowing full well that Meala had only been comforting the child, and perhaps calling Acilius a pet wasn't fair, but her mind was a twisted tangle of intrusive thoughts and Romans were hardly her favorite people.

"Fucking Roman men…" she breathed. She had started the day with combat on the frontier, then fought and killed a Roman man trying to ravish a woman. She had been beaten for her efforts by Roman men and sentenced to death by another bastard of a Roman man, then nearly nailed naked to a fucking cross, and likely much worse would have followed once she had been completely helpless and at the mercy of yet more piss-drinking fucking Roman men. She had finished her night by killing a dozen Roman men or more as she fled her old life, leaving everything she knew yet again, just as she had as a child. As she considered it, she realized how much she had been through, and that sleep might be her best friend.

Of course, there was still the problem of the spell. Oh, her foolish spell that had likely started all of this. Six months later, she still wasn't sure how to process the signs and events following that invocation. Her words from the spell returned to her as she watched the small oil lamp flame dancing under the cooling night sky, each teasing her mind.

Mother of Fire and creator of all, I tire of these ways... this life. I asked you once for a chance to flee, and you filled my body with hope. I beg you once more, spare me this prison. Pierce my heart with death or warm my spirit with love, but don't leave me as I am. My path is overgrown, and I cannot see the way... Burn my path clear, and I shall sacrifice the life of a worthy warrior in your name. This I swear.

A warrior had pierced her heart, nearly physically and certainly emotionally. Her spirit teetered on the edge of love, but was it shared? Now calmer than she had been, she realized that particular angst had been her tipping point, rational or not. Each piece of the spell had come to pass, and the realization brought with it a new fear. In full defiance of Rome, she had been spared from her prison, both metaphorically at having left Rome's service and literally, having been spared a death sentence. Her path was even burnt clear as the fires had aided in passing the caltrops.

Indeed, her spell seemed to have worked, and she had been delivered from death and Rome's service. The problem was the final part of her spell: the cost. As the Mother of Fire traded oil and wood for light and heat, everything came at a cost. A life spared required a life given, as all must be equal at the end of things. This was why she faced the pain and spirits of the lives she had taken each night when she closed her eyes. This was why every warm season was followed by the cold. Everything had a cost.

I shall sacrifice the life of a worthy warrior in your name. This I swear. She had sworn—an oath to the highest goddess of all—but whom would this worthy warrior be? From within the roundhouse, she heard the sounds of people laughing, and her dower mood deepened with worry. Life was always a give and take, but it was also far too often ironic. Sometimes, she wondered if she would have been better served falling dead by Meala's hands. At least she had been a worthy warrior, and there in lay the problem. Meala was a worthy warrior – worthy of love but also as a sacrifice to the Mother of Fire. *Fuck... fuck... fuck...*

Worse, she didn't even know if Meala was interested in women. The near kiss normally would have been plenty of evidence, but they had both been under extreme emotional stress... and still were, she considered, sardonically. Cynna was more likely to hit a target at one hundred paces with her bow at a full gallop than to have found such a woman. No, she had likely been overcome by the emotion of it all, simply needing human contact to ground herself. Her tears began to flow as she realized that she was in love with someone who would never love her back. No matter how free she might be, love was something not meant for someone like Cynna.

Of course, none of this might matter as Meala seemed to quickly fancy her own kind or at least those of similar culture. Thoughts of Julia and Meala laughing came to mind – thoughts where Cynna was merely a spectator. Their interactions had felt like magic, as though the Hearth Mother had reached into her fires of creation and adjusted the burning coals of the world to spread the warmth of love between them, yet each time they had come together, it had been forced. She had spared Meala, and Meala had spared her, at least from the Romans. They had saved each other, but what did that mean beyond the battlefield? Lying on the cooling ground under a sea of stars, Cynna pretended she had died that fateful night by Meala's spear and let the darkness overcome her as she cried.

Meala lay on a soft pile of fur upon a wooden platform that served as a bed. She had consumed far too much beer, enough to drown away the memories of the blood, death, and worry over objectifying Cynna… not to mention the pain in her body. Julia had treated her arm with wine, honey, and beer bud (Achillea millefolium), and fresh spearwood tree leaves (Fraxinus excelsior) had been placed over this mixture to aid in healing. It wasn't how her mother would have done it, but the eclectic household Julia had cultivated came from three different cultures, and some oddities were to be expected.

As she lay, she smelled the gentle smell of Damona, who lay sleeping in her arms, the pair spooning on their small bed. The girl had tried so hard to keep her emotions hidden, masked behind the facade of an enslaved person used to hiding their humanity from the violence of oppression. But kindness, human touch, and a little beer, finally broke through her mask to reveal a girl who needed to cry. The pair finished talking and drinking, then lay in bed while Damona wept. After a time and a soft, soothing lullaby Meala's mother used to sing her when she was young, Damona had finally quieted and fallen into a deep slumber.

The sounds of wind, creaking wood, and snoring filled Meala with memories of home. The roundhouse was of new construction and only had three beds, one extra large holding Julia and Erbin, who had fancied a little romance before sleep, while the second held a thoroughly drunk Acilius and what she presumed was the guest bed just large enough to hold her and Damona. Sharing a bed with her mother and later her sister when it was cold was commonplace, and Meala had always found the company cozy, so long as her sister didn't get up to pee too often.

While Damona was quiet and quite warm, Meala couldn't help but wonder what it would be like with someone else in her arms. Someone less platonic, someone like Cynna. Her guilt had lessened with beer, but she still felt uncomfortable with the thought. She supposed that the mighty woman had chosen to sleep outside under the stars, as mighty warrior women must. Meala wasn't sure why, but she hoped whatever troubled the woman would pass. Of course, sleeping under the stars was a magical experience, provided one had a dog or two around to alert them if animals, such as wolves, showed up. She wondered if the proverbial wolves of the empire would be so brave as to even approach the sleeping archer.

On the rare days that it became truly warm, Meala's family would lay furs and hides outside and sleep under the stars, especially during festival nights when the large fires were filled with herbs to ward away insects. Living beside the lake, such a practice wasn't always possible due to bite flies (mosquitoes) and nippers (midges) unless the wind was strong enough, but she had done it several times. With thoughts of Cynna, stars, and a belly of beer, Meala drifted into the world of dreams.

☽○☾

Titus Fabius Vibulanus stood before the destroyed remnants of his bed chamber, calming his mind. He had entered only a short time before to find his wife, the most unfortunately named Vita, lying on the floor with her neck slit from one side to the other. Her lifeblood had been sprayed across the wall like unholy graffiti pooling around her form. So much blood had spilled that it had dripped into the storeroom below, prompting a most unfortunate discovery by a servant.

The entire room had been looted and ransacked. Worse, the gold and loot he had been inventorying from the prior month had been taken, as had a few expensive possessions, including the gold torc from a fallen Caledon warrior maiden captured in battle by the second cohort just a month beforehand. The old swine had led her warbands against several trade groups and he had spent significant resources finding her and nailing her up high as an example. But now her torc had been taken and word of this would spread among the natives probably adding to the unrest.

If that wasn't enough, the Dacian woman had escaped and murdered eleven trained soldiers of the second cohort, a centurion among them, nonetheless, and left nine more wounded. If the reports he had heard were accurate, she had been aided by a local tribal woman, probably from northwest of the wall, and possibly a second woman, though the reports were sketchy. Add to that the need to find a new wife, and his night had taken a rather downward turn.

All around lay broken chairs, smashed pottery, and blood. His desk, a well-crafted piece of furniture created in Memphis and delivered painstakingly thousands of miles to this wretched land, now sat at an angle, its finely polished surface scratched and defaced. In fact, the majority of damage to the room was the result of his own rage upon finding the missing gold and the disrespect of his wife slain. His marriage to Vita had been more of a convenience than any act of love, though he still missed her on some level. She had been important to him, at least as a semi-trusted confidante, even if she hadn't properly laid with him in two full years. True love was one of the few privileges of the plebs. For those of the Equestrian and Senatorial classes, marriage was often a tool for some end, be it power or profit.

Moreover, his wife's ornatrix slave (dresser and hair stylist) had vanished. Stranger still, she fit the description of the third woman seen at the gates, though only barely. If she had fled and had any hand in Vita's death, law dictated that every enslaved person of his household should be nailed to a cross, their dozens of screaming forms stretching along the main road to the fort for miles. If he recalled, such had been done to four hundred enslaved men, women, and children after an enslaved person had taken the life of a senator, long ago. He had read the story as a youth and still found such a massive loss of capital unseeming and wasteful.

Of course there was no way Titus could afford such a loss. Even in the slave-rich lands of Brittania, a female slave like the ornatrix had probably cost him 2000 denarii or more, and his full household and those working his immediate lands were probably worth easily a million denarii. His mines held hundreds more enslaved workers, a few dying each month, requiring a constant influx of captured Caledonians to keep production on schedule, the reason he had considered sending the Dacian to work the mines.

He would lay the blame squarely on the Dacian and her tribal accomplice, and avoid any such laws. Regardless of who did it, the violation of his office, both figurative and literal, murder of his wife, and theft of Roman property… his property that he needed to bribe the wheels of power into turning his way, simply could not be allowed to stand. Without that gold, people like Lucius Volusius Maecianus would have their way in the senate and people like Titus would find themselves without a governorship quickly. With a nearly primal growl that faded into a deep, throaty sigh, he opened the door with one blood-soaked hand.

"Fetch the 'Dog' and four of your best men," he spoke softly, sending chills through everyone present. Behind him, the pilus prior, Marcus Quirinalis, dared to ask a question, wishing the actual legatus was not a full fort away to the West.

"My lord, should we not use the Dacian cavalry?" he dared ask. Titus responded in a slow, measured tone, never turning to look the man in the face. Something about his demeanor was more terrifying than if he had reacted in rage. In his current capacity, he was the governor of Britannia, and his word was law. The laws and doctrines that provided him some restraint were tenuous at best this far from the actual senate, and if he chose to make an example of anyone or simply take out his many frustrations, there would be little anyone could do.

"You would send Dacians to hunt one of their own?" The centurion stepped backward almost involuntarily before answering, a bit embarrassed, not to mention worried.

"No... No, my Lord, that would be a foolish thing to do." The centurion and his nervous guards quickly left the door to the room, heading to find their best tracker, a wild woman and former gladiator from the South known as Ci, which apparently meant dog in one of the barbarian tongues. Titus was known for his displeasure of women in arms, and the thought that he would resort to just such a woman to track his enemies underscored his determination. With four of the finest soldiers from the second cohort, Ci and Titus' men would ride out that night searching for the Dacian and whoever helped her. As the centurion departed, Lucious squeezed his hand upon the door frame until his bones ached. When they returned with these women, the punishments would be so severe that the gods themselves would look away in shock.

CHAPTER X

BELOW A SEA OF STARS

Concepts of and attitudes toward LGBTQIA+ people have changed throughout history. For example, Romans had little concept of homosexuality and heterosexuality as distinct modes of sexuality, instead focusing more on the roles of those engaged in sexual activity. Generally, a man was expected to be the dominant actor, while a woman was expected to be subservient. These gender norms were heavily enforced, and those who stepped beyond them faced societal consequences. Homosexual interactions among males are well-attested and considered reasonably commonplace, even among otherwise heterosexual men. Homosexuality among Roman women is scarcely documented, with only a few hints here and there. Of course, this is an extremely simplified view of Roman sexuality, but an important consideration when examining how ancient cultures viewed such subjects.

But what of insular Celtic peoples? What we know of Celtic homosexuality and gender roles comes primarily from several contemporary accounts of homosexuality being widespread and accepted within Celtic society, such as the writings of Athenaeus and Diodorus Siculus. These accounts must be taken skeptically, given the politics and exaggeration often found in ancient texts. They also refer to mainland European Celts, rather than the insular Celts of Caledonia and the Western Atlantic Archipelago. Thus, we are left to speculate that homosexuality may have been culturally normative, but without much evidence either way.

It should be noted that Cynna might very well identify as non-binary (she/they) and sapphic in our modern era, while Meala would likely identify as a cisgender woman (she/her) and lesbian.

The ride the next morning was initially quiet as the party headed northeast and then along the Slow River, the start of the mighty fjord, looking for a place to cross. The first night they had fled west in the same direction as the Wall, a route no one fleeing Rome would be expected to take. Given the meandering streams and detours, their trip was lengthened by remaining close to the water. But the need to walk the horses through the water and mask their tracks was a suggestion Cynna had made, and Meala had, thankfully, followed. Offhandedly, Cynna had wondered if all the women of the painted people were as headstrong as Meala, a quality she found just as irritating as it was endearing, though more the latter than the former, now that she had finally slept.

She had awoken that morning coated in dew and chilled, yet she felt as though the ground had rejuvenated her, calling the death and decay from her spirit into the Earth, where it belonged, and leaving her quite alive. She had nearly felt whole until she had tried to sit up, suddenly remembering what had happened to her body the night before. Her arms, legs, and head hurt, and her neck and arms were darkened with bruises, though her voice was a bit better. Unfortunately, while sleep had worked to heal some of her body and restore a measure of her strength, her mind remained a battlefield, and Meala a mystery.

Julia, Erbin, and Acilius fed them barley porridge with mutton leavings, butter, and salt, roasted mutton, wild strawberries, and water beer – a truly marvelous breakfast. Acilius explained how he had roasted the meat while Julia and Erbin merely listened, smiles barely masked. Of course, Meala had difficulty paying attention as she adjusted her mutton and strawberries into various faces, a silly thing that even brought the hint of a smile to the still dower Cynna. How the warrior could find joy in something so childish as playing with her food after what they had faced the night before, Cynna could not imagine. Yet, Meala's playful ways were hard to resist, though with that realization came the pain of loss as she considered what could never be.

Before they left, Julia gave the travelers some dried and salted mutton for the road, though Meala had tried to convince them not to, as their generosity was far too much for the honor-bound woman to handle. But she had given the woman money to replace what she had lost, and Cynna had saved Julia from a far worse fate. Somewhat amusingly, before they had left, Meala had taken a stack of ten such gold coins from her small chest and left them beside their door as a secret thank you. It was another example of her caring nature, the sort of woman who looked out for others, be they missing coin, a runaway enslaved person, or about to be executed. One more reason Cynna had trouble getting the Caledonian from her mind.

As the morn had become high sun, the party had paused for a small break. Cynna had kept her eye on Meala for any signs of the woman's intentions, yet she seemed somewhat aloof, speaking more pragmatically than personally and trying her best to speak to a mostly silent Damona. Cynna couldn't deny that Meala's efforts to help the formerly enslaved girl were admirable, a task she probably could not have done, much of her softness made rough and rigid like leather under the weather. Off in the distance strode a grey wolf, its warm-season coat making it look much less impressive than it usually did. For a moment, she watched the creature, feeling a bit of kinship with the predator.

Her emotions were still a complex jumble, and she still had more questions than answers. After six months of wondering, the painted warrior was finally here, yet she still had no real understanding of the woman's disposition toward her. She had seemed so interested as they had made eye contact following her rescue from the cross, nearly exchanging a kiss, yet she had seemed to lose interest as soon as they were free from the Fort, now giving Cynna a nearly cold shoulder. She should never have expected anything more than this, she supposed. She wasn't even sure if Meala liked women, let alone her, though it was hard to ignore the near kiss. Her mind spun in circles as the horses walked across the foreign landscape, Cynna's destination and future unknown.

As the day became eve, they happened on a gully, Cynna's thoughts traveling further than her horse, yet going nowhere. Unlike her, Meala was soft, like well-oiled suede. She had proven herself worthy as a warrior by thrice facing soldiers in what should have been unwinnable situations and by facing her death at Cynna's hands with honor and bravery, twice, yet these moments of blood and death had not broken her nor made her rough. Even now, Cynna watched as Meala playfully folded grass with her fingers to make little dolls, something that seemed to entertain Damona. How she could be so filled with happiness after what had happened, Cynna couldn't imagine… like a single, bright poppy flower growing in a dead field of sorrow. The passing thought that she had nearly taken the joyful woman's life six months before brought with it the pressure and warmth to her face that preceded tears.

She supposed it was best that she would never find someone like the painted warrior, as her glum, serious, and often brooding nature would probably smother such a beautiful flower. Just to her side, she watched as Meala and Damona enthusiastically offered their grass dolls to their horse to consume. As soon as the horse ate the dolls, Meala burst into laughter, her playful personality infectious. Even Damona smiled, though just a little, her outward emotions quite guarded. Meala's laughter was high-pitched, nearly chirpy, almost like a fox. Cynna frowned as she felt herself coming close to joining in, yet quickly rode ahead. She couldn't allow herself to become too wrapped up in what could never be, so with a few deep breaths to stifle any wayward tears, she focused on the path ahead.

As the day grew late and the sky turned a beautiful red hue, Cynna continued to ponder Meala, her future, where she would go, and what she would do when the Mother of Fire finally demanded payment for her freedom. Her goddess demanded a worthy warrior, be it her own life, assuming she even counted as worthy at this point, or another. Who would be the worthy warrior that she must sacrifice?

"Are we resting now?" Damona asked as their horse came to a stop. The girl looked around, staring blankly for a time, as she seemed to do so often. Meala understood this behavior because the lengthy ride had been quiet and boring and because she had found herself blankly staring many times following the raid six moons before. Sometimes, her mind had simply disengaged from life and disappeared into unwanted memories. She didn't know if her experience was the same for Damona, but it certainly seemed so. Of course, her favorite activity was disappearing into her imagination, though that only worked if she was not too depressed.

"Yeah, I think so. I think this is about as much cover as we will find," she said, pointing at the gully. Meala had nearly made better time walking when she had journeyed to the Fort several days before. The packhorse couldn't carry her, Damona, and the loot for the entire day, nor did most folks wish to ride all day, aside from Cynna, who seemed born in a saddle. Thus, the horses moved slowly and at least one person walked most of the way, taking turns. Luckily, the night was clear, as rain would be dreadful even when still warm.

"Wouldn't the forest be better? Less wind?" Damona asked, drawing a smile from Meala. The girl was not a local and seemed to have no knowledge of the world beyond the stone walls of her late Domina.

"Forests are not safe at night. Wolves, boar, and daru'benen (tree spirits) all roam. Well, some daru'benen can be friendly, I think... I have seen some before deep in the wood, but I've never gotten a good look at one. If we had the company of a druid or a larger group, we would be safe, but we do not. No, we should sleep by the gully," she replied, drawing a slight shudder from Damona, though which of the named creatures of the wood most shook the girl, she could not say. Of course, the forest had also been the source of endless warm season days imagining fanciful spirit creatures when Meala was a child, but at night, the real spirits came out.

The usually westerly winds now blew from the South, a natural mercy that left the small gully they now approached shielded. To the East, just over the natural rise in the land, lay a small pond on the leeward side, an unusual configuration. Meala dismounted, a bit better than the night before, then turned to help Damona down. They quickly removed their few possessions, handed the reins to Cynna, and headed down the small slope to examine their night's accommodation. The archer's body language suggested that she had not invited questions.

Meala watched as Cynna led the horses over the hill to the pond where they might drink fresh water and graze. They would need the horses fresh tomorrow if they were to head north. As she left, Meala's gaze followed, worry across her brow. Meala could still feel the heat from Cynna's lips, a memory she savored like spring water in the Sun, so close yet unquenched. But, was Cynna even the sort of woman who liked women? The near kiss seemed like pretty strong evidence, yet the woman had been under immense emotional strain, and such pressure could do a lot to one's mind. Unfortunately, Cynna's poor mood and self-ostracism the night before had told Meala that she needed space, so space she would have.

She had given Cynna the entire day of privacy to come to terms with whatever pained her spirit. She had made her pain evident the night before between her dower mood and sudden need to sleep outside. Contrary to nosey Julia, most of her people believed in privacy, and her desire to comfort the warrior was only barely offset by her cultural need to let the woman be until she indicated that she wanted help. She sighed as she watched Cynna walk away, her slightly bowed legs showing the tiniest limp from the day before.

"Honeybee…" Cynna mumbled as she finished removing Tamura's saddle and gear as depression began to roll in, just like the thin layer of reddish clouds on the western horizon. The name was cute and endearing, just like the rest of the playful Caledonian, making her present situation so much worse. She had hoped to find love and freedom, yet Meala, the woman of her thoughts for half a year, had all but stopped interacting with her. The bee had flown away. At this point, she had little left but her horse, armor, and two bows, so keeping them in good shape was a priority, especially if they needed to make a run for it. Besides, Cynna was hardly the flower to attract a bee, her body muscular, rough, and almost a head taller than Meala. Her mind seemed to remain tactical, and her soldier instincts at the ready, no matter how dower she felt.

Back at the barracks, she had left 347 denarii, 12 aurei, a necklace she had worn as a child made from carnelian, sard, and amber beads, and a relief depicting two women warriors she had been given by Dotos of Korda, a man in her unit who traded the relief to pay off a small gambling debt to her that the betting man would never have the coin for. He had said that he had witnessed a magnificent duel between two women in the arena at Halicarnassus, in a land to the South, and had traded 24 denarii for the memento. The items had been left under the care of her unit's signifier, though she would never see any of it again. Memories of the relief immediately brought back the sight of Meala standing at the entry to the small garden, shield in one hand and spear in the other. She had been like a warrior of the arena that day, not just a stone memory.

In truth, Cynna had little else she could do aside from heading north and starting a new life among the strange painted people. She couldn't return to the legion, nor would she be safe if she headed south. The

Romans would surely send word of her down their lines, and she would become a fugitive in their lands. The North was a peculiar and barbarous land, and aside from a few trade routes and small frontier forts, it was free of Roman influence, mostly. It was also the painted warrior's home… Meala's home.

If she had understood what little she had picked up from Meala, Julia, and Damona's conversation in Latin, only slightly worse than hers, the warrior had rescued the girl from Titus Fabius Vibulanus' wife, Vita. Worse, they had killed Vita and stolen plenty of gold and silver from the man. For such offense, she expected Vita's death would be a driving force behind any pursuit. Of course, it was no secret that Titus' hold on power was weak. Hence the reason II Legion sent a full cohort north from their headquarters. She hoped that the fledgling governor, or ipso facto tyrant, might be left in too distraught or politically precarious of a position to bother with more than a few short-ranged search parties, mostly to appease sensitivities.

Feeling glum, she deposited her gear and the saddle beside a bush where she figured nobody would notice and began spreading Tamura's horse blanket on the ground to sleep. She would leave the painted warrior and Damona alone once more, as her presence was clearly not desired. She had won her freedom and had to accept that for the boon it was. Staying away from Meala also meant reducing the chance that her goddess would desire the painted warrior as her worthy payment when that time came. Besides, if she had to sleep beside her, she might simply give in and try to kiss her once more. Cynna grumbled.

"Here, drink some wine too," Meala said, handing Damona the wineskin and a few pieces of salted mutton. Some of the meat had been flavored with honey, something Julia hadn't mentioned but was certainly welcome. Damona took her piece and began nibbling on the salty-sweet treat while Meala licked her sticky fingers clean. The darkness of a new day was quickly approaching, and Meala had gathered what little wood she could find near the gully, mostly driftwood from the river, and started a small fire for warmth and light.

"May I speak?" Damona asked a moment later, her eyes averted. Meala sighed, the knowledge that the girl's unwillingness to even speak unbidden was the result of her enslavement, a practice she had never accepted as correct, even though her own people were known to do it, filled her heart with sadness. What if a slaver had come by their farm and snatched Rig or Brynen, carrying them away to some other clan to become captive for the rest of their lives? The idea was awful, and thankfully not one her parents had ever considered, though she had seen enslaved people sold at the Stone before.

"You may always speak, now and forever. You do not need to ask anyone anymore," Meala said, hoping to make the girl's life a little easier, though Damona continued to look forlorn. But, after a moment, she cleared her throat and spoke, clutching the wineskin and fumbling with its soft exterior.

"Where will I go after all of this? I have no one." Needing to keep herself from tearing up, Meala took back the wineskin for a sip, then returned it to Damona with a mournful smile, the wine aiding her relaxation, if only a little.

"There's more than enough room at my family's house. If you are willing to help around the farm, I'm sure you could live with us. I don't speak for our house, but my mother is a good woman who wouldn't turn her back on someone in need." Damona lifted her head to briefly match gazes with the painted warrior, her eyes framed with a strange mix of fear and hope. Without another word, she simply nodded her approval, having no other options and finding the idea of such an arrangement to her liking. Meala shuddered to think what had caused the girl to be so shy, though she was pretty sure she knew. For a time, they were silent with only the sound from the fire and the chewing of dried meat.

With the problem of what to do about Damona possibly figured out, Meala turned her attention to Cynna, the warrior from the East. On the surface, she had felt a deep attraction for the woman ever since she had laid eyes upon her on the battlefield. She had recognized her beauty at first sight, but she hadn't considered that much in the face of the terror of battle, only realizing it when reflecting on those memories. It had been as she lay on her back at the mercy of the mighty woman's bow later that night that she had really felt the longing. Sure, it had also been terrifying and still haunted her memories, and yet all that she had wanted at that moment was to throw down their weapons and kiss Cynna. Perhaps these were her later thoughts mixed with her memories. But, on a basic, primal level, she had felt such an impulse, incongruous or not.

Of course, this was a surface-level attraction. As her mother had often said, a metal plow may look shiny and beautiful when new, but it could break if not well made. What mattered was who a person was inside, though Cynna's well-defined physique and commanding prowess were hardly a bad addition. Meala paused, considering what she really knew about the woman. She was strong of will but seemed to have a calm personality, even in battle. She was also brave and willing to make her own choices, even at the cost of her life. Even though she was a disciplined warrior, she had spared Meala, showing compassion and empathy for her enemy. That last part felt most important to Meala, as knowing how to swing an ax was just as important as knowing when not to.

Her mother had tried so many times to pair her with local men she knew nothing of, other than vague references she had heard of them growing up. Her mother had explained that love could be a complicated journey, but it could also be a sudden and unexpected find. Of course, she was trying to encourage Meala to go man-hunting, but she wasn't necessarily wrong. Life was short, and making the best you could with what time you had before that time ran out was essential. Still, she wished that she knew more about Cynna. Her current state of giving the woman ample room and not prying into whatever bothered her made learning more about her... difficult.

What foods did she like? Did she have a family? Did she even like women? After they had exchanged looks, their eyes holding each other far longer than a woman might normally do so with another woman, and the near kiss... yeah, the more she thought about it, the more likely it seemed that Cynna had an attraction to women, at least to some degree. Why did attraction between women have to be so complicated? Growing up, Meala was always quite aware when a local boy liked her. Yet it could be nearly impossible to tell if a woman was being nice or flirting, or both. With a frown, she swallowed the last of her small meal and took a swig of wine.

She wanted to know more about the warrior, but she remained a mystery like an arrow fired into the sea – not far away, but almost impossible to reach. Even simple things like her tattoos were a mystery. When she had rescued the Dacian, she had seen beautiful and intricate tattoos covering her body, but she had been so focused on not dying at the time that she had not gotten a good look at them. Besides, gawking when she was in such a vulnerable situation, even if innocently looking at tattoos, had felt wrong. Cynna's slightly darker skin and thinner tattoo lines didn't help, either. In fact, she still didn't even know what the woman's name meant.

"Honeybee," Meala abruptly said, causing Damona to pause her eating in confusion and start looking about as though such an insect might be present. Meala suppressed a giggle at the girl's confusion.

"My name means Honeybee," Meala said, explaining what her name meant, though the wording wasn't entirely correct. Meala only used Latin occasionally when traders from the South came by their farm or the Stone. She had learned from her mother, who spoke it fluently from her childhood south of the wall and had encouraged her children to learn as a matter of utility. Still, there were so many words she didn't know, and it was far too easy to make a mistake.

"Nominis est mel'apia," Meala said, which actually translated to something like, "the name is the honeybee," but was close enough to "apis mihi nomen est," that Damona understood.

"What does your name mean?" she asked Damona. Normally quiet, the girl seemed to be opening up to friendly questioning, perhaps a side effect from people expressing a genuine interest in her wellbeing, a drastic change from her previous life in the fort.

"Damona was my first aunt's name. She died when my mother was young, and she gave me the name in her memory. If I ever have a child, they will have my mother's or father's names. It is a long tradition we use to honor those we have lost," she explained, looking mournful as the bright flash of interest lit and faded in her eyes. Far from an exuberant conversation, the mood had darkened slightly, almost imperceptibly. Meala felt sad for the girl but hoped her parents would honor her offer to let Damona live with them. It was the least they could do. With that, she leaned back against the soft grassy hillside and let her mind drift.

Meala wondered what Cynna's name meant, something she would ask the woman when she returned. Probing was rude, but perhaps just asking her that question would be acceptable. Oddly enough, Cynna had not returned, though it had been quite some time since she had left with the horses. Damona spoke between chews as if having the same thought or perhaps simply noticing Meala's sudden frown.

"Where is Cynna?" Meala had cared for her family's single horse since childhood and was no stranger to such work taking time. She had initially set up camp as she waited for the warrior to unsaddle and maybe even brush Tamura and their pack horse, though it had been quite some time and Meala was growing concerned.

"Are you angry with her?" Damona asked, her question confusing Meala. She put down the piece of meat she had been setting aside for Cynna and turned a curious glance at the quiet but perceptive girl.

"Of course not. What makes you say such a thing?"

"You have said almost nothing to her since she got mad last night. I wondered if you had spoken or even fought, but I have been near each of you since we left the fort, and I never saw you fight. Did you tell her you like her, and she got mad?" she asked. Meala's face turned redder than the fire.

"What… I never said that I like her," she nearly coughed out.

"But you do, right? You look at her like you do," Damona continued as Meala stared, mouth open but unable to disagree. It seemed that a mixture of her words of encouragement and perhaps a few heavy gulps of wine had loosened Damona's tongue.

"And she likes you too," Damona added.

"She what? How do you…"

"It is how she looks at you when you are not looking. But I have seen it. Is that why she is angry and why you do not speak to her?" Damona finished. Meala wanted to spit back a witty reply or deny Damona's claim, but she did, in fact, like Cynna. But was the perceptive girl correct that Cynna liked her too? Wine was certainly no friend to Damona, but the girl had a point and Cynna's dower mood might explain why she had not returned.

Anyone of her people would know exactly what she was doing: giving proper and polite room for Cynna to heal, as the woman was clearly distressed. Meala had only ignored that rule for Damona because she was so young, and her silent behavior cried out for intervention. But Cynna was not some child; she was an honorable woman, and honor dictated privacy, the same reason her father had not bothered Meala about her experience at the raid even though it had troubled him.

"She is upset and needs to heal. It would be wrong to bother her about such matters," she replied after a moment, unsure of her own words. Damona swallowed the last of her meat, licking her fingers before speaking again. She took what was probably her fifth swig of the wineskin, her eyes starting to look a little glossy from the alcohol.

"That is not what the Romans do. They never leave each other alone. Domina would bother other women until they told her whatever she wanted to know. I don't remember how my people were, but your people's ways seem better," she finished, taking another sip of the tart wine. *My people's ways*, Meala thought, considering what the girl said. Cynna had said to keep their adventure a secret at Julia's, but she had also worried that Julia and her husbands would steal from them. A sinking sensation overcame Meala as she realized what might be happening.

"Fox piss..." she exclaimed, drawing a confused expression from Damona, who didn't understand Meala's native tongue but did understand a curse when she heard it, at least by tone.

"What if her people are different from mine? What if they have strange ways and I have been ignoring her? She will think I am angry with her..." Meala concluded, her mind suddenly pondering the plurality of cultures in a way she never had. She had lived her entire life around one culture and one way of doing things, and never had she considered just how alien Cynna's culture might be. She grabbed the wineskin and took a gulp, then a second that she swished and spit. Knocking over the meat rations and drawing a perplexed look from Damona, Meala leapt to her feet and rushed toward the other side of the gully.

⚹

Cynna's hand reached for the dagger beside her blanket as she rolled sideways and onto her knees. By the time that sleep had banished enough for her brain to fully engage, she realized that she had Meala's head held by the hair with her left hand and the dagger to the woman's neck with her right. The next thing she realized was that she was breathing hard, and her heart was pounding. She had been in another of her nightmares, and the sound of footsteps and the touch of a hand on her shoulder had been unfortunately timed with the imagery in her dreams.

"We should stop meeting this way," Meala whispered, her expression sheepish.

"Mother of Fire, I nearly paid my debt," she gasped in her native language. Meala remained still as she knelt beside her on the edge of the horse blanket, eyes wide and mouth slightly open. Her own heart beat so hard that Cynna could feel it against the dagger.

"Perhaps I should leave?" she asked without moving a muscle other than her lips. Cynna shook herself and released Meala, lowering her blade. A wave of shame passed over her at such a reaction, but she had twice found a man in the barracks trying to creep into her bed and had developed a penchant for sleeping lightly. She quickly sheathed the lengthy blade trying to look away from the Caledonian, yet finding the action difficult.

"I... I am sorry. You just startled me is all... I..." she began but stopped when Meala smiled, her face grounding the warrior. How could a smile fill her with such calm? For that matter, how could a woman who just had a blade to her throat smile so readily, at the woman who held the blade, none-the-less? They both remained still for a moment, each kneeling on the horse blanket below a sea of stars as a small sheet of clouds rolled by. The day was nearly set and the fading light dimmed almost by the moment, a new day on the edge of life.

"I'm sorry, too," Meala said after a moment. At Cynna's puzzled look, she smiled once more, filling the archer with warmth once again as she began to explain herself.

"Yesterday, you seemed bothered. I didn't know what was wrong, but it isn't something one asks about," she explained. Cynna listened, but her face continued to register confusion, partly because of the cultural differences and partly because she was still calming herself from her nightmare and what had nearly become of it. Wishing to cut through the startled warrior's distressed and confused look, Meala adopted her best elder druid voice, lifting a single finger, and began to speak.

"A person's privacy is to be respected. We don't pry into each other's affairs. This is what the druids and elders teach," Meala explained, then lowered her finger, continuing in her normal voice. "It's what my mother taught me." Meala paused for a moment, her fingers now casually playing with the long grass beside the blanket.

"When I saw that you were upset, I gave you space. But now… now I think maybe that was not right. Maybe that isn't how your people live?" she explained. Cynna's confused frown began to soften as she realized what Meala was saying. Had Meala merely been avoiding her because of some odd custom? Meala waited for her to respond, clearly trying to be polite. Cynna was hardly a wordsmith, but not speaking seemed to have caused much of this mess, so she took a chance.

"I saw you speaking with Julia and holding Damona, but you wouldn't speak to me. I thought that…" but Cynna paused. Just what did she think? Meala didn't seem romantically interested in Julia, and Damona was just a child, even if she was close to adulthood. Cynna's thoughts had been erratic and not logical, and they continued to be. She had lived a rigid, defined life for the last seven years, but everything had just been turned upside down. She had hardened herself to withstand legionary life, but what had she given up by doing so? This wasn't orderly and the feelings she was navigating were chaotic.

She was like a rider on a horse with no reins, arms dangling wild and free in the wind as the steed galloped along, heedless. Cynna couldn't focus and control her emotions because she couldn't find anything solid enough in her world to hold on to. But as she knelt there searching for words to finish her sentence, Meala's soft, green eyes and kind smile felt inviting. If only she could reach forward and take hold of the reins, but fear held her back. What if Meala didn't feel the same way? It frightened her how afraid she was of losing something that she really didn't even have.

Women were infuriatingly difficult to understand, sometimes. It wasn't the same with men. A man left little mistake of his intentions. Even if he tried to be nice, his interest would easily be detected as his eyes wandered, often followed by hands. But with a woman, things could be so much more complicated. Women could seem quite flirty and turn out to be just nice. A woman's closeness could be romantic or platonic; even wandering eyes didn't necessarily mean anything but could mean everything. And what if she made a…

"May I ask you a question?" Meala asked, interrupting her spiraling thoughts. Cynna blinked, embarrassed by her pause yet unsure what else to say. The auburn-haired woman's friendly eyes gazed back with blatant anticipation while her fingers continued to play with the grass, her body never seeming to sit still for more than a moment. ADHD would not be understood for millennia, but Meala's hyperactive nature was hardly a problem. Cynna said nothing, her spiraling mind pausing as she considered what the Caledonian had said, but Meala just asked, anyway.

"What is your favorite animal?" Meala said, her smile springing to life with the anticipation of this somehow important fact. That was certainly not what she had hoped the woman would ask. Cynna frowned, unsure of the quirky woman's motivation, but answered.

"The Eagle. It flies high… and free," she said, now so confused by the segway that she had no idea what to do but reply.

"What's yours?" she added, seeing the almost infectious smile on the Caledonian's face, obviously keen on being asked.

"Probably a fox. They are small, fast, and cute," Meala said, her fingers now playing absently with the loose fringe on the blanket. *Just like you…* Cynna thought as she watched her, realizing Meala had some deeper questions on her mind, and the entirely non-sequitur animal question had probably been meant to warm up to her real query. How she could be so friendly, caring, and warm after the horrors they had faced and having just had a dagger put to her throat, Cynna couldn't say, but she couldn't seem to look away from the painted woman.

"May I ask you another?" Meala asked, and Cynna nodded, not wanting this to go on because it was dangerous, yet unable to do anything but walk willingly into the jaws of death.

"Why did you spare my life? I tried to kill you and nearly did." If she had been stunned before, it was nothing compared to how she now felt as her mind decoded the Latin and understood the gravity of what Meala had just asked her. How often did two enemies... or perhaps former enemies... get to ask each other such metalogical questions as why? It was nearly surreal, yet Meala had asked just that and Cynna knew that she owed the woman a response.

"You are a warrior, and so am I. You tried to take my life as I would have taken yours. But what honor is there in killing a wounded warrior who has proven her bravery? I wouldn't have left you for the Romans, either," she said, her expression darkening at the last thought. There had been a dozen crucified after the raid, yet another horror she would never forget. But as she blinked back the nightmare, she found those same wide eyes watching her, without judgment.

"Besides, you were right... this is your land. How can I kill those fighting for their land with honor and still call myself honorable? I asked if you would swear a dishonorable oath, and you would not. That is the answer of a worthy warrior," she replied, speaking the truth, though her eyes began to wet at the thought. A worthy warrior, indeed. A lump grew in her throat as pressure and warmth around her face spoke of tears threatening to burst free. Meala's honor and the cost of her spell continued to haunt her thoughts. It was why she couldn't bring herself to be more assertive or even open to Meala about her amorous thoughts. It was like a dark secret that she couldn't seem to let go of.

Go... just leave before I... she thought, but the fucking always cheerful woman would not leave. She had put a blade to her neck, a boot in her face, and an arrow in her chest, yet she knelt there staring at Cynna like she was the last beautiful flower in the world. All she wanted to do was take the Caledonian into her arms but holding her would directly cross the will of her goddess. Her mind fumbling in the face of the greatest temptation she had ever felt, she asked the first question that came to her mind in response.

"Why did you save me from the cross? You did not know of my crime. I might have earned those nails, but you faced four men to save me, then four more," Cynna asked, and now Meala was on the spot. The painted warrior frowned as though Cynna had said something absurd, her hands now firmly on her hips as she knelt before the Dacian.

"Because no one deserves to die that way. Death of an enemy is the way of things, but the cross is torture and humiliation. No one deserves that. Besides, what honor is there in letting fools take the life of a worthy foe? A worthy warrior must be faced and bested in single combat. Only a coward kills as the Romans," Meala replied, mirroring Cynna's words. Both were silent momentarily as Cynna considered what she had heard. The strange chirping of a quail rang out in the distance, followed by what might have been a seagull off to the East. Cynna closed her eyes for a moment, summoning her courage to continue. How she had gone from sleeping alone and feeling defeated to her heart fluttering as she shared her inner secrets with Meala, she couldn't say, but her body told her to keep talking even if her mind hesitated.

"You have haunted my memories since that night, Sei'ln Meala, daughter of Ail Braide," Cynna said, now locking eyes with Meala. There was a challenge in her stare, a stare driven by deep, primal instincts that cared little for social, cultural, or rational things, nor the will of gods. Every part of her rational mind told her not to continue. Her spell, aching body, and emotional turmoil… but she was tired of the emotional whirlwind and uncertainty. She needed to know where she stood with Meala, and she was going to find out.

"As you have haunted mine, Cynna of Dacia, of the Iazyges. We are bound by a thread between here and the Otherworld. Perhaps because we shared mortality or some other powerful will," Meala said, matching Cynna's gaze and challenge. Unconsciously, Cynna's body moved ever so slightly closer as their verbal and cultural languages were overcome by the most basic of human communication: body language. Yet before they could grow closer, Cynna shook her head, breaking the stare. What she was doing was… was… dangerous. She could barely keep herself from giving in to her most natural of feelings.

"No, you are right, and that is the problem. I… I can't…" she said, looking away. Meala grew frustrated, her need to understand the problem and help Cynna finally overpowering her cultural need to give the woman privacy.

"What does that mean? If there is something, then you must say it. There is no honor in hiding secrets when they affect others," Meala blurted, instantly feeling like she had overstepped her bounds, yet driven by a mixture of frustration and the empathetic need to help Cynna. The earlier silence returned for a moment as the Sarmatian gathered herself, the gravity of the moment starting to weigh heavily on both women as they awaited speaking and hearing that which had been unsaid – the secret.

"The night we first met in battle, I cast a spell asking the Mother of Fire," she began but paused, noting that Meala seemed confused by the goddess invoked. "Tapeti, the Mother of Fire. She is the supreme goddess of fire, fertility, and the hearth, but you probably know of her by another name as she has as many names as there are blades of grass," she added for clarity. Meala glanced down at the grass she was fidgeting and Cynna felt another wave of sorrow. Everything Meala did was so thoughtful and liminal, yet the gravity of what she was about to say would drive the woman away, forever. A lump formed in her throat as she began to explain what she had done and why they needed to stay far from each other.

"I cast a powerful spell asking her to release me from the Romans. I asked her to bring me love or pierce my heart. In exchange, I offered to sacrifice the life of a worthy warrior in her name." Meala stared for a moment, unsure why this was a problem, but Cynna had no patience and spat it out, "… don't you see? You are a worthy warrior. The Mother of Fire will demand a worthy warrior, and you are the only worthy warrior I know. I cannot sacrifice you, and when she asks me to, I will be consumed as punishment as I will not harm you… because… I…" Meala stared, waiting for Cynna to finish, but the Dacian's eyes were now wet with tears. The already oft quiet woman looked down, swallowing hard, clearly unable to finish.

"Quia te amo…" (Because I love you…) Meala finished, whispering the words as she felt her own eyes growing wet. Like an arrow loosed, once said, the words could never be taken back. Each woman had struck the other in the chest with a weapon, and now both of their chests ached not from war, but from peace and love.

"You would give up your life after losing everything else just to spare mine once more, and you hardly know me. It makes no sense, but I understand. It feels like we are connected and it has since we met," Meala said. Cynna looked up, her eyes swollen and tears rolling down her face, but her pained, frank expression of understanding and mutual agreement didn't need words. But then, Meala frowned, whispering the words back to herself once, once more, and a third time, the blades of grass she pinched between her nimble fingers twitching faster and faster as she began to contemplate something. Cynna looked on, not understanding the sudden shift from what had been a devastatingly bittersweet confession but was suddenly punctuated by Meala's growing confusion… wait, suddenly growing smile.

"You fool… you brave, beautiful, fool…" Meala whispered, grass tumbling from her fingers, forgotten as she came to a realization. But before Cynna could react, the painted warrior's face became supremely animated, a smile spreading from side to side and tears of sorrow suddenly turning to motes of joy.

"Do you not realize? You were a warrior! A worthy warrior, of Rome! The only worthy warrior of Rome I have ever met, nor heard of!" Cynna frowned, sniffing back tears and not understanding. Though she was so distraught that her ability to process Latin was slipping, she concentrated, trying to follow Meala's chittery speech, the Caledonian having only the vaguest idea how to conjugate a verb.

"You said Tapeti is a goddess of fertility, right? Julia is pregnant, and the man you saved her from could have caused harm to the unborn child. You sacrificed yourself to save Julia and her unborn child. As a warrior, you gave up your life to defend your goddess' main concern, fertility. Cynna… you have fulfilled the bargain! That is why she has not asked for a sacrifice, don't you see?" Meala concluded. For a moment, Cynna knelt there, processing what she had just heard from Latin to her own tongue, then against the facts.

"I shall sacrifice the life of a worthy warrior in your name." No doubt, Meala was a worthy warrior, and she had bestowed the same honor upon Cynna. She had, both metaphorically and literally, sacrificed her career and even her life when she had attacked the optio, a risk she had willfully taken when she had stood to intervene. Besides, the Mother of

Fire was as much a creator as a destroyer, and why pay Cynna for her many years of devotion with betrayal? She didn't want to hope it was true and kept looking for the flaw in the argument, but her mind quickly realized the truth of Meala's simple logic: She had been freed, and her debt had been paid. That was why Tapeti had never demanded payment.

There was nothing keeping her from love, but her own fear, and Cynna was not a fan of fear. As she looked on, she saw the woman who had lived in her thoughts for half a year, the woman she had been unable to forget since they had first made eye contact on the battlefield. They had saved each other, and now they were both free to simply live, and to do so boldly was the only way Cynna knew how.

Meala wasn't quite sure why she did it, as her conscious mind had little to do with her next action, but she lifted her hand and placed it tenderly against Cynna's emotionally compromised face, instantly feeling the archer's warmth beneath her fingers. Cynna's head leaned into her hand, as though it was the only warmth left in the world, her body instinctually acting and betraying her deeper, inner thoughts. Her eyes drifted from her fingers back to Cynna only to find that the fear, sorrow, and confusion her hazel eyes held was now much softer, changing into something more akin to shocked relief and maybe even expectation, if not overt want.

Quia te amo... the words had been short, simple, and carried more power than an entire legion. Perhaps it was a warrior's brevity or their deepest nature, not requiring more than three words, but Meala had no intention of speaking anymore. Tenderly, she bent forward until their lips were but a finger's length apart, just as they had been the night before. She once more felt the warmth of Cynna's breath against her lips calling to her like cernen (horns) on a festival night. Also like a festival night, motes of excitement and anticipation danced through her body as she stood upon the precipice of something new and exciting.

Meala had only kissed one person before, at least romantically. She had not even been intimate with anyone before the bathhouse. She had no real idea what would happen next, nor if she should go further, but her body all but cried out for the warmth of another. There was something so right, so natural about this act. Seeing that same look of confusion, subtle fear, and oh-so-deep longing in Cynna's eyes, she surrendered to her primal instincts and simply let her body guide her, completing the memory started the day before.

Time seemed to slow as their lips came together. Cynna was warm, and her lips were soft… so soft, like a honeybee landing on her skin. A moment later, Cynna's strong arm gently wrapped around her, drawing Meala closer as their kiss continued. After a moment, their lips parted, and they stared into each other's eyes, seeing the same shock and joy. For the first time in far too long, both of their minds had become entirely calm and liminal. They were warriors living in the moment, the previous day's events having reminded them of why life needed to be lived and not feared. With a gentle push, their lips met again, then again as kiss after kiss sent waves of ecstasy through their bodies. They were equals, their bodies both strong, prowess proven in battle, and their honor intact. They had faced each other, respected each other, and now loved each other.

"Come," Cynna spoke, barely enunciating the word as she softly drew Meala's body down to lie beside her on the horse blanket. As though gasping for air while underwater, Meala returned her lips to Cynna, feeling an almost intoxicating wave as they coupled once more. But then, she felt pressure against her lips as Cynna's tongue pushed against her delicate skin, a desire no words needed to speak. Meala relaxed, letting the soft tongue press into her, cautiously probing at first but quickly gaining confidence. Meala simply let go, letting the larger woman explore as she would, the feeling of intimacy, vulnerability, and erotic expression making her body weak as Cynna's tongue probed. A moment later Meala found herself lying on her back, her arms lying uselessly to her sides as Cynna wrapped one leg over her, mounting the Caledonian with the skill of someone used to riding.

The Sarmatian lifted herself until she was upright, straddling Meala. She quickly unbuttoned her long kaftan shirt, tossing it aside, then fumbled with her tunic. Meala watched as the magnificent woman tore off the belt holding the previously slit garment together and peeled it away, revealing a body that could have been chiseled from stone. Her upper body had nearly the muscle definition of a young man in his prime, and her cloth-bound breasts and soft skin gave her a distinctly feminine shape Meala could barely look away from.

A lifetime of holding her body on a horse with only her core and leg muscles of her legs and drawing a powerful bow had left Cynna's body openly muscular, and Meala's body became weak upon seeing the mighty warrior straddled atop her. Her arms lay aside, her body entirely open to the warrior, body language making her consent as clear as the sky. The mighty woman gazed down upon her with such reverence that it nearly took Meala's breath away. When she found it once more, her breaths came in deep, warm gasps as she lay back. Cynna gently touched Meala's tunic, indicating the garment should be discarded, a sentiment Meala fervently shared.

Meala could hardly take her eyes off the archer long enough to loosen her belt and remove her own bulky tunic, but ended up needing Cynna's help – and help she did, her upper body strength more than enough to raise Meala's body as she wiggled from her tunic. A moment later, they were kissing again, their lips having been apart far too long. Meala nearly gasped as she felt their skin touch, so warm under the cool, humid night air. It was like nothing she had ever felt and so vital she could hardly believe it was real.

Just then, she felt Cynna's hand grasp her linen strophium, the lengthy, narrow band of cloth she had wrapped around her breasts. Cynna had a similar garment, and they remained the final barrier between their upper bodies. Meala felt as if she had consumed a mug of beer, as the warmth in her body rose with the prospect of their intimacy. Perhaps even more wonderful was the tingle of pleasure rising between her legs as her body cried out for more. But Cynna paused her hand on the strophium cloth. Meala opened her eyes, her mouth open and her want growing.

"We cannot undo what comes," Cynna spoke, her Latin barely making it past her lips as she breathed deeply. Meala was obviously not the only one having trouble thinking clearly.

"We can never undo… [moan] what we have done. We must be bold," Meala spoke, reciting something she had heard her mother say. With a smile, Cynna grasped Meala's strophium in the center between her breasts and pulled with one arm, raising Meala's upper body until their lips met for another deep, probing kiss. Meala watched as the woman's powerful muscles flexed to hold her in a sitting pose, just as she drew her heavy war bow, then melted as their lips met. After a moment of kissing, Cynna placed her left arm behind Meala to support her back and thoughtfully unwrapped Meala's strophium, then gently lowered her and quickly removed her own garment.

Breasts were not something uncommon to see in a family home, nor something Meala spent much time considering, but they suited Cynna's form, complimenting her visage. But before she had time to consider this more, Cynna leaned forward and sank into Meala's arms as they kissed once more, as though they had been away for a lifetime. After a moment, or maybe a lifetime, the Sarmatian pulled back, then repositioned herself as she slowly licked Meala's chest from just above her navel to her sternum, sending waves of joy through her body and eliciting a gasp as she sharply inhaled. Meala nearly cried out from need, but Cynna spoke first.

"Tuh aun suraz zalmo," Cynna whispered in her native tongue, but not before using that same tongue a few more times, then kissing her way up Meala's body, passing over each breast and across her neck.

"Tuh unt germaz shze ballas, nelja surras," she whispered into Meala's ear, an unknown statement yet her romantic intent was far from lost as Meala gasped, her body now burning like fire. But then, Cynna lowered her body upon Meala, bringing their lips back together. Meala gasped, unprepared for the feeling of a woman's soft breasts against her chest, as Cynna softly bit her lower lip. It was a strange feeling, yet feminine and powerful. As Cynna lifted her body to passionately kiss the painted warrior, her skillful tongue returning for more, Meala felt their breasts gently brushing, the most sensitive parts causing extra bursts of joy as they found themselves so delightfully in the way.

The night was fully upon them now, with the darkness reducing them to nothing but feel, but this did nothing more than heighten the moment. Just then, Cynna's muscular leg brushed Meala twixed hers, sending a new level of pleasure up and down her spine. Strangely, the pleasure seemed to tickle her entire body, especially her nipples, from the inside. She had never felt that while sitting beneath the tree. A moment later, she found herself slowly pressing her hips against Cynna's strong leg. It was like pressing against the warmest, softest stone, so strong were her legs, forged from a lifetime of riding. Meala began to moan, finding herself unable to remain quiet and frankly no longer caring.

"Cy… nnna… oh…" she all but whimpered as she rubbed herself against the Sarmatian, so warm and wet with need; all the while, Cynna fought to kiss her. The feeling of their soft breasts touching, the hot softness of Cynna's lips and probing tongue, and the shameless, wet movement of her hips against the archer's legs, and Meala suddenly began to feel herself losing control of some sort of new pleasure. It was like a small dam bursting, but with each subsequent movement, the pleasure grew like a trickle of water rising in wave after pulsing wave into a warm flood.

Sensing her climax, Cynna pressed her tongue deeper and pulled the painted warrior's body tightly against her own. Meala stopped moving as the pleasure built far beyond what she had expected – far beyond her ability to do more than let it happen. Meala moaned and cried out, but Cynna held her body tightly against her own, her tongue between Meala's lips and her leg pressed into the warmth of the Caledonian while she jerked and rode her many waves of pleasure. As the crescendo began to calm, Meala's body went limp, entirely held within Cynna's strong grasp while the archer kissed and nibbled and, quite frankly, did whatever the fuck she wanted, as far as Meala was concerned.

For a short time, they lay in each other's arms, basking in the glow of what had happened, while Meala's rational mind slowly began to assert control over what had become her primal nature. It had been like this only the day before, but this had been so much more emotional. Her encounter with Sabina was her first and an eye-opening experience. But nothing she had ever experienced had been quite as intimate nor felt so right as what had just happened. In truth, while the end had felt so wonderful, it was the start and the slow physical intimacy that had been the most memorable.

For all the boasting of the men and the prideful prancing of the goats, she wasn't sure anything could compare to what she had felt. It wasn't just the climax, but the joy of the embrace, the intimacy, and the pure feeling of joy that came from being in another's arms... someone who loved her. They had known each other for so short a time, yet they had done more for each other in that short time than most couples did in their entire lives. Beside her, Cynna gently played with Meala's hair as they lay bare-chested under a sea of stars, their sweat-slick bodies growing illuminated by the rising Moon.

"You did not cry out as I did," Meala asked, concerned that Cynna had not gone quite as far as she, nor had she seemed to wish it. For a time, Cynna said nothing as she played with Meala's hair, seemingly just as satisfied. The powerful and stoic warrior had just opened herself so completely. Sex had been intimate, and there had also been a sort of vital intimacy shared upon the battlefield, yet nothing had prepared either woman for the emotional vulnerability they had just shared.

"When it happens, it happens," she eventually said, a single tear rolling down her cheek. Meala lifted herself on her elbow, giving Cynna a worried look. She had not let herself be so emotionally vulnerable since her mother's passing, but something about the look of concern and adoration from the Caledonian woman slipped past her emotional armor and touched her wounded heart. She smiled, bittersweet as another tear joined the first. Then, a moment later, Cynna burst into tears, falling into Meala's arms. Meala wasn't sure why, but somehow, she felt as though some of the heavy emotional armor the warrior had worn had finally come off. Together, they lay like that for a while as Cynna softly cried in Meala's arms under the now-waning gibbous Moon. They had nearly taken each other's lives, and now they lay in each other's arms – a situation neither woman could even begin to wrap her head around.

Chapter XI

Tisiphone Rises

Ancient Greek accounts of earlier Scythian cultures using poisoned arrows are plentiful, with snake venom, herbs, and even human blood cited as components. In fact, many ancient cultures were said to have used poisoned arrows to strike fear into their enemies and make sure a wounded warrior wouldn't recover to cause them harm, later. As seen in this book, various deadly substances may have been used, such as dried snake venom and herbs. Great care and skill would be employed to keep the archer safe from their deadly missiles and to ensure the potency didn't fade.

One possible practice may have involved decorating the fletchings (the feathery "fins" of an arrow) in a style reminiscent of the toxic substance used to make identification by the archer easier. It should be noted that death by a "poisoned" arrow would rarely be quick unless the arrow found a vital organ or major artery. Few poisons, venoms, and toxins provide quickly lethal effects, though some are quicker than others. For those interested in an approachable book explaining the use of "poisoned" arrows, the 2022 book, Greek Fire, Poison Arrows, and Scorpion Bombs: Unconventional Warfare in the Ancient World by Adrienne Mayor provides a fascinating look into their use.

Cynna awoke startling a leather mouse (Muscardinus avellanarius) who had likely been attracted to their food from a nearby tree where it lived. Ignoring the tiny creature, she took a breath as the last motes of night engulfed her like a blanket. Her body was covered by a thin layer of dew, and her back was quite stiff from her ordeal. In fact, she had many small wounds that ached from her mistreatment by Roman hands. She held a lot of complex feelings about what had happened and would for a long time, she supposed. Still, it was hard to worry about the past when her brave rescuer lay sleeping at her side in the present. For a short time, the Sarmatian lay beside the sleeping woman feeling her warmth as they lay on the cool ground, Meala's wavy auburn brown hair tangled among the pinks and purples of blooming heather, barely visible in the morning light. To Cynna, this often cold, strange land had long held only death and foreboding, yet it seemed that beauty and purpose could be found anywhere.

Memories of Elder Kazakos speaking similar words as he lifted a rock to show the tribe's children a beautiful ash snake (Vipera nikolskii) came to mind. Of course, elder Kazakos was also demonstrating how to find venomous snakes for more pragmatic reasons than beauty. Their venom could be milked and used to coat arrows, several of which Cynna usually kept in her quiver for special occasions. As she lay under the blue sky of a foreign land, her memories drifted back to those childhood days when her mother taught her how to paint her arrows to mimic the patterns of the snakes whose venom they bore.

"The Lady of the Hearth and the Mother of the Earth gave us snakes as gifts. A fool knows nothing of their bite and fears them, yet we women know better. You must paint each arrow so that it can be seen and understood, even when it is dark. Here, like this…" she remembered her mother saying as a young Cynna watched her carefully holding an arrow painted black with tiny grey lines resembling the ash snake's black, shiny scales. She couldn't remember what her mother was wearing nor much of the event other than the lecture about the venom, but she could still picture her mother's face. She had tanned, tawny skin, deep hazel eyes, like Cynna, and several small tattoos across her cheeks and chin. She was a strong woman, kind and loving. She had stood bravely when their tribe was raided, raining death upon the raiders until an arrow finally found her. With a sigh, she pushed aside such memories.

Sometime during the night, the pair awoke and crept down into the gully to find Damona sleeping beside the small, waning fire. The girl had curled up in the cooling night air and seemed cold. Meala had brought the horse blanket for them to sleep on but ended up placing it over the girl while Cynna added the rest of their small supply of driftwood before the pair had fallen once more to sleep in each other's arms, lying on their clothes. But now, as the Sun rose, Meala continued to sleep, drooling slightly on the archer's arm as she lay beside Cynna, holding tightly. She would never tell the brave painted warrior, but the first thing that occurred to her was how cute she looked. That was a thought she would pack away for personal amusement.

Perhaps it was that same bravery that she saw in Meala that attracted her or perhaps it was her spell – the magic of women, cast the very night they met. She sighed, unsure and not sure that it truly mattered. She was funny, curious, and compassionate, even after events that would have left many jaded and broken. Sure, the painted woman was beautiful, if not adorable, but her personality and bravery seemed to attract Cynna more than anything else. She considered this as the smaller woman tightly clung to the archer's body, even in sleep. There was an oddly comforting aspect to being held all night, not to mention the warmth. Most strangely, she had not been flooded with nightmares the way she had expected.

Typically, she would have placed hemp buds by the fire and breathed in their smoke to calm herself, but she had none, only Meala's warmth. That warmth had been enough to soothe her, it seemed. Memories of resting in her mother's warm arms as a girl came back, flooding her with nostalgia and bittersweet joy. She would place a small bronze censor beside the main tent fire with hemp buds and let the pungent smell fill the tent as the family merry made before rest. Fermented mares' milk and opium were also consumed, their smells filling the night and Cynna's memories, relaxing her into sleep. Now, the feel of the warm Caledonian in her arms seemed more than enough to lull her back to slumber.

They had only met six moons before and formally a mere three days ago, yet the painted Caledonian woman had occupied her thoughts since that fateful night at the wall. A pang of remorse washed over her as she realized how close she had come to taking Meala's life that night. How many wonderful people with rich lives, hopes, and dreams died in war? Warriors were not just nameless people, and each arrow loosed snuffed another precious life from the world, a thought that filled her with sorrow. Her mother had been such a person; her life traded for Cynna's, and the thoughtful, brave, and friendly woman lying beside her had nearly been another. Cynna wished dearly that she could swear an oath to never take another life, yet she knew that wasn't something that she could swear... at least not yet. The world was just so chaotic.

It was probably silly, if not a dumb wish, but Cynna couldn't stop wondering–wishing–that someone like Meala could be her wife. It wasn't likely to happen, but it was a profound thought. She might even bring herself to ask, but nothing would happen, be it mundane or fanciful, until they got safely to Meala's home. That thought sent tears to her eyes. There, she supposed there would be some measure of safety... maybe? She sighed, realizing she needed a cold bath to wash such ideas from her mind lest they nag her all day.

She removed the painted woman's hand from her chest and pushed her tattooed leg to the side with a stretch. Some people might not like being so tightly held, but Cynna didn't mind. In truth, she had long desired to be held and had no one who would do so. Sure, she could have asked some of the men to lie with her, but they would want more than just warmth, a thought that sent a shiver down her spine. Grabbing her iron war ax and armor in one hand and her clothing in the other, she quietly left the small gully and headed toward the pond over the hill, leaving her two sleeping companions. She would need to wash, and the cool morning breeze felt lovely. There were good and bad things about this land, but one she enjoyed was the wind, like home.

Her horse Tamura, as well-trained as she, remained by the pond and was currently munching on grass, her presence keeping the lesser-trained pack horse reasonably close. She approached the beautiful animal and gently stroked her well-brushed back. A horse was a valuable commodity where she came from and in every land she had visited. Tamura had traveled all the way from Southwestern Dacia with her, another peculiarity of auxilia. She and Tamura became almost like one when riding, a feat that took a lot of skill from the rider and a significant amount of training for the horse. Not too far away, their stollen Roman horse stood beside the pond having his fill of water. He would never be a war horse like Tamura, but she supposed he seemed friendly enough.

Her saddle lay out of sight behind a large bush near the pond. She had removed Tamura's soleae ferreae (leather hoof covers used before the invention of horseshoes) and the gear from the horses that night but had kept it close by them as a matter of habit, though she had brought her ax and armor to the gully. In the army, each object had its place, and each rule had its reason. She supposed such thoughts were no longer hers to have, as she had abandoned her post and was a fugitive. She tossed the armor and weapon beside the saddle and stretched, then with a laugh, she began to untie her linen braies (subligaculum-like undergarment) in preparation for a swim. The water would be quite cold, but she could use a refreshing dip to wash away the contamination of her previous life, if nothing more.

Ci rubbed her hand once through her short, red hair as her group approached the edge of a small river called the Ites, which fed into the fjord, another lengthy day of tracking awaiting. Her ancestors had been known as the Iceni (eye-seen-eye), a powerful tribe who had long troubled the Romans, going so far as destroying most of Rome's presence in Britannia and burning the provincial capital city to the ground. The Romans regrouped and defeated her people, and they had been subject to retaliation and oppression over the past one hundred years since their last stand. Ci had trained as a warrior like the rest of the youth of her village, but her chief had sold her to a Roman man at the age of nineteen to train and fight in the gladiatorial ring of none other than Colonia Claudia Victricensis: the rebuilt Roman provincial capital of Britannia, otherwise known as Camulodunum.

Trained as a Retiaria (trident and net-wielding fighter), she had fought in the ring using wooden weapons, mostly for the comical amusement of the crowds. But in a few years, she had earned a place in the night games and a name among the crowds: Canicula (female dog). Fight after fight and victory upon victory, Ci pleased the crowds, winning most of her fights. Even when she lost, her honorable fights and prowess saw her granted missio (reprieve) and spared to fight another day. That and the cost of buying and training a gladiator was quite high, making deaths not so commonplace. Her body had been decorated with tattoo after tattoo, symbolizing her victories and in the traditional Iceni style, a testament to her prowess. At thirty-four, she finally earned her rudis, the ceremonial wooden sword of freedom. Taking her earnings, she had left to become a hunter of men for coin. Now, eleven years later, she had plenty more wrinkles, and moved a little slower, but with far greater wisdom.

While the Romans often paid her well for her skills at finding runaway enslaved people or criminals, she generally worked alone. How ironic that she now found herself in the presence of four Roman cavalrymen. At least they were hunters, soldiers specially selected for their skills in hunting food. If she recalled, they had some special title like "immune" or something like that. They were freed from the burden of regular work, unlike most soldiers, and a bit more agreeable, in her opinion, though she would trust a Roman man only so far. As for Ci, she was, more or less, a private contractor and tracker of the enslaved, criminals, or legionary deserters.

She adjusted her wool tunic, keeping it from bunching up under her leather armor. It was a plain outfit, but those who singled themselves out with fancy gear often caught the first arrow. While the Romans accompanying her wore iron banded armor, Ci enjoyed the lighter, more flexible leather. In the ring, she had fought wearing merely a wool or linen subligaculum (waistcloth), ocrea (greaves), galerus (shoulder guard), and manica (padded arm guard), but otherwise bare, just as the men. Over time, her fighting style had adapted to the lighter armor, and wearing heavier protection would have the opposite effect, rendering her off-balance and more vulnerable. Besides, she wasn't likely to find herself at the frontline of battle. But she was likely to find herself brawling on the ground with a thief armed only with a knife. In that case, leather would work just fine. Besides, finally wearing a chest binding certainly made riding and fighting more comfortable.

She sighed, her mind drifting as she rode beside the water. This assignment had seemed rather odd to her from the start – damn odd. Not only by how urgently the request, more like a demand, had arrived but also with the significant payment promised. She had been a bit annoyed at the late hour of her enlistment for this rush assignment, as she had been occupied with a local man at a place of leisure just outside of the fort proper at the time. Worse, the man who had brought the "request" had been accompanied by a quartet of none-to-pleased guards, bursting in on her fun – fun that she had been paying for. It wasn't technically a threat but a message regarding the ramifications of declining the request.

She sighed once more. Ci greatly respected the women, men and others of the brothel, especially having the patience to put up with the Romans. Luckily, the brothel kept a few men around, as Romans had a great variety of fancies. The man she had paid for had been more flexible than a wet worm (European Eel) and with more enthusiasm than she had hoped. But the heavy coin purse and the promise of so much more from the high and mighty ass Titus himself had hurried her from warm arms and into the saddle. It had been abrupt and unsatisfactory, but with 100 shiny gold aurei coins, that was something she could easily remedy. Moreover, the promise of a small fortune in return for the three problems, alive, and their cargo, unopened, was more than anyone could turn down.

Now, she found herself on horseback attempting to find those two women, an enslaved girl, and some missing "cargo." Clearly, it was something of value, likely gold. She considered the possibility that perhaps some of the valuable items might not be able to be retrievable, having found a more dubious outcome hiding in her saddle pouch. She smiled at the thought, though she suspected that any "special tax" she took would need to be minimal, lest she anger the most powerful man in all the region. Even Ci wasn't quite that brave. Her thoughts were interrupted by the highly accented sound of Latin, a language she spoke for business yet found grating on the ears.

"The tracks lead down into that gully," one of the Roman compatriots spoke, kneeling on the ground beside his horse. Up ahead and barely visible in the distance lay a pond with a pair of horses grazing. Just beyond the pond, the land rose slightly, then appeared to descend, forming a natural, low bluff, likely a meander scar from the small river's ancient past. If she were looking for a place to sleep, the gully on the other side would certainly be a good choice and the horses matched the descriptions she had been provided.

They had followed the horses along the river shore, eventually leading them to a farmstead. There, a local farmer had told them that he had seen no such travelers. Of course, his poorly constructed lies were evidence enough that they were on the right track. She had even thanked the man not only because he was unwittingly helpful even as he had tried to deceive them but also because his handsome face had been a pleasant sight in the early morn after the unwholesome company of the emperor's cavalry. They had lost the tracks a short while back, but the bluff and gully were the sort of location one might stop to rest, and certainly worth a look.

Hiding horse tracks wasn't the most straightforward activity, but they had certainly done their best. Most would have run directly from the Fort, but the women had headed west by northwest quite a distance, nearly along the Wall, then northeast, returning to the fjord's edge. Afterward, they had spent some time walking in the shallow parts of the fjord and following the banks of a few tributaries letting the water wash away their tracks. It had lengthened her task a bit, caused two short backtracks, and would have thrown off lesser trackers. Ci knew that one of her targets was a Dacian auxilium, a deadly foe in battle, but she had not expected such cunning skill at evasion. These were no ordinary women, something to ponder as she considered her strategy.

One could generally track a horse's movement by finding a few tracks and guessing which direction the person would travel. People tended to move from one visually significant location to another, even when trying to be evasive. Like animals, humans were subject to many bad behaviors that made tracking and capturing them easy. With luck, she would have these three women shortly, and then she could return to finish what she had left at the place of leisure, her coin purse much heavier than before. Still, the skillful equestrian evasion tactics bothered her.

"Listen up, the three of you go around the far side," Ci said, nodding toward the northern side of the gully, "and we'll come around the South edge." The men frowned, looking at each other, then at the Roman leader of the quartet, quite unused to the idea of a woman in command. The lead Roman shrugged and gave them a nod to obey while Ci repressed an eye-roll. With a curt nod, the three men she had indicated began to lead their horses north before Ci spoke up again, already annoyed by the heavy-handed nature of the Romans.

"Aye! Get off your fucking horses and walk. We don't need our horses making a fuss. Also, if you catch them before we get there, make sure you take all their weapons, too," she spoke with a heavy accent while pointing at the various men, telling them what she wanted them to do. One of the men seemed confused by her last statement, frowning as he dismounted.

"Why do we want their trash barbarian weapons? We should leave them where we drop them," he said, drawing an equal frown from Ci, a local whose own people used those same "trash barbarian weapons." She supposed she should have expected such a lack of forethought from men without honor, yet it was still annoying to behold. With a sigh, she replied, a bit curtly.

"Because your big man Titus lost his wife, Vito," she began, suppressing a more colorful adjective for the vile woman.

"Uh, Vita ma'am… It's Vita," the head of the four cavalrymen interjected with an almost apologetic tone while two of the men fought the urge to smile.

"Sure… Vita. Well, she was killed by one of them, right? You see?" she continued, then frowned as their glazed expressions indicated that they did not see. "Titus might want to kill all three snakes with the same weapon. I know I would," Ci explained, suspecting the man's lack of understanding was a cultural difference. Her many long nights in the ring had taught her that the Romans had a muted understanding of honor, and their culture vastly differed from hers. Among her people, weapons held power, especially after tasting the blood of powerful people, and were not a thing to be left behind. The very spirit of the vile woman likely still tainted whichever blade had cut her down, and using it to execute her killer would clearly appeal to both the gods and someone of power, like Titus. With a look of begrudged understanding, the men nodded, though one decided to add a final thought.

"Three women... It's a long ride back to the fort. Maybe we take 'em and their weapons but leave their clothes behind. Who knows what might..." But Ci cut the man off midsentence, flashing him a deadly glare. She knew what the man wanted. She would take someone's life regardless of gender or age, but there were some things she would not stand for. She had been enslaved and at the mercy of far too many men. She had suffered enough during her time as a fighter for the public and understood that there were things in life worse than death. Ci would have no luck explaining why his thoughts disgusted her, so she instead appealed to their sense of self-preservation.

"Aye… One of them is a Dacian archer. The other is a warrior of Caledonian stock. I've fought Caledonians… deadly bunch. Between them, they have killed nearly a dozen of you lot and the wife of Titus Vibulanus before they escaped a fort filled with lots more of you. That Dacian also murdered the second cohort's prime optio just the day before, as rumor has it. Now I'm not saying she was wrong to do so, but she fought him in single combat and killed the man in an even fight. If you stick your little Roman dicks in her face, she might just bite them off." Everyone in the canaba had heard the rumors. In fact, if the rumors were true, she had done much more than just kill him, something Ci would need to keep in mind when facing the mighty warrior.

"I was told that they were to be returned, unharmed. If I had to guess, I'd say that little…" she paused, reconsidering her original choice of wording, "...that man, Titus, wishes to do the harming. Besides, if either woman got her hands on you, she is just as likely to cut your balls off and keep them as trophies." Several of the men chuckled, while the man who had made the crude suggestion spat on the ground and looked away, clearly not pleased at being scolded by a woman. Ci didn't care the slightest about his ego, nor was she afraid of a Roman soldier. In fact, part of her would relish the chance to face one of these men with a blade.

One of the most aggravating things about the Romans was that they simply didn't understand how deadly a warrior woman could be. As far as she could tell, the women from their lands were absolutely meek as kittens, as Roman men seemed to regard most women almost like children. The women from her land were a different story entirely. Even now, she could remember the legend of Boudicca, a mighty woman from queen of her people who had nearly driven the Roman menace from the land, a tale told to her by her father as a child.

Cynna kept low in the pond beside the tall grass that grew at the edge as she watched the patrol. She had been underwater cleaning her now unbraided hair when they had first arrived, probably the one bit of luck that had spared her life. As strong a warrior as she was, without weapons or armor, no amount of heroics would have spared her if four Roman soldiers attacked her in the water. While she had expected patrols, she had not expected them to range this far. Normally, her unit–well, former unit, she supposed with a strange mix of feelings that she would consider later–would have been dispatched for an assignment like this, but the Romans had probably not trusted them to capture one of their own. In truth, the men of her unit were mostly from Alan tribes and a few smaller tribes east of her people's lands and would likely have few reservations hunting her, but it was a reasonable assumption on the part of the Romans, she conceded.

Still, they had sent four Roman citizen soldiers and what looked like perhaps a local guide. The guide was a woman, a common enough occurrence among the locals but an odd choice by the Romans. Curiously, she swore that she recognized the woman, having seen her entering the fort's praetorium, the main building where higher-ranking soldiers and leadership lived and worked. As for the four men, she recognized them immediately, though she only knew the name of their leader. Only a few citizen equates (cavalry) existed within the cavalry ranks at the fort; the rest mostly foederati auxilia (those of barbarian stock) cavalry drawn up from the treaty-bound local tribes. The lead Roman cavalryman, Numerius Rabirius Tiburtinus, was the second in command of the local cavalry, a senior position and another bad sign. Had Titus actually dispatched his best units this far beyond the Wall to hunt them down?

As she watched, the guide almost seemed to be giving orders, another oddity. A moment later, three men dismounted and drew their weapons, quickly striding toward the hill's northern side. A moment later, after a brief but tense exchange, the "guide" and Numerius dismounted and similarly approached from the South. They were obviously intent on surprising Meala and Damona, and Cynna had missed her chance to intercept them because she had been swimming and cleaning. Anger, helplessness, and self-loathing over her lack of readiness flooded her mind, but she quickly shook them aside as her martial, soldier mind took over. She forced her emotions and fears into a small container, as she had long ago learned to do. This was like any other drill, and she had to be ready for battle quickly but correctly.

She wanted nothing more than to grab her dagger and rush headlong toward the Romans to save her lover and the child, but years in the military had taught her that such emotional and unprepared reactions were nothing more than a path to defeat. If the men had wanted Meala dead, they would have rushed upon her while mounted and killed her. They were likely trying to capture her, and Cynna couldn't stop that. But she could control herself, become properly armed and armored, and then face the men at her most powerful – as a Sarmatian mounted archer.

Drawing herself from the water, she grabbed her clothing from beside the bushes where she had left it and began dressing. She breathed deeply and rhythmically, calming herself as she had learned to do. She had trained for emergencies and knew that letting anxiety and adrenaline overtake her would lead to mistakes. She had to be fully armored and armed to confront four skilled men such as these and whomever their curious guide might be. Quickly, she donned on her leggings and tied them to her waist cord with a slipknot, then pulled her now cut tunic and kaftan long-shirt overhead. Tamura noticed, seeming to sense her anxiety, and approached her rider. With her armor in one hand and her saddle in the other, Cynna dashed to Tamura and began saddling her as she fought to keep her emotions and fears in check.

"Come on, my friend. We are needed," she spoke with gravity as she finished securing the saddle and began tying Tamura's soleae ferreae into place. The pack horse had since wandered away but had no saddle and could safely be left to his own future. Someone would find and claim him, but that was no longer her problem. Cynna performed each preparatory action in a ritual way, as she had been taught. She had spent years learning to do this as a child and could prepare her mount for riding simply by feel if she had to. After mounting, she pulled free her main bow and strung it, returning it to its bowcase, a sort of holster for her bow mounted to her saddle. Unfortunately, as she checked her quivers, she discovered a problem.

"Mingere…" she whispered, her vocabulary of Latin profanity far exceeding that of her native tongue. One quiver was completely empty, and the other had three arrows. One of the arrows was a special poisoned arrow, its iron tip coated with the venom from a local snake, the woven snake (European adder), and an oil Cynna had purchased from a southern trader the past cold season made from a local flower said to take the life of a man in moments (Aconitum napellus). Such arrows had to be prepared several times a year lest their potency fade. The arrow's shaft was clearly identifiable to Cynna by the fletching painted with v-shaped brown lines with blue spots resembling both the snake and flower, lest she forget.

She normally held a few dozen arrows in each, but in times of war, she would fill them with up to perhaps 100 arrows each and likely carry four quivers or more. Unfortunately, she had exhausted one quiver on their way to the gate and the other as they passed by and fled. Most had been fired wildly without aiming, to suppress her foes. Firing roughly forty arrows during her escape had not only been one of her fastest rates of fire but also exhausting, as bows took a lot of force to draw and hold steady with aim, even for a well-trained warrior like Cynna. She had also been exhausted and wounded at the time, complicating things. Regardless, she had what she had, which would have to be enough.

❧❧❧

"She bit me!" one of the Romans exclaimed, punching the back of Meala's head in anger. Ci turned to see one of the equites grasping a set of bite marks, several of them bloody, on his left arm. Unsurprisingly, he was the same lecherous man she had scolded before. The man held the northern woman in front of him on the horse to keep her from fleeing as they began the long trek back to the fort. She suspected the man had reached forward to entertain himself. Fortunately, he had just learned that women of the isle were hardly the sort to let that stand. Even with her hands tied before her, she had fought back fervently. *Serves you right, you dirty bastard,* she mused as the group followed the river's edge headed Southeast for the fort a short time later.

Ci had to admit that she felt a little pride in the locals' resistance. As luck had it, they had come upon her, and the runaway enslaved girl sleeping against the side of the bluff and quickly ambushed them before they could react. She had not seen the actual carnage the women had left at the fort, but the word of several dead soldiers had quickly spread through the village, and Titus' aggressive "offer" to catch the women gave credence to the rumor. The local looked like her tribe was probably from the Northeast, maybe Wenech, given her tattoos, stains from what had probably been body paint, and accent. Ci had taken possession of the small chest of riches, the gold torc, the quality bronze dagger, and the spear, but the rest of her possessions had been discarded. Both had been wearing simple tunics, which was plenty enough until they returned to the fort, she supposed.

As for the enslaved girl, she was from some distant land Ci knew little of. The miserable waif of a girl was too frightened to even try escaping and merely whimpered like a young pup as she was bound and led away, unlike the Wenech woman, who kicked, fought, and took three men to subdue. Whatever fate awaited the pair, Ci couldn't say, but she suspected the girl's fears were justified, if not underrated. The punishment for killing one's master was severe among the Romans, yet these fools had done something far worse: they had humiliated the most powerful man on the entire isle at a critical time in his ascension to power. Everyone knew Titus was barely holding onto his new position, and such a man would be at his most dangerous – like a cornered dog.

Of course, the third woman was nowhere to be seen, and Titus would likely try and send her back out after the bitch. She was rumored to be the truly dangerous one, and Ci was honestly glad not to have run into her. Depending on the reward, she might consider taking what she got for the first two and letting someone else deal with the deadly mounted archer. She had survived the bloody sands of the ring and several years as a bounty hunter by knowing when the price was too high and when to quit. Beside her, the soldier continued complaining, his arm probably sore.

"I told you not to touch them. If you keep trying, she'll likely bite one of your fingers off, aye. You know they say those of the barbara caledonii fancy Roman men's flesh," Ci said with a chuckle, watching the man bristle from the comment. They had traveled through the forest for part of the day to shorten their trek, but it seemed that boredom was catching up with the soldiers.

"Men, huh? Then why did she bite *you*," one of the soldiers jested to his pained companion. Three of the Romans laughed while the man holding his freshly bitten arm simply scowled. If the painted woman understood what they spoke in Latin, she made no indication of it. As for the enslaved girl, she simply hung her head in reservation. Ci suspected both women knew what was in store, probably a very public torture and execution. It was something vile the Romans seemed to enjoy, but Ci would likely avoid. She might be a rotten bitch, perhaps even a bit prideful of it, but even she had limits. Though to be fair, her own people were known for a little torture and death, but Ci wasn't interested in the inconvenience of biases.

The seven initially made quick time from the gully, riding through the woods to reduce the ability for anyone trailing them to set an ambush, lest the captives have some unknown friends. They had already encountered the local farmers who had clearly housed them for a night, so it wasn't as far-fetched as she would have liked to believe. But after spending much of the day slowly making their way back toward the fort, it seemed that the biggest problem Ci would face would be explaining why she had not captured the Dacian. She might have been out hunting to restock their stores. Of course, the black war horse had run off while they were busy restraining the woman and girl, so wherever the warrior was, she wouldn't find a ride when she returned.

That left them with one extra horse and two prisoners, who needed to be kept from escaping, as well as their heavy cargo. To that end, they had purposely not fed nor provided water to either captive. Between hunger and thirst and their lack of anything but their basic tunics, it wasn't likely either would be able to put up much of a fight, even if they somehow freed themselves. Of course, they were now in the open, but it had been half a day, and the chance of…

Her thoughts were interrupted as she heard the distinctive sound of an arrow slamming into flesh, the click of release followed by the whistle of a fletching slicing its way through the air just before a thud. The sound was immediately followed by the pained gurgle of a man gasping for air as his lungs filled with blood, yet another unmistakable and deeply haunting sound. As she turned, Ci noticed the man to the rear of their group was slumped over his horse, gasping for air and pawing at an arrow stuck deep within his neck, a mortal wound by anyone's measure and also a difficult shot from any significant distance, unless the hit was accidental luck. If she recalled, his name was Markos or something like that, though she supposed it no longer mattered.

Her eyes shifted from the dying man to a moving object far behind them. The source of the arrow was mounted upon a horse and standing on a rise at a distance of nearly 200 Roman feet. The archer had fired quite a long way yet had still hit a moving target in his neck, one of the few vulnerable places on the armored man's body from that distance. Wearing scale armor that caught the morning light with her long black hair blowing loose in the wind, their ambusher could be none other than the missing Dacian. In the morning light, she looked like Tisiphone rising from the underworld, a myth from a faraway land that she had heard from a druid as a child about a mighty spirit who sought vengeance on murderers.

At least her ability to use her bow with such skill made sense. Her people were said to be among the best archers in the Empire, especially when it came to firing while mounted. Finding the woman was a mixed boon: On the one hand, this could mean more gold and no need to piss off the powerful governor by refusing his request to hunt down the Dacian, yet on the other, she had just boldly engaged five warriors at 200 roman feet and was so far proving quite lethal.

"Aye! To the Northwest, look," she called, training the men's eyes upon the woman who chased them. At such a distance, if they kept an eye on her, they could likely avoid her arrows, but the mounted archer might not stay so distant for long.

"Marcus has been wounded," yelled one of the men, coming around to assist the doomed man as he now slumped lifelessly over his horse. Marcus… that was his name. She would never get a proper handle on these strange Roman names, but at least that was one less to remember.

"Marcus is dead. He took one in the neck, and so will you if you don't keep an eye on that archer," barked Numerius, the lead Roman, to the approval of Ci, who was glad that at least one of these men had some sense. A moment later, another arrow loosed and flew right for Numerius, who barely avoided the missile, uttering a profane word in reply.

"You, Aula," Ci said, pointing at the man seated behind the Wenech warrior on a war horse. He was more than enough to keep the bound Caledonian warrior from trying to escape. That same man held a rope leading a brown packhorse carrying the formerly enslaved captive and the chest of gold. With her hands tied before her and to a short rope around the horse's neck, the girl was not likely going anywhere, and any attempt to dismount the horse would result in her being dragged.

"It's Aulus," the man protested, and Ci rolled her eyes. Now wasn't the time for speaking their odd language perfectly or worrying over their pointless names.

"Whatever! You keep your well-paid ass behind and guard the box and the women. That Dacian bitch can't focus on two different groups at once. You two, with me!" Ci ordered, preparing for something that was probably not worth the reward.

"You want us to charge an elite Dacian mounted archer on open ground?" one of the Romans asked incredulously. The men had all seen the results of the woman's handiwork at the gate on the way out. Ambushing them while they slept was one thing, but fighting the deadly woman in her full combat regalia with her bow was quite another task. As the men looked, the woman held her bow high in the air and pointed her other hand at them, obviously calling them to the battlefield. While heroines were part of her culture, Ci had never thought she would face such a mighty woman in battle. She had fought only one woman in the ring, wounding her and winning the match. But this was very different. She wondered if the iron armor would have been more useful.

"I only see one woman with a bow. She cannot have many arrows left or she would be firing them while we sit here like quail. Once her quivers are dry, she is just another warrior with a sword. I thought you pompous asses were conquerors. Are you frightened of a single woman, eh? Am I the only one in the group with balls?" Ci teased, suspecting they would make short work of the archer and hoping to convince the soldiers to attack, subdue, or kill her rather than risking her own flesh and playing on their manly bravado seemed like the easiest method.

Firing on steadily moving targets was tough enough, but firing on several charging and evading warriors was another matter. Besides, when they came into hand-to-hand combat, Romans weren't that bad, dare she begrudgingly admit. She had faced a few in the ring and had several scars to attest her belief. Her only real concern was what to tell the bastard Titus when she returned with the woman's head and not a living prisoner for his vengeance. If they were lucky, she might merely be wounded, and she could drag her back alive. Either way, this was why they paid her well. With that, Numerius pulled free his bow to string while Sextus readied his spear.

Meala's legs held her to the horse almost as tightly as the Roman's arm around her waist. She and Damona had awoken to armed men grabbing and lifting them to their feet, a jarring experience, to say the least. Facing four soldiers when she had her shield, spear, and was mentally prepared was one thing, but awaking to armed men grabbing her when she was unarmed and still pained and tired from the past few days had resulted in her quick capture. Worse, they had not fed nor given them water. Meala could handle a day without food, but she had drunk far too much beer at Julia's house, then wine and not much water the night before, and had been intimate, all coming together to leave her feeling dizzy and weak, not to mention the dryest mouth she had ever had.

Worse, the son of a dog now holding her had tried exploring with his hands several times, but a good bite had provided him with an educational experience, though her head hurt from his retaliatory punch. That had only been a short time before, and her mind had barely caught up to the transition from, risk, escape, drinking, cathartic emotional vulnerability, romance, sleep, then suddenly finding herself captured by men who were probably returning her to face unspeakable punishments and death, a man who clearly didn't understand consent… and now Cynna – beautiful, powerful, remarkable Cynna suddenly appearing. Her mind nearly spun from it all as she fought to put it all into perspective.

Gazing back at the distant western hill, the mighty warrior sat atop her black steed, her long, dark hair blowing in the wind as the morning sunlight danced across her scale armor, a single bronze scale over her heart catching the full luminosity of the Sun's light. She was glorious, and she was Meala's only hope. It was breathtaking to see, like a scene from one of her childhood daydreams, but so much more real after their shared passion. The other girls had made up stories of brave warriors, perhaps the chief's son, coming to save them, a common theme. She even remembered one girl who would pretend to be a warrior queen and rescue various men from monsters. Of course, when she was young, she had held a much different hope. She had hoped a warrior woman would save her and carry her away. Of course, her childish fantasies had never been quite this terrifying.

As she watched, two Romans began racing towards Cynna, one angling right and the other left, flanking her. The woman who seemed in charge took a path down the middle yet let the men get a healthy head start. Behind her, the man holding her watched their advance with a nearly unhealthy anticipation as he muttered enthusiastically. But perhaps most importantly, he was no longer watching her. Part of her wanted to watch as though her attention would make some difference, and a lack of it might doom her lover… **her lover?** This wasn't the time to consider that, so she pushed such thoughts aside. Still, what if something happened to Cynna? If she were wounded or killed, Meala didn't want to see it happen, yet wasn't witnessing heroic deeds part of her culture?

Her hands were bound before her while a soldier held her from behind, and her legs were tied together with a cord that ran under the horse. Even if she threw herself off the horse, her hands would still be tied, and she would be with no weapons or armor. Worse, her legs bound under the horse would result in her swinging under the animal, likely slamming her head into the ground. Of course, sitting before the man with her legs over the two forward saddle horns of a Roman four-horned saddle meant that her legs were constantly rubbing against the horse's tack, especially the breast collar with its pair of well-worn phalerae (metallic ornamental discs) adorning the tack. One of the phalera had a sharp edge, possibly from damage, and her leg had already felt its bite a few times.

Everything had happened so fast that she had not yet considered what to do, but as the man adjusted to better see the action, her leg rubbed once more against the sharp edge of the metal disc. Realizing a lucky break when she felt it, Meala began rubbing the cord bound to her right leg at the ankle against the sharp edge of the phalera, hoping the rope binding her legs wasn't that strong. If she were lucky, her preoccupied captor might not notice the motion as he watched his comrades' attempt to murder her lover, a thought that carried its own wave of anxiety and fear. It had to end, one way or another.

"Ancestors hear me… aid me, please," she whispered.

Chapter XII

Cynna's Last Stand

Throughout the Iron Age and Roman Period, one of the most common garments was the tunic, a simple textile resembling a modern shirt but usually hanging below the waist and often to the knees. Cloth pants were also fashioned and worn under tunics, a garment the Romans called Braccae. Single panels of cloth could be folded around the upper body like a large bath towel, the excess hung over the chest, and the two corners secured with metal pins or fibulae (brooches). These simple but elegant garments resembled Greek peplos, the word used in this text. Beneath these garments, some may have worn nothing, while others may have worn cloth wraps around their waists, similar to the Roman subligaculum, a waist cloth secured by a waist cord. Breasts might be bound using a wide cloth similar in shape to a modern scarf but much longer, wrapping several times around the chest, similar to a Roman strophium.

With most clothing likely woven at home from handspun yarns and threads of wool, linen, nettle, or flax and requiring a significant investment of time and resources that had to be diverted from farming and other tasks, the cloth was costly. Thus, tunics were often made of single panels of cloth, rather bulky and wide and not as form-fitting as modern clothing. A belt was generally tied around the waist to secure the excess cloth, making a presentable and practical garment. The author of this book is an ancient textiles weaver and spinner who has made such a garment and worn it without a belt to learn just how practical it is. Without a belt, it is quite baggy, especially if it is slightly oversized.

It had taken time to saddle and prepare for battle, but she had taken the time. Every instinct had told Cynna to immediately rush to save Meala and Damona, but her military training had taught her that those who rush into battle usually rush into the beyond. She was outnumbered five to one against four veteran elite cavalry and one unknown person. Exercising every drop of discipline and self-control, Cynna stayed out of sight, following the Romans for a distance until a good chance for an attack presented itself. Unfortunately, they had spent far too long in the woods, in a bad location for a mounted archer. But now, they were in an open area between forests, and she was ready.

With a subtle movement of her body, Cynna told Tamura to charge angling toward her left. The horse responded, needing no further direction as she operated as an extension of the warrior's body, quickly speeding into a full gallop. Firing a bow at a target directly ahead while mounted meant avoiding the large bobbing horse head before you. That was easily fixed by coming at a slight angle to keep your foe on one side of the horse or the other. But flanking attacks from two different sides meant sweeping her bow from one side to the other, lifting her weapon over the horse's head, and that took precious moments in a battle that might last a few blinks of an eye.

Unfortunately, the two professional cavalrymen fanned out as they had been trained, forcing her to realistically engage only one of them at a time. The third rider, a redheaded woman, someone Cynna was beginning to think was more than just a guide, charged straight down the middle with none other than a rete (weighted throwing net) in hand, though slower than the others, obviously less experienced and not wishing to be the first to meet her blade. Cynna had only seen a rete used in combat once in a depiction of gladiatorial games and never from a horse.

Racing forward, Cynna knocked an arrow and drew, taking aim at one of the Romans. Even as the horse undulated below her, Cynna's body aligned to her motion and her bow became steady, her abdomen and lower body moving with the horse's rhythm. As she let her breath out, so too did she loose her arrow. The deadly missile flew through the air right at the Roman's chest, but the well-trained man leaned aside causing the arrow to deflect off of his armor at a shallow angle. Without thinking and having time for just one more shot, Cynna drew her poisoned arrow and took aim at the woman with red hair and tattoos. She was probably not her most skilled foe, yet she was also probably much easier to hit than two trained cavalrymen.

She whispered to the gods for luck and fired her final arrow. It flew true but seemed to skip off the woman's leather armor, slicing into the boiled hide but deflecting and spinning off into the grass. Cursing under her breath and with only moments until they arrived, Cynna swung her bow into its side bow case in a smooth, well-practiced motion as she nudged Tamura, urging her to break to the right. At the same time, Cynna swung her entire body over the right side of her horse, holding on with a single strong leg and arm over Tamura's back while the rest of her body clung to the right side of her steed.

The soldier with a spear on her left and the woman suddenly had virtually no target, as the Dacian past them and headed directly for the slower Roman with a bow on her right. The Roman to her right dropped his unfired arrow, holding a bow in his left hand, and drew his spatha longsword with his right, expecting the Dacian to make a close pass. Never one to disappoint and completely out of arrows, Cynna lifted herself just enough to grab a passing rider, her body still hanging almost entirely from the right side of her horse. Having already thrown off any likely attempt by the others to attack her, Cynna angled to pass right beside the man as though she meant to catch and pull him from his horse as they passed. Of course, such a move might dislocate her arm, but desperate situations called for desperate measures, or at least she hoped that's what he would expect.

As they passed, everything happened in an instant: The Roman stabbed his spatha at her unshielded neck and face as Cynna threw her dangling upper body backward, ducking under the plunging blade as her powerful abdominal and leg muscles fought to hold her tightly to Tamura. The sword glanced off her armored sternum and passed right beside her face, barely missing her. Ignoring the extremely near miss, Cynna reached out and grabbed a handful of arrows from the Roman's quiver. She passed and quickly swung herself back onto the saddle properly, feeling slightly disoriented but now with a hand full of arrows for her troubles. Tamura angled left and away from the man as Cynna stuffed the fistful of arrows into one of her quivers, the entire charge lasting but an eight count.

"Thanks for the arrows, you motherless pigs," she screamed, followed by a high-pitched, trilling war cry as she raced away from the men, giving herself as much distance as she could. She had finally found a purpose in life and someone to share it with, but it seemed that fate would not let her be at peace. She would have loved to marry someone like Meala, if even possible, and grow old with her. She wanted to drink, share stories, be intimate, and snuggle. But now, she faced what she was sure were unwinnable odds against the elite cavalry men who would not fall for her trickery again.

If nothing more, she could lead them away from Meala and hope the woman escaped. Even if Meala didn't, she would do her best to reduce the enemy as much as she could and make them pay. She might never hold her lover again, but they had at least spent one glorious night together, and she could take those memories to the next life. She wasn't afraid of death, though dying sounded painful. What really made her chest ache was the knowledge of what love she and Meala might have shared, but likely never would, a sorrow far worse than death. A tear streaked down her cheek as she thought of those moments that would never be, yet she would make her last stand and do the Mother of Fire and her late mother proud. Besides, now that she was partly reloaded, she was finally ready to show them what a mounted archer could do.

🐐🐐🐐

"Put a fucking arrow in her!" Ci screamed as they brought their horses around to begin a pursuit. She simply couldn't believe what she had seen. The woman had charged them, ducked the one attack that should have decapitated her, and the bitch had even stolen the arrows right out of the man's quiver while passing at a full gallop. No wonder the Legatus kept a group of these strange people close at hand. Still, the Dacian had only killed one of them by surprise, and none of them when they had charged. With one remaining man more than enough to control the two bound captives and two men at her sides Ci was reasonably confident of victory. Even better, with the archer fleeing, her back was now to them, and they could fire upon her without her returning the favor. Oddly, she felt a pang of annoyance at not having her trident from the ring, a weapon that might have been of use against such a foe.

Only Numerius had a strung bow, but the man had at least brought three full quivers. She was but a thief who couldn't have taken more than a dozen or two arrows, plenty of them having spilled onto the ground as she grabbed what she could. Of course, the Dacian's armor was high-

258

quality iron scale, and Numerius would be shooting from a distance, but eventually, he would score a hit. It was down to a simple matter of numbers. Once she was wounded or dead, they could take her and the trio back to the Fort, and Ci would be free of this burden.

A sharp pain reminded her that the bitch's arrow had sliced partly through her leather armor and tasted flesh. The leather was strong and had caused the arrow to twist sideways, tumbling as it deflected away, but the tip had dug through her arm as it had. She knew the iron tip had left a nasty flesh wound that might take a few moons to fully heal, but she would have plenty of time and comfort to rest and heal after she was paid in gold for the bitch's head. Oddly, there was a strange tingly sensation where the arrow had gashed her upper arm, not something she had felt any of the many times she had been wounded in the ring. She hoped the tingle wouldn't remain permanently, as such wounds sometimes did.

A moment later, Ci and her Roman escort raced at a full gallop after the archer, trying to catch her before she could get too far away. She was fast, but a horse could only gallop for so long before rest. With fatigue came a loss of agility, which was the primary difference between Ci's men and the archer. In fact, they didn't need to actually catch up to her as they could begin firing at one hundred Roman foot's distance with a chance of hitting her or her horse. Ci would hate to see such a beautiful animal killed, but such was the cost of battle. Her mind played through scenario after scenario as she calculated just how fast she could… *what the fu*… her mind snapped into focus, and her eyes grew wide.

"By the bloody moon…" Ci began to say as the Dacian woman twisted her upper body and brought her bow around to point behind her–at a full gallop–and took aim at her pursuers. A moment later, a well-aimed arrow came right at her, nearly catching Ci in the face as she ducked away. Lifting her head, she watched as the woman drew and knocked another arrow, then took aim once more, firing with precision and accuracy at targets behind her and at a full gallop. Worse, the headwind gave her arrows a massive advantage in distance while limiting how far Numerius' arrows could fly. Ci's dread rose at the realization. This meant that the Dacian could hold them within her engagement range until her horse ran out of stamina. While that was probably not much longer, as horses could run but so far without rest, the tables were entirely turned upon them until that happened.

With almost cruel efficiency, the archer fired an arrow at Numerius, yet as the man ducked to avoid it, she quickly knocked, drew, and fired a second arrow faster than Ci had ever seen. Just as Numerius lifted his head once more, he caught an arrow with his face, ending his pursuit and life. The elite cavalryman dropped his bow and fell backward with the strangest look of shock on the unruined part of his previously handsome face. What had started as three wolves hunting a rabbit had become two wolves hunting a fox as Ci and Sextus zigzagged to avoid arrow after arrow.

As she did this, Ci nearly dropped the reigns when a feeling of dizziness suddenly overtook her. Maybe she just needed water, or it was just the blasted back-and-forth motion as she ducked yet another arrow, but she didn't have even a moment to consider as the deadly woman stopped firing, slowed, and rounded on her pursuers, ready to charge. In response, Ci and Sextus slowed their horses, not wishing to get too close as shorter distances meant easier targets. Dizzy and feeling a bit weak, Ci lifted her rete (throwing net), adjusting it for throwing almost instinctually, just as she had in the ring. Before her stood a scale armored warrior on a horse, but Ci knew how to fight an eques gladiator (horse-mounted gladiator) and prepared her net.

She pulled her legs apart as hard as she could as she rubbed the ropes against the metallic disc adorning the horse's tack. Suddenly, Meala's feet came free with a jerk, and the movement caused her to lurch to the side. Her captor tightened his grip, obviously not realizing the significance of the sudden motion and far too intent on what was happening not so far away. He had just watched his men chase the Dacian woman past them, heading roughly in the same direction as the distant fort. He had already watched one of his men fall from his horse as the woman fired backward with considerable aim, a feat of dexterity that none of his men could achieve, his attention quite enthralled.

Meala had seen some of the fight, and her adrenaline had spiked with every near miss, but Cynna was now too far behind her field of view to see, and getting free had to be her priority. Whether or not Cynna defeated the men or was defeated herself, a gut-wrenching thought, she might need Meala's help. Yet even with her legs now free, her hands were still firmly bound. With time running out, Meala could think of only one way to fix the situation. It wouldn't be pleasant, but there was no way she would let Cynna down – not after she had finally met a woman who made her feel such love and looked at her the way Cynna did.

She had fought at the Wall, gone back for more, and literally tore the woman she loved from the very grasp of Rome. Sure, they had only known each other for a short time, but people married and had entire families out of arrangement or a chance meeting at a festival all the time. Love could take seasons or years to build, but it could also happen during the briefest moments shared over a chance meeting at a festival, trading event, or even on the battlefield, a moment shared between two warriors of honor. She had not spent much time with Cynna, but she might get that time if she fought hard enough. No, she would not give in to these men – she would rather face an entire legion of Romans than let such a woman go.

Just then, Meala heard Cynna's trilling war cry and Damona gasp, but she pushed this from her mind and concentrated on what she must do next. With a brief thought for the ancestors and gods, Meala suddenly jerked her head backward as hard as she could, catching the man in the face with a painful thump. Her vision exploded in stars, but the strong arm that had held her let go as the soldier grabbed at his injured face. Without taking a moment to think, Meala lifted her bound arms overhead as she leaned back and hooked them over the soldier's head, then hurled herself over the right side of the horse with all her might.

She landed hard on the ground, her vision darkening momentarily as she lay disoriented beside the horse. She didn't see the soldier but didn't take the time to look, as whatever advantage she might have would vanish faster than beer at a festival. Wasting no time, Meala crawled to the horse, grasped the same phalera ornamental disc she had used to cut her legs free, and furiously tore at the thin, worn hemp rope binding her hands. She could hear Damona gasping again and whispering something, too frightened to raise her voice. But then, not far to her left, came the low, angry sound of the soldier.

"You stupid cunt, you broke my fucking nose! What the… my… my fucking tooth is loose! Fuck that Britanni whore… You're going to pay for that, and when I'm done with you, I'm going to put my blade in you! Titus can have your rotting corpse, you cunt!" Meala cut with a motivation she didn't know was possible as the truth of what would come next if she failed to escape loomed over her in the form of a bloody, violently angry man, twice her size and well accustomed to killing. He was not like her father, Ris, or even the Roman Acilius. He was the still-breathing corpse of what had maybe once been someone good but was now a living weapon, his human decency stripped from him by the legion.

Beside her, she could hear him standing as she sawed furiously at the cord. Her hearing began to wane, and darkness threatened the edges of her vision as her fight or flight filled her body with the singular will to free herself. Behind her, she heard footsteps and the sound of a blade coming free, the metal leaving leather muted in her terror. Just then, the cord broke, freeing her hands. She ducked and tumbled forward beneath the tawny horse, coming up painfully on the other side. Below the horse, she saw a man's bare legs, ending at calcei (leather boots), blood dripping down his leg.

Running wouldn't help as the man was armed and had a horse, but that was when she noticed that her spear was strapped to the other horse. Unfortunately, her shield and most of her provisions had been discarded, but the spear was better than nothing. Rushing over to the second horse, she grasped the leather thong that lashed the men's gear to the pack horse and fumbled to release it. Behind her, she heard the man cursing in Latin but ignored him as she pulled the first cord free, then worked on a second cord. For a moment, he didn't advance, probably fiddling with his broken tooth and pretty confident that Meala had nowhere to go.

Behind her came the sounds of movement, but she focused on the task, her heart nearly pounding from her chest. A moment later, an oval wooden shield of the type the Romans used fell to the ground followed by a sack of food as the packed gear began to come free, but the last cord was too tightly knotted and wouldn't untie. The sounds of objects falling free seemed to change the injured man's priorities. Hearing movement, Meala grasped the cord and pulled with all her might, willing her arms and hands to exceed their normal limits.

"The man!" Damona cried, as the chance of freedom seemed to outweigh her normally timid nature. The third cord had not come free but had loosened, and Meala grabbed the shaft and dove to her side, sliding the spear from its position alongside the horse as she fell upon the fallen Roman shield. Behind her, the Roman's free hand missed catching her by short measure. Grasping the spear and foreign shield, she stumbled away from his reach, then stood and turned to face the man. She was strong and brave, but nothing empowered her more than the feeling of her mother's spear in hand. Before her stood the elite, armored soldier, his face a bloody mess where his nose had broken, and tooth had been knocked free. In his hand he held his spatha sword, his eyes filled with hate.

"Roman pig…" she spat as she stepped away from the horse, wanting to draw the man away from the bound girl. Damona had cried out a warning, likely saving Meala's life, but now the girl's freedom and life hung in her hands as she faced the elite soldier alone. The Roman stood with blood dripping down his face while holding his sword in one hand and wiping blood away with the other. To say he was menacing and angry was an understatement, but he wasn't the only one, nor did he hold a monopoly on rage. Meala held a Roman shield in her left hand and her mother's spear midshaft in her right, slapping both together, then pointing her spear at the man, a challenge to single combat plain as day, if unspoken.

"I was afraid… but no more. I faced your kind at your fort. I tasted their blood and watched them die at my feet. This is my land and my mother's spear!" Meala spat, waving the weapon overhead and issuing a trill, more to bolster her own courage than anything else. Still, she had fought such men, four on one, and survived. That hope mixed with her adrenalin and fear as her dehydrated and hungry body prepared for the fight of her life…for her life.

"You better hope I kill you because if I wound you first, I'll make you beg for death before I am done," Aulus nearly growled, spitting blood from his mouth where his tooth had come loose and cut his inner lip. Meala bared her teeth in something like a vicious smile, but there was no humor, only anger, and fear she tried desperately to mask.

"You will die without honor this day," she spoke in Latin.

Though she had stolen many arrows, she couldn't bring herself to fire at the horses, something her people frowned heavily upon. Most Sarmatian peoples considered horses sacred, and she had even drank fermented mares' milk as a child. This had forced her to fire only at her pursuers. It had taken time and nearly all her captured arrows, but an arrow had finally killed one man and caught the second man, leaving him wounded and out of the fight. But the infernal redhead rode with her head down, her body close to her horse. It wasn't long before Cynna was once more out of arrows, and this time, she would have to face her final pursuer in hand-to-hand combat. Tamura's head dropped as she breathed hard, Cynna having ridden her hard. Slowing to a halt, she glanced back to find the redhead doing the same as the woman worked to prepare a throwing net, both of their mounts tired from galloping. This would be Tamura's final charge of the battle before she absolutely had to rest.

They regarded each other from a distance for a moment, two warriors ready to face off. Only one of them would live, of that Cynna was sure. The redhead held a sword in her right hand and the rete (net) in the other as she flexed her neck side to side, preparing for their final duel. Around her neck hung Meala's captured gold torc. Barely visible in the distance, she could just make out the shape of the two horses where Meala had been held. She couldn't tell from this distance what was happening, but she hoped the painted warrior was well. Even if she defeated this unusual woman the Romans had sent after her, she would still need to return and face the man holding Meala and Damona. Killing soldiers with her bow at night as they escaped was one thing, but she was honestly surprised that she had made it this far against trained cavalry. Still, the job was not over until all work was complete.

Cynna held her breath for a moment and let it out, then slapped her bow into its holder and bayed Tamura to canter back toward the woman. From her side, she drew her war ax. It had a long wooden handle with a small but heavy and wickedly pointed head made for cavalry use. Ahead, the woman raised her sword and began spinning the net, starting her canter toward the Sarmatian. Unlike the Romans, her sword was a little longer and a little heavier, but what worried Cynna was the net. It wasn't a traditional weapon, but the woman spun it with the skill of someone used to using a net, and Cynna doubted that she was a fisherwoman. Though she was hardly a trained rider, easily visible in how she sat on her horse and held her reins with her sword hand.

Another concern was her arms, legs, and face, all tattooed, marks that spoke of a warrior who had seen many battles. Meala had such marks, though nowhere near as many. They were like the sort of marks Cynna had seen on the locals, mostly black ink with a few red designs. A further concern was that Cynna had no shield to block the sword, but she had a plan, though she figured her arm was going to hurt. It would be risky and harm them both, but she was lighter and knew how to fall from a horse. She was hoping the redheaded warrior was not so skilled.

As Cynna raced forward, she pulled free her lasso and deposited it into her lap while she held her ax at the ready, preparing to swing when they passed. It was precisely the sort of attack the ax had been made for, its pointed head designed to penetrate armor. Nudging Tamura into a full gallop, she raced towards the redhead as her blood pumped hard, and adrenaline flowed. Not only would this be dangerous for her, but for Tamura, too. But she had confidence in her horse, and hope that her own skill would hold up to what was to come. Closer they came… closer… and then the moment came, lasting less time than it took to speak her name.

Cynna brushed Tamura's neck in a particular way with her left hand as she reached for her lasso. On cue, the horse obeyed her training and dropped her head forward as Cynna hurled her lasso into the air, using her powerful arm to quickly spin it overhead in a single, accelerating turn. At that moment, the redhead cast her net, her expression cool and calculated – the face of a warrior who had seen plenty of battle. Both women were about to pass each other, each with their thrown weapons in motion and weapons ready to strike, a blur of motion only a trained warrior might have interpreted.

The net flew forward to engulf the Sarmatian as her arm fought to pull the lasso around from a second accelerating spin. Then, much to the redhead's surprise, Cynna swung her ax, hurling it overhead. At the same moment, Cynna released the lasso, letting the hardened loop of rope launch toward the redhead, a nearly ambidextrous feat of dexterity. The faster-moving ax few just before the lasso and impacted the oncoming net, deflecting its upper portion, sparing her upper body and flying lasso. The deadly ax also suddenly and exclusively preoccupied the redhead's focus as she ducked to avoid it. The partially deflected net and lasso passed each other in the air, barely eight Roman feet ahead of the racing horses, all within a single heartbeat.

The net slammed into Cynna, its upper portions deflected, but its lower part sliding over Tamura's lowered head but wrapping itself and its weights around the Sarmatian's lower body with far more force than she had expected. At the same time, the lasso caught the redhead's upper body as their horses passed and the redhead flew by. On instinct, Cynna grasped the rope with her right hand and, using both hands, pulled it over her right shoulder, bracing for what was to come. Well trained, Tamura dug her hoofs into the soft soil at Cynna's nudging, coming to a halt just as the rope pulled taut. Instead of bracing herself against Tamura's halt, she let her bodyweight fly forward, the suddenly taut rope with Cynna's mass tearing the redhead from her horse and sending both women to the ground in a painful misadventure of momentum.

🐕🐕🐕

Ci lay on the warm sands of the ring for a short time watching strange colors and shapes in her vision. All around, she could hear the crowd's scream urging her to stand and fight… or maybe that was just ringing in her ears. She had the urge to vomit but wasn't quite sure why. The wind had been thoroughly knocked from her lungs, and her neck hurt more than she cared to admit. The Dacian bitch had lassoed her, something she had never seen done but had heard of. Honestly, she was surprised that she had not broken her neck. At forty-five years of age, she was pretty sure half of her joints and muscles would need a lengthy downtime to repair. Oddly, even as her vision cleared, her dizziness remained. She was also sweating, her skin feeling clammy and cold, and her heart racing.

With great effort, she pulled the cursed lasso from her chest and dragged herself to her knees. This wasn't the ring. Not far away lay the Dacian tangled in her net, though she also seemed to be stirring. She should have given up and returned with just the two prizes and the loot, but she had put aside her rules against making things personal and not knowing when to quit, and now, here she was. Pausing to vomit, she unceremoniously spit the sick from her mouth, then crawled towards her fallen sword and wayward mount a short distance away. Whether she wanted to or not, the Dacian would rise, and their fight would resume. This wasn't the ring, and there would be no missio given.

Cynna opened her eyes and let out a strange gasping moan. She held the lasso long enough to transfer her forward movement into the redhead but not long enough to tear her arms off, a delicately timed and dangerous move. Her right arm felt like it had almost dislocated, but she could still use it, though the pain was bad. Her hands had painful rope burns, but she had held tightly reducing the damage. If she lived, she figured it might take several moons for the pain to entirely leave, but the tendons would heal. For a moment, she fought with the net wrapped around her lower body but quickly freed herself as the net had not properly engulfed her. She slowly dragged herself to her knees and saw the redhead doing the same. She had hoped the fall might break the woman's neck or harm her more, but it seemed the redhead's luck had held.

Staggering to her feet, she stumbled on stiff joints and called out to Tamura. The warhorse had already approached, curious why her rider had suddenly been snapped right out of her saddle. Cynna winced as she popped her joints and gasped for air. Her ax was lost in the high grass, and she was out of arrows. Her long sword had been missing when she found Tamura in the stables, probably stolen by someone sure she would no longer need it. That left her without a reasonable mounted option for combat. With her aching right arm, she reached into Tamura's saddle and pulled her dagger free of its sheath. The iron weapon was a little over a pes (Roman foot), more like a cubitum (44 cm) with a wooden handle and a ring pummel to which a loop of braided hemp was attached sporting several agate beads.

She lifted and flexed her arms, popping joints and wincing at the pain as she readied herself for melee combat, something she detested. Fighting on foot was for the common soldier, not an elite Sarmatian cavalrywoman. But if this woman wanted to test her mettle against Cynna's blade, she would oblige. Curiously, as the woman approached, Cynna noticed that she looked rather ill. At first, she attributed it to the rather violent method she had used to dismount the woman, but somehow, it didn't seem to add up. In the back of her mind, she remembered seeing someone who looked similar when she was much younger. That time, the person had been bitten by a snake and the unlucky man had passed at least a day later, if she recalled correctly.

It was how she should have looked if the poisoned arrow had penetrated her armor, yet it had deflected, which meant the woman's ragged look had to have come from something else. She wanted to chalk it up to age, silver hair clearly visible here and there in the woman's vibrant mane. Yet, despite her wrinkles and age, she was clearly skilled and a deadly foe. Either way, she slowly approached Cynna with her reclaimed sword in her right hand, held point forward, and a second rete net in her left hand, like some sort of retiarius gladiator… (a gladiator who uses a trident and net) a retiaria, she supposed. With the dagger in hand, Cynna gave Tamura a pat on the rump for her to step away and spat onto the ground as she turned to face the redheaded warrior the Romans had sent for her.

With a grunt, Meala staggered back, feeling a dull, numb pain in her left hand. The spatha had struck her shield with enough force to bruise her hand through the shield, a disturbing realization. She had wanted to leap forward with her spear as she had seen men do when dueling at festivals and at the raid, but the force of impact had left her reeling. Her left arm tingled and felt numb, but she kept it securely bound to the shield as she stepped back and regained her composure.

"You think I'm scared of a little girl with a stick? I saw your face when you blocked my sword, like a baby tiro. You could barely take the hit. How many more can you take before your arm goes limp?" the man taunted as he flexed his broad shoulders. He towered over Meala, nearly a head taller and twice as wide. Worse, his body was protected by iron banded armor, not nearly as nice as Cynna's, but good enough to block any direct hits from her spear. Her tired, hungry, and thirsty body was clad in a woolen tunic, her feet bare, and not even a belt to secure the overly large garment. The tunic was too long to be practical, but too short to properly gird. It was as far from ideal as she could imagine, but she was no coward.

She dashed forward again and attempted to strike with her spear, thrusting the weapon at the man's head. But he stepped sideways, swiping at the shaft with his left arm and driving the spear aside. She tried to move with her spear, but the excess tunic cloth caught between her legs, nearly tripping her. At the same time, he stepped forward and swung his spatha overhead, causing her to throw her shield up in a desperate attempt to stop him. Unfortunately, when the blade hit the wood, her shield was cleaved in twain from its side and causing it to come apart in her hand. Meala leapt to the side and scurried a few feet beyond his striking distance as she shook her now quite numb left hand, the remnants of her shield tumbling to the ground. Glancing down, she noted how red and swollen her left arm already looked and winced.

"You were lucky when you got free, but you should have run. Ci said that the women from the north were deadly, but it's looking to me like you're still just a simple girl with a toy spear," he said with a laugh. Meala snarled at the man, angered both by his words and her annoying problem with her tunic flapping loosely, making movement difficult. Tunics were cut from a single panel of cloth with square sleeves and often a width nearly twice as wide as their intended wearer. This meant they could grow with the wearer, but this was also why a belt was tied around the garment to hold it tightly against the body. Unfortunately, the Romans had left the rest of her clothing, even her shoes, at the gully, leaving her wearing only her mother's borrowed, oversized tunic. It was like wearing a giant blanket to battle. Without a shield, dexterity was her only armor, but how could she be dexterous in a woolen tunic?

"I'm going to watch when they nail you to the wood. I'm going to be there smiling. Both you and the girl. Just think how lovely the day will be," he quipped with a bloody smile. Meala's spirit burned like a flame at the flippant mention of such a death and the inclusion of Damona, a girl who had been nothing more than a victim. This man wasn't just a creep; he was a disgusting monster. The problem was that life wasn't fair, and a disgusting monster could win. She had no idea if Cynna still lived, and her only hope now was a single spear against an elite soldier. She needed a way to get around his slower but savagely powerful attacks by leaning on her natural dexterity. Suddenly, an idea came to mind. It was less than appealing, but at this point, she had nothing left to lose… and neither did Damona.

"You have nowhere else to go, woman. Drop your weapon, and I promise to be gentle," the man said, tauntingly. She was done listening to his taunts and had an idea of how to finish this. Silently, she whispered a prayer to the gods and ancestors for aid, though what she really needed was help from Damona. Stepping back a fair distance, she suddenly stabbed her spear point into the ground and grabbed her tunic, pulling the garment overhead and tossing it to the ground. The cool wind blew across her body, quickly removing what sweat she had and replacing it with a refreshing reprieve. She now stood as her ancestors, a proper warrior of the highest honor. Her magical bee tattoo lay bare under the blue sky, and she could almost feel the ancestors looking on with respect.

"I am Sei'ln Meala, daughter of Ail Braide, lover of Cynna of Dacia, of the Iazyges, and friend of Damona of Veluniate. My mother fought with honor before me as I now fight in my family's name!" she spoke aloud in her own language. Behind the man, Damona looked on in fear. Slapping her chest the way she saw several of the men do before the raid that late dark season, she grasped her mother's spear with both hands and approached the man, her nerves a wreck and fear seeming to replace her blood as she stepped toward the giant armored Roman. At least she was now free from the flappy tunic.

"You are already stripped for me? Such a friendly barbarian," the man teased in his cruel way as he approached the painted woman. Normally, the local women of Brittania and Caledonia were a modest group, at least by Roman standards, yet he had seen many of her kind fight this way before. Whatever ritualistic and meaningful expression of her culture this was, it was merely a momentary amusement for him. He began to laugh, but his smile vanished as Meala abruptly rushed forward, now suddenly much quicker than before.

He positioned his sword slightly angled and before him ready to defend or attack, but Meala sprung forward, the sharpened edge of her spear tip slicing a small, red arc across the man's face. He threw his hand and sword up to deflect her spear, but she lifted a foot high into the air and kicked forward, catching the man right between the legs. He sliced his blade back her way as he grasped his loins, but Meala used part of the kick's energy to spring back, prancing away on her now unencumbered, nimble legs, though her lack of a chest wrap certainly made things less pleasant.

While the man ignored the facial laceration, he had trouble ignoring the kick. Still, a moment later, he lunged at Meala, stabbing his steel blade. No longer burdened, the painted warrior easily sidestepped the stab, returning the favor with a single jab to the man's exposed arm with her spear. Like the face, it did little real damage, but she was starting to finally make some progress. The only problem was that she was tired, hungry, and dehydrated. Worse, her opponent was just so large and powerful. She was like a bee stinging a wolf, and if she didn't do something soon, she would run out of stamina, or he would get a lucky strike. Unfortunately, the same bare skin that gave her such speed and flexibility also left her vulnerable, and a single good hit, and she would be dead. Though she supposed her woolen tunic hadn't offered any real protection, aside from possibly deflecting a glancing blow.

The man and Meala circled each other for a few moments longer as each looked for a way to strike. Meala began to feel a little dizzy as her lack of water and food and exhaustion from non-stop action began to set in. Even at her age, there was only so much a person could take. She leapt forward once more, but nearly stumbled as her leg gave way, her spear missing its mark. A moment later, the deadly spatha came rushing for her abdomen, a lethal strike. Just as it was about to hit, the man made a strange sound, and his thrust missed its mark by barely a hair's width. He turned to find the timid girl, her bound arms held oddly out as though she had just awkwardly thrown something.

Realizing that Meala was in mortal danger and was losing her pace, and knowing that horror awaited them both if Meala failed, Damona had briefly overcome her fears and painfully learned conditioning just long enough to throw a single bronze dagger she had found in the gear lashed to the pack horse – Meala's dagger, captured by the Romans with the rest of their weapons. The bronze dagger had tumbled through the air and slapped the man's shaved head with its hilt, causing little harm. The ability to throw a knife that bit into an opponent took luck or skill, neither of which Damona had. Still, the force of this impact had negatively affected his thrust. But more importantly, he had turned briefly on pure instinct to see who had thrown the weapon.

Seeing a lucky break for what it was, Meala dashed forward and ducked as she stabbed her spear into the man's exposed knee with all her might, ignoring his heavy armor. Hearing her movement, the man's sword came in a blind swing over her head, barely missing. The blade caught the upper part of her spear, slicing clean through the handle just as the spear's iron tip bit into his knee. Unfortunately for the Roman, the force of the sword's impact and his sudden twisting motion violently tore the spear tip from his knee, along with part of his kneecap, which saved Meala the effort and caused untold damage to the joint. In a scream of profound agony, the Roman collapsed onto his side. Meala lifted the now slightly smaller spear and stepped around the man, looking for an opportunity.

"Ahhh! You bitch! Ahhh! My knee!" he screamed in complete agony as he slashed several times with the sword while holding his ruined knee with the other hand. Meala agilely avoided the sword as she stepped in from behind and stabbed the man in his trapezius muscle, which connected his shoulder to his neck. A moment later, she stabbed him in his thigh and then in his other leg. One bee sting after another until the man finally dropped his sword. Sting after sting found its way past his armor while the man screamed and clawed at the air, but eventually, he stopped fighting. A moment later, Meala had kicked away the man's spatha, then found herself standing over his body with her foot on his chest. She gazed down upon the man, feeling little pity for such a beast.

"You... you... cunt... you..." he mumbled as his blood pressure dropped. Meala stared the man in the face, never breaking eye contact as she slowly pressed her mother's spear into his exposed neck. Using her fleeting strength, she pressed the weapon down while she watched him die. His was not a face that would haunt her because his was a death she would feel no moral confusion over. Not all the guards had likely been bad people, some having the possibility of one day becoming another Acilius. But not this one.

"Well, your leader did tell you what would happen if you touched one of us..." she said, then spit on the Roman with what little spittle she could manage. She pulled free her spear as the man's wide eyes slowly went dull, pupils dilating for the last time, and turned to find Damona. Both woman and girl were shocked, and Meala was so full of adrenaline that she could nearly retch, yet again. As she stepped away, she stumbled and fell to her knees. A moment later, Meala crawled to her discarded tunic and pulled it on. She ripped the leather belt from the Roman and tied it around her waist, finally free from the excess cloth that made the movement troublesome. Stumbling to her feet, she approached Damona's horse and grasped the waterskin with shaky hands, gulping from it hungerly. Offhandedly, she wondered if drinking so much at Julia's had been a good idea. She was dizzy, so she handed the skin to Damona and stumbled away to lay down on the ground in the high grass, hoping it would pass.

"Thank you… Damona. You have saved my life twice, and that alone should be enough if anybody questions your right to live among my family. That is if we make it out of this and you still want to… and if I can get a little more water and food…" she mumbled. The girl finished gulping water with bound hands, then stared back, nodding slowly but looking a bit pale. Damona was no warrior and never would be. People came in all shapes and sizes; some were willing to fight, while others were not. Nothing was wrong with that, as all kinds of people were needed to make a society, and someone like Damona would be much happier on a farm herding sheep. The thought nearly made Meala laugh, though she supposed that her body was just reacting to fatigue and stress more than any real humor.

Her body was rife with pain and stress, and she could feel the flashbacks and intrusive thoughts probing for a way into her mind's eye. They were banished by the adrenaline in combat but came back soon afterward. Only her exhaustion seemed to be keeping them at bay. Unfortunately, after she got some rest, they would likely return in force. She smiled, her mind tired enough to find humor in what was not humorous as her fingers found and played with little pieces of grass. Her thoughts drifted as the adrenaline crashed; no food or water that day, and mostly water wine the night before and beer the previous night having caught up with her. She needed a few moments lying on the ground to… well, to ground herself and to get past the mixture of nausea and low energy. Oddly enough, she was starting to understand why some of the most brazen warriors chose that form of heroic expression, though she hoped never to do it again.

She dozed in and out of rest for a moment, but Damona's sudden and excited sounds jerked her back from her torpor. As she looked up, Meala noticed a horse-mounted figure standing once more on the rise. Cynna...

Cynna!

The woman burst into her mind as she suddenly remembered what she had been trying to recall as she had faded into slumber from exhaustion. Cynna had been locked in mortal combat. How could she have forgotten. Damona called out something in her native, guttural tongue while Meala's blurry eyes fought to focus on the figure in the distance. Was that a final Roman come to finish the job? As she squinted, shock once more flooded her tired body...

Cynna grabbed her stomach, feeling intense pain where the sword had impacted her armor. Realizing that she didn't have time to escape the redhead's swing, she stepped into it, causing the entire blade to hit her stomach rather than a small portion, which might have concentrated more energy in one small place and penetrated. While her superior iron scale armor reflected the blade, her stomach had absorbed the physical blow leaving several scales bent. She had strong abdominal muscles, and she had tensed them, but she could tell there would be bruising. With a swipe of her arm she deflected the poorly aimed net, used more as a distraction at the moment, though she had no doubt the wielder could do much more with it.

So far, she had failed to hit the redhead even once, but she had already hit Cynna's armor three times. She carried herself like a veteran fighter, specifically one trained in melee combat. Instead of coming hard and fast like an inexperienced fighter, she had begun by probing Cynna with simple attacks to find her weak spots, and with her muscles and tendons pulled here and there, she had plenty of weak spots. Now, she seemed to be pressing for the kill. Curiously, while tearing the redhead from her horse had caused the woman injury, evident from her slight limp, it seemed that something else was sapping her strength. Instead of following up with a second strike, the redhead stumbled backward, looking weaker by the moment.

"I don't know what magic you have cast upon me, witch, but as soon as I take your life, I suspect it will end," she spat, looking rather grim. It was the first thing she had said to Cynna, and her voice carried the thick accent of a local. A moment later, the unknown warrior paused and vomited, wiping her mouth and spitting for good measure. What had started as skillful probing had quickly turned into a more aggressive attack as the woman's health seemed to waver. Just then, the woman sprung forward, swiping her net at Cynna's dagger while plunging her blade at the archer's abdomen. Yet again, the scale took the blow, but this time, the net caught her dagger.

Cynna realized that the net had switched from a distraction to the main attack while the sword had become the ruse. The woman drew the sword back to capitalize on Cynna's caught dagger. Instead of fighting to free her weapon, Cynna released the blade, bending her arm back and sliding it out from the net as she took one long step toward the woman. The redhead's blade lifted just behind her head and changed direction, returning for a slash. But Cynna's next step brought her right before the redhead as her now free arm snapped forward, and her fist caught the warrior in her jaw. Cynna punched straight threw, her powerful arms made strong from a life of drawing a war bow.

The redhead staggered back, her eyes rolling back in her head for a moment as she nearly lost consciousness, but she slashed the blade before her a few times to dissuade attacks while she fought to recover. But Cynna didn't pursue it. Instead, she stepped back, her feet squishing against the soft, muddy ground, and put her hands beneath her kaftan longshirt. With a quick tug, she pulled free the two simple slipknots holding her blue and white woolen leggings to her waist cord, then bent down to pick up her dagger from the net. As she looked back, the woman shook her head, trying to recover from the mighty blow, her nose bloodied and her anger seething. Cynna was running low on stamina and her opponent was a far superior melee fighter. Now, it was time to use the environment to her benefit.

The Sarmatian rushed forward, her leggings still held to her legs by their cords and tight waist cord, but no longer tied. As she approached the redheaded warrior, the woman's dizzy focus locked onto Cynna, and she plunged her sword forward like the trident she used to use, its steel tip aimed right at Cynna's torso. At the last moment, the Sarmatian dropped to her knees and threw back her head, sliding across the muddy ground at the warrior. The redhead barely sidestepped Cynna, nearly skipping over her. But, as she passed, the archer swung her dagger backward, reversed grip, plunging it deep into the former gladiator's back.

Cynna took that moment to catch her breath, already rather tired from the exertion, as the redhead stepped forward and stumbled to her knees. Cynna turned to find the woman reaching for the dagger but not having much luck removing it. Slowly, the Sarmatian stood on pained legs, her leggings lying on the ground near the wounded warrior where they had slipped off while sliding across the muddy grass. As she approached, she noted that there was indeed a cut on the woman's leather armor where her poisoned arrow had hit, and from that cut ran a small trail of blood. That explained the woman's degenerating health, which was fortunate for Cynna as she was sure this skilled brawler could have taken her in a fair melee fight.

She had stabbed at an angle, and the blade had slid between ribs as it entered, penetrating at least four unciae (roughly 10cm). Hearing Cynna approach, the woman released her grasp on the blade and struggled for her sword, but Cynna wasn't about to let that happen. With a front kick, the Sarmatian drove her boot into the dagger's ring pummel, forcing the blade in much deeper and driving the woman to the ground. Cynna knelt, pressing one knee into the woman's back and tore the blade free with both hands, an act far harder than it seemed and producing a sound she would not soon forget. The dark blood coming from the dagger wound told Cynna that she had hit something vital.

"Fucking equis bitch," Ci mumbled in her native tongue. Cynna stood, walked a short distance from the warrior and dropped once more to her knees, her body weak. The redhead rolled over, her body too weak to rise. Cynna regarded her as the woman's life blood poured from the gaping wound to her back. Some might take a moment to monologue or gloat over a fallen enemy, but something about this woman had earned her a little respect in Cynna's eyes. She despised the woman, but whoever this nameless warrior was, she had fought well and without fear, something Cynna had to respect. Besides, people who wasted such time sometimes got stabbed by a crafty enemy.

"Who are you," Cynna asked in Latin as she knelt before the dying woman with her bloody dagger in hand. Now on her side and casting Cynna a wry look, the warrior forced something between a grunt and a laugh before replying.

"You may take my life, but you will never know my name," she breathed, her voice waning by the moment as the dark blood flowed.

"Very well. You have earned that honor, if nothing more. I will end it quickly or leave you to the gods," Cynna offered, noting that the woman's sword was out of reach, and she no longer seemed to be trying to get it.

"Give me the iron," she said, slowly lifting herself into a kneeling position and bending her head to expose her neck. Cynna frowned, unsure what the woman was doing but willing to give her a quick death in exchange for her bravery, hated foe or not. She stepped beside the woman holding her dagger and grasping the woman's upper body, then placed her dagger against her neck, ready to plunge the blade. The warrior grasped Cynna's leg but continued to hold her neck open for the kill.

"Moriar quia vixi," the woman breathed as Cynna plunged the blade through her neck and into her chest cavity, stopping her heart and taking her life in an instant. Cynna had no idea that Ci had been trained as a gladiatrix nor that she had just performed the ritual death of a defeated gladiator, a death of honor in Roman culture. But as the woman's body slid to the ground, she knew that there was another woman she cared for and potentially one final warrior to defeat before they were free.

"May the Seven Divines salute your bravery before they roast your soul in the fires of oblivion..." Cynna whispered as she reached to retrieve Meala's gold torc from the woman's neck, then called for Tamura, leaving the body on the ground for the birds to pick clean.

She retrieved her leggings and secured them around her legs again, finding the garments were now quite dirty and would require careful cleaning, but they were otherwise unharmed. Seeing no quiver on the woman's horse, she removed the saddle and bit, letting the animal run free. She might return for the horses if she survived but now wasn't the time. Horses were considered a precious resource among her people, and one never freed a saddled horse as the animal could not remove the saddle and tack by itself. She would pass by one of the other riderless horses and take what arrows she could find on her way back to the tiny specks on the horizon that were probably Meala, Damona, and a dead man who simply didn't know it yet. If the man they had left behind to guard Meala was still there, she would pepper him with arrows from a distance and turn him into a human porcupine.

Meala lay gazing at the mounted Sarmatian warrior woman upon her horse high up on the opposite rise, staring down at her. The woman looked as though she had seen a fair bit of combat, not to mention some mud, but she otherwise seemed okay. Perched atop her horse with her bow and a freshly acquired arrow knocked, her long, dark hair blowing in the wind, and her scale armor catching the midday sun, Cynna was once more a sight to behold. With great effort, she rose to her feet and called out.

"Cynna!"

Meala stumbled to Damona as fast as her exhausted body could, pausing to grab her trusty bronze dagger from the grass and use it to free the girl. She had wanted to rush to Cynna, but the mounted woman could realistically come to her much quicker, and leaving Damona tied to a horse–the girl who had just saved her life–seemed a bit gauche. She finished cutting Damona's cords and flashed the girl an encouraging smile before turning to meet the warrior she could hear rushing up behind her atop the mighty Tamura.

As she turned, the two women momentarily caught each other's gazes before their eyes fell and rose, taking in each other's condition. Meala's hair was a mess, and her tunic was dirty. She didn't even have shoes, and there were several splotches of blood on her clothes, though thankfully not hers. Cynna was equally disheveled, though she was covered in more mud than blood, and her ax was missing. With a frown, Meala noted that the woman's normal arrows were gone, replaced with longer Roman arrows. The pair needed baths almost as much as water and food. Lying nearby was the body of the Roman man, the final obstacle to their freedom, his body covered in the many bloody stings of battle.

"Heia, bellatricem pulchram," (hello, beautiful warrior) Meala said, a smile creeping across her tired, dusty face. Cynna looked from the Roman to Meala and then to Damona, who looked more relieved than anyone Cynna had ever seen. The Sarmatian nudged her horse, who gracefully sidestepped to stand right beside Meala as the mighty warrior gazed down from atop her majestic steed. When she spoke, she did so with a strange finality.

"You have fought your captor and taken his life. As for the others, I drove them to the underworld, where the snakes drink their blood. They dared to harm the woman that I love, and I taught them the price of that dare. When I was bound, you stood upon my deer skin and swore an oath by action. We both tasted blood, the seal of that oath, and now it is done. Your honor is unbroken," she finished, reaching into her saddle bag and removing the gold torc. She handed the precious item to Meala with a nod of respect. Whatever the deer skin and oath were, Meala was unsure, some sort of cultural reference, she supposed, but she thought that she understood the basic message.

"Those who oppose us lie dead at our feet," Cynna added. Meala gently bit her lip as she heard the confidence in Cynna's voice. The death part she could do without, but neither she nor Damona would have survived without Cynna's help, even if Meala had technically defeated the man who had held her bound. Regardless, this was the sort of warrior she had dreamed about as a child but never dared to hope could exist. A warrior maiden who could fight by her side, be her friend and companion, her lover, and share her bed. Blood and mud were not the most romantic, but she was so tired that she could no longer process the worst of it and was far past caring.

For a moment, Cynna sat there contemplating something she wasn't sure how to say. Meala waited patiently, curious what the woman might say, though she needed more water and a long nap. In truth, they were both tired, dirty, and mildly wounded. Cynna glanced down upon the painted warrior, seeing the charming certainty and bravery in her green eyes, like the steppe in spring. There was nothing more attractive to Cynna than mutual respect and bravery, and the look of mutual respect they shared was the richest form of this she had yet beheld.

Meala stood looking shaky and tired, but she had clearly fought and killed the Roman assigned to guard her and emerged victorious. Even after all of it, her wide-eyed, almost playful look was hard to ignore. It was so out of place for the moment, yet she seemed to nearly stand beyond the dirty, bloody reality of the day, like a beautiful flower in a muddy field. With a deep breath to steady herself, she spoke once more, her voice formal but kind. She would have to be brave once more today, and this next part carried with it more fear than her battle with the unknown warriors moments before, yet an arrow never fired, never struck.

"I, Cynna of Dacia, of the Iazyges, and daughter of Syon, offer my bow, my sword, my horse, and my very life to you as a wife," the Sarmatian said boldly, her body armored yet her heart naked and vulnerable in that moment. Meala's hands fell to her side in shock, another wave of feelings passing through her already exhausted body, leaving her instantly weak. Behind them, Damona held onto the horse, watching the glorious moment in awe, perhaps hoping that one day her lover might stand before her and make such a proclamation as Cynna continued.

"Life is short, and our end stalks us, even now. But until that time comes, we must make the most of it. All that I own and am is yours if you accept," she finished, speaking a modification of ritual words passed down by her people. While she spoke with great confidence, a bead of sweat dripped down her forehead as her heart seemed to pause, waiting to know if it should continue beating or simply surrender to death.

Meala stood utterly still for a long moment, hearing only the wind as it played across the grass. As a child, she had long dreamed of a dashing hero, either rescuing her or vice versa. Her dreams had dared to explore the idea that this dashing hero might be a woman from her tribe or another. She had once even imagined rescuing a Roman woman. Still, she had never expected a Sarmatian archer from so far away as this mythical steppe of Dacia. Moreover, she had never expected they would save each other, two warriors, not a warrior and a helpless maiden. Ultimately, they didn't know each other very well, but was this not true love? What kind of fool she would be to turn down what was obviously a gift from the gods. As she looked into Cynna's dark, hazel eyes, the flutter in her chest was all the answer she needed.

Meala replied, using the same wording Cynna had used. It wasn't the way of her people, but that hardly mattered to her. The marriage ritual was meant to make one's mother happy, and they could handle that later. Its other use was to please the gods, but the improbability of their meeting and success told Meala that the gods had already smiled upon their union. In truth, she was doubtful anyone would believe their tale.

"I, Sei'ln Meala of the Flooding Lake, daughter of Ail Braide, of East Wenechon, of clan Wood Owl offer all that I am and all that I own, what little that is, to you, as your wife," she spoke in finality, tears rolling down her cheeks from the sheer emotional enormity of it, though the tears were muted by her dry lips. As she looked on, Cynna, too, shed her tears, her lips quivering as she spoke.

"Then it is done. We who were two are now one," Cynna spoke, lowering her right hand for Meala. She grabbed ahold of the archer's outstretched arm and leaped up. It was a struggle, as Cynna's arms were both quite wounded, and lifting an entire woman onto a horse was hardly easy, but with the cooperation of Tamura and a little work, Meala climbed into the saddle to sit before Cynna, their bodies pressed tightly together. Cynna wrapped her strong arms around Meala as the pair began to slowly trot away from their final battlefield. As they passed, Cynna took Damona's horse's reigns and led it behind them, the girl having no real skill at riding and looking equally emotionally exhausted.

As they headed toward the river for water, washing, and perhaps a nap, Meala closed her eyes, secure in the strong arms of her lover... no, that was no longer an accurate description. Cynna was not just her lover – she was her wife. She whispered the word, feeling it on her tongue as tingles of ecstasy danced down her spine. Behind them, Damona closed her eyes and held onto her packhorse as they left the bloody lands.

"Mother and father are going to have... Questions," Meala whispered as Cynna chuckled.

Chapter XIII

Honey and Flowers

Love at First Sight – a fanciful notion and oft mocked component of romantic literature, but is it really a thing? According to science, yes. Studies from major universities consistently demonstrate that human romantic expression is complicated and has many forms. But warriors on a battlefield? Meala and Cynna were enemies, but Cynna only reluctantly so, her feelings openly hostile to Rome. Perhaps her non-Roman identity was a moderating factor. Studies suggest that love, at first sight, is less of a fully formed love and more of a recognition of compatibility and a readiness for such a romance to form. Having a shared experience of love at first sight under such emotionally powerful conditions, not to mention the compassion and empathy to spare or save each other, probably enhanced such feelings.

Another consideration is one of pragmatism. Meala had a limited ability to find love, as did Cynna, given their rural settings. With sapphic-attracted women (lesbian, bisexual, etc.) making up only a few percentage points of society and strong socio-economic pressures to form heteronormative pairings, coupled with a significantly shorter life expectancy, finding a lover was not easy and likely came with a sense of urgency. These facts should be considered when interpreting the motivations of these ancient women, especially under a modern paradigm.

Braide Homestead, western shore of Flooding Lake (Loch Leven), 64 km northeast of Antonine Wall, Caledonia – 7 AM, September 5, 160 CE

Ail methodically scraped a goat hide stretched between two wooden poles as the morning sun rose over the lake, flooding the landscape with light and painting the clouds carnelian red. She paused, placing her hand upon her back and bending to stretch the raw pains of labor from her muscles. Not far behind, her youngest son Brynen sat on the edge of the crannog just above the calm waters while he diligently wrapped sinew around an arrow shaft, securing a costly bronze point to the wood as he finished his 10th arrow of the morning. His feet dangled over the lake, kicking back and forth playfully while he worked. The seasons were already starting to change, but if the day's warmth held, Ail was sure to find Brynen swimming by midday.

A short distance away, the sound of her husband Uuen's ax could be heard in the forest as he worked to fell yet another tree in preparation for the dark season to come. The family worked when it was warm to make sure they were warm when it was cold. Her older son Ris lay inside the home complaining of a headache. However, he had worked at an almost feverish pace over the last few days repairing the fence in the Western field at her request, given that he and his wife Eilun were once more spending a few days at home after a successful market day by the Stone. Off in the distance, she heard the sound of beavers while a lone osprey sailed overhead on the hunt for a morning meal.

Ail suspected Ris simply wanted a day off after his hefty work, but he was far too proud to admit it. Eilun had spoken with him just that morning and had confessed that she shared Ail's suspicions. Either way, both mother and wife had agreed that it was a well-deserved break, though she wished he had asked. She rolled her eyes, wishing sometimes that her elder son had not picked up so much of Uuen's pride. It could be charming, but oh so annoying after a fashion. She paused, holding her iron leather scraper to the light to judge its sharpness as it had seemed a little dull on her last few scrapes. Her younger daughter Rigandona was likely also in the crannog, spinning wool for weaving when the nights grew colder. And then there was Meala...

"Now I understand... oh yes, I do," she whispered, remembering how she had initially fought with her husband when she was younger. He had wanted her to remain home and raise a family, but she had wanted to leave on a raid against the Wall. She had a particular hatred for the Wall. It had been the place where her mother had died in the most horrifying of ways and where she had spent the first part of her life. Memories of her mother brought a smile to her face. She had been a shepherd in town, having never been one for the martial pursuits of her caste. Ail was born in a modest roundhouse in a small village near what would later become

Hadrian's Wall and spent the early part of her life around Romans. They had been her childhood friends and the friendly townspeople who formed the early part of her life, a mixture of happy memories that stood in stark contrast to what had come next.

She had left the village when she was seventeen years old, following the death of her mother at the hands of the local Roman magistrate. Even now, thoughts of what had happened brought a small surge of anger that quickly washed away with the soft sadness that came with time. Her mother had sneaked into the enslaved pens at the Fort and freed several dozen of their people who had been captured from unallied lands and were set to be transported back to the empire. The Roman soldiers had discovered her act of defiance. As the enslaved fled, her mother, Brigid, had drawn her sword and stood her ground against their steel. It had cost her life, but she had saved so many others.

Uuen was a good man and had treated her properly as the warrior she was, even though she had long put down her spear. She had met the young man when she was nineteen and chosen a life of peace at his father's farm, finding herself carrying baby Ris and then baby Meala two years afterward. He had filled her head with notions of a life free from war, instead simply enjoying the harvest of life. Unfortunately, word of Roman atrocity and memories of her mother's final, horrible end had driven Ail two years later to seek the taste of vengeance when her clan had drawn up warbands and as many as they could for a massive raid. Uuen had argued and even begged her to stay, but when she finally made her choice, he respected that choice and wished her luck as she left with her spear and shield.

She could still remember the fear in his peaceful eyes as he watched her leave, terrified that she would end up killed in battle or far worse. It was that fear that had caused the typically good man to lash out at Meala for fear that she would follow in her mother's footsteps. It was the same fear she felt right now, the worry for her eldest daughter that Uuen had held for her. In fact, that raid had been a success, and she had lived, resulting in her warband raiding another, smaller fort a few days later and Ail returning with the head of a Roman soldier. It had felt at the time like vengeance for her mother and her people, but when she had come to face her husband, he had stood there with her four-year-old son at his feet and little two-year-old Meala in his arms and wept.

Instead of bravado over her victory, she had felt shame in the moment. Though she never doubted that her raid against the Romans was justified and Uuen supported her, she had buried her spear and shield and agreed to live in peace, her vengeance as satisfied as possible. They had lived together as farmers, enjoying a rustic, vital life ever since. Oddly, Meala had been somewhat of an enigma, possessing both Brigid and Ail's warrior streak, but also one of the most playful imaginations she had ever seen. To watch her weave flowers into decorations or add little artistic touches to even the most mundane of things would leave most unwilling to believe the woman could be a warrior, yet she was. She had never told Meala the details of her early life out of fear that it might attract the girl to follow in the foolish footsteps of her lineage, but now she wondered if she might have spared Meala from a rift with her father if she had.

She had wept the entire morning after finding the empty hole at the base of the tree where her shield and spear had been buried. Her emotions had been a mixture of fear and anger, but also a sense of pride in her daughter. In truth, she had all but told the young woman that she could leave if she wanted to, though Ail had hoped she would not. Her husband had made the same request of Ail all those years before, and she knew how she would have felt if Uuen had not respected her final choice. Now, all that was left was to wait, just as her husband had waited for her.

The worst part of all was not knowing. What if she simply never returned? Could she be dead, or perhaps a Roman slave, taken to some distant land to labor or worse. Ail wiped her eyes and tried to return to scraping, though probably a little too hard, as her emotions took over. It had been like this, her mind wandering since Meala had left many days before. It was the burden of family and lovers left behind, a burden Uuen had borne for her, and now she bore for her daughter, a bitter reciprocity, she supposed. On the breeze, she swore her nose caught the musky scent of horses, though the family horse was clearly visible far downwind in the Southern field.

"Ris, Ail! Warriors and horses have come!" came a cry from Eilun as she raced from the Western meadows with a basket in hand, nearly tripping over her sandals.

"A raid?" Ail called back, worried another clan might have come to take their few sheep or loot their stores, a terrible calamity this close to the start of the dark season.

"No! There were three, but I only saw one clearly. Metal armor like fish scales and horses," Eilun called back. A visitor was one thing, but "warrior" likely meant someone dressed for battle and unrecognized. The family reacted quickly upon hearing the alarm. Most rushed to grab what they could and head for the crannog for defense. Brynen nearly fell into the water but stumbled to his feet, his arrow lost as it fell into the lake. A moment later, the crannog door burst open, and Ris came rushing out with his old iron sword, followed by Rigandona, her tunic covered in wool fibers from spinning and a distressed look in her eyes. Ail dropped the scraper and reached for her tunic belt, pulling free her long dagger as she made her way to the home, all while keeping her eyes on the tree line between them and the Western meadows.

The small house built on stilts was just far enough from shore that when the bridge connecting it to the land was separated, it would be troublesome to access, especially if armored. Of course, it was easy enough to swim to in the warm season or even walk to if you were tall enough, but few Romans were willing to take their armor off and try, and those who did would find a spear in their face. The only real danger was that someone might fire burning arrows, something a crannog was not so good at repelling. Luckily, it was easy enough to get water, but hopefully, that wouldn't happen. Ail rushed down the small wooden bridge as Uuen emerged from the wood, ax in hand and quickly surveying the scene.

"Eilun says she has seen warriors in the Western meadows. Come quickly," Ail called to her husband, who nodded and jogged to the bridge and then to the crannog.

"What is it? Is it Romans? The Glen?" he asked as he cleared the bridge, but Ail had no answer as she held her dagger. A few moments later, Ail and Uuen stood at the edge of the wooden bridge connecting the land and the crannog as the family worked to pull the hemp cords, lifting the small wooden drawbridge and separating their home from the land. They were hardly warriors nor prepared for confrontation, but hopefully, the warriors would pass them by, simply be interested in trade, or find their farm not worth the effort.

Ail frowned, unsure what to expect from Eilun's description of the armor, like shiny fish scales. It didn't match anyone she knew, aside from perhaps some of the foreign cavalry she had heard of at the Fort long ago. If it were the Romans, it could mean some final northern invasion. But Eilun had only mentioned seeing three warriors and several horses. Perhaps the intruder was a scout or some sort of outrider? Either way, her sorrow and fear over the fate of her daughter had been forced aside by this immediate threat. Just then, she caught sight of movement among the oak trees to the West, her hand tightening on her dagger. Beside her, she could hear Uuen reflexively squeezing his ax handle.

"Mother! Father!"

The sound from the tree line rang like a clarion call across the land, grasping Ail's emotions like the force of an arrow to her chest. It couldn't be… But she would recognize that chirpy voice anywhere. It was the sound of one of her children, a sound too primal to ignore… it was the sound of her honeybee. Just then, a horse stepped from the small trail running through the thick bushes and trees and emerged into full view.

Sitting high atop a beautiful brown steed came none other than Meala, her familiar smile beaming as she waved to her family. Ail searched her daughter, her eyes scanning over every piece of her, looking for anything wrong. While she seemed intact physically, her woad-dyed tunic was filthy and stained with the unmistakable brownish color of blood. Oddly, she had no shoes and really nothing else but an oversized belt, her old spear tied across her back, and… gold? That was when the morning sunlight caught the gold torc around her neck. Ail stared, her mouth coming open in shock. Her dirty, blood-stained, unkempt daughter was riding the horse of a Roman cavalryman, judging by the look of the tack, and wearing the torc of a chieftain.

Just then, the next horse emerged, a gray horse carrying what looked like an older girl, no more than fourteen or fifteen. The girl wore the tunic of low birth or even an enslaved person, and her facial features gave her away as foreign, perhaps Germania Inferior or Gallia, though she hadn't traveled enough to know. The girl looked apprehensive but otherwise in good health. Strapped to the back of her horse was a small wooden chest and plenty of supplies. The girl kept her head down, only glancing up a few times, briefly.

But then came the last rider. Her horse was black as night, its coat smooth and shiny, like polished iron, and clearly, it was of a prized breed. But the horse was not as impressive as her rider. Atop sat a woman with long black hair running down her back. She wore a strange, long, blood-red shirt, open in the front to reveal a grey, knee-length wool tunic. Draped over the horse's withers was a scale armor cuirass, what Eilun had seen. Her feet were booted with blue and white striped leggings, though these were coated in mud. As she emerged, she made direct eye contact with Ail and Uuen, holding their gaze like a proud warrior, of which Ail had no doubt she was. Each side of her saddle held quivers, mostly empty, and two bowcases, while around her neck she sported a silver chain like that of a great warrior.

As the warrior woman emerged, she led a train of four more horses, their riders missing but their tack and gear unmistakably Roman. Just then, her shock subsided enough to think, and Ail grabbed the small drawbridge pushing it downward, assisted moments later by Uuen. As soon as the wood slammed into place, she rushed across the small bridge with the rest of their family at her heels. As she stopped before the horses, Meala plopped out of her saddle, far from graceful but at least not falling this time and rushed to her mother.

"Meala... I..." Ail began, but she was swept into a deep embrace. Moments later, her legs gave out as the true realization that her daughter had survived and returned overcame her. As Ail slid to the ground, Meala held her firmly to lessen the drop and followed her mother to the ground in a mutual kneeling position. Ail returned the hug, burying her face into Meala's shoulder while Uuen stared, alternating his own tearful look between both of them and the two odd people who had accompanied Meala.

"You made it back... my honeybee!" Ail whispered between tearful gasps. She had been so worried about the unspeakable things that could happen, memories of her mother's fate underscoring each terror, yet Meala had returned.

"Mother, I am here, and I was victorious," Meala whispered, causing Ail to renew her sobbing. For a moment, no one spoke as Ail released more pent-up emotions than she had realized that she carried. Beside them, Uuen wiped away his tears, moved by his daughter's return and wishing he had not played a part in driving her away. At least she lived, which meant he would have a chance to make amends with her, though he couldn't deny that her choice to fight still angered him, just as Ail's had those years before. A bittersweet smile crossed his lips as he realized that Meala was far too much like Ail for him to handle. Slowly, other family members approached to see their sibling, though each kept a weary eye on the unknown people patiently mounted before them.

"Our daughter has returned, but what is the rest of this? Meala, who are these people?" Uuen asked after a few moments more had past. He wasn't sure who would answer the question, but he was hardly the only one curious. Cynna didn't understand his words, but she could clearly understand their meaning: a demand for some kind of explanation. Seeing that Meala was now crying with her mother and confident that Damona wouldn't speak up unless directly addressed, Cynna decided to explain, hoping they understood Latin. She wasn't a fan of speaking to groups, nor was she a fan of awkward situations.

"I am Cynna of Dacia, of the Iazyges, and daughter of Syon. The girl behind me is Damona of Veluniate, and we…" she spoke in Latin, but paused upon seeing Meala's tear-streaked glance, her wish understood and unspoken. Ail clearly understood her while everyone else seemed to roughly follow her words. Ail was fluent in Latin, while Meala was mostly fluent, followed by Ris, then Uuen, and so on. Cynna ceased speaking, knowing that Meala would wish to explain the rest, part of her people's strange, self-aggrandizing culture, and tell her parents the most important part. With that, Meala released her mother and stood to face her parents as she wiped her tears of joy and relief away and then spoke.

"Mother, Father, my sister, brothers, Eilun," she said, nodding at each in turn, then sniffled and wiped again.

"I traveled to Veluniate and sneaked into the Fort. It wasn't my smartest choice, but that is what I did. I took the life of a noble Roman woman and rescued her body slave. She was a monster, and no gods will weep for her," she paused, turning to nod at Damona. "I found and took loot from the Fort. Gold, silver, and this torc. It is enough to ransom a king, and it is a spoil for our entire family. I took them fairly in kind (from those who had previously stollen them), and with honor. As we escaped, we found Cynna… well, we rescued her from the Romans," she explained, skipping the details, much to Cynna's relief. Upon hearing of the treasure, Meala's brothers' and sister's mouths nearly hung open while her parents and Eilun looked on in shock.

"We fought many Romans to escape, and I took the lives of several in single combat," she explained with a forced stoic expression and standing tall, her thick, gold torc adding more weight to her story than its two libra (~660 g, or 1.5 lbs.) of gold did to her neck. Her entire family stood shocked as they listened while she provided a synopsis of her tale, likely something that she would explain in far greater detail at some future point over a cup of beer. In truth, Meala wasn't in the mood to discuss the more troubling details of her exploits, but she felt that she at least owed her family something, especially with how she had left many days before.

"Four Roman cavalrymen and some strange warrior woman from the South chased us, but I fought one and took his life, and Cynna killed the others. Damona saved my life, twice," she said, taking a moment to breathe and looking back toward Cynna, who waited patiently, though the mostly serious-looking Sarmatian flashed her a wink for support. Before her, Meala's family looked like they couldn't take any more suspense.

"Mother, Father… Cynna is my friend, my lover, and a fellow warrior… and now she is my wife. We joined on the field of battle with the gods and ancestors as our witnesses," she said as a fresh set of joyful tears came, her eyes' quivers never seeming to run dry.

"You are married?" Ail blurted out, a bit shocked.

"To a woman?" Uuen added, even more shocked.

"Called it," said Brynen with a smirk. Homosexuality was hardly a problem in their culture, but her father had never really expected Meala to actually wed a woman. Cynna didn't understand Uuen or Ail's words as they had replied in their native tongue, but their expressions and body language took little imagination to estimate, a flash of annoyance passing across her hazel eyes.

"It is true. I took this woman as my wife before the blood of Rome had dried on my blade, and she took me as hers," Cynna spoke, glaring down at Uuen and then Ail, her voice sending delightful shivers down Meala's spine. Her look was not anger, but it held a challenge should either parent wish to stand between them. Uuen swallowed hard while Ail cocked an eyebrow, thoroughly impressed that her daughter had found a warrior so mighty that she couldn't deny that she felt a bit intimidated. Ail had never held an eye for women, but this one certainly had a rustic, commanding presence. Had Cynna been a man with such dark, strong features, stoic looks, and towering command, she might have asked Uuen if he minded her dalliance. Instead, she nodded approval, holding eye contact with the warrior as she had been taught, being raised as a member of the Highermen caste.

"I will explain it all tonight, but we are…" Meala began, then paused and turned to flash a smile at Cynna before restarting, "My wife and I are tired, soiled, and in need of food and water. Mother and Father, we are joined, but Cynna has no home for me to go to, and Damona is also without a home. Would you let us stay under your roof until we fix this?" Meala finished. Per custom, now that she had wed, she was no longer a resident of Ail's home, at least by default. For a moment, Ail and Uuen shared a look, though it seemed like each was making sure the other wasn't opposed. A moment later, Uuen nodded.

"Damona of Veluniate, Meala tells me you saved her life," Ail spoke, to which Damona lifted her head and briefly nodded before lowering it once more.

"Cynna of Dacia, of the Iazyges, and daughter of Syon, my daughter says you also helped her escape. But even more, you are now her wife and now my daughter by union (daughter-in-law). You may stay at our home for as long as you wish. Please, join us for food and drink, baths, some fresh clothing, and beer," Ail said with a warm smile, her tears finally subsiding as her need for a stiff drink rose.

🏹 ❀ ❀ ❀ 🐝

Ten nights after they had arrived at the Braide homestead, Meala and Cynna rode out over the lake in a small wooden dugout boat the family used for fishing and harvesting reeds. There were several small islands and one reasonable-sized one in the lake. Luckily, Meala knew a small island with plenty of grass, trees, and the perfect environment for a romantic evening with her wife. It was a bit of work rowing that far, and Cynna was begrudgingly forced to let Meala do the work as her arms were still quite sore. Still, the pair finally set foot upon the pebbly ground, pulling the little boat ashore past the wall of brambles, tall grasses, and rocks that made up the shoreline.

The air smelled fresh with the scent of water, various trees, and the smell of the cool lake air. Small fires could be seen in the distance from the various homesteads around the lake. The late light season air was warm, though the temperature was already dropping for the night. Within a moon, it would no longer be comfortable without a longer tunic or leggings and not at all after the Sun set without a fire or warmer clothing. Meala smiled as they removed their bag of provisions and some seasoned wood her father had given her for the night. There were several obviously used camping areas, the little island being a popular spot for locals to come and celebrate events.

They had spent ten days recovering and introducing Cynna and Damona to the family. Unexpectedly, Meala's parents had embraced the Sarmatian and had accepted their union, though Meala shuddered to think how Cynna would have responded had they not. Meala suspected returning with enough gold to buy an entire clan's loyalty, and the well-earned torc of a warrior probably had something to do with it. That and her mother and father seemed a little intimidated by the mighty Sarmatian. She hoped their decision had also been based upon true acceptance and love. Either way, her mother had demanded at least a simple ritual in the ways of the Gods the very next day. It was not much for a wedding, but Meala could hardly say no.

In truth, Ail had initially asked for a massive celebration, which would have taken many days to prepare and involved dozens of people from the homesteads. Meala had worked hard to compromise with her mother over the wedding, knowing that Cynna would not approve and honestly not really caring so much for a second event, as her real marriage had been in that unknown field covered in mud and grime as the woman of her dreams looked down upon her. No joining ritual could ever top that memory. Instead, they washed, wore clean clothing, and let Ail perform a cozy ritual in the old ways just before sunset. Afterward, they rested, recuperated, and Cynna had spent some time with a hammer and Uuen's tools working on repairing her armor.

As was tradition, the newly wedded couple would leave the family and find a place of solitude where they might consummate their love.

Many traditions involved a child born from such a pairing and other religious and fertility-related aspects. Of course, those were hardly considerations in their case. Either way, this was their moment, and she planned to enjoy every bit. If her mother wanted grandchildren, she had Ris, Rigandona, and Brynen to do the hard work, not to mention their newly adopted daughter, Damona.

Meala smiled as she considered such things while she placed a few of the dried logs they had brought and dried brush and sticks as kindling into a neat little pile, stacked correctly for airflow, and quickly brought them to light by blowing on some smoldering peat kept safe in a pair of mussel shells. Beside her, Cynna worked laying out furs, unpacking some food and drink, and preparing for a night under the stars with her wife in peace. Finally, they could relax without worrying about wolves, strange warrior women from the South, Romans, or even interruptions from Meala's family. It was just Meala, Cynna, and the world beyond.

As she turned, Meala saw Cynna standing and stretching, her body still sore and hurt, something she could help alleviate. They were now both clean from bathing in the lake, their wounds cleaned and tended. It would probably be a moon or two before the aches and pains fully healed, and Cynna's bruising would take at least half that long to heal. But after ten days of being cared for by an overly attentive Ail and Rig and dealing with Uuen's constant attempts to strike up some sort of cathartic conversation, both women were excited for some alone time.

Cynna's long, thick, black hair flowed loose in the traditional marriage style, though she normally wore it tied into a single braid. Her soiled clothing needed cleaning and mending, and Meala thought she looked dashing in armor, but that was not to be worn to bed. Instead, the Sarmatian wore a light gray, ankle-length, woolen peplos secured at her shoulders with two bronze pins and a hemp cord at her waist. Around her neck, she wore the thick silver chain she had taken in battle. While not quite as large as Meala's torc, it had been taken in single combat and spoke of honor and bravery, much like the woman who now wore it.

Meala wore a woolen tunic dyed green from some yellow flowering plant (Cytisus scoparius) from the North, or so her mother had said when she had traded for the cloth at the Stone. In fact, the tunic belonged to her mother and was on loan for her marriage night. The tunic was simple and knee-length but complimented her hair and gold torc. Upon her head, she wore a chaplet of purple purse flowers (Calluna vulgaris), while a single streak of black paint crossed her face from ear to ear beneath her eyes, a little something her father had given her in recognition of her victory. Meala required a touch-up as her father's accepting act had brought tears, though she could tell he wasn't a fan of warfare.

To be honest, neither was Meala. She had become a warrior originally for the naive adventure and the chance to escape being wed to a man. While she had indeed escaped such a union, she would never again look upon battle in the childish way she had. War had seemed glorious and exciting, but terror, pain, and death had taught her otherwise. She would accept the warrior title and keep a sword on her hip, but she had already decided to never again seek conflict beyond protecting those she loved. Luckily, Cynna had expressed similar sentiment as they had rowed the little boat to the island, the wives far more interested in lives of peace. She supposed that meant her father had won the argument, but she wouldn't fight him over it... instead, coming to peace with it, the first peace in what she hoped would become a tranquil life.

Memories of war would continue to nag her mind, but she hoped that time and peace would help them fade. Of course, seeing her wife stretching certainly helped keep her mind from them. Cynna's face caught in the moonlight, revealing a few nicks and bruises but no such paint. Cynna had refused the paint because it was too similar to a war ritual of her people and painting the body for reasons outside of warfare or magic was not a custom of her tribe. But, as she turned to regard her openly gazing wife, her wide pupils and relaxed countenance told Meala that the paint looked good on her.

Both women stood barefoot in the waning warmth of the late light season, as shoes were costly and often unneeded around the farm. Meala smiled, almost buzzing and visibly excited, not being very good at hiding her emotion. They had planned a late meal, things to say, and two skins of wine to drink, but their plans turned to smoke like the burning lake brush as they regarded each other. Cynna stood almost valiantly before her with a sly smile and way too much confidence for Meala to hold herself back any longer. A shiver of joy rushed through her as she once more considered that she was married... not just to a woman, but to such a dashing warrior with a face cut from stone and a stoic personality that made her want to kiss the noble grin off the woman's face.

Meala stepped forward, gently placing her arms upon Cynna's shoulders. With a smile of consent from Cynna, she gently untied the hemp cord holding the Sarmatian's peplos, letting it fall to the ground, all thoughts of dinner lost in spontaneity. As her eyes returned to Cynna's, she saw that irresistible confidence, yet she could make out a hint of urgency – a vital need behind it. With a teasing giggle, Meala placed her pointer finger and thumb on the ends of the two bronze pins holding the peplos in place and slowly pulled them free, their eyes never parting. The garment spilled to the ground, revealing Cynna, a woman who had curiously not worn her linen braies or strophium chest wrap, a bold move from a constantly bold woman.

Before her stood the finest statue in the world, made flesh. Wearing only her thick silver chain, she was almost a head taller than Meala, her soft, lightly tawny body thick with muscle. Her form wasn't curvy, her hips more like a man, yet her strong features did nothing more than entice. Her arms were defined from drawing her war bow, and her legs were extremely strong from a life clinging to a horse. Her skin sported perhaps a dozen scars, a few fresh bruises, and cuts, a warrior's body. Meala found herself breathing hard, her face, chest, and lower body feeling oddly warm. She had seen nude people her entire life, from people swimming to those farming the fields on a hot day, but the context made all the difference, and this was the most erotic context she had ever experienced.

Her confident personality and muscular form were enough to make a woman swoon… well, perhaps just a woman who liked women, she supposed, yet it was only now that she truly appreciated just how tattooed Cynna was. She had seen the ink when Cynna was tied to the cross, but she neither had the time to look nor felt it right to do so, given Cynna's situation, and it had been far too dark the night they first joined. But now, in the dancing firelight, her beautiful light tawny skin revealed the complexity of her Sarmatian tattoos, a rich tradition dating back long before even the mighty Scythians of old – Her entire body was tattooed. From her feet and spiraling up to her shoulders, around her breasts, wrapping behind her, and down her arms, beautiful vine shapes covered her body, each punctuated by several small flowers with six petals.

Around her breasts, six flower petals had been inked to make them resemble large flowers. The vines were of different thicknesses, and the flowers distorted here and there, probably owing to the work being done over many years. Meala, was shocked by the work, not only with how intricate it was but by how much there was. She nearly winced as she realized the pain Cynna had endured. Of course, she wasn't the only inked woman. Meala's chest sported a magical bee just below her collarbone, stretching from side to side, and her recent exploits would probably result in several more tattoos. Her shoulders were tattooed with spiral shapes, a spiral on her right hand, and her calves and biceps were ringed with black bands, yet her tattoos were nothing compared to the flower garden that was Cynna's body.

"Well, are you just going to stand there and look? Come take what is yours, Meala of the Flooding Lake, daughter of Ail Braide, of East Wenechon, a brave warrior of the Wood Owl clan – my brave and beautiful wife," she dared, continuing to stand so boldly that Meala wasn't sure who the naked one really was. Swallowing hard, the painted wife approached as she unfastened her tunic, then lifted her arms high overhead, closing her eyes. A moment later, she felt the tunic pulled overhead and cast aside. When she opened them, they stood together, their bodies lit by moonlight and the flickering glow of a growing fire. Meala's chest rose and fell as her heart pounded in anticipation, but a challenge had been made, and she would not back down.

Naked before the Moon and hearth, Meala's eyes caught sight of the darker skin forming the scar beneath Cynna's left breast where her spear had nearly proved fatal. Delicately, she extended a finger toward the scar, pausing to see if Cynna reacted negatively, but the Sarmatian merely watched. As she touched the discolored flesh, a feeling of sadness passed over her, realizing how close she had come to ending all of this before it had even started. But then, a strong hand softly embraced hers and drew Meala's finger toward her own abdomen, where a pair of entry and exit wounds were clearly visible against her pale skin. Meala looked up, the unspoken acknowledgment that both women would forgive their scars clearly understood.

Just then, Cynna stepped back, bending down to fetch something beside her spilled peplos. Meala watched, curious and breathing heavily with anticipation. A moment later, Cynna returned holding a small bronze scale connected to a waxed hemp cord before her, making it a pendant, its golden luster catching the fire's light. Someone had engraved the scale with a simple linear form of a woman with a bow held overhead and a woman holding a spear overhead, both women holding hands. Beside the scene were Roman symbols. As Cynna presented the scale pendant, clearly a gift, Meala recognized it… it was the very scale Cynna had used to replace the one Meala had destroyed with her spear. That must have been what she had been working on over the last ten days.

"It reads, NVPTA CMXII (Married 912), which means nine hundred and twelve years since the founding of Rome. They normally write the names of their leaders to record the date, but I would not dirty our love with such names. I had to learn these numbers in my old life and your people have no way to write a date," she said, looking a little apologetic over the use of Latin and her inability to spell the more correct word, conubium. A feeling of warmth filled Meala's heart as a cool chill of elation danced down her spine while the gravity of the gift sank in.

A bronze scale featuring an etching of Meala and Cynna

"We do have numbers, but I don't care… I love it!" Meala exclaimed, not bothered by the Latin, not being able to read it, anyway, and simply touched that Cynna would have worked to make such an item and do so secretly to surprise her. Given Cynna's story of the spell to her goddess, the resulting spear to the heart that same night, and the subsequent events, the scale held more meaning than she could even consider, her mind nearly lost in a daze of joy.

"It would not have been a surprise if I had asked," she replied, a little sheepish, but then quickly restored her stoic look as Meala placed the pendant overhead, letting the bronze disk fall between her breasts where it dazzled in the firelight. Meala was filled with such love and respect for her wife that it nearly pained her, and she could barely hold back her need to kiss the sweet woman and feel her warmth, a feeling it was clear that the warrior shared as the firelight reflected from her body.

"Cynna of Dacia, great warrior of the Iazyges and worthy daughter of Syon, I accept your challenge," she whispered and pressed her body against the Sarmatian, their lips coming together in a kiss. Almost immediately, Cynna pressed her tongue against their shared lips, and then she was within. Meala was instantly lost in the joy of their shared warmth, the strange and yet wonderful feeling of breasts pressing against each other, cozier than erotic, or the Sarmatian's curious use of her tongue. Instead of worrying, she closed her eyes and let it happen all at once, a synchronized cacophony of sensations, from the touch of warm skin and the taste of her lover to Cynna's faint but now comforting smell, followed by the sounds of gentle kisses and the resulting vocalizations.

The pair slowly sank onto the furs beside the fire, finally at peace. But a moment later, Cynna pressed Meala back until the Caledonian could see the stars above and skillfully mounted her, as was her steppe rider instinct. Meala was almost heartbroken to let her lips leave Cynna's, a feeling like a cool cup of water from the lake on the hottest day being taken. But then, Cynna's fingers touched her abdomen and began tracing their way up. The sensation tickled but also sent waves of euphoria and growing anticipation through her body. Higher and higher, her fingers explored, around her breasts, and up her neck, the shudders making Meala giggle and moan with delight. But all thoughts ended as seductive Sarmatian lips returned, this time upon the soft flesh over her hipbone.

"Cynna…" she whispered in a breathy gasp as the mighty warrior softly kissed her skin, tongue flicking once before releasing each kiss as she methodically traveled along Meala's body, higher and higher. As she reached the Caledonian's sternum, Cynna's warm hand found Meala's inner thigh, softly rubbing her where she was already growing so sensitive. Meala nearly gasped as she felt kisses around her breasts but let out a moan as the playful, warm hand slid from her inner thigh over her abdomen and slowly up to gently cup her left breast. Yet, even as she tried to consider how they felt, the kisses reached her neck, and her desires began to take control as need and wanting became all encompassing.

"You tempt me…" the Caledonian whispered, her breath deep and haughty with want. She had experienced her own touch after many a pleasant thought while alone, yet nothing could have prepared her for the sheer intimacy and desire she felt. It wasn't just pleasure, it was joy, warmth, and a shared intimacy that caused her to bloom like a flower in the light season.

"I see the honeybee finds my flowers to her liking?" Cynna purred as her right hand slowly rubbed down Meala's inner thigh, down her leg, and then back up her body. Her low, husky voice made Meala wish for more than her warm touch, her needs coming out as a moan. Needing to learn how far these vital, physical feelings could go and so desperately wishing for more skin contact, Meala grasped the Sarmatian and pulled her to the ground until the lovers lay together. Meala lifted one leg and wrapped it around Cynna so that each woman straddled the other's leg, so they lay beside each other, Cynna on her right side and Meala on her left. With their sudden union, each felt the wet, hot core of their lover's deepest needs pressing into their leg as Meala hungrily pressed her lips to Cynna's, her need for more kissing akin to her need to breathe.

They lay upon the furs, hands gently probing as they kissed, but slowly, movement below began to evolve. First, it started as just accidental friction, but soon, both women were moving their legs and hips as their primal feminine instincts took over. Meala released Cynna's kiss with a moan, returning it as quickly as she could. Then, Cynna released her lips, but instead, she lowered her head and placed her soft, warm lips onto one of Meala's firm, pink nipples, her tongue suddenly flicking across the sensitive flesh. Meala nearly lost it for a moment as waves of pleasure seemed to transfer from her nipple, down her body, and between her legs, but Cynna wasn't quite done. Lying on her side, Cynna took her right hand, strong from a life of pulling the bowstring, and softly pinched Meala's other nipple.

"Oh, oh, I… ohhh…" Meala whispered as both nipples, stimulated at the same time, created a geometric increase in sensation, not only of desire and pleasure but also a romantic, emotional need as oxytocin flooded her body like an overrun river after a rainstorm. And like a river, her banks were now flooded as their rocking and grinding began to feel like it was approaching some point, some sudden, deep feeling that spoke of something wonderful.

"Cy… naaa…" It came like a gentle warm-season rain as the pleasure began, and Cynna released her nipple with her mouth and returned to kiss her deeply. With skill and cunning, the Sarmatian worked to coax the gentle rain into a growing storm as the pleasure came in waves, building as Meala cried out. Like all storms, there was lightning, thunder, and so much water, but soon the storm faded into a light drizzle as Meala relaxed. Strangely, she felt as though her body could do that same thing again and might want to, but only after taking a moment to breathe. They had only just started and neither woman had any other plans for the rest of the long night.

"How could you cry out so soon? I have barely touched you, yet," Cynna playfully scolded as Meala lay in her arms and giggled.

"Where did you learn such skills," Meala asked a few moments later as Cynna returned to softly kissing her neck, the pair still entangled. After another gentle kiss, Cynna replied.

"Have you never taken a lover?" she asked, confused by how a woman of Meala's age could be a stranger to intimacy.

"I have lain with one other, once," she replied a bit sheepishly. Cynna smiled and kissed Meala on the forehead, caring little for experience. At the very least, Cynna was a good teacher.

"My first time was not pleasant, nor most times. It was with a man, and he was far rougher than he needed to be," Cynna recalled, a slight frown crossing her face. Before she could journey too far down that path, Meala gently touched her cheek, returning Cynna to the moment.

"I am sorry that happened. But we are now joined, so this will be our first time as wives. Maybe we should think of it that way? If so, then my first time is beautiful," Meala said, returning the kiss. Cynna's frown vanished and was replaced by a pleasant smile, her eyes wet in the corners. After another passionate kiss, Meala drew from her lips, her expression thoughtful.

"Your tattoos are so beautiful, like morning flowers covered in dew," she whispered, her urge to resume their activities growing as her body relaxed. Cynna had yet to let herself be the center of attention, and Meala hoped she could fix that. Their previous time, Cynna had been tired and not as receptive, but tonight, she had already ground her body against Meala's leg, and her wetness betrayed her body's needs. In truth, the romance, kisses, and the intimacy were far more important to Meala than the climax, but she wanted to watch the brave warrior lose her composure in ecstasy, and she had a feeling of just how to do it.

"That is where you are wrong, Caledonian. My flowers are not covered in dew… they are covered in nectar," Cynna said in her low, husky voice, her eyebrow lifting slightly, perhaps an invitation from a woman sharing Meala's same thoughts. Meala giggled and leaned in to begin kissing deeply once more. But between kisses, Cynna separated to speak, Meala instantly feeling the separation.

"Iris (Pronounced ear-ees, in Latin)," Cynna spoke between sharp inhales. Meala paused for a moment, unsure of what the woman had meant. Cynna smiled, her face relaxed in the calmest Meala had ever seen.

"It is a purple flower from where I come. It is what my name means," she spoke, then resumed kissing. It was a beautiful name with a lovely meaning, something Meala considered as she released from Cynna's kiss and slowly descended downward, leaving her own trail of kisses and playful giggles over the Sarmatian's body. Meala nearly laughed at the symbolism as the "honeybee" approached the Iris flower's bud for nectar. It was something she had seen a man do to a woman behind a bush on a harvest festival night. It had been so different from the usual activities she had seen, and the woman had seemed to find it remarkable.

Cynna breathed heavy, deep moans as Meala, the bee, crawled her way along her body until she found the warmest of all places. Meala felt a little awkward, but Cynna gave no indication that she was bothered and spread her already bowed legs in anticipation. Meala would never have started so boldly, but both women were already quite worked up. Meala delicately kissed around the outside of the Sarmatian's flower as her hands gently stroked the woman's legs, each little kiss causing a tiny reaction from Cynna, more and more nectar appearing at the prospect of Meala's touch. With a flutter in her heart and a lick of her lips, Meala began to kiss the warmest place.

"Meala, toe… toe… Dua, peh…" Cynna whispered in her deep voice, far too aroused to remember Latin, instead reverting to her Iazyges tongue as Meala used her Wenech tongue. It seemed that Cynna's want came from bringing Meala to the edge, and the warrior wasn't interested in taking her time. Meala pressed her lips into another form of kiss, using her tongue at first as Cynna had but quickly adjusting to what made her wife sound the most aroused.

Within moments, Meala's fingers had found her own petals, as they had several times when she had daydreamed. Yet this time, it felt so different. This time, her pleasure came from another, her desires a reflection of Cynna's, and when the mighty Sarmatian warrior suddenly cried out, it pushed her over the edge as she felt a second wave of building pleasure. It wasn't as strong as the first, feeling deeper, with warmer tones, and with much less urgency. But the same could not be said for Cynna, as the woman's upper body bucked, her own river waters flowing freer than Meala could have imagined. She softly giggled as she left the flower's center and began working her way along the wet petals, kissing their nectar and dew.

Wiping the wetness from her face, Meala kissed her way back up into Cynna's warm, now slightly sweaty embrace. She could feel herself satisfied, yet the early day (early night) was young, and they had so much more firewood, wine, and nothing to do but enjoy each other in the blessed joy of simple peace. As they softly kissed, Meala looked up to see the stars overhead and the faces of her ancestors and gods. No Roman gold or glory could possibly top the simple, joyful love she had found with Cynna, her wife. Somehow, she was sure they would grow old together, never parting, their hearth always warm with loving fire.

"I need water… then I need you," Cynna whispered, grasping at the waterskin as Meala's finger traced a line over the archer's visible abdominal muscles.

Meala laughed.

Epilogue

South Bank of Lock Leven, Scotland, – 2 PM, May 19, 2017, CE

"Hey, Isobel, you have the file, ae?" called Alexander, his low voice rising above the sounds of the team of undergraduates learning to use a metal mesh to sift excavated soil for artifacts, the "young'uns" laughing far too much. Sighing, Isobel dropped her metal dustpan and trowel and looked for the file. How Alex's trowel could already be dull, she couldn't imagine, but this was the second time today. She paused to secure a piece of wavy brown hair behind her ear, the rest bound in a ponytail, and took that moment to shake her tank top to remove the dirt that had accumulated in its built-in bra, yet another hazard of fieldwork.

Assistant site director Alexander Bishop was a hard worker and a good "small finds" archaeologist who specialized in knowing what every tiny little thing one found in a dirt sifter was, but the man was far too obsessed with his tools. Isobel's own trowel was now noticeably smaller than when she had bought it, its metal lost in the sands of time. It had already been a year since she had moved to Scotland to work on her graduate degree in archaeology. Unfortunately, her master's thesis subject had hit a dead end. Alex had been one of the few on her team to show interest and support for her thesis; while many of the others just smiled and issued platitudes like, "That sounds well good."

"Are you scraping granite or something?" she called back in her thick Virginia Appalachian accent, her chocolate brown eyes scanning the dirt around the excavation unit, looking for the metal file. The file's steel caught her eye as she looked over her shoulder, so she leaned back and grabbed the metal tool, unwilling to stand after finding a comfortable position in the dirt. It had been comfortable enough of a spot for a pair of skeletons to spend the last two thousand years in each other's embrace, so it was good enough for her worn-out jeans.

"Okay, lunch in 15," called Fiona Taylor, a woman more than twice Isobel's age and with the wisdom to match. She was the site director and a skilled experimental archaeologist, not to mention the connoisseur of more romance fiction than Isobel knew a woman could read. She also ensured that everyone ate lunch and stayed hydrated and safe. Instinctually, she glanced about for any loose shovels or dust pans, lest "Gran Taylor" notice them and come to scold. She repressed a smile, considering Fiona one of the better people she had known.

Sparing a look to ensure that Fiona wasn't gazing her way, she tossed the file two meters to where Alex sat, examining his new trowel in the light like some sort of overly dirty samurai examining his katana. His short, brown hair and grey eyes had made Alex popular with many of the graduate students, but Isobel barely noticed. Instead, she simply enjoyed his ability to identify nearly anything she pulled from the ground, whether a strange-looking stone or a ceramic sherd, or even the chicken gastrolith she had found her first day. She sighed, her thoughts drifting toward her graduate thesis and the growing problem with her topic. Intrusive thoughts of her graduate advisor, Dr. Olivia Grayson, returned to nag her.

A study of female warriors in Roman Period Britain? And how many female warriors do we have evidence for? Why don't you either pick a single set of remains and make an analysis of it or pick something else? Maybe something approachable? This female warrior business always causes a stir. Are you sure you wouldn't prefer a less... controversial subject? She had grown to seriously dislike Olivia's constant push to force her mainstream. The woman was a product of a very different time, yet she had a point. This was a graduate thesis, not her doctoral work. At this point, she needed to get a solid topic and get working, or she would never finish. Yet, she had already worked hard on her current topic, her frustration growing.

Isobel had long had "amazons" on the brain. As a child, she had played Amazon Warrior Queen with her dolls and had always found the idea of warrior women an exciting topic, much to the chagrin of her mother, the amusement of her father, and the horror of several "sacrificed" Ken dolls. The discovery of a well-preserved Iron Age crannog with a gravesite north of Edinburgh with several inhumed (buried) individuals, two of whom some had interpreted as the remains of two female individuals sharing a single grave, had lit the fire in her studies. Even stranger, both individuals had signs of long-healed antemortem (before death) wounds consistent with battlefield trauma, and both had been buried with weapons among their grave goods.

Yet, the principal investigator of the site had made a statement that, in his opinion, the remains were of a Sarmatian man and a local woman based on their grave goods and sex approximations. He had even speculated that the graves were younger than the other site finds, given the flat stones lining the graves perimeter, something seen more commonly a few hundred years later. Isobel's eyes had nearly rolled from their sockets upon hearing this fiat. It wasn't that she refused to believe good science – it was that this wasn't good science. It was an estimation of sex and gender based on inadequate information, and far too speculative. Unfortunately, the principal investigator was not affiliated with the university and getting fired from the site for speaking up would land her back in a teaching assistant job, so little could be done.

She had applied to work on the site and had been lucky enough to be accepted as a student technician. The site had closed for the season just after exhuming the remains, and now, after several months of lab work cleaning and cataloguing, Isobel sat in a waist-deep excavation, scraping one thin layer at a time from the soil just north of where the skulls of the pair had been found. She returned her attention to context 45, which sat just beside contexts 32 and 33, where the pair of human remains were discovered. Had water or tunneling creatures disturbed and moved any of the grave goods, context 45 was the most likely location to find them, so she scraped.

The pair appeared to be lying in each other's arms and had quickly become sensationalized by the news as the "Pictish Lovers," or a "Sarmatian warrior and his Caledonian lover," yet always a "warrior" "man" and his "wife." She frowned, considering how ridiculous the assumptions of the media had been. The smaller individual had worn a gorgeous gold torc of a more southern style, yet another sensationalized media event, an iron spear point buried beside them. The tip had been heavily oiled, but the outside had oxidized badly requiring the object to be sent to a conservator. The larger individual had been buried wearing scale armor with dozens of iron and bronze arrows, the remains of three bows, and a lovely silver neck chain. The slightly smaller remains had been sex approximated as likely female, while the larger remains had been approximated as indeterminate.

The media had simply assumed a man and woman, with something entirely underdetermined, harkening back to the days when remains were "sex determined," often using just the grave good associated with them. If they had a sword, they were a man, and if they were a man, they had a sword, which did not even begin to address the problems with osteology. Male and female skeletons had sexual dimorphism, sure, but it was not something absolute, and plenty of overlap existed. That was why sex approximation was now used and why something as culturally specific as gender was not determined. Worse, the site, so far, was dated before the Pictish people even emerged as a distinct cultural group, and such headlines had made it much harder to protect it from looters.

The soil was dry in the summer sun, though Isobel was thankful she wasn't back in Virginia. She had spent her undergraduate days at Longwood University. The campus was beautiful with it's Joan of Arc statues, lovely buildings, and even the dreaded black crown painted into the walking path that was to be avoided at all costs. But one summer of archaeology field school in Virginia had taught her just how hot and sweaty a person could be. If she ever saw another clay pipestem again, she might scream. Thoughts of the big stone with painted handprints near her dorm apartment signifying her class of 2015 came to mind, bringing with them a smile. Her mind often wandered to the past as she sat on the warm soil scraping layer after layer of soil.

Now in Scotland and working on finishing her graduate degree in archaeology at the University of Glasgow, she found the Scottish summers quite pleasant. Lovely Scottish accents, beautiful weather, when it was warm, and a quick day trip to amazing sights. Even better, no more poison ivy and cottonmouth snakes, though she kept an eye peeled for bracken and giant hogweed, two generally disagreeable plants that would rival Virginia's poison ivy and ticks. Scotland had ticks too, but not like the nasty ones in Virginia, a thought that sent a shiver down her spine.

Returning her attention to the three-meter square of excavated soil where she sat just south of Loch Leven, she placed her trowel on the sandy loam soil and began scraping a new layer. At least she could look forward to dinner tonight with Emily. She'd need a shower first, but that was also something she could share with Em's. Just as she drew her trowel back, a coppery-greenish shape emerged from the soil. Isobel paused, then reached for the offending object, her thoughts over files, media, and Virginia lost. Normally, one sifted everything, and being "grabby" was frowned upon, but she had fully dislodged the small object, and Isobel was feeling rebellious at the moment.

"Is it bronze, or is it cake?" She lifted the small object, instantly realizing that it was indeed bronze. The flat metal object looked to be roughly four centimeters by two centimeters and only a few millimeters thick, punctated at the top (small hole). Isobel immediately recognized the object as an armor scale, something she had worked with before. The larger individual from contexts 32 and 33 had worn what had likely been a set of iron scale armor… but this was bronze. She frowned once more, turning the scale over in her hand as she considered the oddity. Her thoughts vanished like fog on a moor the moment she did as the incised lines of an engraving caught the light.

"No fucking way… Oh my…" she whispered as she realized what she was looking at. The scale clearly depicted two female figures, one with a spear and one with a bow, their weapons held above their heads, their hands joined. Below them were the characters NVPTA CMXII, "married, 912." Isobel closed her eyes as she processed the date. *Rome was founded in 753 BCE… so that's 160 CE.* That was one year before Marcus Statius Priscus became governor of Britannia after Titus… something, she couldn't seem to remember his name, had been deposed and executed for theft and incompetence. It was just fifteen years before Marcus Aurelius famously sent thousands of Sarmatians to Britain. Gazing at the scale, Isobel realized that what she held might very well be a marriage token. The symbology was odd, to say the least, but the figures were depicted as female, and the scale clearly said, "Married."

Just then, her phone rang, initially provoking a grimace as she dug the annoyance from her back pocket and saw that it was from Emily Harper, a first-year doctoral student at Glasgow's SUERC studying carbon dating using Bayesian analysis and other mathematical musings, the person with the largest manga collection she had ever seen, and most importantly, her fiancé. She had met Emily remotely during her undergraduate in a manga forum, discussing their shared love of Ranma

½ and Red River, the two manga series being a shared interest that had sparked a relationship that eventually led to her choice to come to Scotland to be near her soon-to-be wife, and the discovery she had just made.

"Hey Em's, sup?" she said, her Appalachian accent twanging a little harder than normal. She wanted to tell Emily about her find, but her mind had barely processed it yet. Of course, her cell battery was also at 3%, and her powerpack was back in her Suburu, but Emily sounded terse, so she supposed it would be enough to finish the call.

"Sup? Have ye been in the Sun a little much? Do ye need a kip before we chat, ae?" Emily asked, her Scottish accent a stark contrast to Isobel. The Sun? Em's was questioning her heat tolerance? This came from the people who had no concept of putting ice in drinks and barely knew what air conditioning was, let alone had any." She suppressed a laugh as Emily continued not waiting for an answer, her tone suggesting that she was probably busy, a fate that awaited Isobel if she chose to pursue her doctorate, a choice she had yet to make. *Married, 912*, the implications began to sink in as the back of her mind processed the information.

"I am looking at the results of the latest cohort and I think ye are going to like it. Oxcal says both samples from contexts 32 and 33 came back as 207 BCE, plus or minus 18 years. AMS is in a good mood. Oh, I have to go, but see you for dinner, ae?" Emily said, the sounds of shuffling papers nearly as loud as her voice.

"207… 207! You are the best Em's! See you tonight," Isobel chirped.

"With priors like mine, you know it, babe," Emily said, her Bayesian math joke barely registering. Isobel finished with a kissing sound and stuffed her phone in her pocket. Her mind became a sudden wash of thoughts as she worked to fit it all together. The armor was likely late period western Sarmatian, probably Alan, Roxolani, or Iazyges. The warrior wore a silver chain of local origin. The other person wore a more southern torc but her grave goods more closely conformed to the local cultural assemblages… her mind worked hard as the pieces began to fit together. If they married in their mid-20s, say 25, then lived together for another 40 years and died at 60-65, that would make their deaths roughly 200 CE, right in the middle of the 207 CE +/- 18 years Emily had stated.

"Fuck you, Oliva!" Isobel screamed so loudly that the entire site went completely quiet, all heads turning toward her. But she didn't care as she fist-pumped a victory. Not only had she just likely found the evidence to confirm that two warrior women had, in fact, lived and died in Roman-occupied Scotland, but she had also discovered they were married. The implications and the romantic nature of it all were overwhelming, and the emotion from finding such an ancient love that would end up on display in a museum for all of humanity to know about moved Isobel. The words of an ancient fragment of poetry came to mind as she reverently placed the small item into a collection bag.

"Someone, I tell you, will remember us, even in another time..." she whispered as her eyes grew wet.

The End.

ABOUT THE AUTHOR

Ishtar Watson (she/they) is a professional computer scientist with an academic background in both computer science and archaeology. Her archaeological focus is on portraying the Stone Age and ancient history through media for educational and scientific outreach purposes, and the use of EDXRF (Energy-Dispersive X-Ray Fluorescence Spectroscopy) to determine the chemical composition of artifacts. Ishtar has worked in the field and the lab as an archaeology student and hopes to continue her advanced education in the field of archaeology. Ishtar experiences Autism, ADHD, PTSD, CPTSD, Tourette's Syndrome, <u>Dyslexia</u>, and Misophonia.

Ishtar lives on the east coast of the United States with her super-smart spouse and a handful of cats. She has written several adventure-romance novels, short stories, and novellas set in the Stone Age, all of which feature LGBTQIA+ characters. Her hobbies include archaeology, especially Neolithic clothing and adornment, astrophotography, model rocketry, weaving and spinning Stone Age textiles, nuclear physics (specifically gamma spectroscopy), mineralogy, archery, Dungeons and Dragons, sapphic poetry, and writing.

Thank you for purchasing an independently published literary work. Writing, editing, and publishing a novel entirely by oneself is quite a lot of work (especially when the author has dyslexia). I appreciate you as the reader – you are why I write. **Please consider leaving a review and rating**, as this is the most important thing you can do for any author. Words cannot express how much a review means to an author.

~Ishtar ♡

As (plr. asses) – Roman coin made originally from brass but made from copper by the time of the story. 16 asses makeup a denarii. A single as might pay for a cup of inexpensive beer, depending on the location.

Aureus (plr. aurei) – A Roman coin made of gold and having a value of 25 Denarii.

Brigante – A tribe from Northern Britain, roughly near modern Yorkshire, as described by the geographer Ptolemy in 150 CE.

Celtic – A term used to describe several cultures who shared the use of the Celtic family of languages. Importantly, Celts were not a distinct ethnic or cultural group, simply being grouped by their shared use of the same language group. "Celt" describes Celts from mainland Europe while "Insular Celt" describes Celts from Brittian. As a side note, the author pronounces celt with a hard K, not an S sound, as in (K)elt.

Crannog – A wooden home built upon stilts over the water. Crannogs were roughly cylindrical-shaped structures with conical roofs built upon a platform suspended over the water on stilted wooden piles. During their five millennia of use in the Atlantic Archipelago, countless variations in size and construction resulted from a wide variety of conditions, building materials, and needs. A typical crannog structure might be made from wood, while the inner walls could be made from wood, sticks, brush, mud, clay, and other local resources. Roofs were typically thatched.

Dacian – The name for people from the region of Dacia and the culture associated with that region. Dacia occupied lands roughly corresponding to modern Ukraine, Moldova, Romania, Serbia, Hungary, and even parts of Poland.

Denarius (plr. denarii) – A silver Roman coin used as the base currency of Rome.

Gather Hall – A wholly invented place, the gather hall is based upon a common theme among Celtic peoples to create communal structures for social, governmental, and religious reasons.

Language – The insular Celtic language Meala speaks is unattested, so I drew upon the most ancient words I could find from attested Celtic "P" languages, those most likely to be like what Meala would have spoken. Still, her words are invented. Cynna's language was similarly invented from Iranian language groups. In case the reader wants to know what she says in chapter ten:

> "Tuh aun suraz zalmo." – *You have salty skin.*
> "Tuh unt germaz shze ballas, nelja surras." – *You are warm and strong, my brave warrior.*

Latin – Latin is used throughout the story both as a mechanism of adding realism and as a practical means for characters from vastly different places to communicate. While I took two years of Latin, formally, I ended up hiring a historian who studies Latin to aid my poor attempts at period-accurate speech. Of course, those who study Latin may find errors in what is written, but please know that great effort was made towards accuracy. The Latin in the book represents 2nd-century frontier Latin, sometimes known as vulgar Latin. Of course, many differing opinions exist over whether a spoken "vulgar" Latin is even a legitimate concept. Regardless, I hope you appreciate the inclusion of (hopefully) accurate Latin.

Iazyges – (Eye-az-ah-geez) A Sarmatian cultural group whose influence extended throughout what is now eastern Europe. Often nomadic, Iazyges interacted with Rome in the lands of Dacia, the homeland of Cynna.

Longwood University – Longwood was the school I had wished to attend, though fate brought me to several others. I once visited with an alumna friend and toured their lovely campus. In fact, a large boulder painted white and covered with colorful handprints and the words "Making H15tory" exists near the apartment dorms. As of the time of writing, Longwood does, in fact, have a lovely undergraduate archaeology program.

Novant – A variation on the name for a tribe from northwestern Britain who the geographer Ptolemy named the "Novantae" in 150 CE.

Peplos – The Greek name for a textile garment, sometimes called a "palla" in Latin. The peplos is created from a panel of cloth wrapped around a person and fastened at the shoulders using pins. Often, a belt is worn to bind the excess material to the waist, making movement easier.

Picts – A name given to the various iron age cultures living in approximately the land now known as Scotland, from 297-841 CE. However, this term is not academically meaningful. These cultures shared many similarities, including their use of the Celtic-language-family. The origin of the Picts is unknown, though tribes such as the Caledones and Venicones may have been their predecessors.

Sarmatians – An Iranian-language-speaking group of Iron Age peoples related to the earlier western Scythian cultures spanning over 700 years from the 5th century BCE to the 4th century CE. Sarmatians were acclaimed for their riding and archery skills, which many Sarmatians learned from a young age living on the European steppe.

Slavery – While in dialogue, the term "slave" or "slaves" is used, the more proper term is "enslaved," as we are describing a condition people are experiencing, rather than something intrinsic about them. This is the modern convention, as it humanizes people rather than objectifying them. Of course, in dialogue, the characters do not use this modern convention.

Steel – Though the Roman Empire was an Iron Age civilization, they used steel quite extensively. At the most basic, steel is iron with carbon added to enhance strength. Modern steel contains other metals and is far stronger, but Iron Age steel was not uncommon.

Subligar/ subligaculum – The Latin name for a class of clothing serving to cover one's groin. These ranged from a wrap of cloth or loincloth to garments resembling a modern bikini.

Strophium – The Latin name for a cloth wrap that secured breasts. Usually, the strophium resembled a scarf, but much longer, allowing it to be wrapped several times around the upper chest and tied or pinned into place.

Taksalee – A variation on the name for a tribe from eastern Britain who the geographer Ptolemy named the "Taezali."

Torcs & Chains – The use of thick metal jewelry around the neck as a signifier of station, wealth, and bravery has been documented at length among Bronze and Iron Age northern Europeans, and other cultures. The torc, a C-shaped, rigid metal necklace, often made from silver, gold, bronze, electrum, or iron, surrounded the neck leaving an opening, usually in the front, to allow it to be removed. The ends of torcs, called terminals, were often large and more ornamental than the torcs themselves.

Women Warriors – While often overlooked or dismissed as legend, much evidence for warrior women exists, worldwide. From the Scythians of antiquity to the Dahomey Amazons of the 17th century until the start of the 20th century, regular military forces containing or even wholly made up of women have been documented. This should be no surprise as the United States military has nearly a quarter million women. Adrienne Mayor discusses in her 2014 book, The Amazons – Lives & Legends of Warrior Women Across the Ancient World, pages 81-82, that in 2004, previously unearthed skeletal remains of what appear to be Sarmatian warrior women buried near the Roman fort of Brocavum, circa. 200-300CE provided the first significant evidence for Sarmatian warrior women at the walls. While this is still a debated find, it bears striking similarities to well-documented examples of Sarmatian warrior women from their native lands.

Wenech – A variation of the name of the Iron Age insular Celtic tribe called Venicones, according to the geographer, Claudius Ptolemy, c. 150 CE. The name Wenech was imagined for the story.

Woad – A yellow flowering plant native to Europe (Isatis tinctoria) that can be cultivated and processed into a rich, blue dye. Woad does not apply well as a paint, both easily flaking and potentially causing skin irritation. Contrary to popular depiction, woad was likely not used for tattoos or body paints as the coloring does not retain well and woad tattoos tend to scar due to the plant's caustic nature. If blue paint was worn, it was likely only for short periods.

Artwork by Alexandra Filipek © 2025

- *Cover Art – Cynna (left) and Meala (right).*
- *Cynna of the Iazyges, of Dacia – Cynna holding her bow as she calls her enemies to single combat.*
- *Meala (foreground) preparing for single combat. Damona of Gaul (background) stands behind Meala.*

You can find more from Alexandra Filipek at her website, Alexandra.Filipek.us

Artwork by Mary Watson © 2025

- *Marriage Token*
- *Triskelion Symbol*

I cannot thank Alexandra and Mary enough for their efforts to bring my characters and story alive with their amazing illustrative talents.

~Ishtar

Suggested Reading

Below is a selection of books and papers I have found of great use while writing this novel. The actual bibliography for My Mother's Spear is nearly four times this size, but I selected only the works I thought might be relevant to the typical reader. I hope this knowledge inspires you and brings you a sense of academic and scientific joy.

~Ishtar

Antheunis, M. L., Croes, E. A. J., Krahmer, E. J., and Schouten, A. P. (2020). The role of eye-contact in the development of romantic attraction: Studying interactive uncertainty reduction strategies during speed-dating. Computers in Human Behavior, 105, 106218. https://doi.org/10.1016/j.chb.2019.106218

Aruz, J., Farkas, A., Fino, E. V., & Metropolitan Museum of Art (New York, N.Y.) (Eds.). (2006). The golden deer of Eurasia; perspectives on the steppe nomads of the ancient world. Metropolitan Museum of Art; Yale University Press.

Barelds, D. P., De Wit, C. Y., Haucke, M., and Zsok, F. (2017). What kind of Love is love at first sight? An empirical investigation. Personal Relationships, 24(4), 869–885. https://doi.org/10.1111/pere.12218

Brzezinski, R. & Mielczarek, M. (2003). The Sarmatians 600 BC – AD 450. Osprey Publishing.

Chittock, H., Gosden, C., Hommel, P., and Nimura, C. (Eds.). (2020). Art in the Eurasian Iron Age: Context, Connections and Scale. Oxbow Books.

Cowan, R. (2003). Imperial Roman Legionary AD 161-284. Osprey Publishing.

Cunliffe, B. W. (2018). The ancient celts. Oxford University Press.

Dillon, S. and James, S.L. (Eds.). (2012) A Companion to Women in the Ancient World. John Wiley & Sons, Ltd.

Gardiner, S. R. (1892). A Student's History of England. Longmans and Co., London.

Gleba, M. and Mannering, U. (2019). Textile and Textile Production in Europe from Prehistory to AD 400. Oxbow Books.

Hudson, T. P. (2014). Variables and Assumptions in Modern Interpretation of Ancient Spinning Technique and Technology Through Archaeological Experimentation. EXARC Journal, Volume 1, 2014, ISSN 2212-8956.

Johns, C. (1996). The Jewellery Of Roman Britain: Celtic and Classical Traditions (1st ed.). Routledge.

MacKillop, J. (1990). Dictionary of Celtic Mythology, Oxford University Press.

Marlize, L. & Riede, F. (2024). Hunting with poisoned arrows during the Terminal Pleistocene in Northern Europe? A tip cross-sectional area assessment and list of potential arrow poison ingredients, Journal of Archaeological Science: Reports, Volume 59, 2024, 104757, ISSN 2352-409X, https://doi.org/10.1016/j.jasrep.2024.104757.

Martin, T. F. and Weetch, R. (Eds.). (2017). Dress and Society: Contributions from Archaeology (1st ed.). Oxbow Books.

Maslen MW, Mitchell PD. (2006). Medical theories on the cause of death in crucifixion. J R Soc Med. 2006 Apr;99(4):185-8. doi: https://doi.org/10.1177/014107680609900416. PMID: 16574970; PMCID: PMC1420788.

Mayor, A. (2022). Greek Fire, Poison Arrows, and Scorpion Bombs: Unconventional Warfare in the Ancient World. Princeton University Press.

Mayor, A. (2016). The Amazons: Lives and Legends of Warrior Women Across the Ancient World. Princeton University Press.

McCullough, A. Female Gladiators in the Roman Empire. In Budin, S. L., & Turfa, J. M. (Eds.). (2016). Women in antiquity: real women across the ancient world. Routledge, Taylor & Francis Group.

Murphy, E. M. (2003). Iron Age Archaeology and Trauma from Aymyrlyg, South Siberia. BAR International Series.

Nelson, S. M. and Rosen-Ayalon, M. (2001). In Pursuit of Gender: Worldwide Archaeological Approaches. Altamira Press.

Rebay-Salisbury, K. (2016). The Human Body in Early Iron Age Central Europe: Burial Practices and Images of the Hallstatt World (1st ed.). Routledge.

Schultheis, E. M. (2019). The Battle of the Catalaunian Fields AD 451. Pen and Sword Military

Wagner, P. (2002). Pictish Warrior AD 297-841. Osprey Publishing.

Wexler, P. (Ed.). (2019). Toxicology in antiquity. Academic Press.

Wisdom, S. (2001). Gladiators: 100 BC–AD 200. Osprey Publishing.